I met M.C. Quince, the author of Street of Secrets, in a writing class several years ago. Each week she would come in with a chapter and eventually I was coming to class not to learn more about writing but to find out what was happening to the characters. This book will take you back to a time that was not so long ago. It is a story of family and friends, of life, of love, of prejudice, and of war. It is a story that once you begin you won't want to put it down. It is a story that will make you laugh and cry and want to tell all your friends about. It is a story you will never forget.

Ginny Lennox, ED.S
Kaizen-Muse Creativity Coach

STREET OF SECRETS

A NOVEL

For Larraine

M C Quince

M.C. QUINCE

I owe a special thanks to the late writer and friend C. Robert (Bob) Kuehn for his tenacious encouragement and support during my first attempt to write Street of Secrets more than twenty years ago.

Thanks to my fellow writers Ginny Lennox, Marilyn Ryan, and Lois Magline. Their support and presence was crucial during the past three years as I finished the final draft of Street of Secrets.

I will be forever grateful to my husband Fred, for his love, support, and belief in me.

In memory of my grandfather

Francesco Cundari, Sr.,

who raised twelve children

on a ditch digger's pay

PROLOGUE

STREET OF SECRETS is the story of a special place in a Northern city where people lived during a time when political correctness was unheard of, and severe prejudices were held about anyone different from one's own race, nationality, and religion. With the advent of World War II and specifically with the attack on Pearl Harbor, the barriers between nationalities and religions began to disappear.

Families lived in enclaves of their own nationalities, clinging to the security of the familiar. It usually took several generations for them to venture out of their safety zone. The attack on Pearl Harbor hastened that change, giving rise to the slogan, The Great Melting Pot. The story centers on children coming of age when the country was at the brink of war. It's about rebellion, secrets, and forbidden love as they try to free themselves from their parents strict control. The attack on Pearl Harbor brings both sacrifice and redemption.

This is a Chicago story. The families live in a real place during real time, and their feelings and attitudes represent the times in which they lived, a time of different morals, beliefs, and expectations. It was a time when parents had the final word. It was a time of innocence, great bravery and patriotism. It was a time that has passed, and those who still remember will soon follow.

This is a work of fiction; any resemblance to persons living or dead is purely coincidental. Churches, schools, and a few other institutions are named to give homage to organizations that once served a vital neighborhood that no longer exists.

M.C. QUINCE

STREET OF SECRETS
1945

She heard the bell ringing. She thought she was late. Running, she slipped and fell on the wet pavement. When she looked up at the entrance to her school it began to fade away.

"Rosemarie! Rosemarie!" a voice called from somewhere in the distance. She opened her eyes and the ringing bell stopped. It was all a dream, but the voice was real. Lillian was standing at her bedside. She touched her shoulder and said, "Are you awake?"

She turned over and rubbed her eyes so she could see more clearly as she stared up at Lillian's form in the dark. There wasn't any light coming from beneath the window shade. It must still be night, she thought. She turned the nightstand lamp on and looked over at the clock beside it. It was 3:00 a.m. Startled at seeing the worried look on Lillian's face, she sat up straight.

"What's wrong?"

"It's your Mother; she's called and wants to talk to you."

"My Ma's calling at 3:00 in the morning?"

She was now fully awake and worried. She threw off the covers. It was a cold January morning as she ran barefoot into the hall to the telephone.

"Hello Ma, why are you calling so early?"

Nora's voice sounded husky, like she had been crying.

"Rosie, it's Grandma, she had a stroke during the night."

"Granny had a stroke? She's going to be ok isn't she Ma?"

"No, she died about an hour ago and I'm sorry if I woke you up. I thought you might have just gotten home from your night shift."

She could hear the sadness in her mother's voice. "Oh Ma, I can't believe it, not Granny!" It never occurred to her that one day Maria, her grandmother, would not be with them.

"I'll come home Ma, don't worry," she assured her.

3

"No, no you can't!" Nora's attitude changed; fear replacing the sound of sorrow she heard when her mother spoke.

"You can't come home, and you can't come to the funeral either."

"What do you mean; I can't come to the funeral? He can't keep me from saying goodbye to Granny."

"Please, please," her mother pleaded." If you come, I can't promise what will happen. I'm sorry Rosie; he won't let you in if you come."

"You have nothing to worry about Ma, don't get upset."

After she hung up the phone, she started to cry as Lillian helped her back to bed.

"Don't get yourself all upset; forget what your father thinks," Lillian said, pulling the covers around Rosemarie. "How long is he going to hold a grudge?"

"You don't know my father!"

"But you're his daughter, he can't disown you forever."

"You don't know my father!"

Rosemarie cried, as Lillian sat on the edge of her bed trying to comfort her. When she left the room, Rosemarie lay awake thinking of how her life used to be. She had a family once, and they were a close family. Now everything was different. She couldn't change it or turn time back; she wished for that. She cried for the grandmother she loved, and the loss of her father's love. She thought back to a more pleasant time. Back to when she was a child, and didn't have a care in the world.

CHAPTER 1
1931-1932

Eight-year-old Rosemarie Nuzzo was standing on the sidewalk in front of her home. Her eye hurt from the impact of a snowball that had turned to ice. It wasn't the first time he threw snowballs at her; his aim was pretty good for a ten-year-old. She didn't like this funny-looking, redheaded, freckle-faced boy who delighted in tormenting her. When her family lived on Taylor Street, she wasn't the target she found herself to be in this new neighborhood. Her father had promised they would move to a new home by her eighth birthday and he kept his promise. Standing in the snow with her cheeks smarting from the cold and tears freezing on her cheeks, she wished she were back on Taylor Street.

The redheaded boy disappeared into his home across from hers. She ran up the stairs to her family's second floor flat and kicked off her wet galoshes in the hall. The house was quiet, except for the ticking of the mantle clock. She took a deep breath; she loved the aroma of her grandmother's fresh baked bread as it filled the kitchen. She hurried to the table where two plates covered with napkins were placed for her and her ten-year-old brother, Joey. She barely had a half-hour to eat lunch and return to school. It was Monday, two weeks before Christmas, and her mother and grandmother would be in the basement doing the laundry. The home they lived in was a rented flat; it was as old as the flat they had moved from. She remembered how the old neighborhood smelled like her mother's kitchen, but here on West Congress Street everything was different. There weren't any redheaded boys with ugly spots on their faces on Taylor Street. Her father said the move out of the old Italian neighborhood would be good for her grandmother. It would help Maria to speak English more clearly. "Grandma will never learn in the Italian neighborhood," her father said. Yet, it was he who continued to speak to his mother in her native language when he lost patience with her. The street they lived on was an oasis, a mosaic of people of different nationalities. It was the only street that acted as a buffer between the more recent Italian and Irish neighborhoods, two volatile groups that were known to clash on a hot summer day. In 1931 the effects of the Great Depression were very visible. It was a terrible time of struggle, and people felt most comfortable living among their own kind.

Rosemarie heard the hall door open and close with a bang. Her brother Joey rushed in, disheveled and breathless as usual.

"You're late," she said.

"What happened to your eye? It's all red and puffy," he said.

"That bad boy across the street hit me with a snowball again," she cried, rubbing her eye.

"Oh, you mean Patrick McCann?"

"Is that his name?"

"Yeah, I'll take care of him."

She smiled, "Don't get into anymore fights. Mama will be mad at you if you get into trouble again." Nora entered the kitchen.

"Who's in trouble?" she asked. They both looked up to see their mother and grandmother carrying a huge bucket of coal into the kitchen.

Nora was upset and looking at Joey, she said, "Didn't I tell you to make sure you filled the coal bucket and brought it upstairs before you left this morning? Wait till I tell your father!"

Maria tried to calm her down. "That's okay, that's okay, he gonna do it, we no tell Papa, okay?" She patted her grandson's cheek. Joey knew he would be in trouble if he forgot to do his chores, especially since his mother was about to give birth soon and she needed his help.

Nora looked at her son with a frown and shook her head. "I promise Ma, don't tell Pa," he said. He knew his father came home irritable from trying to find work, mostly day labor jobs, which were scarce.

Nora watched her two children eating their lunch. She had always wanted a larger family, but it wasn't to be. She was a stocky woman, an inch taller than her husband, and expecting her third child after eight years was a blessing she never expected. She was thirty-eight-years of age. She never thought she could have another child. Her husband Benny was forty. Not many couples they knew of their age were still having children. Maria, her mother-in-law, called it a blessing from God. She was happy to be a grandmother again. She missed how she doted on Rosemarie and Joey when they were babies. When the children had finished lunch and returned to school, Maria put the coffeepot on for a cup of fresh coffee. Nora let her mother-in-law do whatever the old woman wanted to do; it was a way to keep the peace. Nora was good at that. Mrs. Katz lived downstairs and owned the building. The landlady would often tell Nora she should have control of her own kitchen, but asserting herself between her husband and his mother was the one thing she couldn't do. Mrs. Katz was a short stocky woman who wore thick-lensed glasses, a necessary aid for her diminished eyesight. She was a kind woman, a widow who lived alone. Her married son, David, seldom visited. For lack of anything else in her life, she would attempt to involve herself in the affairs of the neighbors and although she meant well, her meddling wasn't appreciated. Her husband, Sol Katz, had been the neighborhood tailor. His shop closed because of his death several years before. The Katz's were Jewish and the only Jewish family to ever live on Congress Street. The Jewish neighborhood was south of the Italian neighborhood. In 1931 people of the same nationality stayed in their own neighborhoods, but the Katz's wanted to live near their tailor shop, which was on Van Burien Street at the edge of the Irish neighborhood. The neighbors appeared to be tolerant of each other, but inside the privacy of their own homes true feelings about anyone different were freely expressed.

Benny Nuzzo was a little man, five feet five at most, and

at the age of forty his hairline was receding. He feared becoming bald. He was a man full of doubts about his station in life and his place in society, but not of his position as head of his family. He was frugal with money to a fault. He abhorred waste. Nora tried to make a little extra money knitting for the neighbors or helping her sister Rose in her bakery, which added to his insecurity along with deep feelings of inferiority. Since the crash of 1929, he went out to the worksite that hired day laborers. He was fearful of not finding enough work. Jobs were scarce, especially in winter. He knew they gave him the worst kind of work and he didn't dare complain. He meekly went about what he was assigned and kept his feelings to himself. He was lucky to find work only a few days a week and when he returned home he would unload his frustrations to the detriment to his family.

Maria would always put her son in his place, so Nora let him complain and she let Maria handle the explosions that would surely come if he had a hard day at work, or if he returned home without work. Maria knew how far she could go with her son. Because Nora was a gentle soul, she was unable to deal with him. She kept busy knitting for the new baby; little sweaters, bonnets, anything to keep out of her husband and his mother's heated discussions.

"You want I makea you a cupa coffee, huh?" Maria asked.

"No, that's ok Ma," she answered, with a frown.

Maria ignored her and poured the coffee anyway. Nora sighed; all she ever did was sigh. It wasn't in her nature to complain about anything.

A knock on the kitchen door brought Nora to her feet; she looked out between the curtains on the window. It was Mrs. Katz, and she had the empty sugar bowl in her hand as usual.

"Come in Sylvia," Nora said, as she opened the door. Mrs. Katz was quite busty. Her dresses seemed too large for her, but Nora and Maria thought she wore large sizes to hide her ample figure. Benny made fun of her, telling Nora that the old lady looked like she would topple over forward when she walked

8

because she was so top heavy. Nora hoped the poor women hadn't heard his remark. He was on the back porch when he said it. Nora had a soft quiet voice, but her husband's natural speaking voice was loud.

"Sit down, Sylvia," Nora pointed to one of the kitchen chairs. "How've you been?"

"Oy, mine feet hurt today, so I come and do some kvetching." Nora knew it meant complaining in Yiddish.

"A little bit sugar you have, maybe?" she asked, holding out the empty bowl to Nora.

Maria smiled and took it to fill. Between Maria speaking broken English and Mrs. Katz throwing in Yiddish words, the two older women had difficulty understanding each other so most of the conversation was between Nora and Mrs. Katz. Nora longed to tell her of her concerns and problems, but with Maria there it had to keep for when she was downstairs in Mrs. Katz's kitchen. If she stayed too long, Maria would find an excuse to go down and ask for her.

The two women talked mostly about Mrs. Katz's only child, David. When he was fifteen, the family moved to Congress Street and David didn't mind as well as he had when they lived on 12th Street. She had a hard time getting him to attend Hebrew school. When David was twenty-three, he eloped to marry a Christian girl and quit going to the temple. His father took the news badly and a few years later Mr. Katz died. Mrs. Katz's only brother and his family lived in Germany. She had cousins, but they also lived in Germany. She came to America in 1905 to marry Sol Katz. David was born in New York City where Sol's family lived, but her husband wanted to move west so they came to Chicago when David was five and Sol opened his shop. They lived in the Jewish neighborhood, and years later after his shop had become established, they bought the 2 flat building on West Congress Street. The owner who sold them the property thought they were German, which they were, so with Sol speaking fluent English and Sylvia keeping silent, they bought the home and moved into the goyish neighborhood (as Sol referred to their street) to be near his shop. They blended in and at first no one knew they were Jewish. They were fair and appeared German. Davie, as they called their son, was blonde. It was a time of severe prejudice, not just between races but also between nationalities and religions, especially if one were Jewish. Nora found Mrs. Katz to be a warm person and felt most comfortable with her, more so than with the rest of the neighbors. By the time the Nuzzo's moved upstairs from Mrs. Katz, most of the neighbors knew the Katz family was Jewish, and although they appeared polite towards them, they kept their distance.

Joey and Rosemarie running up the stairs broke up the visit between the women.

"Oy! Too late I stay," she exclaimed when she heard the children returning, "I go now," she said. Nora showed her out the kitchen door with the borrowed sugar and turned to her children.

"Do you have homework?" she asked, looking at Joey. "Start doing it now before your father gets home." They used the kitchen table to do homework. The dining room table was always kept with a lace tablecloth, ready for company.

"So, how did school go?" Nora asked.

"Okay Mama, I still have spelling to do." Rosemarie answered.

Joey sat down and started right in, but with Maria looking over his shoulder, he became annoyed. "Granny, please!" he complained, "You can't help me." Maria continued to check on what he was doing even though she didn't understand any of it. Before they finished, they heard their father's footsteps on the stairs. Nora looked at the clock; it was too early for him to come home, so she worried. As he came into the front hall with snow on his boots, Maria yelled for him to remove them because he was getting the floor wet.

"Aw hell, what a day!" he groaned. Coming into the kitchen, he asked for a hot cup of coffee. Nora ran around the table to the stove, her stomach large with child getting in the way of her usual speed when it came to waiting on Benny. She was afraid to ask him why he was home early; he didn't find work for the day, she thought.

Maria saved her that task. "Figlio, perche?" was all she managed to ask before he yelled at her, "Speak English, Ma!

I'm home early because the snow is deep and it's freezing outside! They sent us home! When I get work, it's outside. I work outside!" he yelled.

"No yell!" Maria shouted back and the words between mother and son erupted half in English, half in Italian.

Nora poured his coffee and went into her room and closed the door. The children had fled to their rooms before he had his boots off. This was another evening, with mother and son yelling at each other as usual. Nora would usually try to calm him, but since she was close to giving birth, she could not tolerate his outbursts and would withdraw from whatever room he was in.

Rosemarie was named after her Aunt Rose, her mother's sister, and her Grandmother Maria. The whole family called her Rosie; she hated to be called Rosie. She liked her full name. The teachers at school used her proper name, but her family addressed her full name only when they were cross with her. She lay curled up on her bed holding a doll she received as a gift from her Uncle Nicky, her father's brother. She put her hands over her ears to shut out the loud shouting coming from the kitchen until it became quiet. When her grandmother called her to supper, she knew it was safe to come out.

"Looka here," Maria pointed to her granddaughter as Rosemarie came into the kitchen. "You scare her," she said, looking at Benny.

"What do you mean I scare her? You spoil her Ma. She's eight years old, you treat her like a baby, she's not gonna be the baby no more, soon we have a little one again, huh, Rosie," he said, as she sat next to him. He put his arm around her. "What do you want, Dolly? A baby brother or sister?" He

11

always called her Dolly when he thought she was upset.

"A sister," she answered.

"I want a brother," Joey said. Nora smiled; she knew one of them would get their wish soon.

Four weeks later on January 14th, 1932, Joey got his wish. Nora gave birth to an 8 pound 9 ounce son, and Benny was beside himself with joy. He wanted another son, a brother for his cherished son Joey, a real brother, not like his own brother Nicky. Benny and Nicky never got along. The children loved their Uncle Nicky, but Benny considered his younger brother a good for nothing, spoiled by Maria. He was the son of her second marriage. Benny's father died when he was six-years-old. Maria and Benny were in Italy, waiting for her husband Joe to send for them. Joe died soon after coming to America, and as was the custom in the old country when a husband died, his brother, if single, married his widow. When Maria and then twelve-year-old Benny arrived in America, her brother-in-law Frank met them in New York when the ferry from Ellis Island arrived at the Battery Park pier. Frank was Joe's younger brother, but he was taller and more handsome than Joe. Maria fell instantly in love. She had feelings for Joe, but this was different. Joe was twelve years older, and it was an arranged marriage. With Frank closer to her age, she didn't expect to feel the way she did. Frank was smitten with her also. She was a pretty woman, petite in stature. Soon after they were married she was expecting their son, Nicky.

When Frank became ill, Nicky was only two-years-old, and Maria counted on help from Benny. In order to help them, he had to quit school at fifteen-years of age. He never attended school in Italy because Maria sent him out to be a shepherd boy. His wages were their only support after Frank's illness. Benny attended school in America, but only for a few years. He took evening classes to speak proper English. He was proud and didn't want to speak with a thick accent. He wanted to feel like a real American. Benny resented having to fully support his mother and eight-year- old brother after his uncle died. By then, Benny was twenty-one and a married man. He felt his uncle had given all his love and attention to his own son. Benny had his own ideas on how brothers should be, full brothers, real brothers. Baby Sammy, named after Nora's brother who perished in the First World War, was the answer to all his dreams. He loved his daughter, but to an Italian man, having sons was everything.

When Nicky was born, Benny was just a little older than Joey and he looked forward to having a brother. His feelings towards his brother changed when he realized Maria favored her younger son. Frank was crazy about his son, but he was hard on Benny. His feelings changed toward his uncle. He disliked him and later resented his brother. Maria would yell at him, "You be ashame, you big, the bambino, he small, whatsa wrong wit you?" Benny knew it wasn't the kid's fault, but as Nicky got older it was easy to see how spoiled he was. Benny couldn't get away with much as far as Frank was concerned. He grew resentful; he had to work for everything he wanted. At age thirteen, a newspaper route paid for the bike or the baseball glove. Nicky got all that at a much younger age and didn't have to lift a finger to get it.

When he met Nora, he was twenty-years-old and a year later he felt lucky to marry a girl who was quiet and compliant. She didn't mind sharing her home with his mother and brother. As time went on, it was Benny who found it intolerable, and when Nicky turned eighteen and was working, he asked his brother to get a place of his own. Their relationship didn't improve after Nicky moved out. When Nora had trouble having children the first ten years of their marriage, Maria blamed her. "She too heavy," she would tell her son, "She no stronga girl. She eata too much." She blamed it on the fact that Nora's sister, Rose owned a bakery. When Nora had the first couple of miscarriages, Maria blamed it on the morning sickness and that her daughter-in-law didn't eat enough. Nothing Nora did was right by Maria. Benny would lash out at his mother after seeing how upset his wife became.

13

"Just ignore her," he would tell Nora. "She's old, let her talk."

When Nora was expecting the first child she was able to carry beyond the third month, Benny was beside himself with joy. She was twenty-eight-years-old and he was thirty. He thought it would never happen. When they had a son, he felt his life was complete. Nora knew he wanted to name him after his father, the father he barely remembered, so Joseph it was. When Joey was two, Rosemarie was born. Benny couldn't ask for anything more. At the birth, he cried and thanked Nora over and over for his children as though he had nothing to do with their existence and it was her gift to him. He was a happy man, and now eight years later to have another son was more than he had ever expected.

The year went by quickly, and Benny looked forward to coming home from work each day to see how one-year-old Sammy was doing. He had something to look forward to, something to take his mind off of the hard work. The mornings near the Outer Drive in downtown Chicago went by quickly enough, but the afternoons went slowly. It was almost spring of 1933; the weather bearable, but soon the summer heat and humidity would come and make his out-door job what he dreaded. Mr. Bruno, the foreman on the WPA job, gave Benny the worst job. He had to crawl into the smallest places, but it was Benny's size that determined where they could use him. His mild demeanor on the job also put him at risk. He never complained for fear of getting fired; he had seen it happen to men before. When he first started working full-time in late 1932, many men were out of work. He was grateful to have any work at all, even if it was a WPA job developed by the government, a job he hated.

The workers were preparing for the Chicago World's Fair that was coming and for the crowds that would descend upon Chicago. Laying water pipes deep beneath the ground was work that had to be done. In 1933, the fair would show Chicago's hundred years of progress.

Years earlier in 1919, when Benny was twenty-eight, the Eighteenth Amendment was ratified.

Prohibition had arrived in Chicago. The city became dry. With the Volstead Act, liquor was outlawed. In 1920, there were places where drinks could still be obtained in secret. Speakeasies sprang up all over the city. His only job had been working as a bartender in a neighborhood bar, and he also emptied spittoons and cleaned floors. When prohibition became law, he lost his job. After he was unemployed, he had to find work quickly. He had a wife to support, but he also had to provide for his mother and fifteen-year-old brother. He wouldn't work unless it was legal, but he only qualified for terrible jobs or dirty jobs; his lack of education kept him a ditch digger. A job no educated person had to do. It was against this background that he struggled with low wages and anger. When the crash of 1929 came, he found himself out of work with a wife, children and a mother to support. His new job with the WPA was a means of putting men to work by the new president elected in 1932. President Roosevelt called it the new deal, and that is when he went to work full-time. Having to support his mother and brother all those years wore him down. He didn't have much choice, his uncle passing away left him angry and overburdened. He became short-tempered and expressed misplaced anger towards his family over any infraction, real or imagined.

Nicky worked as a punch press operator, and he made more money than Benny who had a family to support. Nicky's money ran through his fingers like water; he was always broke. Maria didn't help matters; she would slip her favorite son a few dollars whenever he asked. Benny would give his mother spending money, and it would go to his brother. The brothers quarreled often. By the time Sammy was born, Nicky was twenty-seven, but not ready to settle down. He was always going out dancing or to the racetrack, and there were the women; he always had women around him. Benny considered his brother spoiled and thought of him as a useless squanderer.

15

Nicky would come to visit his little niece and nephews whenever he thought Benny wasn't home to avoid a confrontation with his brother. Nora accepted Nicky and was kind to him, but Nora was kind to everyone.

When Nicky came to visit his new nephew for his first birthday, he couldn't avoid Benny. He looked at Sammy and said to Maria, "He looks like Nora, doesn't he Ma?"

Maria agreed. The first child to favor Nora, he was a chubby baby, fair and angelic with the blue eyes of his mother. Joey had dark brown eyes like Benny and Rosemarie's were greenish-hazel like Maria's. Joey was average size for his age, and Rosemarie was a petite girl like her father and grandmother. Benny was uncomfortable with his short stature; he wished he had taken after his father and uncle. Nicky was the taller son.

The visits never lasted as long as Nicky would have liked; Benny had to ruin it.

He was lifting his little nephew up when Benny said, "When are you going to settle down? You don't want to wait until you're too old to have children!"

Nicky turned around and faced him, "I'm not old. You were thirty when Joey was born!"

Benny yelled back, "I was married at twenty-one, Nora lost three babies, and what do you have at twenty-seven?"

"Stop, stop," Maria yelled, "you makea nicea time no good!"

"I'm going Ma," Nicky said, and as he left the room Nora came in.

"Don't go," she pleaded. "Sit down, and have something to eat."

"No thanks Nora, I have to go," and he left as quickly as he had come.

Maria glared at Benny, "Why you makea you brother go?" Like her son, she shouted whenever she was upset.

"I didn't make him leave; did you hear me ask him to leave Ma?" Benny threw his hands into the air above his head,

16

"I'm going out for a paper," he yelled as he left the room. As time went on, Nicky's visits were always the same and as Benny became bitter over his frustrations in life, he directed his hostility mostly towards his brother.

CHAPTER 2
1939

In the heat of a blistering summer, the foreman blew a whistle at lunchtime. Benny stopped his digging and pulled out the slightly damp diaper he kept hanging from his belt. It was the only cloth that would keep his face dry from the ever present perspiration. The salt from the sweat burned his eyes, and he had to wipe his face often. A man's handkerchief wouldn't do; it was too thin. Nora talked him into using one of the few diapers she had saved from their youngest son. At first he thought she was crazy to offer a baby diaper, afraid the men he worked with would laugh, but soon such fears disappeared; a few men liked the idea and did the same. He expected better employment since leaving the WPA job and finding work with a construction firm. In 1939, more construction jobs were becoming available for putting men back to work, but the only work he qualified for was the same kind of work he had when he worked for the WPA.

The backbreaking work of digging deep trenches left him exhausted, and the grime of such labor buried itself into every crease of his deeply tanned complexion. Mr. Marini was a formidable boss, and Benny felt he was picked on for every infraction, real or imagined. A Mr. Tanner owned the construction company, but he seldom appeared on the worksite, preferring to hold the foreman responsible for the work and the crew. Benny started the day waiting for instructions as Mr. Marini or the straw boss, as Benny referred to him, kept changing his mind on where he should start. Benny resented being used as a gofer.

"Benny, get the water jugs out of the truck!" he yelled loudly. Although he stood next to him, he was making sure all the men would know who was boss. Benny resented being singled out for menial jobs; it diminished his ego and left him feeling less than the man he thought himself to be. He walked up to the back of the truck with his jaw muscles twitching, and the veins in his clenched fist protruding as he held in the anger he felt most days. He thought he worked too hard for barely a livable wage. He labored each day in the hot, humid summers, and the biting, cold winters of Chicago's unforgiving weather.

He noticed men taller and larger than him were treated with more respect. He also realized that whenever Mr. Tanner appeared on the job, Mr. Marini's demeanor changed; he resembled the men he abused. Tony Amato had a very dark complexion, an Italian who Mr. Marini picked on regularly. He treated his own kind with contempt. Most of the men on the job were poor Italian or Polish immigrants just over from the old country, barely speaking English. The men who were non-Italians, Benny knew were treated differently. The straw boss came down heavily on his own nationality, and Benny hated him for that.

After lunch was over, he grabbed his shovel and went to work digging the heavy soil. It was backbreaking work, and he would pause occasionally to dry off his face as the afternoon sun bore down on him. Such pure manual labor demanded very little intellectual thinking, so Benny's thoughts were of his family as his muscular arms automatically lifted the shovels full of soil. He thought of his eldest son, Joey, and what he wanted for him and the plans he made for him. He wanted Joey to work inside. It was the only plan his position in society allowed him to think about, a job inside, not the kind of work, just inside work. As the day progressed, he became covered with dirt. It was on his clothing and his skin, and his work shoes were covered with mud. He would take them off when his workday ended and bang them on the ground to knock the mud off. What he feared most each day was riding the red streetcar to return home. He would race to the streetcar barn to be the first one on in the empty car to avoid what he called the clean Americana's, who boarded at each stop. He would enter at the back of the car and stay behind the conductor where everyone boarded, and not sit where rattan seats held nicely dressed ladies or worse, men in suits with fedora hats, their pants neatly pressed, their fingernails white, their expressions pleasant, until they would notice a ditch digger enter the car. Benny picked up on every nuance, and it made him feel like a bug trying to dodge the footsteps of man. He was never comfortable until he arrived home. Year after year his only refuge was his home, but lately he noticed his children were changing. Since his daughter had become a teenager, he thought she wasn't as happy to see him as she had been when she was small. His eldest son was never home, and he didn't know what to make of his youngest son.

As he rode the car westward toward his home, he stood ready to be the first to jump off at his stop to avoid bumping against the neatly dressed riders. He couldn't wait to get to the safety of his flat where he could discard the dirt and grime of the day, the ever present reminder that he, Benny Nuzzo, would never be anything more than a poor ditch digger. In the safety of his home he was the man of the house, and he expected to be treated with respect.

When the car stopped at the corner of Francisco Avenue and Harrison Street, he got off quickly as others from the center of the car disembarked from the front where the motorman sat. He noticed his Irish neighbor, Mr. McCann, was one of the passengers who got off. Benny slowed his walking pace; he didn't want to run into the man, one he barely knew. He was embarrassed by how dirty he was. Mr. McCann walked briskly ahead of him wearing the clean uniform of a Chicago policeman. Benny thought that kind of work was a job of privilege. A privilege most Irish seemed to acquire. He was relieved when the policeman turned into the alley behind his home. Benny walked faster, intent on reaching his porch before he ran into anyone else. He remembered when he lived on Taylor Street; he was more comfortable. In the old neighborhood he wasn't the only man who came home from a day of toil, covered in mud. He often thought of the reason he moved farther west to Congress Street and regretted the move whenever he clashed with his daughter. She was pulling away from him; the Americanas who lived around them were influencing her, he felt sure of that. He also felt threatened by the influence his Jewish landlady and the Southern neighbor next door had on his wife. Once he was inside the safety of his flat he knew he was the boss, and all his insecuritys disappeared.

CHAPTER 3

Fifty-year-old James McCann entered his home, tired as usual, after walking his beat all day. Katie, his thirty-nine-year-old wife, was sewing and Jean, their baby, was sleeping. Katie motioned for him to close the door gently. He held the door as he closed it quietly behind him. He said very little and went straight for the radio. He flopped down in his favorite chair and turned the radio on for the evening news. His feet burned after having walked his beat as a good cop was expected to do. He was assigned to the Maxwell Street district, a Jewish merchant area bereft with smugglers and thieves. The merchandise was displayed on stalls and tables in the street and in front of stores, easy pickings for the criminal element. Having six children to feed kept Jim working extra hours. Grandpa Casey McCann, a widower known as Pops, was Jim's seventy-year-old father who lived with the family. The McCanns had lived on West Congress Street for the past seventeen years.

Their children were sixteen-year-old twins Michael, and Margaret, known as Peggy, and the eldest son Patrick, eighteen. Nine-year-old Kevin and seven-year-old Brian were the youngest sons and then there was the baby. They were a family of nine. On her way to check on baby Jean, Katie asked Jim if he would like a cup of cocoa.

"No thanks," he answered, as he sat massaging his stocking feet. His shoes lay where he took them off. Katie reached down and picked them up.

"How many times do I have to tell you to take them off at the door?" she asked.

"Woman, don't nag me! Will ya stop with the naggen?"

"I wouldn't have to nag if you remembered to help a little around here!"

Katie kept a meticulously clean home. White lace curtains hung in her windows with little patches of thread occasionally replacing a missing flower pattern. She worked hard to feed and clothe six children on a patrolman's wages. She was in control of her home as much as her husband was in control of his beat. When he came home, he was on her turf. His world was of the streets and back alleys, and she never asked him about his experiences. She didn't want to know. Her father had died in the line of duty, badge 211, so she was afraid to hear about any problems he had. He had no questions about her world; he found it mundane after his experiences with the petty crooks he had to deal with, but his home was peaceful, a place to relax. He was content with that.

He asked where his two younger boys were. He was hard on his boys when it came to chores around the house but most lenient when it was outside the home. As a result, the McCann boys were well-known in the neighborhood for always getting into one scrap or another. For years, Patrick was looked upon as a bully and an irritation to the neighbors, especially the Petersons who lived two doors down from them. Now that Michael and Patrick were grown, Brian and Kevin took up where they left off. Ralph Peterson and his wife Grace owned the home that Ralph grew up in. Mr. Peterson was not tolerant of his neighbors and found fault with everyone on the street. The McCann boys tormented him with boyhood pranks, and just as Patrick and Michael quit bothering him, the younger boys began to harass him in one way or another. They loved making tire tracks when they rode their bikes over his lawn after it rained. The more Mr. Peterson complained, the more the boys enjoyed the harassing. Complaining to Jim about his boys fell on deaf ears. Jim was proud of them. In neighborhood fights with other boys, the McCanns always came out winners.

Boys will be boys was Jim's attitude. Katie was more concerned with keeping her floors clean, and she let her husband handle any complaints about their sons.

Mr. Peterson didn't think much of the McCanns; he didn't like any of the neighbors who lived on a street that was as diverse as a patchwork quilt. His father had built the home he lived in and then the neighborhood was new. In the late 1800s the residents were a people of upward prosperity, mostly white-collar workers that were referred to as WASPs, White Anglo-Saxon Protestants whose ancestors came to America decades ago. Ralph now found himself living among newly arrived emigrants or first and second generation Americans, people he disliked and didn't understand. The neighborhood was built on the heels of the Great Chicago fire of 1871. With booming new construction finished in the area nearest the lake, the city expanded westward. In the last fifty years, what was to be known as the Near West Side or East Garfield Park had fallen into a state of deterioration due to age and the poor economy. An influx of poor laborers, some barely speaking English, and others of poor backgrounds would start its downward spiral. Most of the original occupants had moved on. The financial crash of 1929 also brought southerners up north looking for work. Food on the table was a priority over painting a house. The street was interspersed with many lower economic earners and out of work poor people of different nationalities. Homes were in need of repair; lawns had turned to weeds or bare dirt, and except for the Petersons, no one seemed to notice or care.

Ralph Peterson worked for the Chicago Tribune newspaper as a journalist. He kept his job during the bad times. He was nearing age forty-five in 1939, and he was lucky his only child, nineteen-year-old daughter, Lorraine, had a job working for Sears and Roebuck. The lawn in front of the Peterson home was well-groomed. It was the only lawn. Katie McCann's pleading with her boys to stay away from the Peterson's property was useless. After Jim settled down to listen to the news, she busied herself with getting supper ready. Soon her father-in-law would be coming home from O'Conner's Tavern and it wasn't her favorite time of day. The old man had time on his hands so he chose to get out from under her nagging by spending time with the men who hung out at O'Conner's. He would usually return in time for supper. He knew she didn't approve of his trips there every afternoon, but he had nothing to do or nowhere else to go. He needed the companionship of a few of his old retired buddies from the railroad yards. He worked for the railroad for over 40 years before he retired.

"Hello Pops," Jim said, as Casey entered the house.

"Take your shoes off, Pops!" Katie ordered, as she gave him a look she usually reserved just for him.

He did as she asked. She studied his face and thought, well, at least he isn't drunk tonight. Once in a while he had a little too much to drink and she would blow up at him. He dreaded her anger and so he tried to be a careful drinker, some of the time.

"Wat yer doen?" he asked Jim, as he sat across from him.

Jim turned the sound up on the Philco radio. The news wasn't good; Hitler had advanced on Poland on August 31st and it was now September.

"Pops, things don't look good for Europe. England and France now demand a withdrawal and you know Germany won't," Jim said.

They continued to lean forward towards the radio, as they heard the commentator say that an ultimatum had been sent at 11:00 a.m. the day before the invasion, and the voice of British Prime Minister Neville Chamberlain stated that England had declared war on Germany. Casey had no love for the English; he called them Limeys.

"Well that 'ill do it, bet Hitler will give it to thim Limeys too." Casey rubbed his hands together, as he was enjoying the prospect.

He blamed the English because his grandfather was forced out of Ireland during the potato famine of the 1840s. They left Ireland when his father was a small boy. Casey was born in America, but his family never lost their thick Irish brogue. He finished grade school, but he made sure some of his children went to high school. Jim, his eldest child, had four years of high school before he joined the police force. Jim married Katie when he was almost 30 years old. She was eleven years younger than him. He gave a thought to becoming a priest but for only a moment, and he would often laugh when he would tell the story to his children. "The moment was gone the minute I laid eyes on Kathleen O'Neill's blue eyes and red hair, and any thoughts of the priesthood flew out of my head as quick as a heartbeat," he said. And as he recalled the moment, he would look at Katie and smile.

Jim, Casey, and eighteen-year-old grandson Patrick, a plebe in the fire department, sat around the radio. The news was grim.

"Are we going to get into the war, Pops?" Patrick asked.

"No," Casey answered. "Me minds me own affairs here and that's what er country should do."

Jim wasn't so sure. Katie calling them to supper ended the broadcast on the radio, and their conversation. At the supper table Michael talked excitedly about Hitler's war and how he wished he could go over and join England's RAF which caused Casey to shake his head in disapproval.

Peggy returned from her part-time work, her after-school job, at the dime store on Madison Street. It kept her in lipstick and face powder, the latest records of the Harry James band with a new singer named Frank Sinatra and anything else she wanted. She agreed with Michael and it caused Patrick to laugh and change the subject.

"Why do you buy all that dance music with that new Italian guy singing?" he asked her. He laughed as he said it and mentioned that Joey Nuzzo's sister Rosemarie only bought Bing Crosby records.

"What do you care what I buy?" she asked. "It's my money!"

"Stop it!" Katie yelled, as she couldn't stand bickering at suppertime.

She expected all her children to take their places at the table and to be quiet, bow their heads and say grace, like the good Catholics they were.

Casey started to say something, and one look from his daughter-in-law stopped him cold before he could inject his usual sarcastic remarks, which would cause havoc at the meal with his grandchildren breaking into fits of laughter.

CHAPTER 4

At the age of 16, Rosemarie Nuzzo was awaking to the ambivalence of a teenager. She loved the attention her grandmother gave, the kind of indulgence her father would have arguments with his mother over. When she was a baby and would cry, Maria would pick her up at the slightest whimper until Nora complained to Benny, and he put a stop to it. That didn't stop Maria from reaching between the bars of the baby's crib and holding her little hand. There were times Nora would find her mother-in-law asleep on the floor next to the crib with her hand between the bars.

"Look at Ma!" Nora would complain, and Benny would have to wake his mother up again.

"You're spoiling her, Ma. Let her cry. Don't sit on the floor holding her hand until you fall asleep!" he would yell. Benny did a lot of yelling.

Since Rosemarie became a teenager, new problems arose; she felt the oppressive restraints forced upon her by her strict father. She longed to breathe free, to engage in flights of fancy but she had to be content with Bing Crosby records. Her room was decorated with posters of the singer. His face was everywhere. Her brother Joey teased her.

"He's not Italian, why don't you like that new singer with the Harry James band?" he would say whenever he passed her room. She would tell him to go away, and slam her door shut.

She liked Sinatra's voice, but he was Italian and she was attracted to the Irish. She watched them on Saint Patrick's Day and at the Saint Patrick's Day parade. How proud they were. Her father referred to them as "Those Americanas," the way he referred to anyone who wasn't Italian. She knew her father and grandmother weren't quite removed from their old country ways to accept her adoration of an American institution like Bing Crosby. Even though she was born in America, she often wondered what she was. Everyone on her street was from different ethnic backgrounds, but her father linked them all together when referring to them. She also knew she wasn't allowed to date a boy, especially a non-Italian boy.

Benny was nice enough to the neighbors when he ran into them on the street, but at home in the privacy of his own kitchen, he would sit at the table after a hard day's work and complain about the Irish and everyone else. Knowing what good Catholics the McCanns were Rosemarie hated to hear him talk about how the Irish believed their ticket to Heaven depended on how many children they could bring into the world.

When Nora would remind him of a large Italian family they knew, he said, "Italians had large families because they loved children, not because they were afraid of the Pope."

Benny did the opposite of what the Pope demanded of a good Catholic. He attended Mass twice a year: Christmas and Easter. He said twice was enough.

Rosemarie didn't believe what her father thought of the neighbors, especially the McCann family. Her brother Joey and Patrick McCann had become close friends over the past year. Joey bought himself a 1924 Ford when he started working after high school graduation. It was near the end of September and both boys had jobs and were lucky to get them. In 1939 there were still plenty of men out of work. Joey worked at a gas station, taking classes to become a mechanic. Joey was proud of his car and Benny was proud of his son. Benny never learned to drive because he took public transportation. His brother Nicky had a car, but he would never ask him to drive him anywhere. Now he felt he could count on his son if he needed him. Rosemarie didn't attend the same high school as Peggy McCann, but the two girls were friends. Gone were the days when she would hear words like Mick, Shanty, Dago and Wop coming from the boys. They would yell the words at each other as children, reflecting what they heard at home. The derogatory names evaporated with some maturity and a truce of sorts, a few waves hello and then the shiny black 1924 Ford, a Pied Piper on wheels, something for Joey to be proud of and for Patrick to stroll over and admire. Each time Joey took the car out of the garage the boys got together and went for a drive. Their differences and the wrong perceptions of each other narrowed with each ride around the block.

The relationship of the girls was different. Peggy at 16 was dating boys. All Rosemarie could do was watch from her window when Peggy and her date walked to the neighborhood theater on Saturday afternoons. She wasn't allowed to go anywhere with a boy unless it was her brother. She felt it was unfair. There wasn't much she could do except look out her window or sit on her back porch and watch the elevated train pass through her backyard or the number 6 streetcars go down Van Buren Street. The cars took the entire neighborhood to Lake Michigan to ward off the heat and humidity of a Chicago summer. There was Grant Park, the Oak Street Beach, the North Avenue Beach and shopping on State Street. There were museums and park fountains to go to, a necessary journey from the oppressive heat of the surrounding neighborhoods. All of that was off limits to Rosemarie, unless a family member or a trusted friend accompanied her. Peggy went with her to the beach once, but she had to be home so early that it crimped Peggy's style. There was not enough time to engage in conversation with the sailors from Navy Pier who were often strolling the beaches.

Rosemarie's relationship with her father was changing. She was often angry with him but to Benny she just appeared moody. She couldn't confront him on what was bothering her because she knew it was useless. He was set in his ways. He catered to Joey, his pride and joy, the son he was most proud of and loved without question. Little Sammy, seven-years-old, was an enigma to Benny. Sammy was very slow and had trouble learning. He was kept back in school. He was still struggling in kindergarten and he should have been in second grade. Sammy was labeled slow or dumb. To make matters worse for Sammy, the kids at school picked on him. He was overweight, a little tall for his age, and he never seemed to get enough to eat no matter how much Nora or Maria fed him. Benny handled his disappointment and sorrow over his second son by ignoring him and leaving him to the two women to deal with. It was too painful to face, having a son with any kind of disability, especially to a man that prided himself in having sons. Although he loved his daughter, it was Joey he idolized and allowed the most freedom. Joey could do no wrong.

With Rosemarie, he was strict. In the old world way, he watched over her like a hawk above a chicken coop.

"SKIRTS!" was all her father said when she asked why she wasn't allowed to date a boy.

She complained to her grandmother, "Granny, why can't I go out like other girls my age?"

Maria held her hands palms up and looked at the ceiling as if the answer could be found there. "You Papa, he say no," she said.

She admired Rosemarie's spirit and her rebellious nature, but she also respected her son's decisions regarding his children.

On Sunday mornings, Nora, Maria, and the children attended Mass, but not Benny.

Maria would look at her son with sadness and say, "Onea day you gonna go to the church ana the roof she falla down on you."

Benny would just laugh.

It was on a Sunday morning when Nora and Maria were about to leave for church. Rosemarie wasn't ready, so she told them she wanted to go to a later Mass.

"Take your brother with you" Nora said, referring to Sammy, "It takes all morning to get him ready. What Mass do you want to go to?"

"I'm going to the 11:00 mass, Ma," she answered.

She was hoping to go alone, but having her little brother along wasn't what she expected. He didn't understand what was going on and was fidgety in the pew. She wasn't looking forward to taking him. It took too long for him to get ready and before she knew it, it was too late for the 11:00 a.m. service. She dreaded going at 12:00 noon. That was when the entire McCann family went; in fact most of the Irish familys went to the noon mass. Benny would say they can't go early; most of them are sleeping off the hangover. Rosemarie hated when he would make remarks like that, when she knew it wasn't true. She liked going when there was a mixture of people and then she didn't feel so different.

"Sammy," she called, "Hurry, we're going to be late!"

She ran down the steps of her flat to the porch below. He lagged behind; he never wanted to go to church. He still hadn't made his first communion, and she thought it was a waste of time taking him. When they reached the entrance to the church, she noticed Patrick McCann standing next to the baptismal font. She never remembered seeing him in a suit and tie before. His hair was slicked back with Brylcreem. It turned his bright red hair auburn and he did look different in a suit. She thought, *"It's funny I never noticed how handsome he is."* In all the times he came around for Joey, she had never noticed him in that way.

"Hi Pat!" she said.

He smiled back at her. He took in her brother behind her and gave a quick punch to Sammy's shoulder to acknowledge he noticed him and he followed them in. Rosemarie went up the middle isle, knelt, blessed herself and waited for Sammy to enter the pew first. She turned to look behind her to see if Patrick was seated; she couldn't see him, so she turned back and waited for the Mass to begin. Halfway through the service she felt uncomfortable and turned to look down the aisle again. She spotted him sitting across the aisle about four rows down with his family. She thought he was staring at the back of her head. She tied the blue scarf tighter under her chin to keep it from slipping off. She had spent a lot of time on her hair that morning; it was one of her best features, long and shiny, light brown like her mother's, almost the color of taffy. She wished he could see it cascading down her back, but she had to cover her head in church.

She had not seen Patrick in weeks. He would come up to her porch, usually to call for her brother. Was he really staring at her, she wondered, or was it her own self-consciousness over the strange feelings she had been having since she first laid eyes on him when she entered the church. She felt flushed as though her cheeks were on fire. She thought it was her imagination. She was sure of it. It couldn't be because she felt something for Patrick McCann, not the same Patrick who a few years earlier tormented her as she walked home from school, who threw the largest, hardest snowballs, who pretended to run her off the walk on his makeshift scooter when she tried to skate. She hated that old orange crate he made with scraps of wood and old skates. She thought it was ugly with all the bottle caps and slogans he nailed on it. Her brother had a real scooter and would laugh at it, a cause of friction between two eleven-year-olds, but that was seven years before. No, she thought, *"I couldn't possibly have a crush on that nasty Patrick."* Somehow he had changed. She wondered if it was the handsome demeanor he seemed to possess this particular day in church. Like a chameleon, he seemed to fit his surroundings. *"I dare not look back a third time,"* she thought. She did not want him to think she was interested in the likes of him.

After she went up for communion, he watched her coming back to her seat, head down, hands in prayer and thought she looked different. When did she develop breasts? He wondered. *The last time I noticed her, she looked scrawny, but now she is so pretty; I can't believe it's the same Rosemarie, Joey's little sister*, he thought. Thoughts of Rosemarie followed him out of the church. He stood around after the mass was over trying to get a glimpse of her again, but there wasn't a trace of her. Rosemarie hurried down the steps of the side entrance. She was too embarrassed to run into him again. She was sure her face would give her feelings away. The pit of her stomach felt like it would fall out. She would never be the same around Patrick

33

McCann again. She was sure of that. She wondered what had overcome her feelings as she hurried to return to her home. She went into her room and sat by the window hiding behind the curtain and waiting for the return of the McCann family from church. They made quite a crowd walking down the sidewalk on the way home. As they approached their porch, Patrick seemed to linger and look over at her house; she backed away from the window and watched him follow the rest of his family into their home. She wondered if he was looking back to see if he could catch a glimpse of her.

She entered the front room in time to see her father turn away from the window. He was laughing as he said, "Leave it to those Irish, look how they go single file down the sidewalk to church and back, like sheep. The church ain't going to run my life!"

Maria heard him and entered the room. "Benamino, you shoulda be shame you say sucha tings! Watsa matter wit you? Benamino, you gonna go downastairs whena you die!"

Sunday supper was served promptly at 3:00 pm. Nora hurried around the kitchen as Maria was bringing dishes to the dining room table.

"Rosie! Comea help!" Maria called.

Rosemarie went into the kitchen and retrieved the silverware from the kitchen table to take to the dining room. The family always ate Sunday supper in the dining room. She tried to pay attention to what she was doing, but the memory of Patrick kept creeping into her thoughts.

Nora looked at her and said, "She's in a daze Ma."

"Watcha what you do!" Maria scolded.

"What's with her?" Nora asked, directing her question to no one in particular.

Maria looked at the mistakes. Rosemarie put two forks at one plate, two spoons at another and her grandmother corrected it.

Benny took his place at the head of the table and after several glasses of wine he would become talkative. Nora was still in the kitchen handing out plates of food to Maria who carried them to the table. The women made sure everyone had enough to eat. Rosemarie picked at her food. By the time Nora and Maria were able to sit at the table, Benny and Joey had almost finished. Sammy couldn't get enough food; he ate like he couldn't get it down fast enough. When he reached for more, Benny slapped his hand on Sammy's fork causing the meatball to fall back on to the serving plate.

"You had enough!" Benny shouted.

Sammy whined, pointing to Rosemarie's uneaten food.

"She ain't eaten hers Papa, can I have that one?"

"No!" came the answer.

"Oh comea on!" Maria yelled, coming to her grandson's defense, " Hesa grow up!"

"Yea Ma, he's growing in the wrong direction. You can blame the Scali family for that," Benny said, as he looked at Nora.

He never stopped bringing up the shortcomings of Nora's side of the family when it came to weight. Maria remained silent; Nora wouldn't get any help from her on that remark. That Nora was subservient to both Benny and his mother didn't go unnoticed by Rosemarie.

Joey seldom got involved in family squabbles; he was too interested in spending as much time away from home as possible. Except for his work, he spent most of his time dating girls.

He finished his supper and as he got up from the table, Nora asked, "Are you going out again?"

"Ma, you know I always meet the guys on Sundays," he answered.

"Leave him alone," Benny said, "You know he always goes out on Sundays."

Nora could see that in some way Joey reminded her of her brother-in-law Nicky, but she knew Benny would never admit to it. To Benny, his brother was irresponsible; Joey was just a regular guy, doing what most young guys did. They chased after girls, and that is why he knew he had to watch over his only daughter.

CHAPTER 5

When Rosemarie hung out with Peggy McCann she had occasions to go over to the McCann home. She noticed that Peggy's mother ruled the home. She thought Peggy's father's uniform gave him a look of authority, and when she was younger she was frightened of him because he represented the law until she once viewed him sitting at the kitchen table in his sleeveless undershirt, and then he looked harmless. The past year brought changes to her friendship with Peggy. They started to grow apart ever so slightly. Peggy was allowed to wear lipstick, and she wasn't. Peggy had more freedom, and she felt she wasn't allowed any. She thought about all the past visits between them, how she never noticed Patrick, nor he her. After the encounter at church, she knew she would find it impossible to ever go over to their home again if he was there.

Benny continued to work hard as a laborer, digging ditches for the new water main downtown near the Tribune building. He struggled to make ends meet and with Joey paying some board and Nora taking in sewing for some of the neighbors, it kept them afloat. Every penny counted in 1939, as they were still struggling with the hardships of the depression.

Once he arrived home, Benny expected everyone to wait on him. He worked on his job and that was it. At home he sat and gave orders; he was king of his household, and Joey was raised to expect the same. He would try to make demands of his sister.

"Hey, Rosie!" He called in a singsong voice when he wanted a favor. "Would you iron my shirt? I'll pay you ten cents".

She did it because she needed the money. Her father did not want her to work at the five and ten; he thought that could wait until she graduated in two years because that was all he expected of her. She was a girl. She reluctantly got out the ironing board, put it across two chairs and held out her hand.

She demanded the money first. It never occurred to her to refuse. She had been ironing her brother's shirts since she was twelve years old, since Joey discovered girls. He would then go down to Peppy's Drug Store and Soda Shop with the guys to drink Coca Cola and watch for girls. Then all the whistles and catcalls would start. Rosemarie was never the recipient of such attention. It was an unwritten rule, you never whistle at Joey Nuzzo's sister. She was untouchable. No one ever said, watch out! Don't stare at Rosemarie Nuzzo; they just knew. Patrick thought of that when he stared at her breasts beneath her sweater in church.

Across the street in the McCann home, Patrick was getting ready to hang out. He combed his hair and pondered about going over to Joey's in hopes of getting another glimpse of Rosemarie, but her brother changed that idea by ringing the McCann doorbell first, and then the two boys would stroll over to Peppy's Drug Store. Rosemarie ran to her bedroom window in time to watch them leave. Patrick at six-feet was taller compared to Joey's five-ten, and his red hair glistened in the sun. Her heart beat faster. She thought she could not possibly have a crush on a boy she despised a few years before, but she did. It was a stronger feeling than what she felt when Bing Crosby or even Frank Sinatra sang. Maybe it was the red hair she was attracted to, and he still had some freckles. She thought they looked ugly when he was younger, but now she found them kind of cute.

She sat on her bed and thought of him, how he was off-limits to her even if he liked her, not because he was her brother's friend, but because he wasn't Italian. She told herself that maybe it was her imagination that he noticed her in that way. She felt safe in enjoying the new feelings that stirred within her. No one would know. She would never tell Peggy, especially Peggy. Peggy might tell her brother, and he might laugh or worse tell Joey. Joey thought of her as an extension of her mother and grandmother, not the person she was becoming.

After reaching Peppy's, Joey and Patrick ran into a few

other guys that hung out. One character, by the name of Billy, had a blonde girl hanging on his arm. She wore shoes with high heels, open-toes and ankle straps, and her skirt was above her knees. Her lipstick was bright red, too red. She wore her hair in a high pompadour in front with a red hairnet holding the back of her long hair in a large page; it was called a snood net. Joey could tell she was one of the put-out girls by just the way she hung on Billy and chewed her wad of gum, blowing bubbles as she listened to the guy's conversation.

"Puttana," Billy whispered to Joey.

"What did he say?" Patrick asked.

Joey laughed, "That means tramp in Italian" he said, as both boys entered Peppy's store, the slightly battered screen door slamming shut behind them. They sat in a booth by the window.

"Leave it to Billy to find all the live wires," Joey said, as they looked out the window.

They drank their Cokes while the Jukebox was playing Moonlight Serenade by Glenn Miller's Band and watched a few more guys circle the blonde outside. In their neighborhood, her kind was hard to come by. She was the butt of jokes between most of the guys. They didn't even know her real name. It didn't matter; it could have been any name.

"I guess she wasn't worth introducing," Patrick said, laughing.

"Maybe he was afraid we would make a move on her," Joey said.

Patrick shook his head from side to side, "Naw, not me Joey, she's not my type."

On Monday night after Joey and Benny returned from work and supper was over, they sat next to the radio to hear the latest war news. Canada had declared war on Germany. It was the end of September and Hitler's troops were deep into Poland. The German-Soviet Treaty dividing Poland into eastern and western zones was complete. Benny thought of Mrs. Katz downstairs. She was from Germany, and there were

39

rumors that Hitler had made things tough for the German Jews. He knew she had family there. There was a Polish family on their street, but they didn't know them. They were a young couple with a baby.

"I hope they don't have family in Poland," Benny said.

The Nuzzos along with the McCann family and most of the neighbors spent the evenings around the radio. The news from Europe held their full attention. Benny was upset because the news reporter said there were attacks by the Italian press against England.

"You don't think Italy will join Hitler do you?" he asked Joey.

"Pa, haven't you heard what they're saying about Mussolini? They're calling him Hitler's Faithful Jackal!"

Benny shook his head, "No, Italy will never join Germany!" he said, but he was worried.

"Yes, they will and they have, and we'll get into the war sooner or later," Joey answered.

"Never!" Benny yelled, "Italy will never fight America!"

He couldn't imagine that ever happening when he had family still living in the old country: cousins, and second cousins. No, that would never happen, he told himself.

"President Roosevelt will never get us involved," he said, but he was talking out loud to himself. Joey had left the room.

CHAPTER 6

The first week in October it rained for three days. Everything in Maria's garden needed weeding; it was the end of the growing season, and the carrots and lettuce needed attention. Maria was proud of her little patch of vegetables that grew between the garage and the back porch. For being in her seventies, she had a strong back. With the help of her daughter-in-law, she managed to turn the ground over and plant the seeds she so carefully cultivated in pots on the kitchen windowsill. She planned on working in the garden that October Saturday when she heard Brian McCann come into her backyard calling for Sammy.

"Hey Sammy!" he called.

Sammy looked over the porch railing down into the yard. Maria eyed Brian suspiciously. She knew he usually got into trouble on the street, and Sammy was gullible when he played with him. Brian was on his scooter.

"Get your scooter," he told Sammy.

Sammy retrieved his from under the porch. The boys started towards the street when Maria reminded Sammy to stay on the sidewalk. She stood with her hands on her hips, and her forehead wrinkled as she watched the boys until they were in front of the house and out of her view. Then she turned back to her garden.

Maria looked back towards the front of the property when she heard a loud wail; she threw down her hoe and walked quickly down the gangway and met Sammy pushing his scooter and crying. Brian was running home. She looked up to see Mr. Peterson yelling from his porch and yelling at her. She understood the word dummy and that she should keep Sammy on his side of the street.

She yelled back in Italian, "He's no dummy!"

Sammy did everything Brian did. They were the same age in years only. Sammy didn't remember Maria's words of

41

caution. He had trouble remembering rules or time; this forced members of his family to search for him before supper each night until Nora made him come in much earlier than his playmates. Sending him to bed without supper wasn't a deterrent. He had trouble paying attention to anything for long. He had lost his footing and control of Brian's homemade scooter. When he did what Brian told him to do, he ended up on Peterson's neatly trimmed lawn with the metal skate wheels attached to the orange crate which dug a long path into the soil beneath the grass. Brian thought it was amusing with Sammy lying on the ground. He found it easy to talk Sammy into trading scooters when they played. Sammy's scooter was store bought by Joey. Maria put her arm around her grandson who was now crying uncontrollably. Sammy's feelings were touchy. He cried often.

"You no follow thata bada boy," she said, as she consoled him.

Mr. Peterson closed his door behind him and entered the front hall. His wife Grace met him with a dishtowel over her shoulder and a large spoon in her hand. She heard the shouting but dreaded confronting him about it.

"What's wrong?" she asked, even though she didn't want to know.

Swinging his arm in the direction of the door, he said, "Those damn Dagos across the street should keep that dumbbell of a kid on his side of the street. No use telling them; the old lady doesn't understand a word of English."

"Ralph, the boy can't help the way he is," she said.

"Then all the more reason they should keep him home," he answered.

"I can tell that flatfoot down the street what I think of those brats of his, a lot of good his badge does him! What kind of an example do his kids set in this neighborhood? They are the worst of the lot."

His face still red and flushed, he sat down in the nearest chair and shook his head from side to side.

"And another thing, I'm sick and tired of seeing this neighborhood going to hell. There was a time it wasn't like this you know!"

Grace knew she was better off keeping quiet. She let her husband rattle on until he had spent himself. Any type of reasoning she tried with him only succeeded in flaring up his temper even more.

"This street has never been the same since those damn Shanty Irish Micks, Dagos and Hillbillys started moving in; and the Jews should have stayed in their own neighborhoods!"

He went on ranting as his wife left the room to do her chores. She didn't get upset over his anger and bigotry; she was used to it. She paid little attention to the things he said about the neighbors. She didn't feel that way about them, but she couldn't convince her husband to see them as she did. She thought of how kind Nora was when she became ill one winter. Lorraine told Rosemarie and in no time at all Nora was over with a hot plate of manicotti. None of the neighbors rang the Peterson's doorbell when Ralph was home, so Grace knew her neighbors in a way her husband never would.

Grace had a quiet way about her; she appeared subservient to her husband on the surface, but unlike Nora Nuzzo, she was able to go and do as she pleased. Where she and her daughter were concerned, Ralph's bark was all hot air, blowing off steam. He never followed through with all his threats. He was kind and gentle with his wife and daughter, but with the neighbors he showed an ugly side. Everything bothered him when he looked out his window. He had derogatory names for everyone on the street, and he received much pleasure in using them. Mr. Peterson referred to Mrs. Katz as a kike or that putty-nosed Jew. He called the Nuzzo Dago and the Wood families Hillbillies. He made fun of the neighbors who went to church. He was not religious; he didn't believe the Bible was the word of God, just a fairytale he would tell his wife and daughter, but that never stopped Grace and Lorraine from attending Sunday Service at the Little

Messiah Baptist Church in the neighborhood.

Grace tried to make up for his gruffness by being sweet and kind to all the neighbors. Nothing he said amazed her; nothing he said upset her either. It was just the way he was. Later that evening as Mr. Peterson stood leaning on his rake, looking at the ruts in his lawn, Jim McCann was returning home. He walked towards Jim, and as he neared the McCann porch, Jim knew it was about one of his boys again.

"I want you to take a look at what your boy is responsible for," Ralph said.

He pointed to his lawn.

Jim looked over at the lawn and laughed, "Oh that's not so bad, I thought maybe my boy broke a window or something worse."

Jim tried to laugh it off, but Mr. Peterson continued to complain, all because of two hardly noticeable little lines in the grass.

"I haven't got time to listen to such nonsense," Jim said, as he walked up the steps of his porch, his back to Mr. Peterson.

"What did you say?" Mr. Peterson asked.

Jim turned to look down at him, "If you haven't heard me, I don't repeat," then he walked into his door leaving the enraged man standing on the walk.

"You're no officer of the law," Mr. Peterson called after him, "You're a disgrace to the police department!"

People walking down the street were watching the exchange, so he walked back to his house and disappeared into it as quickly as he could. Looking disappointed, Grace admonished him.

"Ralph, you made a spectacle of yourself out there!"

"That shanty Mick, did you see how he walked? I think he was drinking. They shouldn't have any Irish on the police force!" he ranted.

"If that were the case dear, we wouldn't have a police department. The whole department is Irish and Mr. McCann is not a drinker. The old grandfather is, not him." Grace said.

Lorraine joined her mother in the kitchen; she whispered to her, "I get so embarrassed when Dad gets that way. None of the kids on the street like him, that's why they pick on our house. Why does he hate everyone?"

"He doesn't understand them, dear," she said, putting her arm around her daughter, "He doesn't really hate people, deep inside I think he cares, I know he does."

"Too bad everyone else doesn't know," Lorraine said. She didn't agree with her mother, but said nothing more.

CHAPTER 7

Joey spent the month of October working on his car, getting it ready for winter. The garage opened to the alley in back of his house. He hung curtains in the backside windows, polished and buffed the old car until it shined so bright one could see his reflection. Whenever he went into the garage to work on it, Rosemarie followed hoping to run into Patrick. Finally, the weekend Patrick walked across the street and down the gangway between the houses to Joey's garage, she was on an errand with her grandmother. As she climbed the backstairs, her arms full of groceries, she heard laughter coming from the garage. She recognized Patrick's voice. The boys were in the garage so she hurried to put the groceries away.

Joey was in his usual place on Saturday mornings, working on his 1924 Ford. He loved keeping it highly polished. When Patrick came over, Joey was happy for the help.

Patrick bent down to Joey who was tinkering under the car. "Find anything wrong with her?" he asked.

"Just greasing her a little. She has a squeak in the front wheels." Joey got up and wiped his hands on a rag hanging from his pants belt.

"She sure looks great!" Patrick said.

"Well, I keep her inside as much as possible; it's the original paint job you know."

Patrick changed the subject, "Did you hear the latest news? Looks like we might still get into the war."

"No, I don't think so," Joey frowned. "We're not sending any help in arms, and Roosevelt promised to keep us out of it, so far he has."

"But if Mussolini's made a pact with Hitler," Patrick said, "if we did send army material it wouldn't be enough."

Joey turned away from what he was doing inside the car and looked at Patrick, "My father thinks Mussolini has been good for Italy."

"He's a dictator."

"Yeah, but he helped all the poor send their children to school."

"How's that?" Patrick asked.

"Well, he made a rule that every child had to go to school. When my father was a boy, only the rich could afford to send their children to school, mostly boys, girls not at all. We got relatives there, cousins. Nah, I don't think we'll fight them."

"If we get sent over there, I think I'd join right up, go into the navy maybe; if you join first you get to pick what branch of service you go into. Wouldn't you go Joey?"

Joey looked at Patrick, shook his head no and said, "I don't know Pat, I don't know." Then he crawled back under the Ford.

Patrick looked around the garage and through the garage window over to the back porch of Joey's house hoping to catch a glimpse of Rosemarie. He couldn't get her out of his mind since running into her at church. He wondered why she never came over for Peggy like she had before.

"What are you looking for?" Joey asked, coming up behind Patrick, as he was looking out the back window of the garage.

"Oh nothing, thought I saw Michael follow me here."

Joey had no reason not to believe him, so he went back to the car. Patrick turned away from the window and knelt down to help.

"Hand me that wrench Pat."

"Sure thing."

Patrick reached into the toolbox that lay on the floor. He was still on his knees next to Joey who was under the car when a pair of brown and white saddle shoes topped with white Bobbie socks appeared. Patrick looked up; above the socks were a pair of shapely legs. He raised his eyes to see a pleated plaid skirt just at the knees; he stood up and her white sweater caused his heart to beat faster.

"Hi!" he said. She just smiled. She had a beautiful smile.

His eyes went from her smile to her eyes. Their eyes locked, somewhat like they did at the back of the church that Sunday. Now that he had a second look at her, he realized how much she had changed from the past few years.

All he could think of to say was, "How old are you now?" but before she could answer, Joey crawled out from under the car.

"What are you doing here?" he asked, with a look of disapproval.

"I just came to see what you were doing," she said, never taking her eyes off of Patrick.

Patrick stared back at her. Joey looked from her to Patrick and back to her. Patrick remained silent.

"I just wanted to see what you were doing," she repeated.

"Since when did you care about what I'm doing?"

"You polished her up real good Joey," she said, as she ran her hand across the fender.

"Yeah, well you never bothered about my car before."

Sammy came into the garage, "Mama wants you!" he said.

"Ok," she answered, not moving.

"Mama wants you! Mama wants you!"

She got irritated, and gave him a stern look.

"Rosie, Rosieee!" he whined, and pulled at her sweater.

"Don't do that!" she said, anger creeping into her voice

"Mama wants you!"

"Ok, Ok," she said, annoyingly, as she gave Patrick one last look. "Bye," she whispered.

"Bye, Rosemarie," he said, as he looked at Joey, fearing his face turned the color of his hair, but Joey didn't seem to notice, and Patrick was thankful that Joey wouldn't know how his heart was pounding.

Sammy paused at the door after Rosemarie left. "Her name is Rosie!" he said loudly, correcting him.

Patrick just smiled and continued to hand Joey tools while trying to watch Rosemarie climb the porch stairs. Later that night, Rosemarie thought only of Patrick. She was sure he felt something for her by the way he looked at her. She would be seventeen on her next birthday. She knew she just had to date a boy, any boy, because she feared appearing so juvenile on a first date. She was fearful of a first date being with Patrick, that he would realize what a child she was if he ever asked her out. She found it difficult to concentrate on anything. She was afraid of what her brother might have guessed.

She wondered, *Would he be angry with me, and mention to Pa that I flirted with a boy?*

She was afraid to face Joey across the supper table that night. But Joey showed no knowledge of what had gone on between her and Patrick. If he did, he didn't mention it.

Later that night, Joey would go into the garage, take out the Ford, swing around the corner and pick up Patrick for their usual drive. The boys cruised around the neighborhood in the evenings and she would watch from her window. She watched between the trees and buildings to the street south of her street; it was a busy street. Van Buren to the north had a streetcar line that ran downtown. Harrison Street to the south was also a streetcar line. Congress Street, a residential street, was set between two busy streets with the schools and businesses that served the neighborhood. The boys stuck to the two busy streets when cruising. Too far to the south and Joey would have been teased about driving a Mick around. Two streets to the north and Patrick would have been kidded by the Irish he knew for riding with Joey.

Rosemarie attended Marshall High School, the same school Joey graduated from. Patrick graduated from St. Phillips, and Peggy attended St. Mary's school for girls. Benny often wondered how his Irish neighbors could afford to send their children to private schools. The economy was still struggling in 1939. One day, when he wasn't at work due to bad weather, he watched from the window as the McCann children walked to school wearing their school uniforms.

He became agitated and said to Nora, "The church has no business teaching reading and writing or telling a family to keep having so many kids. Look at the Irish, like sheep; they follow like blind men, letting the church lead them. They have no mind of their own!"

"Oh, Jesus, Mary and Joseph!" Nora said, making the sign of the cross. "Maybe they'll go to heaven, they believe, you don't Benny. I say a prayer every night for Mr. Peterson; maybe I should say one for you too?" She crossed herself again.

"Ahhh," he answered, throwing his hands toward her in a wave, "What do you know?

Did the priest ever come here with a food basket when I was out of work? No! But they went over there!" He pointed to the McCann house, "The Irish take care of their own!" he shouted.

"Maybe if you showed your face in church once in a while, we might have had some help," Nora said, as she turned away from him, hoping to escape his tirade about the church.

"You went, and did they help you? No! We're Italian!" he yelled. "You know what the Irish think of Italians? They think we're all crooks and gangsters. Well I work hard for what I got. I never did a dishonest thing in all my life, but still, that's what they think. You know what they are? They're all drunks; look in O'Connor's Tavern on Van Buren Street. They're all there every night, elbows on the bar, singing their silly songs. That McCann is tied to his wife's apron strings. After he gets home you can hear her yelling at him; he gets no respect in his own house. His kids pay no attention to him; that's why he can't control them in the neighborhood. Look at the trouble they get into. Yeah Nora, you should understand that a man is a man, and he deserves respect. That McCann is useless in his own home."

Benny switched his thoughts suddenly and shouted, "Where are my brown shoes? I'm going out to get a newspaper; did you see my hat anywhere? You got my shoes shined?"

Nora quickly retrieved them for him. She couldn't wait

50

until he left. The last thing she heard him say as he went out the door was how useless Mr. McCann was in his own home.

CHAPTER 8

Jim McCann had a hard time convincing Katie that Patrick should have a driver's license. He would be nineteen soon, and Jim was thinking of buying a car. With public transportation on two streets less than a block from his home, he never felt the need for one, but now with Patrick grown, he thought it was time. Katie looked at him like he had gone daft; Peggy entered the room to hear her mother voicing her fears.

"Aw Mom, Pat's old enough to drive," she said.

She agreed with her father.

Katie had a worried frown on her face, "I don't want him cruising the streets like that Joey across the street; that's all I see him do, cruise the streets and look for girls in that old Ford. It's just a trap for the girls."

Turning to Jim, she said, "I warned Peggy about that car, and I warned her about Italian boys." Addressing Peggy, she said, "Stay away from Italian boys, they only want one thing from you, and then they marry their own kind."

"Joey's ok Mom, he's just a friend. Pat's friend and mine, that's all."

"Well, just stay out of his car. You know the rumors I hear about that car?"

"No Mom, I didn't hear any rumors, what rumors?"

"I heard he gets a girl into it, and drives her through the alley to his garage and he drives right into the garage because the door opens and closes by itself. He fixed it to do that."

"Who told you that Mom?" she asked, a wide-eyed look of surprise mixed with amusement crossed her face.

"Never mind who told me, I'm telling you! Watch yourself. You know what father O'Malley said; protect your innocence at all times."

"Mom, I know who tells you these things, it's old lady Katz, she has nothing better to do than imagine what goes on in the alley behind her house."

"Well that's what I heard, and besides you better be careful if you want a pure life like your Aunt Margaret."

"Wait Mom, I'm not going to be a nun just because you have a sister in the convent."

"Well, they lead a good life."

"And you expect Patrick to be a priest because Uncle John is a priest, right mom?" Her mother's staunch belief in the merits of the religious life was irritating Peggy.

"Pat isn't going to be no priest Mom!"

"How do you know?" Katie asked, her voice sounding a little edgy.

"Because he likes girls too much, that's how I know," she said, as she went to join her father in the front room where he had escaped after he mentioned a car for Patrick.

The last thing she heard her mother say was, "He'll get that out of his system in a couple of years, you'll see."

Peggy and Jim smiled at each other, a knowing look between them. Father and daughter were on the same page as far as their thoughts about Patrick.

CRUCRUCRU

Across the street, Rosemarie was waiting for her brother's car to come down the alley. Once the boys got together it could be hours before they returned. It was almost suppertime and Nora was at the stove preparing the meal, so she went back in to help her mother.

"Is your brother back?" she asked.

Rosemarie shook her head no.

"Well, Aunt Rose is coming from the bakery in a few minutes with bread and your favorite blueberry pie."

"Is she staying for supper Ma?" Rosemarie loved when her Aunt Rose brought bakery items.

Her family never lacked for desert from Rose's bakery.

"Yes of course, and I invited Mrs. Katz to eat with us, you know how she loves her sweets. I feel sorry for her because she's so alone. Ever since her son moved to Skokie she doesn't see as much of him."

"Why not Ma? That's all she ever talked about was her Davie."

"I don't think since he married out of his religion, he comes around as much to see his mother, it's too bad but what can she do?" Nora's expression was sad as she talked about her landlady.

A knock on the kitchen door interrupted their conversation. Rosemarie opened the door to find Mrs. Katz; she seemed upset. Nora led her to a chair.

"What's wrong Sylvia?" Nora was concerned; she knew it was too early for supper and Mrs. Katz came early.

Maybe she's sick, Nora thought, waiting for her landlady to answer, but she was too busy wiping her eyes and blowing her nose to answer.

Maria came into the room, "Maybe shesa sick," she added.

Mrs. Katz shook her head no. The three Nuzzo women felt sorry for her; they knew she was alone and seldom had visitors. Nora patted her on the back.

"Tell us Sylvia," she said using her first name as she often did when it was just between them.

"What could be so bad? Is it that you don't feel well?"

"Nein, Oy, the bad news, the bad news I got," she cried.

"Is it about your Davie?" Nora asked.

"Nein, today from mine cousin I get the letter, from England she write. From the friend in Germany she get the letter. Mine cousin, she run avay from Germany after Hitler take over, oh vat he does! The letter, it say mine brodder's store vas broken into, they smashed all the vindows that belonged to Jews and now mine brodder and his family are missing, they vas taken avay. I don't know vat happened to him, his vife and the children, he vas mine only brodder, Oy, such terrible tings over there."

"Maybe he'll write soon," Nora said, trying to console her.

"Such terrible tings that Hitler vas doing to the Jewish

people, they take avay their verk and stores and den they disappear too. You don't vead about that in the papers or hear about such tings on the radio, but the Jews here, vee know vats going on, vee get letters. Mine cousin vas lucky she left Germany ven she did. My Papa, he vas run out of Russia at the start of the first vorld var and now mine poor brodder," she continued to cry.

Maria had a sad expression on her face, and all she could do was offer the poor woman a cup of coffee.

Nora put her arm around her, "You have your son Davie!"

"Oy, Davie, Davie," Mrs. Katz went on," Ven he's not busy, I have Davie. All the time he is too busy for his own mutter."

"You have your daughter-in-law and the two grandchildren." Nora kept her arm around her. "They come to see you don't they?" Nora knew it was seldom but she was trying to comfort the poor women.

"Daughter-in-law?" Sylvia asked, anger in her voice.

She slapped her cheeks with the palms of her hands in frustration, forgetting that Nora wasn't Jewish, she said, "She's a Shiksa! Mine grandchildren, Shiksa, they don't go to temple. Davie don't go no more, only mine poor brodder Jake, kosher he keep the home and now he has no home. In Europe they vun you out, here in this country they mix you up, until you become like a pot of borsht. Who's who, vot's vot, who knows vot he is, only my poor Sol, may he rest in peace, he knew who he vas!"

Nora hugged her with sympathy and looked at the clock. Benny would be home soon. It was one of the few Saturdays he had to work. Maria carried dishes to the dining room; they would need the larger table with Mrs. Katz and Aunt Rose staying for supper. Sylvia kept a kosher home in the early years when her husband was alive, but time and loneliness caused her to become lax. She enjoyed Nora's cooking and never asked what was in the dishes put before her. She was grateful for the invitation and the company.

Next door lived a young family, Bob and Twyla Woods; they came up from Kentucky and lived next door to the Nuzzos the past five years. They had two young children when they arrived, and they took to Nora and Maria as if they were family. Mrs. Katz was kind to their children and between the Nuzzos and the Woods family, Mrs. Katz had their company to look forward to. When she left the Jewish neighborhood, she lost contact with her old neighbors. A few old friends passed away, and others moved to Skokie. In later years, the synagogue on 12th Street was too far for her to walk, so she quit going.

Rosemarie helped her grandmother set the table, and soon after the footsteps of her father could be heard on the front stairs. He entered the door with his usual crabby expression. He expected everyone to jump and tend to his needs. He stared at the dining room table set for company and his expression turned sour.

"What's all this about?" he bellowed, "Who's coming over today? You know on Saturday I wanna to come home and relax!"

Nora rushed into the room to explain, "We have Mrs. Katz for supper tonight," she said in a whisper hoping Sylvia hadn't heard his loud remark. Rosemarie added, "Aunt Rose is coming too."

"Oh hell, bringing all that bakery stuff again?" he asked, knowing that she never came empty-handed.

He could eat anything and never gain weight, but Nora and Sammy were not as lucky. A slice of pie showed up on both of them, especially Sammy, he wouldn't be content with one slice. Maria took Benny's jacket and hung it on the hall tree where he would throw it and miss. She gave him a look he knew well; it meant more than behave, we have company, and don't embarrass us. She picked up his shoes and brought them to the kitchen; they were caked with mud and he insisted on using the front stairs, making extra work for the women. He said he was too tired to walk around to the back of the house.

56

He got off the streetcar on Harrison Street; it was closer to the front of the building. He grumbled to himself and went into the bathroom to wash up and change his clothes. He then went to the front room dragging his tired feet to his favorite chair, sat down and closed his eyes. He would remain that way until he was called to the table.

When the doorbell rang, Rosemarie ran down to meet her aunt to relieve her of the heavy shopping bag. Together they came into the hall before the dining room. Rose peeked into the front room and seeing the back of Benny's head, she retreated into the kitchen. She wasn't too fond of her brother-in-law. She greeted Nora, Maria and Mrs. Katz. Rosemarie put the bag on the kitchen table; Mrs. Katz peeked into it and took a deep breath. The aroma of fresh baked goods and the arrival of his aunt brought Sammy in from the front room floor where he had his lead soldiers lined up.

When he got up to run into the kitchen, Benny yelled at him, "You better pick these up before I step on them!"

He didn't move from his chair or bother to greet Rose. He hated when it was too quiet in the kitchen; he felt like the women were plotting against him. He strained to hear if they were talking about him.

When he was called to the table, he walked in like his feet were weighed down with lead. Rose tried to keep the smirk off her face.

He never bothered to say hello first, so she said, "How's work Benny?"

It was all she could think of to say, which was the wrong thing to ask him.

"Don't get him started," Nora whispered to her as they took their places at the table.

She told Sammy to sit between Mrs. Katz and Maria, as far away from Benny as possible. With Benny at the head of the table, Rosemarie and Joey would end up on each side of him, except Joey wasn't home yet. His chair remained empty half way through the quiet meal.

"Where's Joey?" Aunt Rose asked.

"He's not home yet," Rosemarie answered. "He's never home on time; if I was late I'd catch hell, but not Joey."

Rose stared at Benny, "Joey gets excused because he's a boy?" She asked.

Benny slammed his fork down, "What do you know Rose? You don't have any children, so don't tell me how to raise mine!"

Everyone remained silent; Nora looked over at her sister's face and saw sadness. It wasn't Rose's fault she was childless, she never found the right man to marry, and she had to care for her parents. After they died, there wasn't anyone to run the bakery except Rose. Nora thought it was an insensitive and cruel thing to say to Rose, but she kept her feelings to herself. She looked over at Maria who would never get involved in any confrontation with her son about anything that didn't pertain to her or her son Nicky. Mrs. Katz appeared uncomfortable and ate in silence. Sammy broke the tension-filled moment to add to it.

"Papa, how come I get punished when I'm late for supper?"

"Joey's a grown-up boy, he can do what he wants."

Turning to Nora, Benny said, "Save a plate of food for Joey and make sure it's heated up when he comes home."

All the women glared at him except Maria who was busy eating and thinking it was normal to warm up food for a son who was late. Mrs. Katz thought she wouldn't mind warming up food for Davie if only he came to visit more often. Aunt Rose and Rosemarie smiled at each other. Rosemarie had a partner in her Aunt Rose.

CHAPTER 9

"Bobbieeee!" Twyla Woods called; a towheaded boy came running to his mother with his little sister Betty following behind him.

They observed Nora standing at the door with Sammy. Bobby knew why they were there.

"Do you know who the kids are that pick on Sammy?" Nora asked.

Bobby was a year younger than Sammy but a grade ahead of him in school. Bobby was gentle and Nora preferred Sammy to play with him instead of the McCann boy. Bobby went to the John Ericsson Grade School with Sammy. Bobby knew who hit Sammy, so he nodded yes.

"Well, who are they then?" Twyla asked.

Bobby looked down at his scuffed-up shoes and mumbled, "I don't know the names, but Sammy knows what they look like."

Nora could tell that Bobby was afraid of the boys. "That's ok," she said. Tomorrow I will go to school and find out."

She thanked Twyla and took Sammy back home. He had come home from school crying, with a red puffed-up eye and a small cut beneath it. All the children on Congress Street knew Sammy; they might tease him a little, but mostly they left him alone. It was his classmates, the boys from his school, he was afraid of. The public school was predominately filled with Italian students, and was on the edge of their neighborhood. Maria had opened the door to a crying and red-faced Sammy. She called for Nora,

"Looka what the bada boys do to Sammy!"

Nora took him into the bathroom, she pulled his shirt off; it had blood on it and it was torn.

She cleaned his face and asked, "Who did this?"

"I dunno," he cried.

"Why they no leavea him alone?" Maria said, wringing her

hands as she watched from the bathroom door.

Both women felt frustrated and helpless over the situation. He would be afraid to go outdoors to play. He would sit in the window overlooking the street and watch the children play, as he munched on the fresh baked bread and butter Maria gave him to stop his crying and calm him. It added to his weight problem. Nora knew she would have a difficult time getting him up for school in the morning. He would be afraid to go. When he was younger he was picked on less often, but with each passing year they found him a more vulnerable target. She had hoped Bobby would know who the boys were, but he seemed afraid to tell.

When Rosemarie returned home from school and saw her brother's face, she said, "Sometimes I think you just stand there and let them insult you." Turning to her mother, she said, "Ma, quit babying him. If you treat him less like a baby, maybe he wouldn't get picked on so much."

It upset her to watch her mother and grandmother treat her younger brother like he was still a baby. She thought he was slow because of their treatment of him. After he was cleaned up, Nora sent him into the front room and she turned the radio on for him. It was time for his favorite after school program, Little Orphan Annie. Rosemarie followed her mother back to the kitchen.

"Wait till Pa sees his messed up face," she said.

Nora dreaded facing another argument at suppertime over Sammy, with Benny yelling and demanding to know who did it, expecting Joey to do something about it. Rosemarie helped her mother get supper ready.

"You know Ma, if he wasn't standing around whenever he saw trouble and just ran home when he plays with Brian it would be better; instead he just stands there and takes the blame." She remembered when he was younger, how they gave in to his terrible temper tantrums when he would throw himself down on the floor inside or outdoors, oblivious to all who happened to stare at him. Rosemarie loved her little brother but was often embarrassed by him. It was Sammy's unflinching trust, his being naïve, and slow in maturing that brought much sorrow to both him and his family. Nora and Maria made excuses for his condition, and Benny blamed them. When Benny came home from work and noticed Sammy's bruised face he became very angry.

"Do you know who the boys are?" he directed his question to Sammy, who nodded yes.

"Who are they?" Joey asked.

"Go ahead, you tella Joey," Maria ordered.

"I dunno," Sammy whined.

Joey patted his brother on the back and said, "After supper we're going to take a ride and you point them out to me if you see them." Sammy's eyes lit up and he smiled.

"You put a stop to it," Benny said, looking at Joey. "I mean put a stop to it! No more of this!"

Joey laughed, "Don't worry Pa, I'll stop it, they won't bother Sammy no more."

"What are you going to do? Beat them up?" Rosemarie said, laughing.

"I'll scare the hell out of them, that's what I'll do; they won't come near him again."

Rosemarie laughed, "Maybe you can get Uncle Nicky to scare them."

"What's that supposed to mean?" Benny asked, in an angry voice.

"Nothing Pa, nothing," she said.

She knew her father was touchy when it came to his brother. He was sensitive about the lifestyle he thought Nicky kept. He had a good job, but he knew he spent too much time at the racetrack, and he was sure he ran into unsavory characters there. He wasn't sure how he spent his free time. It was a source of contention between the brothers.

Later, Joey drove the Ford around the neighborhood south of Congress Street pointing to a group of boys gathered together on a street corner.

"Is that them?" he asked.

Sammy shook his head no. They went up and down several blocks until Joey spotted a few boys in an alley, so he turned the car into the alley and stopped. The boys looked surprised; they were attracted to the shiny car and walked towards it.

As they got closer, Sammy said, "That's them!"

Before the boys could run, Joey was out of the car. He grabbed the smallest boy as the other two managed to quickly scale a fence. He held on to the frightened boy's shirt by the back of his collar and pushed him against the back of a garage door, knocking over a few garbage cans. The loud clatter and Joey's expression frightened the boy and he started to cry.

"I didn't do nuttin, I didn't do nuttin," he cried. His nose started to run along with his tears.

"You've been picking on my brother Sammy?" Joey yelled into the kids face while the boy looked over at the car where Sammy sat looking out at him with a smile.

"It wasn't me," he pleaded; Joey shook him again to get his attention as the frightened boy looked up at him.

With his face brought up close, Joey said in a menacing voice, "You better tell all your friends that Sammy's uncle is a big powerful man and he can have you kids taken care of just like that," he snapped his fingers as he said it.

The look of fright on the kid's face turned to terror.

"Tell all your friends that the next time Sammy comes home crying because one of you so much as said an unkind word to him, his uncle will make a phone call. He knows some powerful men."

He bounced the kid against the garage a couple more times.

"Did you ever see Sammy's uncle? He wears a white hat and he can make punks like you guys disappear."

He let go of the kid and watched the terrified boy run off, falling as he went.

Joey started laughing as he walked back to the car. He

thought of his Uncle Nicky who played the horses and maybe placed a few illegal bets. He knew the only thing his uncle could make disappear was a sawbuck and maybe a glass of wine.

Driving Sammy home, Joey said, "You don't have to worry about those boys bothering you anymore."

Sammy smiled. When they returned home, Benny was waiting.

"What happened?" he asked, "Did you find the boys?"

"Yea Pa, don't worry, they won't bother Sammy no more."

Benny looked worried, "I hope you didn't mention your uncle," he said.

Before Joey could deny it, Sammy excitedly said, "Uncle Nicky is going to make them disappear."

"What!" Benny shouted, "It's bad enough what I think, but now you make the whole neighborhood think my brother is a crook?"

Joey laughed, "Pa, they're only kids; they'll hide out and forget about Sammy's uncle."

Benny wasn't convinced; it was one thing what he thought of his brother, but he didn't want the whole neighborhood to think that of Nicky. He knew those kids were from the Italian neighborhood; he also thought some questionable characters might live among them.

"Don't worry Pa, you and I know Uncle Nicky wouldn't hurt a soul; he couldn't step on a crawling caterpillar. He's too good natured," Joey said.

Benny knew it wasn't his nature he worried about; it was who he really hung around with at the racetrack. He couldn't imagine any decent men spending his time and money betting on horses.

CHAPTER 10
1940

It was late summer of 1940 when Rosemarie, having turned seventeen in early August, asked her father if she could go out on a date with a boy. The answer was a loud "No!" Peggy McCann had a steady boyfriend for the summer, but Rosemarie had to be content with staying home helping her mother and working at Woolworth's Department Store for the summer. Her senior year would start after Labor Day and her senior prom would be a real problem. She wasn't allowed to go to her junior prom unless she let her brother take her. It was a terrible time and she didn't want to repeat it. She remembered her father's words, "You go with an Italian boy like Vinnie Russo or your brother or you don't go." She would rather die than be seen with either of them at her junior prom, so she refused to go. She knew if she went with Vinnie, the short stocky son of the neighborhood shoemaker, the embarrassment would have killed her. She cringed at the thought of a date with him. She was determined to fight for her senior prom and attend with a proper date. She made up her mind to find a way to go; it meant too much to her.

After she arrived home from work Friday, she planned on telling her father she was going with Peggy to a birthday party on Saturday for one of the girls from St. Mary's school. She was home early, and she was happy to see that both Benny and Joey had not arrived home yet. It would give her time to prepare herself for the lie she would have to tell. She went into the kitchen where her mother and grandmother were starting the evening meal.

"Ma, I'm going out Saturday to a party with Peggy," she said.

"What party?" Nora asked, her back to Rosemarie.

She turned and shook the fork she held in her hand at her daughter. "You know if it's at night, he won't let you go."

"It's in the afternoon Ma," sounding annoyed, she went to her room and sat by the window looking out at the street below.

Her father was too strict and she felt like a prisoner in her own home. She hadn't gone over to the McCann's ever since she had seen Patrick in church. Except for the time she ran into him in her family's garage, she had only seen him from a distance, and it had been almost a year since she first realized she had a crush on him. She was so sure it was only her that felt that way. Since Peggy was dating, she hadn't seen much of her in the past year either. She thought of how close she had come to making a fool of herself when she encountered him in the garage with her brother, but the last time she got up the courage to go into the garage, the boys were gone before she got there. She was almost relieved.

After supper, Benny and Joey sat listening to the news on the radio. The war was getting worse each day as Hitler invaded more countries. The Italian dictator, Benito Mussolini, had predicted that his country would be involved in the war, and he did just that on June 11th by joining forces with Hitler. Benny was beside himself with anger. Dutch forces surrendered to the Germans. The French and English were in full retreat towards the French and Belgian coastline. In May of 1939, German troops had marched into Paris after the fall of France. The English had their backs to the sea at Dunkirk waiting to be rescued. All the war news came from London, usually a few days after the events took place. It was now August of 1940, and some in congress wanted to send war material, called lend lease, but not get involved with sending men. The English were fighting alone. America had not sent supplies openly but clandestinely through Canada.

Benny's ears never left the dial on the radio as he tried to tune in each station.

"You see Pa, all they're doing in congress is talking. We need to do more," Joey said.

"What more? It's not our war, and now England has a new

prime minister, Winston Churchill, so maybe he'll make a difference," Benny said.

"Remember what happened to the English at Dunkirk Pa?" Joey worried that England might fall.

"Oh that won't happen." Benny said.

Joey and Benny argued loudly about the direction the war was going, the news was always about what was happening in Europe.

"If England loses, Pa, Hitler will come after us next."

"Never!" Benny said loudly, "It's not our war."

Rosemarie sat in her room listening to her father and brother's voices grow louder as they disagreed. It was the same every night when the news came on. She dreaded telling him she was going to a birthday party, so she casually went into the front room and asked if he was working on Saturday. He was so busy with the news on the radio that all he said was yes. It was all she needed to hear. She wouldn't have to mention the party at all, just pretend to go to it. Later that evening, she sat on her front porch with Peggy. The girls began plotting how Rosemarie could go out on a date. Rosemarie started working after school was out for the summer, and Peggy would often shop at Woolworth's and walk home with her after her shift was over. A boy from Rosemarie's class asked her to the movies for Saturday afternoon; the Kedzie Theater was only two blocks from her home. They made up the story about a birthday party.

Patrick looked over at the girls sitting on the porch. He wanted to walk over, but didn't. He had to get ready for his shift at the fire station. He thought about Rosemarie often since the day they met in the garage. He knew how he felt about her but wasn't sure if she felt the same for him. *What good does it do if I think about her?* He thought, *she would never be allowed to go out with me.* He was sure it wasn't him personally; it was her family, and they over-protected her. He knew there had to be a way to see her alone. He laughed to himself when he thought of how his mother expected him to follow in his uncle's vocation. He always knew he would never be a priest, but he didn't have the heart to tell her, not yet.

On Friday night, Rosemarie thought about the boy in her class who would be her first date and how she would prepare to go over to Peggy's for the so-called birthday party. She was relieved that her father would be at work and also that Patrick would be at the fire station. She seldom went to the McCann home, always making sure he wasn't home when she did. The boy from school was a nice enough boy, and he seemed shy when he asked her out, so she felt comfortable saying yes. She liked him but not in the way she liked Patrick. Peggy suggested the plan about the birthday party.

"How are you going to get out?" Peggy asked, "Would your parents let you go? You can say we're going to a birthday party, you come over to my house and I'll tell my Mom we're going and I'll leave with you out our back door, and you can meet Pete in my backyard."

They made plans as they sat together on the porch.

"What about your mother?" Rosemarie asked. "Won't she question when she sees Pete with us?"

"No, she never questions, she trusts me, and she'll think he's going to the party with us. I'll walk a way down with you and then go over to Lucy's and stay until the movie lets out. Let him drop you off at Lucy's after the movies."

On Saturday Rosemarie was nervous.

She looked herself over in the hall mirror and with a fake little gift-wrapped box in hand said, "I'm leaving for the party."

She flew down the stairs to avoid a last minute question from her mother, or worse, see her mother's expression as she lied to her. Her heart beat fast; she had never gone against her parent's wishes. She was afraid of her father. He never laid a hand on her, but he could give a look that was worse than any punishment she could think of.

When she arrived at Peggy's, she applied as much lipstick as she wanted. At home, she had to wear light lipstick. Her father equated dark red lipstick with fast girls. Both girls walked out to the back alley behind Peggy's yard. Pete walked up a few minutes later and Peggy walked to the next corner with them and then went the opposite way. On the walk to the movies, Pete held her hand. It was the first time a boy held her hand, except her brother when she was younger. Pete's hand was warm. It felt nice.

In the theater, Rosemarie sat as straight as a board in her seat. He tried to make small talk, but she could hardly answer, she was nervous. She was in unfamiliar territory. Half way through the second feature, *The Bride Came COD* starring Betty Davis, (Rosemarie's favorite movie star) she felt his arm go around her shoulder. What was she supposed to do? She wasn't sure; the screen in front of her became a blur. She hardly knew what she was viewing. She couldn't concentrate on anything except his hand on her shoulder. He pulled her closer to him. She was shaking and she didn't even like him at that moment. She was seventeen and had never been on a date; she hated herself for feeling so nervous. She started to regret saying yes to the date. She wondered what he thought of meeting her in Peggy's backyard instead of picking her up at her house like most girls expected. He didn't seem to mind meeting her there; he never asked her any questions about herself, or why he didn't pick her up at her door. *Does he really like me?* She thought. Pete's thoughts were on necking; why else did he talk her into sitting way up in the back of the balcony. He didn't even buy popcorn or candy. Maybe he didn't because he didn't have the money, she thought. His hands started to move around her neck, then her arm. She could hear him breathing. His breathing became heavy and then he grabbed her and forced a kiss on her lips. The kiss was wet. She tried to push him away, but he kept forcing her. She felt like she couldn't breathe; his hand found her left breast and she pushed him away as hard as she could.

She was crying and he said angrily, "Oh come on, if you didn't want to do this you wouldn't have come up here."

She thought he wanted to see the movie, but he looked at her like a bird of prey waiting for the kill.

She felt nothing from the kiss except disgust. She hated him now. She waited for so long, anticipating her first kiss and it was awful. It didn't feel anything like what Frank Sinatra or Bing Crosby sang about. She felt cheap; she sprang out of her seat and ran down the steps to the lobby, and she couldn't get out fast enough. All she could think of was what a laugh the boys at school would have over her when he told them. She ran, crying all the way to Lucy's house. She felt so taken advantage of. What was she told at Catechism class in church? Never let boys touch you in that way. What would her parents think if they knew? Would her father call her the names he called her Uncle Nicky's girl friends?

When she got to Lucy's, Peggy couldn't believe she was back so soon. "What happened?" she asked. She could see Rosemarie was crying.

"He touched me."

"He touched you where?"

Rosemarie pointed to her left breast.

"Oh maybe he just bumped it. That's no tragedy; a boy touched me there once," Peggy laughed.

"He did?" Rosemarie looked surprised, "You didn't feel bad?"

"No, I thought it felt good, I felt warm all over."

"But Sister Veronica said…"

Peggy looked at Rosemarie and continued laughing.

"What does Sister know? She never dated a guy." Suddenly she felt bad for laughing and making light of what Rosemarie was taking so badly.

"I'm sorry Rosemarie, I didn't mean to laugh at you, it's just that I don't think it was that bad; you're not going to hell if that's what you think. At most it's a venial sin, no big deal; those sins are forgiven in the confessional, besides, I don't think it's a big sin."

Rosemarie looked surprised, "You mean I have to confess

in the confessional that he touched my breast?"

"Only if you want to."

"I couldn't do that, it would be too embarrassing."

"Did he kiss you?"

"Yes, once, it was awful."

"You didn't feel anything?" Peggy looked surprised.

"I felt nothing but lousy. What was I supposed to feel?"

"Wow!" Peggy laughed, Maybe you'd make a good nun. God knows I won't, and my mother thinks I'm going into the convent like her sister."

The girls were almost to the McCann's home and Rosemarie was still crying.

"I can't go home, looking like this," she said, pointing to her eyes. Peggy led her into the McCann home. Katie heard the door slam shut and peaked into the kitchen to see who had come in. Rosemarie had her back to her.

"Are you girls back already?"

"Yeah Mom, it was a short party." Peggy said.

Katie didn't question and went back to the front room.

Looking at Rosemarie's red eyes, Peggy led her to the sink.

"Splash some cold water on them," she said.

Rosemarie looked at the clock on the wall. She had left at 1:00 p.m., and it was now almost four. She couldn't go home until her eyes were back to normal. Unlike Katie, Nora would notice everything that was a little off, and she would question over and over.

The running water in the sink shut out the sound of the kitchen door opening and closing.

Patrick walked into the room; Rosemarie didn't see him at first. When she turned around, only to face him, she thought she would die. At that moment, he was the last person she wanted to be near. He looked at her, surprised to see her there and more surprised to see she had been crying.

"What happened to you?" he asked.

"She got something in her eye," Peggy said.

He smiled; he knew it was more than that. Rosemarie looked embarrassed, not at all like the friendly girl he last encountered. She remained silent; her head down looking at the floor, she wanted out of there badly but was frozen to the spot, unable to move.

"Sit down and have some milk and cookies," Peggy ordered, pushing Rosemarie into a chair.

She thought her demeanor was due to what had happened on her date. She was unaware it was now about her brother. Patrick sat across from her. He thought she looked so venerable; not at all like the girl he had remembered who flirted with him in her family's garage.

"The cookies are fresh; my Mom just baked them," Peggy said, sitting next to Rosemarie.

Rosemarie stared at the plate of cookies, anywhere but at Patrick. He stared at her; he couldn't take his eyes off of her. He noticed how the tears in her eyes made them shine and look greener than he remembered when he first noticed them in her garage. He looked at her shiny brown hair. Her long hair hung in her eyes and fell around her shoulders as she looked down at her glass of milk. It seemed to him that she grew up overnight. She was afraid to look up; she could feel him staring at her. He thought she was so much prettier than he ever remembered.

"How old are you now?" he asked.

"Seventeen," she said, finally looking up at him.

"You shouldn't cry; it makes your eyes all red and you have pretty eyes."

He wondered what she seemed so upset about. She didn't know what to say, except thank you. When their eyes met, neither of them was in a hurry to look away. Peggy stared at them, looking from her brother to Rosemarie with her mouth open and her eyebrows arched. She looked amused, and a little shocked. She was witnessing something but not quite sure what. She felt the tension and thought something was happening between them. She sensed it, maybe even before they did.

There weren't any more words between them. Rosemarie broke eye contact to drink her milk. As she stood up, she thanked Peggy and said she had to leave.

"Take care," he said.

She smiled and left.

Patrick turned to Peggy, "What was she so upset about?"

"Nothing," Peggy answered, hunching her shoulders.

"A girl like that doesn't get upset over nothing."

"It's none of your business Pat, but I can tell you she had a date, her first date, and you know how the Nuzzos are, they're so strict and over protective when it comes to her."

Patrick shook his head in disbelief. "So a first date, that's something to cry about?"

"Well, she had to sneak out and she was nervous about it."

He didn't press her for any more information...

CECORECORDES

Back in Rosemarie's room she lay on her bed thinking about Patrick. She knew she would never be allowed to date an Irish boy. She admired the Irish; they seemed so sure of everything. They paraded wearing green on St. Patrick's Day for the entire world to see. They were a cocky bunch and they seemed so sure of themselves; she admired that. Most of all she admired Mrs. McCann's control of her home and the freedom Peggy seemed to have.

CHAPTER 11

Nora rang the doorbell at the Woods home.

Twyla answered, and seeing Nora with Sammy she called to her son, "Bobbieee! Sammy's come to play with you."

Nora preferred Sammy to play with her gentle Bobby and his little sister, Betty.

"Y'all come on in now," Twyla said, leading Nora to the kitchen. Bobby entered the room and soon both boys disappeared to play in another room.

"It's my Sammy," Nora said, "You see how he is?"

"Yes, he's a very nice boy; is anything wrong Nora?"

"You know, the boys at school pick on him, they laugh and call him names and they hit him. But Joey took care of it; he scared the boys, now maybe they will leave him alone. He's a little slow you know; when he was born the midwife told me the cord was around his neck, and he had a hard time breathing at first, then he seemed to be okay. He's a good boy; it takes him longer to learn things. Ever since he came home with that black eye and cuts, he's been afraid to go to school. My mother-in-law has to walk him to school now, or he won't go."

Twyla looked concerned, "Sammy is welcome to play with Bobby anytime; I'll make sure they stay near the house, in the backyard or inside. I sure do understand Nora; I have a younger brother back home who's the same way. I understand, don't worry."

Nora thanked her and left Sammy to play, "I have to go make supper soon," she said, and she left.

As she was coming down from the Woods' front porch, she noticed her brother-in-law parking his '39 Ford coupe at the curb. He had this cocky walk as he walked up to her porch. He was always neatly dressed, his dark hair slicked back under the white fedora hat he always placed at the back of his head. He looked like what Benny would sometimes say he looked like, a hoodlum. It was what their American neighbors thought he was, even if it wasn't true. Nora never believed it was true. She sighed, another evening of tension is coming, she thought. He always managed to appear in time for supper.

"Hi Nora," he called to her, as they both met at the bottom of the porch steps. "How's everything?"

She hunched her shoulders and gave him a smile; he followed her up the stairs. Benny wasn't home yet; it would give him time to visit with Maria and the kids before the usual arguments erupted between the brothers. There were times when Nicky would storm out after an argument or Benny would ask him to leave. He always came back to visit like nothing happened; he appeared happy-go-lucky and Benny would let it pass. Neither man held a grudge for long, but no words were spared in their arguments.

A neighbor passing an open window on a night they were yelling at each other would think they would never speak to each other again. When their voices could be heard above the usual neighborhood noises, it always brought Ralph Peterson to his feet. He was tall and lanky as he bent over near his open window and with his Adam's apple protruding from his neck as he laughed; he tried to catch the sounds of anger coming from the Nuzzo's open windows. He never failed to hear every tone of voice, every shout; it fed his prejudices and confirmed his impressions of Italians as a loud and volatile group. Nicky's visits were an evening of entertainment for Mr. Peterson.

"Hey Ma!" Nicky greeted Maria at the top of the stairs and the old women's face lit up.

He was her baby, the son of her great love, the source of all the tension between her and her eldest son. He gave her a hug and she followed him into the front room, Nora trailing behind.

"You gonna stay to eat?" Maria asked.

"No, no Ma, I ate already."

Nora thought, *That's what he always says, and then he ends up at our table.*

Maria looked at him admiringly.

"Whata you beena doing? We never seea you. You shoulda comea over more."

"I've been working Ma, you know, I'm busy."

Nora laughed; she knew he came sporadically, whenever he needed something. If he had a good day at the track, he would slip Maria a few dollars only to borrow it back when he was broke. Money passed back and forth through Maria's little black purse more often than any transactions made at the neighborhood bank. She always had a few dollars for Rosemarie's hair curlers, for Sammy's ice cream or Nicky's little deals at the track, not to mention streetcar fare for whoever needed change. Saturdays were busy for the women; they would prepare a large supper if Benny worked on a Saturday. When Joey and Rosemarie heard their uncle had arrived, they greeted each other affectionately. Nicky put his arm around Joey.

"How are things going Joey?"

"Great, Uncle Nicky."

"Got a steady girlfriend yet?"

"No, no one special."

"That's good kid; don't tie yourself up to one. Date them all. How's the old Ford coming along?"

"I've been working on it; it needs a couple of new parts."

Nicky put his arm around Joey, "Hey, I know someone who can get you the parts real cheap."

"No thanks, Uncle Nicky, remember? I work at a gas station; I can get what I need."

Nicky turned to give Maria a hug, and then he followed them into the kitchen. He finally took his hat off and looked at himself in the mirror above the sink. Slicking his hair back on both sides with his hands, he said, "Do you think my hair is thinning?" he asked Joey, who sat at the table behind him.

Joey looked at the large bald spot on the back of his uncle's head and said, "Nah, it's still thick."

"He better geta married before he havea no hair," Maria said.

Nicky turned around, "Why should I get married, I'm having too much fun to get married."

"You getta old, you needa the wife," she yelled.

"I'm not old, I'm only 37."

"You better finda the wife before itsa too late."

She took out her tortoise comb from the back of her hair bun and combed a few strands of hair away from her forehead and just shook her head at him, with an expression of sadness.

"Ma, why are you always on my back about a wife? When I find the right one, I'll get a wife!"

"When you find the right one?" Nora laughed, "You have to hang around where the right ones are. What about Antoinette Jollia or Amelia Falula? They're nice girls."

Nicky laughed, "First, Antoinette is too fat, and second, Amelia is, you know, slow," he pointed to his head.

"But they nicea Italian girls," Marie added, "Ana they stilla no married."

"Well, that's why they're still unmarried," Nicky said, waving his hand as if to shoo his mother away. "The only ones left my age are the fat and dumb ones." She looked at her son and shook her finger at him. "You gonna die witha no family, you gonna die witha no son to carry the name."

"Oh Ma, so I die without a son! Joey can pass on the name; doesn't he have the same name? I'm having too much fun to get married; besides I don't want the dumb ones."

He looked at Nora's expression and realized what he had said.

"Oh, I didn't mean that," he said, then looking at Joey, he said, "Tell her I didn't mean"… but each time he tried to explain, it sounded worse. Joey knew Nicky loved Sammy, and didn't want to hurt Nora by using the word, but to Nora it was like mentioning her son.

Maria gave him a stern look. "What kinda son you geta from the kinda girlsa you goa with?" she shouted. "You be lucky to havea son likea Sammy. The girlsa you see, they no good."

It never occurred to her that Nicky fit that same description as far as what some of the neighbors thought about him. Joey tried to calm everyone down.

"Hey! Cool it! You know Uncle Nicky didn't mean it that way." Joey was always the peacemaker in the family.

Nora went to the phone to call Sammy home and Rosemarie entered the kitchen, "What's all the yelling about?" she asked.

Nicky looked her over, "Hey Rosie, you're growing up!"

"Thanks Uncle Nicky, I'm glad you noticed, maybe you can let my father in on it too," she said.

Joey watched his uncle hug his sister, and thought he was a good guy. He didn't see him as the ne'er-do-well his father saw him as, or the precious son his grandmother thought she had, just his happy-go-lucky Uncle Nicky who took him to carnivals and bought him ice cream when he was a kid.

"There he is!" Nicky said, as Sammy rushed into the kitchen, his face red from running up the stairs.

Sammy's face lit up with a big smile; he loved his uncle unconditionally.

"Put r' there," Nicky said, as he slapped palms with his nephew.

He ruffled the boy's hair and grabbed him to wrestle. Sammy screamed with laughter just as Benny came in from work.

"What's all the racket?" he shouted, and when he saw Nicky his expression changed. Always around mealtime, he thought.

"Hi," Nicky said, "How've you been?"

Benny glared at him, "Like I've always been," came the answer, then silence. Maria held her breath. Later at the table as the food was passed, only the clinking of forks and serving spoons could be heard in the silence. Two plates were heaped with food, not surprisingly, in front of Sammy and Nicky. Rosemarie hated when her father and uncle were both at the table. She felt like she couldn't breathe. Benny reached down to retrieve the gallon of wine he kept on the floor at his feet and poured himself a small jelly glass full, returned the cap to the bottle, and was about to put it down when he looked over at Nicky.

"Oh, do you want some wine?"

"That's ok," Nicky said.

"What do you mean? That's ok, yes or no, that's ok yes or that's ok no?"

"I don't care." He avoided eye contact with Benny.

"You don't care what? You don't care to have some or you don't care if I give some to you?"

Joey looked up from his food. It starts again over nothing he thought. His father was baiting Nicky.

"He wants the wine!" he answered for his uncle.

"No, that's ok," Nicky said, looking at Joey as if to convey to him to stay out of it.

Maria stood up. "Enough! Givea the wine," she shouted.

"You want it?" Benny held the bottle up and looked at Nicky, "You want it or no?"

Nicky was getting angry and wouldn't give in. "No!" he shouted.

Maria glared at Benny, "He can't eata the spaghett without the wine, he needs it to wasa down, it will sticka ina hisa throat," and then she reached over and took the gallon from Benny.

"No Ma," Nicky protested, "I don't want his damn wine!" but she poured it anyway. "There!" she said, and put the gallon down by Benny and gave him a look he understood.

"Mangia," she ordered, "shuta up and mangia!"

The tension was bad; they all ate in silence for a few minutes and then Rosemarie made the mistake of asking her mother a question.

"Ma, when can I go out with a boy? There's a school dance coming up soon and I want to go."

Before Nora could answer, Benny answered gruffly with a firm "No!"

"Why not?" she pleaded, "All the other girls are dating already."

"What girls? What girls?" Benny asked loudly, "Not nice girls, you mean the puttanas!"

"Are you calling Peggy and Lorraine hookers?" she screamed.

"Give them time," he yelled back, never looking directly at her.

She looked at her brother for help, "Tell him Joey, you know Lorraine and Peggy and that girl you like, are they all hookers like Pa thinks?"

Joey turned to Benny, "Pa, not all girls that date are fast. You act like you're still in the old country." He was hoping to get his father to relent.

"Tell him Uncle Nicky," she pleaded, "All the girls go out on dates at this age. I can't go anywhere or do anything, why? Why?" she asked, wiping the tears that had fallen down her cheeks with her napkin.

"You're a girl," Benny said.

"So what, that's what I'm supposed to be; I'm a girl; I'm a girl; I'm an American girl!" She looked to Maria for help, "Tell him Granny, I'm an American girl."

Maria was confused. She felt sorry for her granddaughter but years of loyalty and indoctrination into the culture from the country of her birth left her unable to side with her granddaughter. She felt sorry for Rosemarie but couldn't come to her aid. She tried to reach out to her by putting her arm around her but watched helplessly as Rosemarie fled the room in tears.

"Why must we always have our mealtime ruined by these fights?" Nora asked of no one in particular.

It was the first words she spoke since the argument started. When it came to voicing her opinion, she was unable to, and she was docile, especially in front of her husband. She sought peace at any cost. Nicky kept silent through the meal, trying to avoid any more escalation of the hostility Benny felt towards him, but he couldn't remain indifferent, he loved his niece.

"You know you can't keep her a child forever," he said, looking down at his plate. Then looking up at the women, he said, "She's not a pickle that he can preserve."

He said it in a whisper, ignoring Benny's demeanor, but he heard Benny's chair scrape away from the table. Benny stood up in a rage as the chair fell back behind him to the floor.

"You, mind your own business, and get the hell out of my house!" He shouted.

Maria ran behind Nicky and pushed his shoulders down as he tried to get up.

"NO! You no leave!" she said.

Benny knew he couldn't fight Maria; he threw up his hands in the air and left the room in a rage.

"Uncle Nicky, he isn't going to change his mind and you know how stubborn he is," Joey said.

"What about a nice Italian boy taking her out?" Nicky suggested.

"What nice Italian boy? Uncle Nicky, you know any?"

Both Joey and Nicky laughed.

"There's Gumba, Gus' son," Nora suggested.

"Oh forget him," Nicky said.

"What about the Russo boy?" Nora asked, she wanted to help and with Benny out of the room she felt brave enough to join in on a solution for her daughter.

"Vinnie? Vinnie Russo? Are you kidding Ma!" Joey laughed, "He's short and fat with a big nose. Rosie would never go out with him."

"Yeah," Nicky agreed. "And he's a Mama's boy too."

Nora had to turn her face away so Nicky wouldn't see her trying to stifle a laugh at his expense.

She started to clear the table of the half-eaten plates of food in front of her place and her daughter's. Who could eat a whole meal in this family, she thought, except for Sammy and her brother-in-law.

Rosemarie sat in her room, pondering her dilemma. She

looked out the window and watched as Mrs. Katz was walking her dog. The dog strained at its leash, trying to run, pulling the old women along. *That's me,* she thought. She felt like that dog, straining at the leash her father held. She wiped away a tear.

CHAPTER 12

Patrick and his father met on the same streetcar after work, which seldom happened because Jim usually worked extra hours, but it was Friday, and he looked forward to coming home at the same time as his son. They savored the little time they had to talk with each other alone without the rest of the family's interference. It was a short block from the streetcar stop to their door.

"How's everything going?" Jim asked. He was interested in how his son was making out at the fire station as a plebe in training. He would have been proud of his son if he had become a rookie in the police department, but he was just as happy he wasn't. It was Katie's idea for her eldest son to become a member of the fire department. She felt it was safer. Jim had to agree with her.

"Do you like your work, son?"

"Fine Dad, I'm doing ok. Today they dumped a bucket of water on me from the upstairs window. I was standing below in front of the engine, you know, polishing her up. That's a plebe's job."

"That's their way of initiating you into the brotherhood of fire fighters. At the police academy they do crazy things like that too."

As they approached the front porch, they spotted Ralph Peterson tending his lawn.

Jim started laughing, "Look at that screwball, always working on that postage stamp of a lawn."

"Aw Dad, what else does he have to do with his time, and he can afford it, he doesn't have a lot of kids, only Lorraine and she works and takes care of herself."

Patrick couldn't understand the prejudices of the grownups. Both he and Joey often talked about their parents not understanding others who were different from them. They entered the house and went to the kitchen where Katie was sweeping around Jean's high chair.

"Wipe your feet!" she said, with annoyance in her voice.

She had just finished mopping the floor and she put clean rugs down near the door.

"How many times do I need to tell you guys to come around the back instead of coming through the front hall and tracking in all this dirt?

"What dirt?" Jim said, as he brought up his shoe to look underneath it.

"There's no dirt here," he said.

"Lord knows, I have enough to do around here!" she raised her voice as she commented, and looked at her father-in-law who sat hunched over at the kitchen table, holding a cup of tea with both hands to steady the shakes.

"I'm nobody's slave," she said, looking at her father-in-law.

Casey remained silent drinking his tea. He had learned to tune her out. Jim kicked off his shoes, not so much to keep the floors clean but to relieve his aching feet.

"Do you have to do that here?" she scolded. "Your feet are sweaty and they smell."

Ignoring her, Jim sat across from his father and said, "She won't be satisfied until she nags me to death."

"Yup," Casey said, "Like ya Mama nagged me ta death."

Katie stopped her sweeping, leaned on the broom handle and stared at Casey, her face taking on the color of her hair. "Old man, what are you saying? I think it's the other way around, cause you're still here and your wife, she ain't!"

Katie was a tall, thin, serious woman, traits that were more pronounced in the presence of her father-in-law. Patrick remained silent, pouring himself a glass of milk and taking in his mother's tone of voice, the inflections, the underlying anger that his family expressed from time to time. It bothered him. He was more like his father. He couldn't stand friction in the family. The only thing he inherited from his mother was the color of her hair.

"If ever I come into this place and it's quiet, I'll think I'm in the wrong house," he said.

He sat next to his grandfather and smiled at him.

"How's things Pops?"

He always called his grandfather, Pops; it was what all the McCann children called him since they were little and mimicked their father. Katie referred to him the same way unless she was angry with him, which was often, and then she referred to him as the old man.

Casey smiled at Patrick, "Thins are thins, ya know! Me gits up in da morning and me ets somethin, me reads somethin, den me goes to O'Connor's and gits me a pint and me comes home for supper and ets somethin agin. The day is full of somethins," he said, sounding facetious.

"You forgot one thin!" Katie said, mimicking him sarcastically, "You spend your time doing nothin! You don't even pick up after yourself."

"Now Katie, stop it!" Jim ordered, "You know Pops legs are bad, and he can't be lifting and bending; he's old, have a little compassion woman!"

"He doesn't seem too old or his legs too withered to take himself over to O'Connor's every afternoon to drink with those old sops he hangs out with; he seems to manage that ok," she said.

"Please Mom," Patrick pleaded, "That's all he's got left; a short visit every day, at least he's not under foot here in your kitchen every afternoon, you would complain about that too."

Baby Jean started crying and it put an end to Katie's presence in the kitchen. As she picked her up and left the room, Casey shook his head in frustration at her intolerance of him. He did everything to stay out of her way, but the old man knew she barely tolerated him.

"She's tired; she works hard with all the children to care for, and she doesn't mean to be harsh with you Pops," Jim said.

"Her ways is different din your dear old mudder, aye, God rest er soul, ginteel she was, she never let anythin upset er.

"I know Pop, I know."

Patrick admired his father's ability to handle the tension between his wife and father to try to keep the peace, but he was upset with his mother. Although he understood her feelings, he loved his grandfather. Nothing she would say about Casey could change that.

"Ya got a girlfriend yet me boy?" Casey asked Patrick. "Yer old enough now ain't ya? Yer nineteen ain't ya? Me was married to yer grandma when I was yer age."

"You were married at nineteen?" Patrick looked surprised, he knew his father and uncles married later in life, more like the upper twenty's and early thirty's.

"All da lads at da Rail yards was single. Me was da only married one."

"How come you got married so young Pops?"

"Well, yer grandma Molly, may da saints protect er soul, a bitty ting she was, real Irish lass, straight from County Cork. Come over wit er brothers after er Mama died. I met er brother Joe Murray at da Rail yards. Thim was bad times, and I met er once and den sees er agin. Well, they didn't know wat to do wit er when she come over and she cooked a good pot o stew, so's I upped and married er."

Katie returned and stood in the doorway, giving Casey a look of disapproval,

"What kind of yarn are you spinning now?" she asked.

"Aw Mom, let him talk," Patrick said.

"He's said enough," she said.

Casey got up from the table and throwing his arms up wildly above his head said, "Pat me boy, da men in dis family can't have a decent talk amung em."

He quickly left for O'Connor's and Katie knew she might be in for another night of his drunken ramblings when he returned. She would start supper without him; if he drank too much before he could eat she dreaded his return.

Patrick looked disappointed, "Why do you always pick on Pops, Mom?" Katie just smiled at her son.

"Gosh, he was only telling a story about Grandma Molly cooking stew; what harm did he do?"

Katie didn't answer, she watched her son go out to sit on the porch and she knew he was annoyed with her. She busied herself in the kitchen and thought, *that's not all Molly had cooking.* She found that out after she married Jim. It seemed Casey and Molly just managed to say their I Do's a few weeks before Jim was born. She kept that bit of knowledge from her children and intended to keep it that way. She was going to make sure her children grew up the right way in spite of her husband's inferior family background. No child of hers would bring shame upon her family, she would see to that. The condition of their very soul depended on it.

Jim was sitting in the front room when Patrick came back in to sit with his father, he appeared upset with his mother, and although Jim heard the conversation, he chose to stay out of it. He turned the radio on. They both listened to the news.

"Sounds bad," said Jim."London is taking a beating."

Back on the 11th of June the news was about Italy declaring war on Britain and France. It was now September and the news report was grim. On July 12th the British Air Force had bombed two cities in Italy in response to the declaration of war by Mussolini in June. Italy's first offensive in North Africa took place on September 13th with plans to lock the Suez Canal. It was now the 17th of September.

"That's bad!" Patrick said. "I bet Mr. Nuzzo is very upset. Joey and his father fight over the news reports all the time."

"How's that?" Jim asked.

"I think Mr. Nuzzo is afraid we'll have to fight Italy; he still has family living there. I bet they're going at it again tonight; he has the news on every night," Patrick laughed, although he knew it wasn't a laughing matter.

After supper, Casey came home. He tottered in with too much drink in him. Jim and Patrick were back in front of the radio joined by Michael. Jim got up to help his father sit in a chair. Better to keep him out of the kitchen for now while Katie was washing the dishes, he thought. He would warm his father a plate of food later if the old man would eat. Usually he would go straight to bed. Jim blamed Katie for driving him out to stay at the tavern before he had any food in his stomach. The news on the radio was always the same, all about the war. Casey sat and said nothing for a while and Jim hoped he would fall asleep in his chair.

"Me poor grandfather, he knew what it was like under dem Brits," Casey exclaimed loudly. "He tried goin north for work but all dem jobs was taken by dem Orange Men. Really Brits in disguise, they was. No more Irish den dem Dago's across the street. They was all under the Church of England ya know, so's me grandfather left Irland. Yep, when er potato crops went, he went. He worked in America building dem railroads alongside dem Dago's, Polocks and Chinks. Me father was a boy when he come over and he worked right along wit em." Jim tried to quiet him down so they could hear the news but he just rattled on.

"He died a poor man, me father, but a happy man, ya know? He died in his parlor chair, holdin a rosary in one hand and da empty whiskey glass in da otter. He died wit a smile on his face, yep, he was a happy man, me father."

He stopped his recall just in time as Katie peeked her head into the room, her pursed upper lip displayed distaste for his ramblings.

"Do you think we'll get into the war?" Michael asked.

"I don't know, I hope not," Jim said.

"Well, I think we should. I'd go."

"Yep, just like me father," Casey said, with a wide grin as he tried to get out of his chair.

Jim had to help him, and as he led the old man out of the room, Casey looked back at Michael and said, "Yer just like him, ready fer a good scrap."

Peggy came home late in the evening.

"Where have you been?" Patrick asked, hoping had been at Rosemarie's.

He wanted to ask her a few questions. She told him she guessed how he felt about Rosemarie and he denied it but wondered how Rosemarie felt about him. He couldn't ask her any questions at supper with everyone present. She had gone out like she usually did to see her friends and just hang out. Rosemarie wasn't allowed to hang out anywhere, especially after dark.

"Who were you with?" he asked.

"I was at Lucy's, why?"

"Just thought you might have gone across the street," he said.

Peggy smiled; she didn't have to guess what he was thinking.

After everyone had gone to bed, Patrick stayed up reading some firehouse manuals. He had to study for a test and he liked it when the house was quiet without his brothers running about. Peggy came out of her room in her bathrobe and slippers; she went to the kitchen for milk and cookies. He followed her into the kitchen. He had questions to ask her about Rosemarie but didn't want his mother to know he was interested in any girl, especially an Italian girl. He knew he would never join the priesthood, but didn't have the heart to tell her, not yet, there was plenty of time for that he reasoned. With the war in Europe raging on, he felt it was just a matter of time before America was in it. He was sure of it. In that case, he could put off telling her anything indefinitely. Peggy poured herself a glass of milk and stood leaning against the sink, staring at him.

"What is it Pat? What do you want to talk to me about? Rosemarie?"

She had a slight smile on her face. Patrick's face turned red and now he knew for sure she knew about his feelings.

"Uh, oh, you got it bad for Rosemarie, huh?" She snickered a little laugh.

"No I don't," he lied. "I just wondered why her parents won't let her date, she's seventeen, and she's old enough isn't she? Well maybe when she's eighteen they'll let her, do you think?" he asked, not really believing it himself.

"I doubt it," Peggy said. "It has nothing to do with her age. I think they would let her date if they could pick out the person. You know how Italian's are."

No, he thought, he really didn't know. He only knew how the guys his age were, all wolves, like the ones that hung out at Peppy's. They were after any girl they could get. He was never attracted to the type of girls they went after.

"If you're thinking of dating Rosemarie, forget it!" Peggy said with a laugh. "Not unless it was on the sneak, besides, how do you know she even likes you?"

"I think she does, she flirted with me in their garage."

"In front of Joey?" Peggy looked surprised.

"No, he was working under the car, I don't think he noticed."

"Well you better be careful. Joey might be your friend, but when it comes to his sister, I don't know," her face took on a look of concern. "Do you want her uncle to beat you up?" then she laughed.

"He's not like that," he said. "He's really a gentle guy; you don't know him like I do."

"Pops said you can't trust Italians, if they aren't all in the rackets they know someone who is, that's what Pops believes, but I don't agree with him," she said.

"What does Pops know? He's an old man with all his prejudices, he thinks bad of everyone who isn't Irish. He isn't much different from Mr. Nuzzo or Mr. Peterson. You wouldn't say anything if I did meet with her, would you? Because if you did, I'll tell Mom about seeing you coming out of Johnny Kelly's place on Whipple Street. You're not supposed to be there when his parents are at work."

"When was that? I was visiting my friend, Lucy." She seemed surprised he knew but thought he wasn't half as bad as Joey was, watching over his sister.

CHAPTER 13

It was the first week of December, the last month of 1940, and the school Christmas dance was coming up and Rosemarie needed a date for the dance. She was in her senior year and in June of '41 she would graduate. She worried about her senior prom; who could she go with? But that was months away. The Christmas dance was coming up soon. She spent a lot of time in her room, thinking, plotting and crying. She kept harping on her father to please let her go with a boy to the school dance. She wasn't getting anywhere. The more she begged, the more stubborn Benny became. The only time she could bring up the subject was at suppertime when he couldn't avoid her. As a result, it produced anxiety and anger when everyone was trying to enjoy eating. Mealtime used to be important in the Nuzzo family when the children were small; it was a time for conversation, unlike the Peterson's where Lorraine had to eat her meals quietly as her parents would rarely discuss anything for fear of setting Ralph off on a tangent about the neighbors.

The Nuzzo's used to use suppertime to communicate, but lately communication had turned to very angry words, which produced outbursts of shouting and many tears, mostly running down Rosemarie's cheeks. It never used to be like that when the children were young but with Rosemarie straining for some freedom and Joey clashing with his father over the war in Europe, it made mealtime unbearable for Nora and Maria.

Another Friday night supper I have to look forward to Benny thought, as he rode the Harrison Street streetcar on his way home. What would await him this time? Many nights he dreaded going home at all. As bad as his work was, he began to prefer the job he hated to having to face his family each night. As he entered the downstairs hall, he could hear loud voices coming from upstairs. He took his time ascending the stairs. He recognized the high-pitched voice of his sister-in-law Rose. He viewed her with suspicion because he thought she was influencing Nora, and he dreaded how they would gang up on him. He had to fight for his rights on the job, and he didn't intend to fight his own family at home. He would demand respect. He was the husband, father, boss; it was time he let them all know. He wasn't like his neighbor, Jim McCann, or like the other American husbands on the street. He thought they were tied to their wives apron strings, *no, not me,* he thought.

Rose was instructing Nora on how she should speak up for Rosemarie, "After all, she's your only daughter," she said. "How could asking a boy to a school dance be of any harm?"

Before Nora could answer, Benny came in the door with a crabby expression on his face. As he was taking off his work shoes, Rose whispered to Nora, "I see the crape hanger is home."

He went into the bathroom to wash up without saying a word to either of them. Rose helped to set the table. She was staying for supper. Maria cooked a large batch of veal parmesan. Nora thought it was enough to feed an army, but Maria was expecting Nicky and it was his favorite dish. When Benny finally entered the kitchen and realized Rose was there for supper and his brother's favorite dish was about to be served, he wasn't too happy. With barely a whispered hello to Rose, he turned to Maria,

"Ma, is Nicky coming over tonight?" She nodded yes, her back to him, appearing busy at the stove.

He looked at Rose and thought, *just what I needed, first her and now my brother.* He couldn't tolerate the two of them at the same time.

Nicky arrived when they had all been seated at the dining room table. Late as usual, Benny thought. Nora waved him in towards an empty chair. No one said a word as Maria got up and filled his plate from the large oval serving platter in the middle of the table.

"Is he crippled Ma?" Benny asked sarcastically. "I'm sure he can serve himself."

91

Maria ignored him and continued to pile food on Nicky's plate. They all ate in silence for a few minutes until Rosemarie spoke.

"I'm the only one who isn't going to my school dance," she said as she pushed her fork around the plate without picking up any food.

She looked across the table at Joey. Their eyes met. She hoped he would take pity on her and take her side.

"That's not an important dance," he said. "It's not like it's your senior prom."

Didn't she iron his shirts for him when he needed her help, and now he wasn't helping her and he owed her, she thought. "Joey, tell him, you went to all your school dances," she pleaded, never taking her eyes off of her brother.

Joey looked away, down at his plate. He thought for a minute before he said, "Pa, I can take her to the dance."

"What!" Rosemarie was shocked; it wasn't the kind of help she expected. "I can't have you, my brother, take me! I'll be laughed at. Are you crazy?" she directed her anger towards Joey.

She didn't expect that kind of help from him. The tears came again.

"OK, OK!" Benny shouted, "How about Vinnie Russo?"

The picture of Vinnie came into Rosemarie's thoughts, she cried even more.

"He's ugly, he's—Oh God please, not him, Why him?"

"I could trust him, to honor you," Benny answered.

"Honor me?" She shouted back, "I honor myself. I do my own thinking. I don't need that fat slob to honor me!"

She looked around the table and watched Sammy eating away, unaffected by the conflict. She was sorry she said fat slob when her eyes settled on her little brother but the derogatory remark went unnoticed by him. Nora had a pained expression on her face but said nothing as she left the room and went to the kitchen. She was always getting up for something, trying to avoid the conflict as much as possible. She never seemed to sit still long enough to put a fork full of food in her mouth. She hardly sat down during pleasant meals; lately she tried to avoid the table all together.

Maria put her hand on Rosemarie's and patted it. "You goa with thata Vinnie. He'sa gooda boy. You no hava to likea him, justa go so you cana go."

"Granny, please! I can't stand him," she cried. Looking at her father, she asked, "Why him?"

"Because, we know his family. They're good people, his father owns the shoe store, he's a shoemaker," he answered gruffly. He avoided looking directly at her.

"That's not the reason," she said, "Unless you expect to get free shoes... that's it! You'll loan me out for a new pair of shoes!"

"Don't be silly," he said, waving his hand for her to sit down.

She had been standing, gripping the edge of the table, almost hysterical with rage. Nicky couldn't believe the spunk his niece had. She certainly didn't take after Nora he thought.

"I know the reason," she continued, "It's because he's Italian, isn't it? If Vinnie were a murderer, just out of jail, you would trust him with me because he's Italian. Isn't it so Pa?" She glared at her father, "Well I was born here, I'm an American and I want to go with an American boy to the dance, not some cartoon all the kids would laugh at."

It pained Nicky to watch his niece become hysterical. He waited for Joey to say something and when he didn't, he spoke up.

Turning to Benny he said, "You're still living in the old Country and this is America. What could happen when she'll be at the school and the boy will bring her right home after the dance?"

Benny glared at him, "When you get your own daughter, then you tell me how I should raise mine. She's not your daughter! It's my business how I raise my daughter. It's my house! My daughter! Where's your house? Where's your

93

daughter?"

With that outburst, Rose decided not to say anything. She would only make things worse if she spoke up in defense of her niece.

"Stop!" Maria yelled at Benny "You shuta up!"

Nicky got up from his chair; he knew when he had overstayed his visit. To remain would only make things worse.

"I'm going Ma," he said, and went into the hall to retrieve his hat off of the hall tree.

Rosemarie came up to him.

"Uncle Nicky thanks for trying to help."

"Don't worry kid, I'll talk to Joey. I'll make sure he figures something out, so you can go to the dance."

"Joey won't help me," she said, with sadness, her head down.

Nicky put his arms around her.

"He will, you'll see Rosie."

After Nicky left, Rosemarie called to her mother that she was going across the street for a while. She couldn't stand to go back in and face her father again. The days she would go over to Peggy's were seldom unless she was sure Patrick wasn't home, but she had to talk to someone so she went to see Lorraine. Mrs. Peterson was always kind to her and Peggy whenever they stopped to visit Lorraine. Lorraine was like a big sister to the younger girls and would share her secrets on how to apply make-up or give advice on their crushes. Ralph Peterson didn't have a problem with the children on the street if they were girls. He found them less troublesome and enjoyed teasing the teenage girls. Lorraine was a year older than Joey and Patrick, she was too old to tease anymore and he missed that.

Lorraine answered the door. She wasn't surprised to see Rosemarie; Peggy had been filling her in on all the problems Rosemarie was having trying to date boys.

"Hi!" Lorraine greeted her, "Come on in."

Rosemarie stepped into the hall and seeing Mrs. Peterson,

peeking her head into the hall from the kitchen to see who it was, Rosemarie said hello and followed Lorraine upstairs to her room.

"What's wrong?" Lorraine asked. She could see she looked troubled.

Rosemarie started to cry, and in between the tears she told her how badly she wanted to go to her school Christmas dance. The Peterson's home was a two-story one family home. Lorraine could keep her bedroom door ajar and still retain her privacy.

"My father is so foreign. He won't let me go out with any boy unless it's my brother or someone like that stupid Vinnie."

"You don't mean Vinnie Russo?" Lorraine laughed. "He's got to be kidding! Right? Not Vinnie who lives down the street? The shoemaker's son?"

"He won't let me go because he doesn't trust any boy. He makes me feel stupid, like I can't take care of myself."

"You know there's something wrong with Vinnie, don't you?" Lorraine laughed. "He's a big baby, besides he's repulsive looking."

She couldn't stop laughing, she looked at Rosemarie and then they both started laughing.

"Did you ever notice how he walks, like a duck, he waddles," Lorraine said.

Rosemarie added, "And he always has an ice cream cone in his hand whenever he walks home from Peppy's."

Still laughing in hysterics, Lorraine asked, "Who always stops the ice cream truck when it comes down the street?" "Vinnie," they both said.

"He beats all the little kids to the ice cream truck, what a big galoop," Rosemarie said.

Lorraine looked concerned, "You'd be better off going with your brother."

"My brother? It would seem like I couldn't get any boy to take me. I would rather not go at all. My father came to this country when he was twelve years old, but he acts like he's still

95

in the old country."

"He went to school here, didn't he? He doesn't have an accent like your grandmother."

"He had to quit school after three years and go to work because my grandfather was sick, but he took classes in English at night, that's why he doesn't have an accent, but he had very little education, enough to read and write. I'll explain it to you sometime; it's too complicated. My Father lived for too long in the old Italian neighborhood where everyone doesn't speak English at home because of the old people, so they lived like they were still in Italy."

Lorraine looked at her with sympathy, "At least he doesn't embarrass you in front of people like my father does. You know how he is, finds fault with everyone, doesn't keep his feelings about religion to himself, and he insults everyone he comes across. He'll say things like: I hope you don't date one of those holy rosaries; that's what he calls Catholics. He dislikes Catholics the most."

"How come?" Rosemarie asked.

"Oh, I really think it's because of the McCann boys and them being strict Catholics, but he doesn't like Baptists or Lutherans either. When I hear my father say, there goes that old Jew. I know he means, Mrs. Katz. He can't just say there goes Mrs. Katz, no, he has to refer to her as that old Jew."

Rosemarie sadly shook her head, "What does he call my family?"

"Oh, you know," Lorraine said, not sure if she should say it. "Those Dago's across the street. Sometimes he uses the word Wop. I'm not sure what it means." She looked embarrassed for having said the words.

"That's ok, I never knew what it meant either until my Uncle Nicky told us that Wop means With-Out-Passport. Joey was called that once when we were kids and he came home crying, but after Uncle Nicky told us what it meant, it didn't hurt when we heard it. My grandmother and father had a passport when they came to America.

"I don't think my father knows what it means either, but he uses it." Lorraine said sadly.

"Do you want to know what my father calls your father?" Rosemarie asked, still uncomfortable over hearing the words Lorraine had just used. "He calls him That Crazy Atheist. My grandmother thinks anyone who doesn't believe in God is the devil. Why can't grownups get along? At least, you're not told you're something other than American."

"My father never mentions his nationality, and anyway, my mother is Welsh," Lorraine said.

"I think that makes you a real American, if you're mixed, maybe that's what you have to be; mixed, to be a real American. My father thinks of himself as Italian first."

"I don't think it should matter, look at the McCann family, they think of themselves as just Irish and they are real proud of being Irish and it irritates my father," Lorraine said.

"Well I'm not going to marry an Italian when I marry, that's for sure; I want my children to be mixed. To be real Americans." She touched Lorraine's arm affectionately, "I just have to go to the Christmas dance or I'll die if I can't go. I have to find a way." Both girls tried to think of a solution to Rosemarie's problem.

"Did you ask Peggy for help? Lorraine asked. "She knows plenty of boys. She's seeing Johnny Kelly."

Rosemarie couldn't tell her who she really wanted to go with. She knew it was impossible. She didn't want anyone to know how she felt, especially Patrick, and besides she thought, "He was out of school and might not want to go to a high school dance."

"Before you go, I need to show you something," Lorraine, said.

She opened a dresser drawer and took out a small box. Rosemarie could see it was a ring box. Lorraine opened it.

"See this!" She held the box open and a diamond ring appeared. "I'm engaged, but don't tell anyone. My parents don't know yet."

97

"Oh my gosh!" Rosemarie gushed, bringing her hand up to her month, hoping Mrs. Peterson hadn't heard her say it so loudly, "Why haven't you told your parents? Who is the guy?"

"It's Michael Donovan, and you know how my father hates the Irish. I can't tell them yet. If I tell my mother she'll be upset not because of Michael but because of how my father would react. I want to spare her that worry for awhile."

"Does your mother know you're dating him?"

"She knows I've gone out with him a few times, but I didn't want to burden her with knowing we were serious. We've dated for the past year, and last week at dinner he presented me with this engagement ring at The Palmer House, where we usually go, and I said yes."

Rosemarie looked at the ring more closely. "It's beautiful, I'm happy for you and I won't tell a soul."

She gave Lorraine a hug and on her way out she called "Goodbye Mrs. Peterson," as Lorraine let her out the door.

On the walk back to her house, she felt better. She wasn't the only one who had to keep secrets from their parents.

CHAPTER 14

Peggy walked over to Rosemarie's porch where she was waiting. Together they sat on the inside stairs to Rosemarie's flat. It was too cold to sit on the outside porch, and the girls needed privacy. They met to plan what they could do about a date for the dance. Peggy had an idea. She knew how her brother and Rosemarie felt about each other, even if they themselves weren't acknowledging it. She thought she wasn't mistaken when she witnessed something between them that day in her kitchen.

"Why don't I ask my brother to take you?" she said.

Rosemarie looked surprised, "What makes you think he would want to take me?" She couldn't believe what Peggy just proposed.

"Because I know he likes you, and you have a crush on him. Don't deny it; I know about it and Pat asks me questions about you all the time."

"He does?" Rosemarie's eyes grew larger, "Well, how is that supposed to happen?"

Peggy started laughing, "Don't worry, we'll figure out something."

"That's what my uncle Nicky told me, not to worry, but it might take a miracle. I won't go to the dance if I have to go with who my father chooses; I'll just say I don't want to go."

"I have a better idea," Peggy said. "Let Joey take you. You know that girl Francie Kruger; well she has a crush on your brother. Pat can take Francie; she goes to your school. Don't worry, it'll work out. Just let Joey take you. When you get there, you both switch partners. Let me take care of it; I promise it'll work. I'm sure my brother will welcome the idea."

The night of the dance, Rosemarie took her time dressing as her father watched from his chair in the front room. He couldn't believe she agreed to go with her brother. Joey didn't appear too happy over the situation, but he knew he was the one who offered to take her. Nora helped her dress. Twyla Woods made the dress for her. Twyla was quite the dressmaker and Rosemarie picked out the pattern. It was light blue with puff sleeves. Nora thought it was cut a bit low at the bosom, but the dress would be covered with a short imitation fur cape that Twyla lent her to ward off the cold that December evening. Nora made Twyla add a little piece of lace at the cleavage. It wasn't low-cut, but Benny would never let her leave the house unless she was properly covered.

When Rosemarie first tried it on, Twyla whispered to her, "You can remove the lace after you leave the house. I won't sew it; I'll just tack it on with two little threads. The lace doesn't really go with the dress, but that's what your Mama wants." Rosemarie couldn't thank her enough. Ever since the Woods family moved in next door, Nora seemed to become more understanding of modern ways. Twyla and her husband Bob were a younger couple living on a street of mostly the elderly and middle-aged. Twyla understood Rosemarie's frustrations and lent a sympathetic ear whenever it was needed, usually when Lorraine or Peggy weren't available.

"Call up Mrs. Woods so she can see how it looks with my purse and shoes: I need her to tell me it all goes together," Rosemarie said when she finished dressing. Both Nora and Maria said in unison, "It goes, it goes," but Rosemarie knew they didn't have the sense of style a younger person had.

"I want her to see the effort of her hard work, and to tell me it all goes together," she said.

Tears glistened in Nora's eyes and Maria held her hands to her cheeks and shook her head from side to side in disbelief that her granddaughter could look so beautiful. By the time Rosemarie was ready to leave, not only Twyla, but also her Aunt Rose had come to see how she looked in her gown. Benny wondered why she was going with Joey after all. All Joey told him was she agreed to have him take her. Benny wondered if Joey was acting for someone else. Nothing got by

Benny in his own home, but the expression on Joey's face told him that Joey didn't really want to take her to the high school dance.

Rose lived through Nora's children; she smiled and made ohs and ahs as she walked around her niece, inspecting the dress, touching it here and there, brushing hair away from Rosemarie's face, clapping a few times, saying ... "How, beautiful! Beautiful! She is." Maria joined in and said, "Bella, Bella!" Benny grumbled something to himself, but Rosemarie didn't care what he thought. She was angry with him and for the past week hadn't spoken to him. He didn't look too pleased as she walked back and forth in front of the long hall mirror; she told herself she didn't care if he didn't like the dress, it was too bad if he didn't approve. She didn't need his approval. She was allowing Joey to take her; she wouldn't compromise on anything else, especially the dress.

On the ride to the school, only a few blocks away, Joey didn't say one word to her. She sat thinking about how he really didn't want to be with her and she hoped he wasn't angry with her. She checked her face in the compact she took from her little evening purse, and applied fresh lipstick a little darker than she had put on in the house. Joey looked back at her; he had a look of disapproval on his face but said nothing. After he parked and they were about to climb out of the car, he said, "Don't make a spectacle of yourself at the dance, behave yourself."

She stared at him with an angry expression and said, "Don't tell me how to act; you're not my father. It's my school dance; I'm seventeen and you can't order me around."

The frown on Joey's face disappeared when they entered the school gymnasium. It was all decked out in paper decorations for Christmas. A blonde girl standing near the entrance drew his attention, and he hung back as Rosemarie entered the room. She scanned the room for Patrick. Joey finally came in behind her, a girl on each side of him. He was talking to the girls, ignoring her. He passed her with the girls, and she followed them to the punch bowl. Joey was laughing, he never looked back at her, just engaged the girls that seemed to gather around him. She watched him resentfully. Boy! What a charmer he could be, she thought, *If only the girls who swooned around him knew him like I did.* She knew how he threw his clothes on the floor for her mother to pick up or the terrible mess he would leave in the bathroom for her to clean up. She didn't think he was so great. She didn't know what the girls saw in him that they would flock around him. Joey could always charm the girls; he was what one called, tall, dark and handsome. The blondes went for him big time and he went for them.

The band started to play a lively jitterbug, and couples drifted to the center of the floor. Joey was now down to one blonde. The others went to find their dates. A few girls came alone. Joey turned to her and said, "I'm going to dance now, and you can do what you want, but don't get into any trouble." She didn't answer him. She worried that Patrick wouldn't be at the dance, maybe he changed his mind, after all, Joey didn't want to be there either, but to watch him on the dance floor with the blonde expelled that idea. She had to admit he could really dance. She looked in the direction of the door and poured herself a cup of punch. Standing there, she felt like a wallflower, someone who couldn't get a date. She searched the crowd. A couple of her classmates came up to talk to her, but she was too distracted to give them her full attention. She felt ridiculous standing there alone, watching her brother dance. A crowd was forming around him and his partner. The others stopped dancing and watched the pair jitterbugging; they were that good. Just as she was about to sit on one of the chairs lining the wall, Patrick walked in with Francie. A sudden urge to flee came over her. She turned toward the punch bowl table pretending she didn't see them. With her back to the dance floor she waited until she heard the music stop. The music started again, a Tommy Dorsey tune. A slow dance started. Joey came up behind her.

"You wanna dance?" he asked. She turned around and there standing next to her brother was Patrick and Francie. She didn't answer; she was too nervous. She just stared at her brother speechless, trying to avoid looking at Patrick. Joey asked her again, "Do you want to dance?" She nodded yes, and her brother took her toward the other couples that were already dancing. When he made a few attempts to twirl her around, she could see Patrick dancing with Francie. He never said a word to her, not even hello when they were all standing together. Maybe Peggy was wrong about how he felt about her; maybe it was Francie he liked. All these thoughts went through her mind, and as if in a trance, she danced with her brother, whom she thought earlier she would die before she was caught dancing with him. At that moment she wished she were at home, anywhere but in this place.

When the dance ended, she thought of escaping to the girl's room, but she knew if she did she would remain there unable to come out. She felt humiliated to have danced with her own brother for all the kids to see. She walked back towards the wall expecting Joey to follow, but when she turned around Patrick came up to her, and he was alone.

"Hi Rosemarie," he said. He was standing too close to her; she felt like she couldn't breathe. She managed to say hi so softly he barely heard it. He looked down at her and she appeared painfully shy, not at all like the same girl he remembered in the garage. More like the girl in his kitchen with tears in her eyes. It was her shyness that really turned him on. He liked that in her.

"Would you like to dance?" he said. Not looking up at him, she said yes, and he took her hand and led her to the dance floor. They waited until the end of the music and another dance started, another slow dance. They were playing *Green Eyes*. How appropriate, Patrick thought as he took her in his arms. She thought she would faint. She hated herself for being so nervous. Patrick ignored her silence and did the talking for both of them.

"So you're graduating in June?" he asked. She was sure he knew she was in her last year, but he was trying to engage her in conversation to put her at ease.

"Yes," she answered, looking to see where her brother had gone. She spotted him dancing with Francie, and she began to relax. Patrick looked down at her and she managed to smile up at him. When their eyes met she didn't look away; they looked at each other both knowing how they felt. Words were unnecessary. The dance ended, and holding hands they walked over to where the chairs were lined along the wall and sat down.

"I'd like to take you out," he said, "But I know you're not allowed to date."

"It's my father."

"I'll talk to Joey about it, he can cover for you. I'll tell him how I feel about wanting to date you, Rosemarie. Would you go out with me?"

He didn't have to ask, he already knew how she felt about him, and what they felt was mutual.

"I would like that," she said. The rest of the evening went the way she dreamed it would go. She relaxed and they talked and danced together like they had always been together. She didn't want the evening to end. Joey stayed busy dancing his feet off with numerous girls, but he always came back to Francie for a dance. Rosemarie knew how Francie felt about her brother, but he wasn't ready to settle on any one girl. When he wasn't dancing with her, she was talking with Patrick and Rosemarie between dances. She didn't seem to mind; she knew why Patrick took her to the dance.

Later in the girls' room where they both went to touch up their makeup, Rosemarie thanked her.

"Don't worry about it," she said. "Peggy told me the whole story and I was glad to do it. I got to be close to your brother for awhile, even if he did dance with others."

"What did my brother say about Pat and me?" Rosemarie asked. She was worried about how her brother would feel about her and Patrick dancing together all evening.

"Oh, he told me that you have a thing for each other."

"He did?" Rosemarie looked surprised. "I don't know how he could know," she said.

Francie laughed, "When we were dancing, and you were dancing not too far from us, he said, 'Look at my sister and Pat; they think I don't know what's going on.' He told me how strict your father is. He thought it was stupid and he felt sorry for you."

"He said that? Wow! I never thought that would come out of my brother. He never said much at home in my defense." Maybe he can't, she thought. She knew at home everyone walked on eggs around her father, except her grandmother.

On the way home Joey said, "I know you both want to date each other and I trust Pat, he's my friend, but it still feels weird that you two, of all people, want to be together. Remember, it's my head the old man will cut off if you do anything wrong." He looked at her with an expression that reminded her of her father whenever he was suspicious.

"Don't worry, Pa will never know you had anything to do with covering for me."

Joey laughed, "You and Pat McCann? My God! That's enough to start another war, right on our street. Sooner or later, someone is bound to find out. Let's hope it's later, after you're eighteen."

CHAPTER 15
1941

Benny's job with the public works system, digging underground for the city's water and sewer line, was exhausting work. He would walk up the stairs to his flat each night slowly, hitting each step hard with feet that felt as heavy as the clay he dug and the cement he occasionally helped lay along the city walks. It was the pure manual labor of an uneducated foreign-born immigrant. He was always strapped for money with a family to support, including his mother; he worked as many hours as was offered to him. Coming home this particular evening, he was in a foul mood.

Things didn't go well at work. He kicked off his shoes and went straight to the bathroom. Nora could tell by the way he climbed the stairs and slammed the doors as he passed through the flat, that it would be another one of those nights she would dread. Hearing his footsteps as he came up the stairs each night, the women would quickly run about the kitchen making sure the sauce was coming along for the meal he expected, taking the freshly baked bread from the oven, setting the table, looking at the clock, and expecting all the kids to be home in time for supper. Nora hoped they were all accounted for to stave off an explosion from him when he came to the table and someone was missing, especially if it was Rosemarie.

Maria didn't bake every day; and when they had to eat the bread the second day, it became dry and he would complain. Once Maria wasn't feeling well and Nora ran out of time to bake. When that happened, she usually went to her sister's bakery for the bread. With the bakery bread he wasn't satisfied. It had to be Maria's bread. They never had store-bought bread. Once Joey brought home a loaf of sliced American bread from the grocery store, and Benny yelled, "This isn't bread! It's made with paste; it sticks to the roof of your mouth!"

Later, when all were accounted for at the table, they

sensed his mood and ate in silence. Sammy never caught on to the nuances of the family dynamics. He would look around at all the sober faces eating away and break the silence.

"Rosie! Can I come with you to the library tonight?" he asked. He was nine years old; but Sammy was still two grades behind in school. Rosemarie froze; she had been using the excuse of going to the library to study for her exams. Graduation was two months away. She would meet Patrick and they would spend the time together when she was supposed to be at the library. The weekends were worse. Unless her father worked on a Saturday, they were unable to see each other. They hated to be sneaking around, but it wasn't just her father they had to keep their relationship from, it was Patrick's mother as well.

"No, I don't think so," she answered.

"Why can't he come with you?" Nora asked, not helping the situation. At that moment Rosemarie thought her mother was as dense as her younger brother. She couldn't take the chance of her ever knowing. If Benny ever suspected anything he didn't like and he pressed Nora for the truth, she might give it to him out of respect or fear, mostly fear.

Benny felt he was losing the respect of his children. He came home dirty; the gray Chicago clay clung to his shoes, his clothing, and his skin. They knew he was just a common laborer and he would never be anything else. He looked around the table at the family he tried so hard to provide for. Despite his line of work and his lack of education, he didn't feel he had to apologize to anyone for the way he made his living, least of all his own children. He knew most of the men who lived on his street had what he called clean work. Newspaper people worked inside; he didn't consider a few spots of ink getting dirty. Milkmen, shoemaker, policemen, to him, all had cushion jobs. They didn't know what real labor was; he told himself. Working outdoors, his medium complexion turned brown and his hands became rough and callused. He was an angry man. On the job, and around his boss, he was like a fallen leaf at the mercy of Chicago's ever-present wind. In his home, he was the wind.

"You take your brother with you," he said, directing his command to Rosemarie.

"Do I have to Pa? He fiddles around and makes noise; you have to be quiet in the library."

"Then you study at home!"

Rosemarie looked at Joey; her expression was a silent cry for help. Joey finished a few more bites of food as she waited for some response. He drank half his bottle of Coca-Cola before he responded.

"Pa, I'll take Sammy with me, I need to stop at the station tonight to check out a few things. He likes going to the station and watching the guys work on cars; he would get bored at the library and Rosie needs to study where it's quiet, besides they have the books she needs for research."

Benny looked confused, he didn't understand what needed to be researched, but if Joey said it, it must be true. After they all left, he parked himself in front of the radio. He hated when there was static as he fiddled with the dial while he was trying to listen to the news. Maria and Nora stayed in the kitchen cleaning up. They seldom joined him in the front room. Nora wished her mother-in-law would sit with him and leave her alone so she could run next door to Twyla or downstairs to Sylvia; she needed a break from both of them, but she knew it seldom happened. She was beginning to feel like a prisoner. Maria didn't understand that she needed her own space; she would follow Nora to the landlady's and sometimes to Twyla's. Nora was caught between the old world of her mother-in-law and her husband and the new world her children were striving toward. It left her nervous and exhausted. They could hear Benny's grunts and groans. He was talking back to the news report about the war. "Did you hear this?" he hollered to the women. Maria ran into the room to see what he was yelling about.

"That damn Hitler will declare war on America if we give

Japan any trouble," he said. "And he's invaded Greece and Yugoslavia and that stupid Mussolini. I don't know, Ma. I don't know what's going to happen. If he declares war on us, we'll have to be in it." He was sitting close to the radio, his nose almost touching the dial. He was talking out loud to himself; Maria had gone back to the kitchen. She didn't want to hear any of it.

When the month of May arrived, Rosemarie's prom was quickly approaching. As far as her father was concerned, she still refused to let her brother take her, especially to her Senior Prom, so he took it upon himself to invite the Russo's for Sunday supper. When her mother told her, she was beside herself with anger. She knew the reason. She went down to the garage where Joey was working on the Ford.

"Do you know what Pa just did?" she asked. "He invited the Russo's over; he thinks he can get Vinnie to take me to the prom. I'd rather die first."

Joey started to laugh at the prospect of Vinnie and his sister together anywhere. He knew it wasn't going to happen.

"Don't worry about it Rosie" he said. "It won't happen. Go along with it and let me handle the rest."

Later at the dining room table, Benny and Joey were discussing the war news when Rosemarie walked through the room to her bedroom. She had been crying again; they could see that her eyes were all red. Lately her eyes were always red.

"Why does she put on that long face? And all the crying she does," Benny said, looking at Joey for an answer.

"She wants to go to her prom Pa, you won't let her, you said 'No,' remember?" Joey had a look of disbelief on his face as he stared at his father. "Remember? You said 'What's a prom? What's the big deal about a prom?'" Joey gave his father a disgusted look as he started to get up to leave. It's no use trying to talk sense to him, he thought, the old man just doesn't get it.

He walked toward Rosemarie's room, stopped and turned to Benny and said, "Pa, it's an important school dance. I went to my prom, remember? I even brought my date up here so you and Ma could see her dress. You didn't tell me I couldn't go or that I couldn't take that girl, Helen O'Connor, who by the way, wasn't Italian."

Benny sat speechless for a moment; he knew Joey was angry with him.

"You're a boy, she's a girl, and I never said she couldn't go, but not with anybody, with you or someone we trust, someone we know. She can go with the Russo boy."

"Vinnie Russo is not a boy, he's older than I am," Joey said.

"I trust Vinnie!" Benny's voice was rising.

Joey yelled at him, something he had never done before, "She doesn't want to go with Vinnie Russo!"

Maria joined in, "Sure, you yell, you yell so everybody hear you say the name. They no deaf you know, the neighbor, they tella the Russo's."

Nora had taken Sammy outdoors into the backyard; they stood talking over the fence to Twyla. Nora hated when warm weather came and the windows were open; the whole street could hear her husband and he didn't care who heard him. She was always embarrassed by him and now her son started to sound like him, both of them shouting at each other. When Maria joined in it was too much. Nora came from a quiet family. Her parents ran their bakery in a neighborhood where everyone knew them as gentle and reserved. They raised three children above the bakery, two daughters and a son. During the First World War when their son Sam was killed, it was up to the two younger children to help them. Rose was the eldest daughter and Nora was the baby of the family by five years. When Nora met Benny she was seventeen and she liked that he was very talkative and even fun to be with. He was different from her and she was attracted to someone different. Her family warned her that he was like most Calabrase, coming from a region in the south of Italy where they were considered loud and stubborn. The Scali's came from Milan, it was in the northern part of Italy. Her parents came over when Sam was a baby and adapted well to the new culture making Nora's parents a little more removed from the old country ways. Rose ran the bakery after their parents died.

"Nora, is anything wrong?" Twyla asked, as they both met at the fence. She could hear Benny shouting.

"Oh no," Nora said, but she knew they had moved to the kitchen; the window was open and now Twyla could hear everything. "You know my husband, he doesn't know how to talk; he has to yell."

"Is it about your daughter's prom again?" Twyla asked sympathetically.

"Who knows," Nora shrugged. "It's this; it's that; it's everything. He has to make a big thing out of everything."

"He won't let her go?" Twyla asked even though she knew the answer.

Nora looked down at her fingers that tightly gripped the top of the wooden fence, "Oh he'll let her go, but he has to choose who she goes with."

In the kitchen Benny was shouting, "What do you mean, I'm old fashioned?"

"Pa, she wants to choose a boy on her own," Joey pleaded.

"What boy?"

"I don't know, maybe a boy from school."

"What boy from school?"

"I don't know, a boy from her class. You know Pa, one of the boys she's graduating with. It's the boys' prom too."

"No, No, she goes with Vinnie. We know his family. It's a good family."

"Pa, Vinnie isn't even in school anymore; he's twenty-five-years-old, and she doesn't want to go with him."

Joey didn't agree with his father about Rosemarie; he knew how serious his sister and Patrick were about each other, and he was worried about what would happen if his father ever found out about them. Also, he had started dating Francie Kruger since the Christmas dance. Francie was German and blonde, and he found her attractive. There were very few German families living around their neighborhood and though Benny didn't know any, he never had anything good to say about the Germans. He usually called them Krauts, but since the war, he referred to anyone German as a Nazi. Joey was afraid if he knew about her, he might find something crazy to believe because Hitler was German. He and Francie began to date often, but he still hadn't brought her around the family. He wasn't fighting just for his sister's rights, but also his right to date what his father called "Those Americanas."

"Pa, I don't think Vinnie has ever dated a girl, how do you know he would want to take her?" he said lowering his voice and hoping his father would do the same.

"He'll take her. He's a good boy; he don't run around with those puttanas like your uncle runs around with."

"Ok, Ok!" Joey said, and left the kitchen, and left Maria to deal with his father.

He went to his sister's room. He knocked on her door. "Rosie!" he called. When she opened it he could see she had been crying. She knew what they were arguing about; she could hear everything through the closed door.

"That's it! I'm not going to my prom," she said, wiping her wet cheek with the back of her hand.

"You don't want to miss your senior prom; it's the only one you'll ever have." Joey felt sorry for her, more now than he ever did when they were growing up. He sensed her struggle was also his own.

"I'll be the laughing joke of the entire class, and I can't stand the Russo's, especially Vinnie. He makes me sick the way he breathes, like he's always out of breath and he always smells of garlic. His mother treats him like Ma and Granny treat Sammy. He's a big baby."

"I know, I know," Joey said, patting her on the back. "That's because he's overweight."

"He's fat and ugly, a Mama's boy, the only thing we have in common is being Italian, and right now I hate it when Pa thinks of us as only Italian, when I feel like I'm as American as anyone." She started crying again. "I'm never going to marry an Italian, much less date one, even if it kills Pa, I'll die first."

Joey looked at her and laughed, "I'm Italian; am I that bad? Francie thinks I'm great."

She started to laugh, "You know what I mean."

"Don't worry; Pat and I will think of something," he assured her. "Let Pa think Vinnie is taking you and be nice when the Russos come for supper Sunday."

CHAPTER 16

Nora and Maria were preparing Sunday afternoon supper, but Rosemarie kept her distance and wouldn't help. She stayed mostly in her room dreading the visit that was due soon. She would try to pretend everything was fine in front of her father, but she wasn't good at pretending. She thought of Angie Russo and how bossy she was. She knew her mother would sit quietly while Maria and Angie did all the talking, mostly in Italian. She felt sorry for her mother. Nora didn't carry much weight in family decisions, but Angie Russo ruled her house like a queen. Her husband, Salvatore, appeared meek around her. Rosemarie wondered if her father ever noticed how Mr. Russo catered to his wife whenever they were together. They were the only neighbors Benny had as friends.

Maria whispered to Nora as they cooked together in the kitchen, "I thinka Rosie be ok. She no cry today. She looka nice, she brusha the hair when I goa to the bedaroom."

Nora just smiled; she wondered why Rosemarie didn't seem as upset the past few days as she had been. Benny was putting on his best tie; he stood in front of the sink trying to tie it in front of the small mirror over the sink. He loved to impress the Russos. They owned a shoe store and repair shop. To Benny, they were big time. Nora had to drain the spaghetti in the sink and he was in the way.

"Do you have to do that here? I have to drain the noodles; get out of the way!" she said.

He continued to stand at the sink while she held the hot pot with her dishtowel.

Maria shoved him aside, "Goa to the toilet, the glass, shesa ina there too!" He left to go into the bathroom. Nora shook her head in disgust, as she poured the hot water into the sink. She thought he was getting worse. Lately, he was deferring more to his mother, treating Nora like she was one of the children. His behavior was noticed by her sister Rose, and relayed to her many times, but she felt intimidated with Maria living with them.

Rosemarie sat in her room watching at the window; she spotted the Russos coming down the walk. Mrs. Russo was almost hiding the two men behind her because she was so large. Mr. Russo, a skinny little man, was walking next to his son. A perplexed look was on Mr. Russo's face as Vinnie was talking nonstop to him. Vinnie didn't walk, he waddled, and his legs from the knees down seemed to be at opposite angles, his thighs rubbing together. The sight of him made Rosemarie cringe. She couldn't believe her father was so ridiculous that he would want someone who looked like him to take her out. She thought her father had lost his mind. She wanted to feel like a real American. She didn't feel that way when her family entertained the Russos. They would all talk in Italian, except her mother. The Russo's English was as good as her father's, but they wanted to include Maria in the conversation, so they spoke in Italian most of the time. Like Nora, Rosemarie could understand a few words here and there, but couldn't speak it. She worried about what they would be plotting, but Joey told her not to worry, he would take care of the problem. She hoped he was right. She made up her mind not to engage them in conversation or answer any questions. She would not make this comfortable for her father.

When the doorbell rang, Benny went to answer with Maria following behind him. They were in the hall saying hello, as the Russos entered. Rosemarie sat on her bed; she would stay there until she was forced out to greet them. She could hear all the endearing words her father used to ingratiate himself to them. It made her sick. Their chatter, mostly in Italian, was drifting closer to her as they entered the front room. She got up to close her door, but found Benny in front of it, and he asked her to come out and say hello to them. She walked into the room and said hello. The senior Russos were seated on the sofa. Maria was in the chair next to the fireplace where Benny usually sat. Nora had brought a couple of dining room chairs into the room. Vinnie was still standing, looking like a lost soul. He looked down at the floor and never looked at Rosemarie or anyone.

"Sit down," Nora said, directing her request to Vinnie; she pushed the chair closer to where he was standing, bumping into the back of his legs. He sat. Rosemarie deliberately walked behind him, her back next to the doorway to the dining room for a quick getaway to the kitchen. The hall door opened and Joey came in; she was relieved to see him. After all the pleasantries were said, there were a few moments of silence. Sammy stood in the middle of the room wondering what it was all about. The tension in the room didn't go unnoticed by Nora; she felt bad for her daughter to be trapped in the situation, but all she could do was sympathize.

"Look how pretty she looks, Bella, Bella," Angie Russo said half in Italian, half in English, directing her comment to her son, as she pointed to Rosemarie.

Rosemarie hid behind Vinnie's chair waiting for an excuse to leave the room. They must know why they're here she thought, otherwise why would Mrs. Russo be singling her out. She was sure her father discussed the reason they were invited to supper with them before they came and now she was really angry. She wouldn't engage them in conversation. She wouldn't say a word to anyone. They couldn't make her. She would stand there like a statue. She looked at her brother leaning against the fireplace; she couldn't help noticing a half-smirk on his face. When they made eye contact, he winked at her.

Benny was proud of his only daughter and when he looked at Joey the same look came over his face, the same feeling of pride, and the love he felt was boundless. He never had that expression when he looked at Sammy; in fact he avoided looking at the boy much of the time. She knew his dreams rested on her and Joey, but they were her dreams that mattered to her, not her father's.

"How's everything, Benny?" Mr. Russo tried to make

116

small talk to break the silence. Benny welcomed the question.

"Joey's in the mechanic's trade. He's doing real good, and he got a raise last week, huh Joey?" He turned to his son for confirmation.

Joey looked embarrassed. "Yeah, yeah I did," he answered. He thought, No use telling them all the mechanics received a raise and break the illusion his father was trying to portray; that his eldest son was smarter than their son and he was going to amount to something he could be proud of.

"Yeah, Joey will never have to work outdoors in the winter and freeze or get wet when it rains," Benny said, smiling at Joey. Salvatore agreed and shook his head up and down.

Sammy was restless. He walked over to Vinnie. He noticed a shiny ring on his finger.

"Where did you get that?" he asked, "Is that Little Orphan Annie's ring?"

Vinnie smiled, "No, no, it's my high school ring."

Benny looked at Nora and the expression on his face prompted her to remove Sammy from the room.

"I'll go make coffee," she said, as she took him to the kitchen.

"I'll go help her," Rosemarie announced following them out of the room. It was the excuse she needed to leave. She would help her mother carry food to the dining room. In the front room she felt like a spectacle on display.

Benny looked at Vinnie "So how's the job going?"

Before Vinnie could answer, his mother said, "He works hard you know; he works with his father in the shoe shop!"

Benny looked pleased, "So maybe you can afford to take a girl out, no?" He was still looking at Vinnie, waiting for an answer.

Vinnie was sweating, the sweat started to bead up on his forehead, little drops falling down on his eyelids. His fat cheeks glistened as he took out his handkerchief to wipe his brow and cheeks, but just as he was about to speak his mother's words filled the room.

"Oh my Vinnie, he don't date no girls; there's no good girls anymore!"

Vinnie had an uncomfortable feeling, like he was a tomato, ripe for the picking, and Mr. Nuzzo was the picker.

"But my Vinnie, he make a good girl a nice husband someday," she said excitedly.

Joey was still in the same spot, standing at the fireplace, leaning on it, watching the scene before him. He had to hold the laugh back that was about to escape his mouth. *I can't believe this*, he thought. *First my old man implied a date, if there was enough money for a date, and now she mentions her son would make a good husband?* He was glad Rosemarie was out of the room.

Benny fingered his chin; he did that when he was nervous. He turned and directed his attention to Vinnie. "I was thinking maybe you could take my Rosie to her prom?"

Angie popped out of her seat, "Oh sure, he'll take her," she turned to Vinnie who so far hadn't been able to say a word.

"You gonna take Rosie to her prom, that's nice. Rosie's a nice girl." Turning to Benny, she said, "Don't worry, my Vinnie, he'll take good care of Rosie."

Benny smiled, "You get her home when the prom is over," he said.

Vinnie looked confused; his face became flushed taking on the color of his mother's red dress. He was unable to answer; he was too busy thinking that he had never taken a girl out anywhere, and he knew he couldn't dance. Joey could see by his expression that Vinnie was worried and uncomfortable; he wasn't able to talk for himself, his mother had taken care of that.

"Come, sit down, supper is ready," Nora announced. They followed Benny into the dining room. Rosemarie had nicely set the table. Maria eyed her granddaughter suspiciously; she didn't seem upset at all, not like she had been in the past week. Rosemarie made sure she sat on the same side of the table as Vinnie; she couldn't bear to sit across from him where they would be unable to avoid glancing across the table at each other. She waited to see where he sat and then she sat as far away from him as possible. Maria sat across from her; she stared at Rosemarie, nothing got past Maria. All the whispering Joey and Rosemarie did all week didn't get by her, but she couldn't figure it out. The meal was a disaster as far as Rosemarie was concerned. She was the object of discussion throughout, mostly between Benny and Angie. It was unbearable for everyone except Benny, Angie and Maria. Salvatore remained as quiet as his frightened son. Rosemarie could barely swallow her food; she gave up and excused herself, feigning a headache. She fled to her room and closed the door.

After everyone left the table, Benny invited them back into the front room, but Salvatore sensed that Rosemarie wasn't too happy about the prospect of going out with his son. He was a quiet man, but he was sensible. He realized his son wasn't the type of boy that a girl who looked like Benny's daughter would go out with. *Why can't my wife and Benny realize how ridiculous it all is*, he thought. Salvatore held out his hand to Benny, "Thanks for the nice meal," he said, "We have to go now."

"Wait!" Benny said, "I'll call Rosie." Salvatore shook his head no. "She don't feel good, it's ok," he said. After the Russos left, Nora went into the kitchen. She knew why Rosemarie left the table and she wanted to say something to Benny, but after he drank a few glasses of wine she knew she couldn't say anything to him that would make a difference for their daughter. All she was able to do was clean up the dishes and stay in the kitchen. Maria kept bringing in plates from the dining room, talking away about one thing or another. Nora didn't feel like talking. She began to feel like she couldn't breathe. She felt anger, but didn't know what to do with it. The pit of her stomach felt heavy. Once the dishes were washed and Maria left the kitchen to be with Benny, and Nora was sure Rosemarie was in her room, and Joey had gone out, she looked into the front room to check on Sammy who was playing on the floor, she slipped out to go downstairs to visit Mrs. Katz. She knew it was just a matter of time before Maria would notice she was missing and look for her. She wanted to leave unnoticed, so she went out the kitchen door and hurried down the back porch stairs.

Mrs. Katz wasn't surprised to see her. She knew the Nuzzo's had company. "Come in, come in," she said motioning for Nora to enter. She could tell by Nora's expression that something was wrong. "Vat is it darlink?" she asked. With Mrs. Katz being much older than her, she didn't feel so alone; she had someone to lean on during bad times. Her sister Rose gave her emotional support, but Rose was judgmental and excitable, so she wasn't as calming as Mrs. Katz. Rose expected her to stand up to Benny, but the landlady could see how he was on a daily basis and how difficult it was for Nora to assert herself.

"Come sit," she said. She put her arm around Nora's shoulder. "You talk, I listen."

CHAPTER 17

The week before Rosemarie's prom, Joey waited until he arrived at the gas station before he made the phone call to Vinnie. They were to meet at Peppy's that evening. When Joey arrived he wasn't surprised to see that Vinnie was already there. Most evenings he would be found at Peppy's, with a bottle of Pepsi in his hand, leafing through the paperback books that lined the back wall. Vinnie lived his life between the pages of the Maxwell Grant Detective novels. He would read a chapter or two while he finished his Pepsi, so he never had to actually buy a copy. Joey called to him, and they sat in a booth. Vinnie guessed it was about Rosemarie. After greeting him, Joey made small talk until Patrick came in and sat next to Vinnie. Patrick said a few words to get him to relax. Vinnie was nervous, and even with the large ceiling fans whirling above, he was sweating profusely. Joey looked at him and felt sorry for the guy. When he wasn't at Peppy's, the poor sap spent all his time in his father's shoe shop, Joey thought. He knew he didn't have much of a life. He was sure he was frightened at the prospect of taking a girl out anywhere.

"I know it wasn't your idea to take my sister to her prom," Joey said. "You can get out of it Vinnie, we'll help you."

A look of relief crossed Vinnie's face. "What do I do?" he asked.

"All you have to do is show up at my house in a tux to pick up my sister; I'm driving both of you in my Ford."

"When you get to the school, I'll be waiting for Rosemarie; you don't even have to get out of the car," Patrick said.

Vinnie looked confused, turning to Joey he said, "Where will I go?"

"You stay with me; we could go to that diner on Lake Street and wait out the evening. When it's time for my sister to come home, we pick her up at school and you ride back with us. My old man knows I'm driving you there and bringing you back. You don't have to get out of the car when we pull up. I guarantee that my old man will be at the window watching. All he'll see is my sister getting out of the Ford and you and me sitting in it. He'll think nothing of me driving you home, even if you live just down the street. That's the plan. Is it a deal?"

Vinnie looked relieved, nodded yes and took out a damp handkerchief to wipe his face.

Joey pulled out a few bills and threw them on the table in front of Vinnie.

"I don't expect you to pay for the tux," Joey said.

Patrick stood up and shook Vinnie's hand, "Thanks Vinnie, you know without your help Rosemarie wouldn't be able to go to her prom."

Vinnie felt relieved, he smiled for the first time since he entered Peppy's.

"It wasn't my idea, I can't dance. I never took a girl out; no girl would go out with me anyway."

Joey put his hand on Vinnie's shoulder, "It'll be ok; you'll see," he assured him.

After Vinnie left, Patrick said, "Thank God for your car, without it, it would be impossible."

The night of the prom had come and Rosemarie was dressing in her room with Maria looking over her; she loved her grandmother but she wished to be alone to dress. Maria made her nervous slapping her hands together and saying, "Bella, Bella!' over and over again.

"Please Granny, leave me alone now," she said, just as her mother came into the room. *Oh no!* she thought. She hoped it wasn't a repeat of when she went to the Christmas dance. She felt self-conscious with everyone hovering over her. All she wanted to think about was seeing Patrick. She dreaded facing Vinnie in front of her father; it would be awkward, her father not knowing what Joey and Vinnie knew, that her date was all a lie. She wouldn't smile; she had to keep a straight face in front of him, because he knew she didn't want to go with Vinnie. She started to feel sorry for the guy; she didn't want to hurt his feelings. She intended to put on an act, but not too good. When the doorbell rang; she wondered who it could be. Joey hadn't left to pick up Vinnie yet. She looked out of her room to see Aunt Rose come in with her usual shopping bag in hand. "Oh God!" she said aloud. She didn't want anyone else present to see her leave with Vinnie. When Rose entered her room, there wasn't enough room for both of them as far as Maria was concerned, so she left the room.

"You look beautiful Rosie." Rose said, touching her niece on the cheek. "Did Twyla next door make this dress?"

"No Aunt Rose, I bought it."

It was getting warm in the small room so Rosemarie finished looking at herself in the mirror over the dresser and walked out. Benny was sitting in his usual chair and he watched her walk to the front hall. He thought the dress didn't cover her enough but said nothing. Nora and Maria were standing nearby admiring her as Rose smoothed out any wrinkles she thought she spotted on the pale sea foam green chiffon evening gown. The color brought out the green in her hazel eyes and her light brown hair shined as it flowed down her back. She pinned the sides back with little green berets, which had tiny green chiffon flowers glued to them. She looked at herself in the hall mirror and was pleased with what she saw. With the three women fawning over her, she couldn't wait to leave and was thankful when Joey came into the room.

"You really look nice," he said. He thought she looked more than just nice, but he was her brother, he thought telling her she looked beautiful would sound goofy.

When the doorbell rang again, Rosemarie gave a sigh; she said to Nora, "Now who that could that be?" Joey opened the door to Nicky. It was all she needed, and she looked at Joey with a look of "What gives?"

Nicky greeted everyone and looked at Rosemarie. "Wow, you look beautiful Rosie!"

"What are you doing here Uncle Nicky?" She wasn't sure he knew about the Vinnie situation. She would die of embarrassment if he thought she was actually going with him.

"I came to see you going to your senior prom; that's a big deal Rosie. Vinnie is taking you, huh?" He said it loudly so Benny would hear. He winked at her as he said it. She relaxed; sure he was in on the deception.

Benny never left his chair; he turned it to face the hall where he could view them all around his daughter. He would wait until Rose and Nicky came to him to say hello. He watched as they were taking pictures of her. He waited for Rosemarie to come into the front room; she went into the kitchen instead. They all followed, ignoring him. It was a small kitchen and he wondered how they could all fit in it. Rose was taking pictures of Rosemarie on the back porch, on the swing, everywhere but in the room where Benny was. Finally, Nicky went in to say hello to him. Benny grunted a barely audible hello.

"Don't you think Rosie looks great?" Nicky asked. Benny just sat there and nodded. He wasn't in a mood to talk. Nicky tried to engage him in conversation, but it wasn't working, so he went back to the kitchen where they were all gathered around the table. Rose never said hello to Benny, she avoided him. Joey looked at the clock; it was time to pick up Vinnie. Rosemarie wanted to leave with him, but she knew it wasn't possible. Her father had to witness Vinnie coming for her and to give last minute instructions.

After Joey left, Rosemarie whispered to her aunt not to take any more pictures. She didn't want Vinnie in any of them. Nicky sat at the table drinking the cup of coffee Maria put before him. For a few minutes, no one said a word. Rose looked around at all of them jammed into the small kitchen.

"Let's go into the other room, where we can sit more comfortable," she said. Rosemarie shook her head no and put her finger up to her lips to quiet her aunt. She didn't want to be given a lecture by her father about how to behave herself on what he thought was her first date. She would die of humiliation in front of her aunt and uncle. Benny had a way of looking at her that made her feel like she had done something wrong before she did anything. Rose understood her niece completely. She turned to Nora and pointing toward where Benny was, said, "Is he going to sit in that chair talking to himself with that puss on his face all night?" She said it in a whisper, but Maria caught some of what she said. Maria made a face, like she didn't approve. It was one thing for Maria to talk about her son, not Nora's sister who wasn't part of the Nuzzo family. Nora sensed the tension between Rose and Maria and looked at Nicky, her expression told him to do something to resolve it. There was no love lost between Rose and Maria, or Rose and Benny. Rose's comments didn't endear her to him or his mother, but Nicky liked Rose. Like her, he felt sorry for Nora.

"Come on Ma," he said, "let's go in the front room and sit, it's more comfortable than these hard chairs."

Maria followed him. It gave Nora, Rose and Rosemarie time together, alone, without the comments they were sure to hear from Maria if Nicky had not removed her.

When they heard Sammy yell, "Here they come!" as he stood by the window, they all filed into the front room. Joey entered first with Vinnie behind him. Vinnie looked frightened. All he could see were too many people standing around and staring at him, he put his head down and quietly said hello. Benny stood up for the first time in hours.

"You take good care of my daughter and have her home by twelve o'clock," he said.

Vinnie nodded yes. Joey thought it was a silly thing to say when he was picking them up at that time. Everyone noticed how nervous Vinnie seemed; he was sweating badly and his hand shook when Benny reached to shake it. His eyes looked down at the floor; he was too nervous to look at anyone, least of all Rosemarie, who stood there looking like an angel, trying to act pleased, trying to be kind, wanting to get out of there as quickly as possible.

She gave her father a look of defiance, and then put her arm in Vinnie's and pulled him toward the door. She never bothered to say anything to anyone when she left. Joey followed them down to his Ford, parked at the curb. He held the door open for them to get into the backseat, and when Rosemarie looked up at the front room window she could see them all plastered against the glass, vying for space, trying to watch them leave. She thought of how they all crowded around her in the kitchen, and she felt like she couldn't breathe. Looking up at her entire family in the window, reminded her of a crowd at the zoo viewing the animals behind the glass enclosure. How embarrassing, she thought. She hoped the neighbors weren't watching it all. In comparison, she realized, sitting next to Vinnie for a ten minute ride wasn't going to be as horrible as she had envisioned. Across the street, Katie McCann took in the entire spectacle from her window.

"Look at that!" she said to Peggy who was standing beside her. "I can't believe they forced her to go to her prom, with that Russo guy. What on earth was her family thinking?"

"It's not her family, it's her father. He won't let her date anyone unless he's Italian," Peggy said.

Katie had a frown on her face, "But why Vinnie? I'm sure they could have thought of someone else, one of Joey's friends at the gas station, or any other Italian. There's something wrong with that guy, he's not right in the head, and he's in bad shape, so heavy!"

"Mom, that's exactly why Mr. Nuzzo chose Vinnie, he figures Rosemarie's safe with him." Peggy started to laugh, "You know...he wouldn't know what to do with her."

Katie shook her head and laughed, "Well I guess it doesn't matter who takes that girl out. Any boy who would get involved with a member of that family should be scared off after seeing poor Sammy, how he is and all. He would have to think of any future children that he might have coming from that family. By the way, where did Patrick go tonight? He didn't have a meeting at the firehouse did he?"

Peggy looked away from her mother; she had to hide the smile on her face. "Yes, I think he did. Mom, I'm going down to talk with Lorraine. I see she's sitting on her porch." She hurried out of the house.

Lorraine smiled as Peggy approached her and said, "Did you see how pretty Rosemarie looked when she came out of her house?"

Peggy laughed, "She came down from her porch so quickly all I caught was a flash of her dress. I think it was a pretty light green. I felt sorry for her, having all the neighbors watching her leave with Vinnie."

"Having to have her brother drive her?" Lorraine said sadly. "I'm sure she'll be miserable the whole evening."

Peggy put her hand up to her mouth to hide the wide smile forming on her lips; she had to keep the secret of her brother and Rosemarie, even from Lorraine Peterson. She knew Lorraine would understand, being secretly engaged to Michael Donovan, but she couldn't take the chance of letting anyone in the neighborhood know. Mr. Peterson came to the door and seeing the two girls sitting on the porch steps, he wondered what they were talking about.

"What are you girls up to?" he asked.

Lorraine looked up at him and said, "Oh nothing."

She was relieved that he missed seeing Rosemarie with Vinnie Russo. She would have had to listen to what he thought about it. It wouldn't be pretty to listen to. Tonight she and her mother would be spared his usual prejudiced opinions.

CRISOCRISOCRISO

As Joey pulled up in front of the high school, Rosemarie looked at Vinnie and felt sorry for him. She could see Patrick standing near the door holding a corsage box.

"Thanks, Vinnie," she said, as she patted his hand.

He blushed, "I forgot to get you a flower, I'm sorry."

She got out of the car, and looked back at him, "No problem, Pat has that covered."

Patrick walked towards her, waved to Joey as they pulled away, and took Rosemarie by the arm. He couldn't believe how beautiful she looked. He kissed her on the forehead and handed her the flowers, white carnations with a yellow ribbon. When they entered the school gymnasium of Marshall High, the band was setting up. He wasn't the only escort who wasn't an alumnus of the school. His graduation from Saint Philips High School two years earlier made him the same age as a few other boys who graduated at the same time from both Marshall and Saint Philips. He knew a few of them from the neighborhood. He didn't feel out of place, many of the senior girls had boyfriends or dates that were out of school.

The band started off with a slow dance number, -- I'll Never Smile Again. -- He took Rosemarie in his arms. It was the second time they were at a dance together. The intimacy they felt was different from just holding hands at the movies, or walking in Douglas Park, or sitting on a park bench and kissing when weather permitted. They could feel the love between them deepen.

It was far more than the mere crush Rosemarie felt that day in church. For Patrick, he knew it was love at first sight since he had first encountered her in Joey's garage and noticed she was much more than Joey's little sister.

"When are you going to tell your family about us?" he asked.

She looked up at him, "I don't know, I really don't know. I'm afraid of my father's reaction if I tell them now."

"You have to tell him sometime, Rosemarie. He'll find out sooner or later. We take a chance every time we meet. Someone is bound to see us. You know how news travels in this neighborhood, and now Vinnie knows."

"Joey swore him to secrecy," she said. "I'm sure he won't say a word about it. I felt so sorry for him, having to do this for us. I never could stand the guy, but sitting next to him in the back of the car, I realized how he must have felt being used by us."

Pat looked down at her, their eyes met, they danced in silence for a few minutes, and then he pulled her closer to him.

"I love you, Rosemarie." He said it, the words she was waiting to hear.

"I love you too, but when my father finds out, I'm afraid love might not be enough to suit him."

"How could he object if we love each other, and when you're eighteen, what will he find wrong with that?" he said, knowing her father would find something, the fact he wasn't Italian or because he was a neighbor. He couldn't think of any other reason.

She wrapped her arm around his neck tighter, afraid to let go. She buried her face against his shoulder. She could still hear her father's words... 'Those damn Irish, those crazy drunken Irish, being led by the nose by the Pope.' She couldn't tell Patrick what her father thought of the Irish.

As he held her in his arms, he thought of his mother, what would she say? She expected him to become a priest. He never had the heart to tell her, absolutely No! He realized he should have told her long ago. He heard how she talked about Italians, he laughed when she said, 'All their women get fat,' or because Sammy was slow, she would say, 'It must be something in the family.' She referred to them as Dagos, but she called his grandfather Shanty so he didn't take it too seriously, then. He realized he expected Rosemarie to do what he couldn't bring himself to do, tell his parents about their relationship.

 C380C380C380

Joey pulled up to the curb in front of Tommy's Diner. It was far enough away from the High School, so he was sure no one would see them. They sat in a booth. Joey looked at Vinnie and felt bad about it all, but it was his father's fault he reasoned. If he had let Rosie date who she wanted, none of this would have happened. He could be on a date with Francie instead of sitting in an all-night diner on Lake Street with a fat guy in a tux, and then he felt bad thinking that way. He knew Vinnie couldn't help being overweight, and as he looked at him he remembered how some of the neighbors laughed when Vinnie was the first to stop the ice cream truck on the street. They thought it was funny, so did Joey, but he also remembered how all the little kids who ran up to the truck got an ice cream they didn't have money for, and all complements of Vinnie.

"What can I order for you?" he asked. "A Pepsi? Are you hungry?"

"No that's ok Joey, I ate at home."

"Well let me order you something, I'm going to order a hot dog and fries." He called the waiter, "Two orders of hot dogs and fries please a Coke and Pepsi too."

He stared at Vinnie, "Why don't you remove your jacket and tie and be comfortable?" he said, because he noticed two guys enter the diner and stare at them. Vinnie was quiet. Joey tried to engage him in conversation.

"What do you do after work every night?" Joey asked. Vinnie hunched his shoulders.

"I go home and turn on the radio, nothing else to do. I go to Peppy's for a Pepsi and I go to Farnelli's store for my Ma to get whatever she forgot to buy earlier. Once, I was carrying a bag of groceries and the sidewalk was covered with ice. Some kids were throwing snowballs at me and I fell down, right on top of the groceries. Everything was smashed. Boy, was my Ma mad! I crushed the package of spaghetti. I don't know why she got so upset, once you cook it and chew it, it'll be broken anyway." Vinnie laughed.

Joey laughed with him; it was the first time he witnessed Vinnie really laughing. He couldn't help feeling some shame for all the snowballs and rocks both he and Patrick threw at him when they were children. He now realized he was once no different than the boys who tormented his little brother. He never really got to know Vinnie, and now he could see the real person inside, a kind and gentle, overweight guy with a big heart.

"I can't thank you enough for what you're doing for my sister," he said.

After the dance was over, they picked up Rosemarie and Joey stopped at Vinnie's place.

"You don't have to come down to our house first, it's dark, even if my old man is watching at the window, he can't see into the car. As long as I'm bringing her home, that's all that matters."

Joey and Rosemarie thanked him again. They would never think of him as the neighborhood joke, ever again. They also thought of their little brother, how they had to protect him as he got older. Being with Vinnie made them think of Sammy.

CHAPTER 18

It was about one in the morning when Patrick arrived home after changing out of his tux at the apartment of one of his firehouse buddies. Katie was up waiting for him. She liked the early morning hours. She found them quiet and peaceful, a time when she could be alone without the children underfoot.

"You're home," she said, surprised that he was home so early on a Saturday night. Usually he came in much later when he was with his friends. "I saved you some cake, would you like a piece," she asked. She loved to sit and talk with her eldest son when they were alone. She could feel him slowly pulling away from her. As a little boy, he was the easiest child to handle. He was gentle, unlike her, more like his father. She loved all her children equally, but because he was her first, he was special to her.

"Thanks Mom." He sat down at the kitchen table and she sat across from him. She watched him eating the cake; she looked at him with pride. She loved that he resembled her. Only Patrick and little Jean had her red hair. The other children went from Michael's blonde hair to the other's having different shades of brown

"Peggy and I watched Rosemarie leave with Vinnie Russo for her prom last night," she said. "It's too bad that she had to go with Fatty Arbuckle," she started laughing. Arbuckle being an earlier fat movie star that everyone loved to laugh at in comedies, but Patrick wasn't laughing.

"Mom, Vinnie can't help being the way he is." The expression on his face was sad. It surprised her. He must be in a serious mood she thought.

"Well anyway, I feel sorry for that girl, the way her father is so controlling." She shook her head from side to side. "That girl is going to have a hard time getting a boyfriend with that family. The mother is a doormat. The grandmother and father are always yelling and that uncle, God knows what he's up to, and then there's Sammy. I feel sorry for anyone who marries into that family."

Patrick knew then, if he had any notion of telling his mother he was the one who took Rosemarie to her prom, he could never tell her. His head was spinning with ways to come up with the truth in the future, but right then he couldn't find a way. All he knew is that he loved Rosemarie with all his heart. The fact that they had to keep it from their parents was weighing on him. He knew there would be no one else for him, in spite of his mother, Rosemarie's father, her uncle, her little brother, or the whole lot of them. *It isn't any of them I want to marry, just her*, he thought.

The month of June went by quickly. Patrick was now a full-fledged fireman. On July 4th, he met Rosemarie a block from her home. In order for them to attend the fireworks at Riverview Park, her Uncle Nicky with Lillian, one of his girlfriends, picked up his niece in his '39 Ford coupe rumble seat with the top down and drove to the corner of California Ave. and Congress Street to pick up Patrick, who crawled into the rumble seat and hid until they were safely out of the neighborhood. They were always weary someone would see them together. On the way to Riverview, Nicky stopped the car and Rosemarie joined Patrick in the rumble seat. Nicky looked back at them and then turned to Lillian, a Polish woman he had been seeing off and on for years. She was crazy about him and put up with his indecision on committing to any women.

"Look at them back there," he said, "They can't take their hands off each other. All I know is I'm as good as dead if my brother ever finds out I'm involved in their romance."

"Why can't they date openly? Is it because Patrick isn't Italian," she asked. She didn't understand any of it. "Is that why you never brought me back a second time to visit your family? Is it because I'm not Italian?"

"That's mostly Benny, my set-in-his-ways-brother. He clings to the old ways. I don't know how my sister-in-law puts up with him. Remember when I brought you over to meet my family years ago and introduced you as Lillian Kosinski. Kosinski isn't an Italian name. I never brought you back because he only feels comfortable around Italians."

He couldn't tell her his brother thought all Polish were considered dumb by the Polish jokes Benny heard at work. He couldn't tell her that Benny called her a Polack and a cheap puttana. "My brother is plain ignorant," was all he could say.

The fireworks were beautiful as they watched them from the rollercoaster. Later, they met Joey and Francie and went to Grant Park to watch the boats on the lake. The night was warm and groups of couples sat on blankets watching the fireworks display. Nicky and Lillian sat with Joey and Francie, a little bit away from Rosemarie and Patrick to give them time alone.

Rosemarie knew, without her uncle, brother, and Patrick's sister Peggy covering for them it would have been impossible to be together as often as they were. Winter would be a difficult time. They wouldn't be able to walk in the park as they did during warmer weather. She thought of asking her uncle if they could meet at his apartment once winter came, but she was afraid of what his answer would be. His relationship with her father was flimsy at best. She would turn eighteen in August. She was sure her father would accept the fact that she wasn't a minor any longer and if he didn't, she felt the law was on her side regardless of what he thought.

She lay on the blanket in Patrick's arms, looking up at the night sky, watching the stars. She didn't want the night to end. Later they would all go to their usual place for a late night snack.

On the way home, and a few blocks from their street, Nicky pulled over so Rosemarie could squeeze in next to Lillian in the front seat and Patrick would lay low in the rumble seat while Nicky drove him into the alley behind his house so he could climb out and go in through his back- yard. He knew Benny would be at the window, no matter the time, watching for him to return Rosemarie. The fact that Benny allowed Nicky to take her anywhere with one of the many questionable women he thought Nicky dated was due to Joey. He was coming to his sister's defense more often. Joey meant so much to Benny that he gave in to his demands. With the war looming large in the newspapers and on the radio nightly, he worried that America might get involved. He worried about Joey, his eldest, his pride, the son he always wanted. Lately, Joey was able to accomplish what no other member of the family could by putting some controls on Benny. It wasn't just for his sister; he would also come to his mother's aid more often.

The one person Benny was afraid of alienating was his son Joey.

CЗ∞CЗ∞CЗ∞

When Patrick entered the house at midnight, he entered into an argument between his mother and his brother Michael. Michael, being his mother's wild child, had celebrated his eighteenth birthday on July 2nd and now wanted to join England's Royal Air Force. Katie blamed her father-in-law, Casey, for putting all those ideas of fighting and honor into his grandson's head.

"Tell her, Pat, I'm old enough to join now," Michael said.

"To join the RAF? Are you kidding me, Mike? Pops would disown you. He hates the English."

Patrick turned to his mother, "Mom he's old enough to do what he likes, but he should wait for our country to join the war, then he can be in America's army."

"When's that going to be? I don't think Roosevelt is even shipping arms to the British, he certainly won't send men," Michael said as he left the kitchen.

Katie turned to Patrick, "See how he's itching to get into a fight, any fight. All that talk your grandfather does after a pint about putting up a good fight for Ireland and that stuff about taking Ireland back from the British. The British are only in the north of Ireland and still he talks like it's the eighteen hundreds."

Patrick didn't want to get between his mother and brother so he excused himself and went to bed. Katie couldn't sleep. It was one in the morning. She was too upset to sleep, so she poured herself a cup of tea and sat at the table in the quiet house, and thought about Casey and his wild ideas. She was afraid of the influence he had on her boys. She thought of the first time Jim had taken her to his home to meet his parents. They had been dating only a short time. She knew Jim was crazy about her, but she wasn't prepared for what she witnessed. She perceived his parents as being, what her family would refer to as, Shanty Irish. Casey was friendly enough, too friendly. She could tell he had been drinking, and Molly, her future mother-in-law, meant well when she welcomed her son's young girlfriend with a wild rendition of Irish eyes are smiling on a beat-up old player piano. As Katie stood beside the piano, she noticed Molly was wearing one of her husband's old undershirts, holes and all. It was the hole Katie noticed; it exposed one of her nipples. At first she thought she was mistaken, but when she realized what she had seen, she backed away. She was certain the poor woman was unaware of the calamity in the shirt she was wearing. When she finished the song and stood up, the hole had moved to a more proper spot, to Katie's relief.

She had doubts about the McCann family, but not about Jim. He seemed mild-mannered and he wasn't a drinker. Her family, after having met the McCann clan, warned her about how Jim's family was from a lower class. The O'Neil's considered themselves better, the Lace Curtain class, and they called the poorer Irish, 'Shanty,' and they informed her that they weren't sure if McCann was a proper Irish name. They thought it came from Scotland sometime in the past, but in the end they had to accept Jim because Katie loved him and he was Catholic, and that was all that mattered to her deeply religious family.

After Katie and Jim married, they settled as far away from his family as Katie could get. His family lived in a poor section of Bridgeport, an Irish neighborhood quite a distance southeast from where the young couple lived. She never imagined Molly passing away right after the twins were born and Casey coming to live with them after he retired from the railroad. She always thought about how well her children behaved in spite of being subjected to their rather crude grandfather. Casey's humor caused fits of laughter among his grandchildren, but she found little humor in the things he said or did. Jim would often tell her to lighten up, but she was unable to do that. She was a serious wife and mother and she took pride in that. Of all her boys, Michael was the hardest to handle. Now that he was out of high school, he would need to think about what he wanted to do for a career. She knew Peggy would end up staying at Woolworth's or find a better job at Sears and Roebuck. She wished her second son had half the sense her eldest had. She blamed Casey for some of Michael's shortcomings. She failed to see it was a similar personality and not necessarily any influence from her father-in-law.

The next morning, Katie awoke to Jim and Michael's loud banter about what Michael should do next. She knew Michael was serious, but to tease his father, he was laughing as he threatened to join the R A F. She entered the kitchen and joined them at the table. Jim had poured the coffee for her.

"He's going to join the police force," Jim said. "I told him he could forget about joining the British Air Force. I'll see what he needs to do for the police department, to fill out forms, things like that."

Katie looked at Michael, "Is that what you really want to do?" She wasn't surprised; his temperament fit the profession, unlike his father's, she thought. She could never understand Jim going into the force, but she knew her father had a part in it. He was instrumental in getting Jim a job when they were newlywed. She thought it was a wonderful career, her father being a sergeant on the force. She never imagined that after Jim had been on the force for five years, her father would lose his life in the line of duty. That is when she began to worry about

Jim and said a prayer whenever he left for work. Now she would have to add Michael to her prayer list.

"I guess it's what I better do," Michael laughed, "or I'll never hear the end of it Mom." Michael smiled his crooked smile that endeared him to her. All her children were growing up and pulling away. She knew that day would come for all of them, but she wasn't ready to let them go. Her home and her children are what she lived for. She would attend Mass Sunday with special prayers for Michael.

After she cleaned up the breakfast dishes and her brood had gone to their different pursuits, Katie thought of paying a visit to Grace Peterson. She had not been feeling well. She would bring her a coffee cake and spend a little time with her, catching up on the neighborhood gossip.

Grace suffered from arthritis badly during the cold winters, but for her to get an attack in the month of July was rare. Katie pressed the doorbell at the Peterson's. Grace came to the door to let her in.

"I see you're up and around with no problem," Katie said. "I thought I would find you in bed, with Ralph home answering the door." She was happy he wasn't home. He had left for work as usual. The two would have a chance to talk. Regardless of the bad feelings between Ralph and Jim through the years over the children, it never interfered with the good neighborly relationship between the women. Over steaming cups of coffee, they talked about what was going on with the neighbors and the war. They had plenty to talk about. Grace had the kitchen radio on.

The morning news was very depressing. Hitler's assault on Russia in June was all over the news in July. The two women sat quietly not wanting to miss a word from the commentator. Most Americans worried that whatever happened in Europe would eventually have an effect on America. The news report said supplies were needed inside Russia and they had to be sent by sea. The British Royal Navy was already stretched and only the Soviet Arctic ports could receive them. The route was flanked on the east by German-occupied Norway. During the past winter, ice was a detriment and forced the English ships closer to the coast of Norway. To make matters worse, they only had four hours of darkness at that time of year. There was the constant threat of German submarines.

"Enough of that," Grace said as she got up and clicked the station to another that had the music of Tommy Dorsey. She lowered the sound, poured two more cups of coffee and sat down.

"I think of you with all your sons Katie," she said. "It's during times like this that I am grateful I only have a daughter." Katie nodded in agreement and said, "As long as we stay out of it we don't need to worry, after all, it's not our fight. England should be able to win over Germany now that Russia has joined the fight."

Grace put her hand on Katie's, "I just wish it would all go away; Ralph is glued to the radio every night and he gets his dander up over it all. Well, at least he's not complaining about the neighbors as much. For that I'm grateful."

Katie smiled and said, "You're not going to believe what my Michael wanted to do, he wanted to join the RAF. But of course, if his father and I have a say in it, he won't. Jim will make sure he gets accepted as a rookie on the police force before he gets any fool notion to fight for England."

Grace smiled a strained smile and thought of her aunt and cousins in Wales, relatives she never met, but still they were family living in danger. Katie had no way of knowing Grace had family where Hitler was bombing. The war was affecting many Americans who had ties to Europe, regardless if Roosevelt kept Americans out of the fighting or not. Many Americans had family who came from some country in Europe at one time or another. Many had family living in the countries at war. Both women continued to talk of the war and lately it was taking up most of their conversations. Their talk of neighborhood gossip was becoming less important in their everyday lives.

CHAPTER 19

The month of September brought the same old problems for the Nuzzo family; Sammy was attending school again. Labor Day was celebrated by going on a picnic to Garfield Park. Nora and her sister Rose packed a basket of food and took Sammy to the park for the afternoon. Joey and Rosemarie went off somewhere, and Benny said it was a day of rest so he wasn't getting out of his chair in front of the radio. The park was too far for Maria to walk, so she stayed home with her son listening to the radio and crocheting.

After Labor Day, they had to get Sammy up for his first day of school. He slept late all summer. Getting him up wouldn't be an easy task. Rosemarie and Joey left for work; Benny was gone before them, and Sammy was still sleeping at eight a.m. It would take him the full hour to get ready and Nora was grateful that the John Ericsson Grade School on Harrison Street was less than a block from their home. Nora would walk him there the first day. He was nine years old and would be starting second grade again. It was a grade they hoped he didn't have to repeat. He had to repeat first and now second. Nora was hoping he would be capable of going into third when he finished. After Rosemarie spoke to Grace Peterson about Sammy, Grace arranged for Lorraine to help tutor the boy. Having his sister or any other family member help him was tried in the past, and it didn't work. Having Lorraine, who was happy to do it, was like having his teacher from school; he paid closer attention.

Rosemarie graduated, had her eighteenth birthday in August and was working full time at Woolworths, but Benny still wouldn't let up on his strict enforcement of who she could date and what time she was expected to be home at night. She felt his presence repressive whenever he was home and she loved when he worked on Saturdays, which unfortunately, was seldom. She had planned to meet Patrick on Saturday, but

Benny was home and had other plans for her. Maria wasn't feeling well and he expected Rosemarie to help with whatever Maria needed.

"You're here," she said to his request. "And Ma's here. Why do I have to stay home?"

"What do you mean, why? You're here and you live here, right? You belong to this family; she's your grandma. Don't get so big-headed because you're working and paying board. You stay home when you're needed."

Rosemarie turned and gave her father a look he knew well. She was about to erupt into a rage. Her face turned red before the words came out.

She screamed back at him, "I'm eighteen; I just started to work full-time, and you demand half of my paycheck and now you expect me to stay home whenever you decide? You're home; you can watch Granny. That's just your excuse to keep me home; well, I'm not staying home today. I promised Peggy and a couple girls I'd meet them at the movies. I'm not a child anymore, so stop treating me like one!"

She turned and left the room before he could answer. She went out to the back porch and down the steps to the backyard, worried that he would follow her there. She knew she couldn't go back upstairs. She had to leave while she was out of the house. She would face whatever came later. It was too early to meet Patrick, so she went next door and rang Twyla's doorbell.

Twyla answered with her usual sweet southern drawl. "Come on in honey; how y'all doing today?" She knew the answer. Just one look at Rosemarie's face told her what she needed to know. At the Nuzzo's nothing went well for long.

"Can I stay here until I need to leave for the movies?" she asked, knowing what the answer would be of course, as always. Twyla felt sorry for all the women in the Nuzzo family, most of all Nora.

Rosemarie was growing up and soon she could leave, but Nora was stuck between her husband and his mother. Twyla was a good neighbor, old enough to understand Nora's position and young enough to aid Rosemarie with encouraging her independence.

Later, in Douglas Park, Patrick and Rosemarie sat holding hands, thankful it was still warm in September. They only had the park bench as a place where they could sit and talk when they weren't at the movies. There were few places they were able to go to be alone. Patrick was working towards buying a car but so far had not been able to save enough to match what his father was willing to contribute. Except for Joey, few boys had their own cars at age twenty. Times were difficult; the past twelve years found most people still trying to climb out of the setback caused by the depression.

"I feel silly sitting here," Rosemarie said, "I'm eighteen and you're twenty and we have to sneak around like a couple of little kids."

"Don't you think I feel the same way?" he said, looking down at their hands, their fingers intertwined together as they clung to each other. Their lives were in secret, making them feel like they had done something wrong. To go against ones' parents was unheard of. Her uncle was dating a woman who lived alone in her own apartment. She was considered a marked woman, a woman who was called names, one no decent man would marry. Good girls lived with their parents until the day they left for the church to marry a good boy who lived with his parents, regardless of his age.

He put his arm around her and held her tight as they kissed. They were trapped by their parent's view of the world and by the different cultures around them. They sat for hours until the sun went down. They were unable go out to grab a bit of supper somewhere; there wasn't any place in the neighborhood. They would have to take a streetcar, but maybe someone would be on the car that knew them. They couldn't take the chance. They had to be content to be together alone in the park, shielded by trees and bushes, with squirrels and birds for company.

When winter came, the month of November was bitter

cold and just two weeks before Thanksgiving Nicky relented and allowed Patrick and Rosemarie to stop over to his apartment whenever they wanted to spend a few hours indoors. Except for the movies or traveling downtown to walk around Marshal Fields, there weren't many places to go. They could have gone to one of the ballrooms to dance, but everyone from the neighborhood went dancing and they were afraid of who they might run into. At first Nicky and Lillian were present when they were in the apartment. Later, after several talks with Nicky reminding them that he had to trust them and that he would get the blame if they misbehaved, and to not do anything that would cause him trouble, he would allow them time alone.

Thanksgiving was over, and it was the last day of November when Nicky opened the door to a very chilled Rosemarie and Patrick. They had walked the six blocks to his apartment. It had been snowing all afternoon and it was nearly six in the evening. It was Patrick's day off from the firehouse, but he had to wait for Rosemarie to leave work and meet up with him. They waited for one of the new streetcars that were now replacing the old cars. The new cars weren't as reliable in the deep snow. They took separate seats when they had to take the streetcar and ran into someone they knew. They decided to walk along the route and catch one as soon as it came, but they reached the apartment first.

"Hi, Uncle Nicky." She smiled at him as he met them at the door.

He looked at Pat, "I'm letting you guys have the apartment until eleven, you know my brother will expect her home by twelve and I have to bring her back so I'll come back at eleven. I'll be at Lillian's."

"Don't worry about us, Nicky. I appreciate everything you're doing for us," Patrick said. "I know your life is on the line with her father and I wouldn't do anything to ruin your relationship with him."

Nicky laughed, "Ruin? It's ruined already, been ruined since the day I was born. All he can do now is kill me, nothing left to ruin."

Rosemarie gave her uncle a hug. "Yeah, Yeah," he laughed. "You gonna patch me up if he ever finds out I've been covering for you guys?"

After Nicky left, Rosemarie went to get them a coke. After handing one to Patrick they sat on the couch and Patrick held her, kissed her a few times, drank the coke and kissed her again. Their relationship was getting beyond serious and it was getting harder for him, but he promised her uncle they would behave and in spite of being un-chaperoned, he kept his promise. There were a few moments when she would have thrown caution to the wind if it weren't for him. He knew he had her reputation in his hands. She loved the time they shared in the apartment; she could pretend it would be like this once they were married.

"How was your family's Thanksgiving?" she asked. She thought about how she wasn't feeling too thankful about anything, having to meet like this, not being able to date openly.

He searched her face for a hint that she told her parents about them over Thanksgiving, like she said she would.

"Did you ask your father if I could take you out?"

She lowered her head. "I couldn't do it," she said. "I can't tell him about us or ask him anything."

"You didn't even try? Or at least ask if I could take you out on a date?"

Rosemarie looked up at him. "Joey mentioned it. He asked him if you could take me out and my father had a fit. He said a loud no!"

"He said no?"

Rosemarie hugged Patrick tighter, "That's it, he just said no, gave no reason, just no." She thought about Thanksgiving dinner, and how she had ruined it for the whole family. She couldn't tell him how her father really reacted. He glared at her when Joey mentioned the name Patrick.

He turned on her with anger. "Patrick who?" he shouted.

Joey tried to help her, "You know him Pa, Patrick McCann, from across the street."

Ignoring Joey, he turned to Rosemarie. "What! From that drunken family? You stick to your own kind!"

"You mean like Vinnie?" she yelled back.

"There's other nice Italian boys who could take you out later when you're old enough? You're only eighteen."

"Yes, I'm eighteen and by law I'm old enough. How old do I have to be?"

He banged his fist on the table, "When you're twenty- one; that's MY law!"

She felt the frustrations working its way up from the pit of her stomach and aided by her temper, it reached her mouth full-force. She screamed at him, "Why Pa? Why? Why do you call them a drunken family? Why do you say all those bad things about people you hardly know?"

"I know. I know them; they live across the street, no? And I know!" he shouted back.

She stood up and leaned on the table, her face close to his, "No you don't! You don't know anything about them. You've never been in their home. They have never been invited here, how can you know them?" she cried, tears streaming down her face. Maria stood up and tried to sit her down but she remained standing. Nora fled to the kitchen. Joey gave up and just sat and said nothing.

"They are good people. The father is a policeman; the mother works hard and they go to Mass every Sunday, and that's more than you do," she said.

"They go every Sunday?" Benny laughed, "Like a dog fetches a bone."

"What have you got against them Pa?"

"They all drink, those Irish, it's in their blood; they're different from us."

"I don't want to be different!" she cried, fleeing from the room.

Joey left the table and walked out the door. He couldn't

remain there and witness the insanity of it all.

Maria yelled "Enough!" in Italian, and gave her son a slap on the back of the head; he ignored it, then she went to comfort Rosemarie.

Nora stayed in the kitchen and Sammy sat chewing on a turkey leg; he was used to all the yelling. He continued eating, in spite of it all.

Nora called Sammy out of the room, leaving Benny alone at the table. He sat there hunched over mumbling, "They are all drunks," he repeated to himself as he poured another glass of wine.

The full gallon that was placed at his feet at the beginning of the Thanksgiving meal soon became a half-gallon of wine.

"Rosemarie! Rosemarie!" Patrick called. She looked at him, totally forgetting where she was.

"A penny for your thoughts," he said. "So what else did your father say besides no?"

"Oh, just no. Did you ever tell your mother about us?"

"I tried once. She's under a lot of stress right now with Michael joining the police force, but I promise, I'll tell her soon. You know I hinted at it once, I told her I thought you were a very pretty girl."

"What did she say when you mentioned me?"

"She wasn't pleased that I would notice any girl, she thinks I'm going into the seminary one day."

He thought about what his mother had really said. "You're not thinking of asking out that little Dago girl are you? Look at her little brother, well, I mean, you know, the poor kid, someone could marry that girl and have a kid like that. It must run in the family," she paused. "Besides they're Italian. They're not like us." As an afterthought she added, "But they make good cooks."

He knew the minute she addressed Rosemarie as "That little Dago girl," it was all over, as far as he was concerned, of ever confiding anything to her about how he felt about Rosemarie. She would never accept her in the family, he was sure of that.

"So she thinks you should be a priest, huh?" Rosemarie laughed, "Well at least I know she likes me; she's nice to me whenever I visit Peggy."

On the way home, they sat up front with Nicky. It was a little too chilly for the rumble seat and being late at night they were sure no one would be out on such a cold night, so Patrick was dropped off at the back of his house. As Nicky pulled up to the curb in front of her house, there was Benny, his nose plastered against the windowpane.

Nicky said, "Rosie you're going to have to do something about this soon. You're old enough to tell him, I can't keep doing this for you. I'm going to get in trouble if he ever finds out, and he'll find out sooner or later."

"Don't worry Uncle Nicky, Pat and I will think of something soon."

"Well, the sooner the better."

"Thanks for tonight, Uncle Nicky." She leaned over and kissed his cheek. He watched her go up the porch steps and open the outer door before he drove away.

Benny greeted her in the hall, he opened his mouth to say something, but she rushed past him and the only sound he heard was her bedroom door slamming shut.

She could hear him on the other side of the door... "What's the matter with you? Everybody's asleep. You want grandma should wake up?"

She put her hands over her ears until it became quiet again. Her first thought was, *I can't wait to leave this place.* She lay in her bed across from Maria. She never had the privacy of a room of her own, not since the day she was born. As a newborn she was kept in her parent's room, even after she graduated from a bassinette to a full-size crib. Joey was put in Maria's room because the small apartment they lived in on Taylor Street only had two bedrooms. Later, Joey was sleeping on a cot in the small front room. She was then put in Maria's room until they moved to Congress Street and with three bedrooms in the larger flat she still ended up sleeping with her grandmother. It was larger than the small room off the kitchen her parents shared. Ten-year-old Joey had the small room off the dining room. The front bedroom had less privacy with Benny sitting within sight of the door to her room. As a result, Rosemarie kept the door closed as often as possible. The only redeeming quality about the room was a view of the street below. From her window she could view the neighbors going in and out of their homes. It was of interest to both her and her grandmother. It gave her another place to escape Benny and his lectures and the narrow opinions he held of his neighbors, the environment they lived in, of everything.

She lay awake thinking of Patrick and the dilemma they found themselves in. She knew her twenty-first birthday was a distant two and a half years away. There wasn't any way they were going to wait that long. She would talk to Patrick about eloping to Crown Point, Indiana, where other underage teenagers went to marry. She knew she was of age at eighteen, but maybe Patrick would have to wait until he was twenty-one. Boys were considered less mature than girls when it came to adult milestones like smoking or drinking, so the law was girls were considered adults at eighteen and boys at twenty-one. Crown Point didn't have such restricted rules.

ೞഇೞഇೞഇ

Patrick lay on the top bunk of the bunk bed he shared with Michael. He could hear his brother Michael's heavy breathing, and he looked over at his two younger brothers across the room asleep in their bunks. None of them seemed to have a care in the world. They could fall asleep as soon as their heads hit the pillow but not Patrick. He wished he were more like Michael, more daring and not afraid of anything. He knew if it were Michael caught in the situation he was in, he would have told his mother long ago that he would never be a priest but it wasn't Michael she expected to go into the seminary. It was past two in the morning before he fell asleep.

They would all awaken to the first day of the last month of 1941, a cold snowy December day, overcast and gloomy.

CHAPTER 20

Nora looked out of her kitchen door for the milk delivery, but the milkman was late. The first day of December, a Monday and the weather was unusually cold. The day was overcast and the temperature had dropped severely, unusual for that time of year. January and February were usually the coldest months. Several inches of snow covered the ground, except where the snow was packed down by the few cars that went by or by children who pulled their sleds back and forth. On Sunday, the day before, Sammy was one of the children who played in the street, belly flopping on his sled. His size and weight limited the distance the sled could take him, but he never tired of playing with his sled.

If the milkman didn't arrive soon, she would have to go downstairs and hope Mrs. Katz had milk she could borrow for Sammy's breakfast. He sat at the table with his bowl of dry corn flakes in front of him. He whined and fidgeted. When it came to food, he had little patience for waiting. He was putting on more weight, and Nora felt guilty about it. She herself was overweight and her sister Rose was what Benny called, 'just plain fat.' He never let her forget that Sammy took after her side of the family.

Nora heard Tillie, Mrs. Katz's cat mewing. Tillie knew the milkman by sight. She would follow him from the downstairs porch up to Nora's door. She followed him as he set bottles of milk on the back porches of nearby neighbors. She would walk around the bottles and meow, and if the owner didn't get there fast enough, the milk would freeze and the cat received a treat licking the cream from the popped up cap. When Nora heard her, she quickly retrieved the milk to Sammy's delight. Mrs. Katz was climbing up the stairs to her door just as Nora reached down for the milk. She had been sweeping the snow off the stairs.

"Come on in Sylvia," she said, holding the door open for

her. "Have a cup of coffee with me." Nora poured Sylvia a cup of coffee and poured the milk into Sammy's bowl. "He needs to hurry or he'll be late for school," she said, motioning toward her son. "Hurry up, you're going to be late again!" she said annoyingly.

He finished his cereal, which he usually ate quickly hoping for more, but this morning he would have to make do with one bowl. She helped the boy put on his winter clothing. Pulling on his galoshes was the one thing he found hard to do for himself.

"Oy! Too fast they grow, everything too fast it goes. The children, the years, Nu, vo den?" Mrs. Katz said with a shrug as she raised the cup to her lips, her last line in Yiddish, meaning –"So, what else?"

After Sammy left, Nora sat across from the landlady she had come to love, to enjoy a cup of coffee in the quiet of her kitchen, a first visit alone without Maria's presence in quite a while. Normally Maria would be up and right there with them, but she hadn't been feeling well, so she went back to bed after Benny left for work.

"How've you been Sylvia? I haven't seen you the past few days. I don't know where the time flies to and it's December already," Nora said.

"Oy, don't ask! How should I be? It's terrible times ve live in. It vouldn't hurt, the sun, she come out today." Mrs. Katz looked down into her cup of coffee and sighed.

"Have you heard anything more about your family in Germany?"

"Don't ask, don't ask, nothting, I hear nothting." She shook her head sadly.

"Well, better times will come soon in Europe, don't you think so?" Nora patted her hand. "I keep hoping for better times here in my family. The fighting between my daughter and my husband, I can't stand it no more I tell you, no more!"

Mrs. Katz nodded in agreement "The children, they vant to go their own vay. Vat can vee do? Nuting, nisht do gedakht," she said, which meant, 'It shouldn't happen here.'

Nora looked at her with sympathy, knowing about her troubles with her son. "How is Davie?" she asked. "Have you heard from him lately?" She couldn't remember the last time he visited his mother.

"Mine Davie, he don't vant to be Jewish no more. You can't vish avay being Jewish. You are vat you are, no matter vat! You know ven the neighbor's find out vee vas Jewish, the bad boy's in the neighborhood, they vait for my Davie to get off the streetcar from high school and they beat him up, that's vat they did, they tell him, Go home Jew to 12th street!" She started to cry, bringing her handkerchief up to wipe her eyes.

"Don't cry," Nora said sympathetically. "I know how you feel. It's terrible to see your children hurting. I watch my daughter struggle with her father every day. I'm afraid she's starting to hate him. I don't understand him; he is so set in his ways, so stubborn. She can't talk to him, and I can't say anything without him blowing up at me, and my mother-in-law, she comes to take his side. She fights with him and yet if I say something, she joins him against me. I tell you, they give me knots in my stomach."

"Oy! The knots, I shoult know, like the big fist vight here! I used to have all the time the knot, ven my Sol vas alive. Oy! The fights my Davie and Sol vood have, such fights! My Sol, he vasn't easy to live vit. Always I have the big knot vight here." Sylvia made a fist and tapped her stomach a few times. "Someday it all goes avay."

"When does that happen?" Nora asked, looking sadly at Mrs. Katz.

"Ven they die!"

After Mrs. Katz had gone back down to her flat, Nora sat alone at the table pondering her family's problems. She glanced up at the clock on the wall above the calendar with its November page still visible. It was almost ten-thirty and Maria had not come into the kitchen yet. She thought about going in to check on her, but she seldom had time to herself to put two thoughts together. To be alone in a quiet house was a rare occurrence for her. She got up and tore the November page off the calendar and sat back down and poured herself another cup of coffee. When she heard Maria moving about the bedroom, she looked up at the clock. It was 10:45. Her time alone was as unexpected blessing and now she could feel just a hint of that little knot returning.

At supper that evening, to take the conversation away from anything about Rosemarie again, Nora brought up Sylvia. "That poor Mrs. Katz," Nora said, not to anyone in particular.

"How is she?" Benny asked.

"The poor women, she still hasn't heard anything about her brother in Germany."

"Well he shouldn't have stayed there. He should have got out when he knew Hitler didn't like the Jews."

"It was his home, where was he supposed to go?" Joey said.

Benny took a sip of wine, "Back to where he came from, didn't he come from the East? I thought most of the Jews came from Russia or Poland before they went to Germany."

Joey looked aggravated, "That's where he was born! That Hitler is a monster!" Joey couldn't leave well enough alone, he continued, "And that stupid Mussolini goes right along with him."

Benny stared at Joey with an expression Joey came to know well.

"Mussolini did a lot of good for Italy."

"I know Pa! He made the trains run on time," Joey said, sarcastically. "And now he drags Italy into the war by joining Hitler. What if we have to fight some of your relatives over there, huh? Then what will you think?" He knew it was time to stop baiting his father but he couldn't stop himself.

"Never, it's not going to happen!" Benny shouted. "My Cousin Tommy's son is in the Italian Army; he would never fight America, and besides we're not going to get involved."

Benny couldn't comprehend anything so terrible. How

would he feel? Would he feel American or Italian? He thought about the fact that Maria didn't have her citizenship papers; he had neglected to get hers at the time he had applied for his own. Would she be deported if America went to war? He felt unsettled and a little worried that Joey might be right. He knew he had to take care of his mother's papers soon.

Rosemarie ate quickly and left the table during the conversation between her father and brother. She dreaded mealtime and was happy when Joey engaged him long enough for her to get away. When Joey was absent from a meal, it was terrible for her. All her father's attention would be on her and she was finding it more difficult to sit at the same table with him, or speak to him about anything. When Benny noticed Rosemarie's absence, he called to her. When she didn't answer, he asked where she had gone.

Nora was annoyed. She wanted to say something but she remained silent.

"She went to talk with Peggy, where else does she go?" Joey said.

"Why is she always over there?" he asked. "They can talk here. Why is she always running out of here? Always across the street by those drunks."

Joey knew she would only go over to Peggy when Patrick was at the firehouse. They would sit on the porch steps in warm weather and inside Peggy's room in bad weather, because there wasn't any privacy in the Nuzzo home. Benny was all ears and suspicious of everyone, and of everything going on around him. Joey finished his supper and rose from the table.

"Pa, they're girls, they like to talk, and there isn't any drunks over there. Only the grandfather drinks a little, besides, he's old. He doesn't harm anybody."

Before Benny could answer, Joey had left the house. Benny stared at Maria, then Nora. Sammy was waiting for one of them to pick on him; he was afraid to be the last one at the table with his father. He got up and quickly fled the room

"So where did she go so fast? Always running out of here, the both of them." Benny's mood was getting darker; he poured himself another glass of wine.

"Out, they go out!" Nora said. "They are eighteen and twenty years old!"

"Where is she going when it's snowing out there like it is? Where does she go all the time?" He didn't ask where Joey was going. He never asked where Joey was going.

"All the time she runs; she's never home no more." He was talking to himself; everyone left him alone at the table.

He sat drinking his wine, feeling like he was losing control of something, but wasn't quite sure of what. He drank down the last of the wine in the glass and left the kitchen to go to his favorite spot in the front room. He mumbled to himself as he paused by the window. He parted the stiff white curtains in the middle, looking across at the McCann's house. When Nora looked into the room, she spotted him hanging on to the freshly starched curtains. It upset her.

"Ma!" she called, "he's wrinkling the curtains again, and that's why they don't hang together in the middle no more!"

"Takea you hands off!' Maria yelled, as she rushed to the window. "Looka," she said, as she pointed out the wrinkled curtains to her son. "Looka what you do." She showed him how they hung at a crooked angle. "You ruina the curtains. What you see in the street?"

He looked at her and threw his hands up above his head in a gesture of disgust.

Maria went to smooth out the damage. "What you always looka for? Golda in the street?" she said, as she tried to pull the curtains together, the curtains she had taken pride in starching and pinning on the curtain rack. Her one other chore besides baking bread was the curtains.

Nora listened to the rampage given out by Maria to her son. Nora smiled; if she had said the same thing to him it would have started him yelling back at her. Maria got away with it because she was his Mama.

155

It was half past seven when the doorbell rang. Sammy ran to open the door; he knew Lorraine Peterson had come to help him with his schoolwork. Nora cleared off the kitchen table for Sammy's lesson. Lorraine took off her coat and hung it on the hall tree rack. It was snowing heavily and the white flakes glistened to drops of water when the warmth of the room melted the snow on her coat.

"My coat is wet, I hope it doesn't drip on your floor Mrs. Nuzzo," she said, as she entered the kitchen. Nora smiled and pulled out a chair for her. Sammy was seated next to her.

"I leave you two alone now," Nora said. "How is he doing?"

"Better, much better, Mrs. Nuzzo," she patted the boy on his back. "You're doing real good Sammy." As she praised him, the boy had a big smile on his face.

Nora was proud of her son. He tried so hard, and she wondered why his father couldn't see how well he was doing. Benny thought it was a waste of money, hiring Lorraine to teach him. Nora didn't feel that way. Benny was a generous man when it came to food, but anything beyond that, he considered unnecessary. The movies, the Boy Scouts, magazines, lipstick, the hairdresser, all that was considered a waste of money to Benny. In those items he was downright cheap. Nora paid Lorraine out of her own earnings she made knitting for people. Sammy wanted to join the Boy Scouts and she promised him he could if he made good enough grades on his report card. She would pay for the uniform too.

CR&OCR&OCR&O

Rosemarie and Peggy sat at the McCann's kitchen table. They had spent the last hour in Peggy's room but she shared it with three-year-old Jean, and Katie was ready to put Jean to bed so the girls went into the kitchen. Rosemarie watched the clock; she wanted to leave before Patrick came home from the fire station. They made a pact never to be together in the house

156

with Katie for fear she might sense something between them. Rosemarie loved going over to their home when Patrick was at the fire station, but this night he was due home soon.

"I better go," Rosemarie whispered. "It's getting harder for us to keep our feelings from showing."

"What are you two going to do?" Peggy asked, looking concerned. "It's going to have to come out in the open soon. You're both old enough; it's silly, all this secrecy."

"It's my father and your mother."

"It's not my mother so much; I think she would come around about it in the end, Rosemarie."

"It's not your mother I'm worried about, but if your mother knows then eventually my father finds out and that scares me to death. You don't know how crazy he thinks. How he is, you don't know." Rosemarie looked upset, shaking her head from side to side.

Peggy put her arm around her as they went to the door, "You don't have to do anything yet, but just think about it."

"Peggy, that's all I've been thinking about lately, I can't eat, I can't sleep, and I'm always on the verge of tears."

Peggy smiled at her, "You'll see, things will all work out." She gave Rosemarie a hug and watched as she crossed the street leaving her footsteps in the freshly fallen snow. She stood watching the large snowflakes falling, how still the night was, how beautiful the trees looked, the empty branches were covered with a blanket of snow. How quiet, peaceful and beautiful this December winter was. She closed the door and turned out the hall light. She left the kitchen light on for her brother and went to bed.

When Rosemarie entered her flat her father was sleeping in his chair. The house was quiet. It was almost eleven p.m. Everyone was in bed except Joey, who never came home before midnight when he went out in the evening, even if it was a weekday. She would be real quiet. She didn't want to give him the satisfaction of knowing she was home at eleven. She thought, *Let him sleep, and I hope he wakes up when Joey comes in or in the early morning and race to my room and peek in to see if I'm home.* She didn't want to make things easy for him. *Let him sleep the night away hunched up in his chair, I hope he gets a kink in his neck,* she thought, as she quietly went about getting ready for bed.

Early on Sunday morning, December 7th, Patrick awoke at seven to his mother's voice speaking loudly to his father in the kitchen about how Patrick and Michael never went to mass as often as they had in the past. He looked forward to having his usual rendezvous with Rosemarie at her uncle's apartment. He would leave around 9:00 a.m. on the pretense of going to Mass at a parish near the firehouse, but he would meet Joey. He told Katie he was meeting a couple of buddies from work. The past couple of Sundays, Nicky had invited them over for breakfast. Joey usually drove his sister and Patrick over and would tell Benny they had a right to visit their uncle. He would leave them at Nicky's and then go to Francie and spend the day with her, but this particular morning he would pick up Francie on the way to his uncle's. They were all to have a late breakfast at Nicky's. Lillian would be there also. After having breakfast together, they planned on going their separate ways during the afternoon, except for Patrick and Rosemarie who would stay at the apartment until either Joey or Nicky would return to drive them home. They both knew Benny never relaxed his vigilance when it came to his daughter. Nicky had warned his niece often that they couldn't continue to use his apartment indefinitely. He was taking a big risk. He was sure his brother would never show up where he lived, but he still worried.

Nicky was usually sleeping when they arrived, unless Lillian stayed the night, which was often enough that Rosemarie and Joey thought nothing of it. They were both adults, in their thirty's, and Rosemarie and Joey accepted what at first had shocked them. Without her uncle's help, there wasn't any place to be together in the winter without being seen from someone in the neighborhood or from someone who knew someone who lived on her street. The East Garfield Park neighborhood or the West Side, as it was also called, was a close-knit community where everyone knew someone, all the way to Kedzie Avenue, as gossip traveled quickly, from one block to another. It was the same in the Irish and Italian neighborhoods. Rosemarie and Patrick would have to stay out of both neighborhoods during the summer; they chose Douglas Park because it was in the Jewish neighborhood where they were safe from prying eyes that might recognize them. Nicky trusted Patrick, because he convinced him he was a good Irish Catholic boy and would do nothing to break that trust. He would wait for Rosemarie forever if he had to.

Nicky heard them coming up the stairs to his apartment. Lillian was up making breakfast. She had set the table for six. Joey picked up Patrick a block from their street and then Francie. A blast of frigid air followed them up the stairs and into the open door to Nicky's apartment causing him to wake up from his morning drowsiness and scratch the back of his bald head and yawn.

"Come on in," he ordered, hurrying them in, in order to close the door quickly. "Boy, it's cold out there!" he said, as he took their coats. They sat at the table in the kitchen of the three-room apartment. Rosemarie liked Lillian. She wished her uncle would make up his mind and settle down with her. She thought it would be neat to have her as an aunt. She was happier that morning than she had ever been. She wished her father were more like his brother. She wished for many things, but as she looked at everyone around the table, eating breakfast together, she wanted that time to last forever.

Nicky went to the front room to turn the radio on for some music. They sat and talked until well past noon. Here were the six of them, enjoying each other's company. Rosemarie and Joey always thought their uncle was a lot of fun to be around. Nicky could spin stories, many embellished, to make them laugh. They never heard any of them when he visited their home, not with their father present. Benny could put a damper on every visit of Nicky's, so he would mainly come only for special occasions, or to visit his mother and he never stayed long. Here, in her uncle's kitchen, Rosemarie laughed until she cried. Nicky was much older than the rest of them, but it didn't seem like he was. To Joey and Rosemarie he was just their happy-go-lucky Uncle Nicky.

They talked about Rosemarie and Patrick's problems, about their parents' view of the world, which was quite different from their own. They talked about how much tension there was in their homes, especially around the supper table each night when arguments erupted over the war or over generational views, which were quite different between parents and grandparents, parents and children.

"Times are changing," Nicky said. "For Christ sakes, it's going to be 1942 in a few weeks; it's modern times and my brother acts like time stands still."

Patrick laughed, "It's modern times, but my mother expects me to do what the men in her family have always done."

"What's that?" Lillian asked.

"Go into the seminary," he laughed as he put his arm around Rosemarie. "Does this look like I'm going to do that?"

They all laughed. Nicky would say one word they found funny, and they would laugh. It was a happy few hours to spend together with their uncle, who never seemed to grow older if one didn't count the hairs on his head, which increasingly disappeared with each passing year.

Before they realized it, it was afternoon. The music stopped and they could hear a man's voice excitedly come over the radio, it sounded like important news, something had happened. They all rushed into the front room to hear what it was about. The Jap's had bombed Pearl Harbor, Hawaii.

The announcer said most of America's entire fleet of battleships was in port at the time, and except for the aircraft carriers still at sea, most of the ships in port were hit. He was talking about the many sailors and other servicemen who lost their lives, about a cowardly act perpetrated on a quiet Sunday morning when most service personel were just awakening. Rosemarie and Patrick's fingers grew tighter around each other as they held hands. Joey looked at Francie, she was holding on to his arm; he put his arm around her. Nicky stood in the middle of the room running his hands through his hair; he did that when he was nervous. Lillian never moved from the spot she stood in, her coffee cup still in her hand, the coffee getting cold. They were all frozen in the same spot they came to when they entered the room. No one moved, as the commentator continued with the very bad news. The Japanese had attacked America. They looked at each other in silence. They knew then that their world was about to change; nothing would ever be the same again.

CHAPTER 21

December eighth, the day after the disaster at Pearl Harbor, President Roosevelt declared war on Japan. He addressed congress at 12:30 p.m. and the radio relayed the message to the nation. Some of the neighbors on Congress Street called each other, those that had telephones. The young people and teenagers ran into each other's homes after school, passing the dire news back and forth. Joey was at the gas station when he heard the call to arms from the President. At work, Benny was glued to the radio along with most of the men. They stopped working, whatever their work, to hear the latest news. Patrick and all his fellow firemen sat around the radio at the firehouse. Jim McCann, walking his beat, stopped in front of a clothing store on Maxwell Street with crowds of people, to hear the speech on a radio the store proprietor brought outside. The snow didn't deter folks from standing around after pausing on their way to wherever they were going. Everyone and everything was at a standstill for the President's speech. The roaring motors of some of the factory machines went quiet during the speech. President Roosevelt announced...

"Yesterday, December 7th, 1941, a date which will live in infamy—the United States of America was suddenly and deliberately attacked by Naval and Air Forces of the Empire of Japan. We were at peace with that nation, and how cowardly we were attacked by surprise."

He declared war on Germany on December eleventh. By the end of the week he had declared war on Germany's Allies. There were thirty-three nations involved, twenty-five on the side of the U.S. and our Allies. Eight were on the side of the Axis. At the center were Britain, the U.S.S.R, and the U.S. vs. Germany and Japan. America's industrial machine went on a 24-hour, 7-day a week schedule. Roosevelt had declared war; men were joining the services the next day, and troops had to be trained. The newspapers stopped writing about neutrality and appeasement; they now wrote aggressively about victory. The everyday talk of isolation had changed to fighting not only Japan but Germany as well. Soon there were long lines to enlist in the Army, the Navy, the Marines, and the Army Air Corps. The words...Remember Pearl Harbor... became a call to Battle.

At the McCann's, Katie was beside herself with fear. She knew she couldn't stop her two eldest sons from joining. She pleaded with them to wait until after Christmas. Draft registration had started the year before. Patrick knew both he and Michael would have to join early in order to choose which brand of service they wanted to be in before the Army would call them up.

He was dreading having to tell Rosemarie. Michael rushed into the front room to announce he planned to join the Marines. Casey looked at Patrick who was sitting next to the radio along with the rest of the family the evening of December 12th. "So what will it be, me boy?" he asked. Patrick thought of Rosemarie, he thought of Katie, of getting home safe after the war was over.

"The Navy," he said. He stood up and Michael shook his hand. Katie was standing in the doorway by the dining room. She brought the bottom of her apron up to her face, and covered her trembling mouth as the tears came.

Jim said, "Good choice boys," as he embraced his sons.

"You aren't going to do anything until after Christmas, are you?" Katie asked.

Patrick went to her and put his arms around her; she dropped the apron away from her face, and he could see she was crying. He pushed her back by the shoulders and looked at her, "Mom, that's ten days away, I don't know when my draft number will come up. They already started calling up numbers and ordering guys to report to the draft call. I want to make sure I get into the Navy, it's safer Mom; I'll be on a ship, not fighting on the ground."

"How safe can it be? Go tell that to the mothers of all the sailors who were on those ships at Pearl Harbor," she said.

Benny's vigilance of his daughter began to wane. He worried and he only had one fear, for his son Joey. As far as he was concerned, Joey was the only son he could count on to succeed where he had failed, to live out his dreams, to be the man he knew he would never be. Joey was a son to be proud of. The attack on Pearl Harbor was the worst thing that could have happened to Benny's dreams for his son. That evening at the Nuzzos, Benny was quiet. Nora noticed he ate very little supper. He drank less wine than usual. He was in a hurry to leave the table and to sit by the radio. Joey sat at the table longer than the rest of the family. He dreaded having to tell his father what his plans were. Rosemarie's only thought was about when she could see Patrick again as she helped her mother in the kitchen. Nora was worried and it showed. She wiped her eyes a few times between washing dishes and putting them on the drain for Rosemarie to dry. Nora was thinking of her parents. She remembered when they received the news of their son Sam, killed in the battle of Somme, near Rheims, France in World War 1. After the loss of their son, her parents were never the same, and her mother died soon after, leaving her father and sister Rose to run the bakery. Nora was a young schoolgirl.

When the doorbell rang, Sammy ran to press the buzzer. He had been looking out the window and spotted his Uncle Nicky coming up the porch stairs. Nicky entered the hall; his shoes were covered with snow. He took them off, hung his coat up and went straight to the kitchen. Joey stood up to greet him. Nicky gave everyone a kiss and sat at the table. Soon they were all around the table, except for Benny.

Nicky looked at Joey, "Have you thought of what you're going to do?" he asked.

"I'm sure, Uncle Nick. I want to fight in Europe, that damn Hitler, that's where I want to go. I've always wanted to be a pilot on a B-17. I think I'll try for the Army Air Corps."

"Go for it Joey!" Nicky said, giving his nephew a pat on the back.

Maria stood leaning against the sink frowning; she wasn't sure what was happening and felt helpless. There wasn't anything she could say. She was confused about what would happen next. All she could comprehend was a terrible thing had just happened to America. She understood what war was.

She reached for the coffee pot. "You wanta the coffee? No?" When no one answered, she placed cups on the table and filled them, pushing the cups towards everyone. She had to do something. She had to feel useful while sensing all the tension in the room.

C3℧C3℧C3℧

Across the street at the Petersons, Ralph and Grace sat at their kitchen table; a small radio was turned to the news station. Lorraine was in her room worried about Michael Donovan. She sat looking at her engagement ring which she had placed on her finger. She was twisting it around and around, thinking about how she would break the news to her parents that she was going to marry Michael Donovan. She knew she couldn't keep her engagement a secret much longer, not with Michael being of draft age, and he might be called up at any time. She took a deep breath and went down the stairs slowly as she thought of how to approach them with the news. When she entered the kitchen, her parent's attention was on the news coming from the radio.

"How bad is it?" she asked. She sat down next to her mother. "The news about Pearl Harbor, Mom, how bad is it?"

Grace touched her daughter's arm affectionately, "It's bad honey. They say thousands of sailors lost their lives."

She looked at her daughter, and gave her a hug; she was thinking, *How fortunate we are, that we have a girl*. They would worry about all the servicemen, but their worries would not be as close to home as some of their neighbor's would be.

She thought of the McCann boys and of Joey Nuzzo.

"Mom, I need to talk to you," Lorraine whispered, "It's important." Grace followed her daughter into the parlor. "What is it dear? What's wrong?" She could see her daughter looked troubled.

"Mom, I'm in love with Michael Donovan."

"Michael who? Do you mean Michael Donovan who lives on Washington Blvd.? Isn't he the boy you're dating whose father is a politician?"

"Yes, Mom, he goes to school taking college courses, and he works downtown."

"Oh, Lorraine, he's Irish! And he might be Catholic. You know how your father feels about the Irish."

"Yes, he's Irish and he's a wonderful guy Mom. He wants to become a lawyer, and when you meet him you'll see how serious and good he is. His parents live in a beautiful old house near downtown, and his father is an Alderman. He's in politics and his wife is a secretary in the mayor's office. You know I've been dating Michael and that we met at the Paradise Ballroom a year ago."

Grace gave her daughter a hug. "Oh dear, I hope he isn't Catholic too. I mean it's fine with me dear, but I don't know how your father would take the news. You know how he is. Bring Michael over for dinner soon and leave it to me to tell him before that. We have to break it to him slowly. Don't tell him right away, that Michael is Irish I mean. What does he look like? Does he look Irish?"

Lorraine put her hand out with the ring on her finger, for her mother to see. Grace's hand went up to her mouth and her eyes grew large. "Oh dear, I didn't know it was this serious. Why didn't you tell me this sooner? We can't break it to him after you're engaged. We have to let him get to know Michael first. Don't mention the engagement, make sure Michael doesn't and let us start with the dinner. Please dear, I need time to explain you're dating him."

"Mom, I don't want any trouble, we can't wait too long, he

might get called up, make it soon."

"Just give your father enough time to accept it before he meets Michael."

"They are drafting younger guys first so maybe he won't get called before the holidays, but let's do it as soon as possible. Do you want me to tell Dad?"

"Heaven's no! I know your father better than you do in matters like this; just let me handle him. We have to get him to like Michael first. Oh, dear!" She kept repeating herself. "I hope he doesn't look too Irish."

"Mom! What is too Irish? Michael has black hair and his eyes are brown, he could pass for Italian, Greek, any nationality."

"Oh, dear! That isn't good either."

Lorraine was getting upset, "Mom, I can't make him look different; what difference does it make? He is what he is! This is ridiculous! Mrs. Katz son looks German and he's Jewish. Who cares what anyone looks like, people are people."

"It's not me dear; it's your father. You know I love all kinds of people. If your father doesn't like him, I will never hear the end of it."

"I don't care if he likes him or not, I love Michael and we are going to get married and if he won't accept him, he will never see me again!"

Grace shook her head sadly, as they exchanged words in the parlor; they kept their voices low. Ralph couldn't hear them; the kitchen radio was on loud.

"Let's start slowly dear." She put her arm around her daughter. "I will tell him you're dating a boy named Michael. Make sure you put the ring away, and let's hope for the best."

Later that night as Grace lay awake, she was nervous and worried about how she would approach the subject so close to Christmas. She wished she had more time but regardless of the time, whatever the outcome, it would be the same. She had always been able to ignore his blatant bigotry because it involved other people. It wasn't easy to dismiss when it had come home to her family. She looked over at her sleeping husband and felt resentment towards him for the first time. A few hours ago, she was grateful to be spared worry over a son at war. With Michael in her family, she knew that would all change. She knew she wouldn't sleep this night. She thought of the past dates Lorraine had, how the boys pulled up to the house and never came in but blew the car horn or Lorraine would meet them somewhere. Ralph never cared that she dated, but never had much to say because she never brought a date home. She met her dates away from home because she was afraid of what would come out of her father's mouth to embarrass her and offend the boy. This was different and Grace knew he would have plenty to say. All she could do when she retired for the night was lay staring at the ceiling thinking of what to do and what to say.

That evening, Grace wasn't the only mother on the street who lay awake worried and anxious. If they had sons, they wouldn't sleep well. If they had brothers or husbands of draft age, they would also share the same feelings the mothers with sons had. It wasn't a night for sleep. Sleep for mothers of sons old enough to go away to fight in a war wouldn't come easily.

CRITICAL

On the evening of Saturday the thirteenth of December, Joey went over to Patrick's; together they went to Peppy's Drug store. Michael was already there with some of the other young guys he hung around with. Peppy's was crowded. Most of the time, when Patrick went there with Joey, it was a hangout for guys from the Italian neighborhood, but tonight it seemed everyone was there from both Irish and Italian streets. Everyone was talking together, discussing what had just happened to their country. Peppy stood behind the soda fountain, a big grin on his face. He remembered all the fights he had to break up both inside and outside his shop between different groups, mostly younger boys, but this night, everyone acted like they were brothers. There are no differences on this night he thought, they're all Americans, and if the attack on Pearl Harbor did anything, it brought all the young people together. Michael was praising the merits of joining the Marines; a roar of claps went up from future Marines. Someone mentioned the Navy, which brought Patrick to his feet from the counter he had been sitting at. The same clapping and hollering took place when Joey mentioned the Army Air Corps.

The days were filled with neighbor's discussing what had happened at Pearl Harbor. Neighbors who seldom spoke to each other were engaged in conversation on the street, on the streetcars, on the way to and from work, in the grocery store, the butcher shop, the bakery, wherever they gathered they were friendly, worried and shared their fears with one another. It was true of a street like Congress where many different ethnic groups lived together but hardly knew each other. Pearl Harbor was making a street of strangers forget their differences, which now evolved into, "We are Americans."

CHAPTER 22

On Monday Joey dreaded going home after work. He knew that since he was registered for the draft, he was going to join The Army Air Corps as soon as possible, and he dreaded telling his father. He had to do it soon; he didn't want to end up in the Army infantry. He drove his Ford home slowly, contemplating on how he was going to break the news about his plans. He knew Benny would be home before him in his usual sour mood. He would wait until the family had finished eating before he would attempt to gingerly bring up the subject about joining early. At the supper table too many meals were ruined trying to discuss anything before everyone was finished eating. He had to wait until he was alone with his father.

"Pa, I'm not waiting for the Army to call me up, I'm joining the Army Air Corps as soon as I can."

Benny looked up from pouring another glass of wine, "What! Are you crazy? You wait until they draft you. I heard they'd be drafting the younger guys first, you know, the eighteen and nineteen-year-olds. You're twenty, you wanna get killed right away? Let the others get there in the beginning, maybe the Japs, they give up soon."

"What are you talking about Pa? You make no sense. I'm not going to fight the Japs if I can help it. I want to go to Europe to fight. Didn't you hear that Hitler declared war on us?"

Benny's jaw muscles started to twitch, and looking at Joey he screamed, "Are you crazy, maybe they send you to fight in Italy, then what you gonna do, huh?"

Joey looked back at him like he was crazed, "Italy? your damn Italy! Don't you understand? Italy is our enemy! You're in America now! If I have to fight in Italy, I will. I hope I do!"

Benny's loud shouting brought Maria and Nora back into the kitchen. "What's going on?" Nora asked. Maria shouted back at him to be quiet, "You herta the ears," she said.

"He wants to go join the Army, now!" Benny said, his voice cracking. He was torn between wanting to cry and demanding his son stay put. Deep down he knew he couldn't hold him, keep him home or keep him safe, but he was too stubborn to give in and accept Joey's decision. He chose to remain angry, to berate his son, and yell about how Joey was ungrateful, how Joey owed him for being born.

He said terrible things. He yelled, "I went without eating after the stock market crash so you kids could eat. You have no respect for your father. You owe me."

Joey yelled back, "What do I owe you? I didn't ask to be born! You don't own me, I'm my own person and you're talking crazy! I'm not a kid anymore, it's my life, you're not going to keep me under your thumb like you do Ma and Rosie." Joey turned away from him and left the house as quickly as he could before Benny had a chance to reply.

CR&OCR&OCR&O

It was after midnight but Joey had not come home. When the clock chimed over the mantel Nora worried, but she knew it wasn't unusual for Joey to be out late. It was Monday, she reasoned, he never stayed out this late on Monday night, but she couldn't sleep, she worried because he left without changing his clothing. He wouldn't be on a date wearing his work coveralls from the gas station. She wondered where he had gone. She lay next to Benny, who with the aid of his wine, slept soundly. She wondered how Benny would feel in the morning.

When morning came, Nicky awoke to find Joey sleeping on his sofa; he had come to his apartment during the night, his greasy coveralls were on the floor.

"Joey! Are you awake?" Nicky asked. "What happened? What's wrong? Why are you here?"

"I'm awake," came the answer from a sleepy Joey who sat up and ran his fingers through his hair. "Oh, my God! What an ordeal, trying to reason with the old man. I swear Uncle Nicky, he is impossible to talk to. I can't take it anymore, all the shouting he does about one thing or another, yelling at my mother over Sammy, and yelling at Rosie over anything. He sits at the table every night and we have to hear about his rotten job, how everyone is out to get him, how we are ungrateful kids, and on and on. I don't know how Ma and Granny can stand it."

"Feel sorry for him Joey, he's his own worst enemy. I had to live with his crooked view of the world ever since I could remember. For years I was his scapegoat until I moved out. Well I guess I still am. That's why I don't come around too often."

"Uncle Nicky, I'm going to join the service first thing Wednesday. He's at work and I quit work yesterday and told them I'm enlisting. I'm going home to clean up and then can I come back until Wednesday morning? I don't want to deal with him again until I have to."

"Sure kid, you can stay whenever you like. Just don't ever slip to your Ma or Grandma where you are."

"I feel terrible about ditching Ma, Sammy and Rosie, but I need to go," Joey said as he covered his face with his hands.

"I would be going sooner or later; it's just I won't be there to act as a buffer for them. He always treated me better than the other kids; I knew he put all his hopes and dreams in me. I always knew I was his favorite, but he did me no favors making me his favorite. It's been a burden."

Nicky put his arm around Joey and walked him to the door. "Don't worry kid; it'll be ok. Just do what's right for you, what you want to do, it's your life, not his."

That afternoon Joey began packing a suitcase with a few articles of clothing. The night before when Rosemarie heard the argument, she stayed in her room trying to avoid the whole scene. She was happy to see her brother had come home. She went to his room.

"Joey!" She called, as she entered, "I'm sorry I didn't

come in to help you when Pa was attacking you."

"That's ok, you have enough problems with him without getting mixed up in mine. I can leave, but you have to stay. I understand Rosie; forget it."

As she looked at him, she couldn't stop the tears from coming. He was the only one who stuck up for her when it came to their father. Now she could see he was leaving sooner than she had expected.

"Are you going straight to the recruiting office?" she asked.

"No I'm going back to Uncle Nicky's, until Wednesday morning."

He walked past her to go into the kitchen to say goodbye to Nora and Maria. Maria met him half-way across the room and embraced him.

"You watcha you self," she said, it was all she could say as she burst into tears.

Nora was crying when he put his arms around her. She took his face between her hands and said, "It's so close to Christmas, you can't wait until after?"

"No Ma, I want to go."

"You have to see your father before you go; you can't leave without saying goodbye to him."

"After what he said to me! Ma, how could he say those things to me? He's a bitter old man, look how he treats Uncle Nicky, his own brother."

"You can't leave without seeing him, he wasn't himself," Nora pleaded, "It was the wine talking."

Joey could see she was right, but the thought of facing his father again left him feeling trapped, a feeling he always had around him, but never realized it until that moment. "I'll think about it Ma," was all he could say.

"Goodbye Ma, I'm sorry, but I have to go, you know that! What difference does it make if I go now or a couple weeks from now? I'll be back after training." He held her and patted her back as she hung on to him.

"Please be careful," was all she managed to say between sobs.

"I will Ma, I promise, don't worry about me, ok? I'll write as soon as I get settled and have an address."

He looked at the clock; it was nearly three in the afternoon. He was never sure when Benny arrived home. He had to leave quickly. He turned to Sammy who was standing behind him; the boy was upset and crying after witnessing his mother and grandmother in tears.

"Sammy, be a good boy and maybe I'll send you a German helmet or sword, would you like that?" he said, as he hugged his little brother who wasn't so little anymore. He was nine years old and big for his age. As he put his arm around him, he wondered if he would still be a child when he returned, if he returned, but he kept those fears to himself.

He went to the front hall with Rosemarie. They embraced. He found it difficult to say anything to her except goodbye and gave her a hug as she burst into tears. She knew she was losing the one who supported and defended her the most. "I will pray for you," she said, and then he was out the door. She fled to her room and watched him go down the front porch stairs only to turn and go to the back of the house to the garage. She ran to the kitchen window and watched him enter the garage. She knew he was giving his beloved old Ford a last look over.

He had Patrick come over one night and they covered the Ford with a tarp and set her up on blocks. They both knew it could be years before they would start her motor up again.

When he came out of the garage, she watched him go back toward the front of the house. She ran back to her bedroom and watched him walk down the walk, his heels kicking up the snow as he turned the corner toward the Street Car line that would take him to their uncle's. He looked back at the house and then he was gone. Rosemarie dried her tears and hurried to meet Patrick. He too would be leaving soon. They were going to the movies where they could be together in a warm place and talk between features. She felt guilty leaving her family at that moment but her father would be home soon. She had to leave before he appeared. She looked into the kitchen; her mother, grandmother and Sammy were at the table. Her mother was still wiping her eyes. Maria had her hands together as if in prayer and Sammy was eating a large slice of bread and butter.

"I'm going out Ma, be back later" was all she dare say and she was out the door before Nora could respond.

In the movie theater Rosemarie and Patrick held hands as movie tone news flashed across the screen. They watched how brutal the Japanese attack on Pearl Harbor was. When the second feature was about to start, Rosemarie put her head on Patrick's shoulder. The images on the news report frightened her. She knew Patrick and her brother were heading toward battles like the British were fighting. They both knew, but hid their fears from each other in the quiet darkened theater.

"I'll wait for you Pat, for as long as it takes," she said. They both decided not to mention their relationship to their parents. There was no need now, not until the war was over and he came back home.

When Benny arrived home, his expression was of an angry man. His mouth drooped at the corners and his brow lines were deeper. Nora hated when he looked that way; she was hoping he would have some remorse, but he was more defiant than ever.

"Where's Rosie?" he asked. She was surprised he didn't ask about Joey.

"I think she went out with Peggy, she needed to go shopping." She wasn't sure where she went. She looked at the clock, it was 6:30 and she had hoped she would be home in time for supper. *That's all I need*, she thought, *with the mood he's in, and Rosie not home.* She busied herself getting the meal ready while Benny washed up in the bathroom.

Maria stood in the kitchen watching her and said, "You no saya noting to him. I no wanna hear the noisea he makea no more." Nora didn't answer; she continued to check the pot on the stove.

"Sammy, come in here!" she called. She wanted the boy at the table before Benny had to call for him.

All she could think of was Joey leaving without saying goodbye to his father. She couldn't believe he would do such a thing, so she expected to see him again. Deep down she felt it wasn't the last time she would see her son. He had to return one more time.

Wednesday, the 17th of December, Joey appeared at the recruiting station early. It took all of several hours to fill out the proper papers, answer questions, and he was told to report the next day for a physical. He thought about what his uncle said, about having to face his father again. 'It's the right thing to do,' Nicky said. 'I understand why you don't want to see him but be bigger than that, he's your father, and you can't leave without seeing him. It's not like you're going on a trip and expecting to return in a few weeks. It's war; who knows what will happen? You have to go back home one more time.' He knew his uncle was right. It was the only thing he would be able to live with, going back to see his father one last time.

When Joey walked into the front hall that night, Benny was sitting in his usual place. When he walked into the kitchen, Nora rushed to embrace him. She was still hugging him when Maria and Rosemarie entered the room. Benny turned his head to look towards the kitchen but didn't move out of his chair.

"Go see your father," Nora urged him. She gave him a little push, and he went into the room where Benny pretended to be napping, his eyes closed.

"I'm leaving Pa; I'm all set. I joined the Army Air Corps. Tomorrow I report for a physical and then wherever they send me."

He was standing in front of his father and Joey could see tears welling up in his father's eyes. Benny stood up and they embraced. Benny was relieved that he had come to say goodbye. It was too emotional for both of them, so not much was said.

When Joey backed away, Benny sat down and without

looking up at his son again said, "Take care of yourself and write to your mother." Joey quickly turned to the others; who had followed him into the room.

"Where's Sammy?"

"He sleep," Maria said.

Joey was upset over how distraught they all were, so he quickly went in to see his little brother who was sleeping in the double bed they shared. Joey bent over to kiss his cheek, brushed a curl off his forehead and wiped away the first tears that formed in his eyes. He felt most guilty leaving the boy. "You'll never have to go away and fight in a war," he whispered to the sleeping Sammy. "You'll have enough battles to fight in your life." He always accepted Sammy for who he was, a mildly mentally challenged nine-year-old. He went back to the hall where the three women were waiting, gave each one a kiss and hurried to leave. If he stayed too long, he was afraid he would lose all composure.

"Goodbye Ma, I'll write. Write me Rosie; don't forget to keep me up on all the neighborhood news." He was racing down the stairs as he yelled all this back to them. All Rosemarie could do was race back to the window and watch him walk away, once more.

Later that evening he went to see his Aunt Rose; she rushed out to meet him as he entered the downstairs hall of her building. She knew he was leaving; she spent the evening before with Nora, trying to comfort her on the phone over Joey's departure. She felt as close to her sister's children as if they were her own. She cried and told him to take care of himself. All the emotion was wearing on Joey; he felt drained after leaving his family, and he felt bad when he had to witness everyone crying and he had yet to see Francie. He didn't have much time to spend with her that evening but was glad he spent all day Sunday with her. Their parting was bittersweet. He finally made a commitment to her, telling her they would become engaged when he came home on leave before he shipped out. She promised to write every day. He was to report for his induction on Thursday, the 18th of December. He couldn't bring himself to go back home one more time, so he went back to Nicky's and spent his last night with his uncle.

CRUCRUCRU

At the McCann's, Katie, with glistening eyes, watched her second son getting ready to leave for the Marines. Michael lost little time in joining. He refused to wait until Christmas. Most of the guys he knew were going. It seemed no one wanted to wait for the Army to call, and some feared the infantry. In Michael's case, he hoped the Marines put him in the toughest unit. The fighting infantry is what he hoped for. Just a few years ago he was Patrick's little brother and now she had to face the fact that he was a grown man at eighteen, and he was leaving home. She couldn't change that. She followed him out of his room to the front room where the rest of the family waited.

Casey stood up, holding on to the arm of his chair to steady himself. He stretched his other arm out to shake Michael's hand. "I'm proud of ye, me boy!" he said.

"Thanks Pops." Michael held his grandfather's hand until the old man sat down. His legs were bothering him. The cold winter brought on arthritis in his knees.

Patrick put his arm around his brother, "So you're really going, never thought this would happen, first Joey Nuzzo, he left yesterday and now you," he said.

Katie looked surprised, "Are you telling me Mr. Nuzzo let his son join this quickly?" she shook her head sadly. "The Street won't be the same with all you boys gone. It's so close to Christmas; it's only 7 days away." She started to cry again. It was a sad time. Christmas trees were lit up in some homes, looking festive on the outside but inside there wasn't much to be happy about.

Jim hugged Michael, "Do you know where they will send you, son?"

"I don't know Dad, but I'll let you know as soon as I get there." He turned to his mother, she was crying into the bottom of her apron. "Please Mom, don't worry about me, I can take care of myself." He kissed her and Peggy who stood by unable to say anything to him. He gave Brian and Kevin a hug, and bent down to pick up baby Jean who at the age of three wasn't much of a baby anymore, and then handed her to Katie. He picked up his duffle bag and went quickly out the door. They all watched him from the window except for Patrick who walked him out to the porch. He stood shivering in the cold as he watched his younger brother walk towards California Avenue where he would climb the stairs to the elevated train tracks, and board the train to the recruiting station where he would join the newly enlisted men of the United States Marine Corps. It would be a sad Christmas on Congress Street in December of '41. A custom soon developed, little flags with blue stars were sold to hang in one's window to signify a member of that household was in the Armed Forces fighting for his country. Blue stars would appear in more than a few windows on Congress Street. On Christmas morning at the McCann's, the three youngest children's laughter filled the house, but Katie, Jim and the two eldest, Patrick and Peggy found little joy under the circumstances. At the Nuzzos the same scene unfolded as they watched Sammy open the little gifts they managed to place under the tree for him. They pretended to enjoy the festivities for their youngest member, but their hearts weren't in it. The same was true for many families in their neighborhood and across the nation.

CHAPTER 23

Grace Peterson rushed around her dining room, making sure the table was set properly in anticipation of Michael Donovan's arrival. She waited until the last minute to tell Ralph that Lorraine was inviting a friend to dinner. She didn't want anything to ruin their Christmas, so she waited until after Christmas and until the morning of the dinner to tell him. It was the Friday after Christmas, on the 26th, before she had the courage to tell him. She wasn't sure what his reaction would be. He didn't show any reaction. She failed to tell Ralph the friend was a boy.

When the doorbell rang, Lorraine went to answer it and Michael Donovan stood in the open doorway with a bouquet of flowers in his hand; he handed them to Grace who had followed her daughter to the door.

"Hello Mrs. Peterson," he said, as if he knew Grace. This was the first time they had met and he was already engaged to her daughter. He felt strange meeting her after the fact. Lorraine said, "Mom, this is Michael." He could sense the tension her mother seemed to portray. He hoped Lorraine had told her parents about him before he walked into their home. Grace took them into the parlor.

"Sit down Michael," she said, as Lorraine led him to the sofa. When they were seated, Lorraine reached for his hand. Grace could tell her daughter appeared very nervous, but she herself felt the same way. Mr. Peterson had not come down from upstairs yet, and she took the opportunity to engage her daughter's friend in conversation.

"So, Michael, I hear you work at the mayor's office and you met my daughter at a dance? Is that where you met?"

"Yes Ma'am, we've known each other for a year. I love your daughter Mrs. Peterson; I want you to know that."

"I know you do Michael, but it's not me you have to convince. Please don't mention the engagement until my husband has a chance to know you."

When they heard Ralph coming down the stairs, the room became quiet; they seemed to hold their breath. Michael stood up as Mr. Peterson entered the room.

"Ralph!" was all Grace managed to say, before Lorraine stood with Michael and met her father at the entrance to the front parlor. "Daddy, this is my friend Michael." She didn't mention his last name. Michael held his hand out to Mr. Peterson and Ralph took it. Both men shook hands, but Michael noticed the lack of enthusiasm in the older man's handshake. Ralph sat in his chair across from the young couple and remained silent as he stared at Michael and his daughter. They were sitting apart and not holding hands as they had done earlier. Mr. Peterson addressed Michael.

"So you're my daughter's friend! How long have you known each other?"

"We met about a year ago," Michael said. He was uncomfortable; he had heard all about Mr. Peterson from Lorraine and knew what to expect, so he was very guarded. Mr. Peterson said nothing more and the room became painfully quiet as each was waiting for the other to speak up. Finally, Grace stood up and said, "Let's go into the dining room please." They followed her and took their places at the table. Michael noticed the beautiful china, silverware and crystal stemware set in the proper places. His family's table looked similar at dinner, but he knew most of the people who lived in the surrounding neighborhoods did not have fine china or real silver. He began to think his family had something in common with the Peterson's, and it might make it easier for her family to accept him. Lorraine went into the kitchen to help her mother, and for a few minutes the two men were alone.

Mr. Peterson stared at Michael. He thought of how they introduced the boy, as just Michael. "What's your last name," he asked.

"Michael Donovan, sir."

Mr. Peterson thought for a moment. "Donovan? Are you

related to that alderman, Thomas Donovan? You're Irish? What kind of Irish? You don't look Irish, is your mother Irish too?"

"Yes Sir, Thomas is my father. Among the Irish I'm what they call Black Irish." He could see Mr. Peterson's expression change from quizzical to hostile. "It's just a term we use for anyone with dark hair and eyes," he announced quickly, but Mr. Peterson's expression never changed.

"You look more like Italian or Greek," Mr. Peterson commented. Michael thought he'd better stop explaining while he was ahead of the game. No good would come of explaining that Black Irish could also mean of Moorish decent. He knew he had a tough battle ahead to win over his future father-in-law, just because he, Michael Donovan, was born Irish.

The rest of the evening seemed to go well. Grace relaxed because her greatest fear, Ralph asking Michael to leave or insulting the boy before he was even introduced, hadn't materialized. She was grateful for that. She did take note of how her husband behaved during dinner and later when they retired to the parlor and Michael asked politely if he could smoke; Ralph nodded yes, but he remained too quiet. He didn't ask any more questions. The visit was strained; she could sense that much, and it worried her a little, but she brushed the thought aside as quickly as it appeared. She knew it could have been much worse because she knew her husband. After Michael left, her fears were confirmed. Ralph turned on his daughter as soon as she came in from the front hall where she had kissed Michael good night.

"Do you have any idea who that guy is? His father is the biggest Irish crook in Chicago! I heard he takes money under the table. He's responsible for men losing their jobs, for his cronies getting all the best city jobs, and he looked the other way during the speakeasy days. He got payoffs to keep them from being raided." Lorraine started running up the stairs in tears.

"You can forget going out with the likes of him!" he yelled

up at her. He didn't stop shouting until he heard the door to her room slam shut.

Grace was upset and ran up the stairs after her daughter. She knocked on Lorraine's door, "It's me dear," she whispered. "Please let me in." She turned the knob and opened the door to find her daughter lying across the bed, sobbing uncontrollably. She put her arm around her to comfort her. Lorraine turned to face her mother, "He can't keep me from seeing Michael; I'm twenty-one and in a few months I will be twenty-two. I will make my own choices."

"I know dear, I know. You do what's right for your own happiness. I feel Michael is a very nice boy and I wish you all the happiness in the world."

Grace was crying as she said the words her daughter wanted to hear because she knew it would be she alone who would have to endure what was to come. A few days later Michael sat in his car holding Lorraine in his arms. They were parked in the Sears parking lot where he went to pick her up after work. They were talking and making plans. He had just informed her that he was going to join the Army. He wanted to get into the medics branch of the Army before they drafted him. His father told him to get all his affairs in order in the next two weeks. She was crying because he would be leaving soon and he was trying to console her.

He kissed the top of her head as she buried her face in his chest. "Honey, don't cry. I want to marry you before I leave," he said.

"How is that going to happen? I want my parents there, but my father won't share our wedding with us." She began to cry.

"We'll get our blood tests and then go down to City Hall next Saturday. We can get married quickly without waiting. My father knows people, and at our age couples don't need their parents' permission. I'm certainly old enough at twenty-two. Don't worry Babe; I will take care of everything and we will have a whole week together before I leave."

She started to cry again, putting her arms around his neck.

"What will your folks say? You're older than the guys who are being called up first. You could have waited."

"I'm joining with two of my friends. We want to be trained as medics and I hope we get shipped to England. You know my folks; I've already talked it over with them. You have been to my home many times and they like you honey. They even offered to have a little reception for us at the house, but I told them about the problems with your family, and we don't want any time taken away from our spending the last week together. Just find an excuse for being away from home and your work."

She smiled for the first time since she entered his car.

"Don't worry Michael, I will think of something to tell them. I can't tell my mother about us yet, only because it's better if she doesn't know in case my father questions her. I will tell her later when I think the time is right."

All Grace and Ralph Peterson knew was their daughter had picked a week in January as her vacation week. They thought it strange that she would want to go on vacation with two girls from work in the middle of winter, but after they were told the girls would be skiing in Wisconsin, they didn't ask any more questions.

After the quick marriage at City Hall, with two friends as witnesses, they spent the week at the Edge Water Beach Hotel overlooking Lake Michigan. Due to the winter weather they could only look out at the water from their hotel room window but managed to go to the Chicago Theatre for a good movie. They sat through *The Little Foxes*, starring Bette Davis, went out to eat, strolled along State Street and dreaded when the week would be over. When they arrived at Michael's parents home, Mrs. Donovan managed to have a nice dinner for them and they spent their last night together at the Donovan's before they had to part. It was a terrible parting; both Mrs. Donovan and Lorraine were in tears. Lorraine wished they could have been alone for their last moments together, but she was grateful to spend it with him and to share the bittersweet time with his parents. She knew Michael was their only child, and it was important that she share his departure with them. They went to Union Station to see him off.

"Write!" Michael said, as he held her in his arms. "Don't forget to write," he reminded them, as his parents and new wife stood on the platform waiting for the train to arrive.

As the train approached, he kissed his mother, gave his father a hug and held on to Lorraine tightly, kissing her one last time before he boarded the train. The three of them stood waving until the train was out of sight.

When Lorraine arrived home, Grace noticed she didn't appear too happy.

"Did you have a nice time dear?" she asked. "Yes Mom, I'm just tired. I'm going to lie down." Concerned, Grace said, "Don't you feel well?" Lorraine didn't answer. Grace was puzzled by her daughter's behavior as she watched her climb the stairs.

CHAPTER 24

Rosemarie and Patrick rode the streetcar to Nicky's on a cold Sunday morning in early January. He had enlisted in the Navy, and he would be leaving soon. He waited to join after the holidays, not only because of his mother, but the thought of leaving Rosemarie weighed heavy on him. He would miss her, just when they were becoming so serious about each other, and he wondered if she would feel the same about him if he were gone too long, or if he received any injuries. He was full of fear about their relationship. He knew he wouldn't be leaving with such a heavy heart if he wasn't in love. It left him with a great deal of apprehension. Leaving his family wasn't as bad; they would always love him whatever his condition might be when he returned.

Nicky was still sleeping. They had a key to his apartment and entered quietly. Since winter had come, they were meeting every Sunday morning where they could be together for a few hours in the warmth of the apartment. This would be their last day together until Boot Camp was over. Patrick would spend the evening with his family. Monday morning he would leave for Great Lakes. When Nicky came into the front room, Rosemarie and Patrick were in a tight embrace and kissing.

"Hey, good morning," he said, gave his niece a kiss on the cheek and patted Patrick on the back. "So today's your last day huh?"

"Yes, and it's not going to be easy leaving everyone," Patrick said with sadness in his voice. They followed Nicky into the kitchen and he sat across from them in his pajamas. Rosemarie put coffee on and they talked about Patrick's enlistment. Nicky watched with sadness as his niece laid her head on Patrick's shoulder.

"I'm going over to Lill's as soon as I get dressed," he said, checking the time on the clock on the wall. "I promised to take her downtown to an early show."

He looked at his niece and gave her a look she knew well. Every time he left them alone in his apartment, he reminded them to behave. Rosemarie knew he would have to face her father's wrath if he ever knew his brother was leaving her alone with a boy.

After Nicky left, they turned the radio on in the front room and sat together on the couch. They held hands for a few minutes and listened to the music of Artie Shaw's band playing Stardust. Soon, handholding wasn't enough so they started kissing. It was an awkward moment when their kisses became more intense. Patrick drew away from her, holding her away by the shoulders.

"Remember what your uncle said," he reminded her. "After Boot camp, I'll be home on leave. We'll see each other again before I get shipped out."

She knew she would see him again, so she was content just to be held in his arms. They talked about their plans after the war was over and about Patrick's job with the fire department and how he wouldn't be around to fight his first real major fire as a full-fledged fireman, having just graduated from being a plebe the year before.

When he left for Great Lakes, Rosemarie wrote to him every day. His letters went to her uncle's address. Whenever a letter came for her, Nicky would either slip it to her when he went over to visit his mother or she would go to him to read it. She preferred to go to his place to read them because she was fearful of keeping any mail addressed to her uncle's address with her name on it. If she tried to hide it, Maria or Nora would eventually find it. When he brought them to her, she would go to her room or the bathroom, read the letter and give it back to him before he left her flat. She hated all the secrets she had to keep from her mother, but she knew Nora wasn't able to go against her husband.

When Patrick left, his family didn't make a big thing of it because they knew he would be back again before shipping out, and with him being so close at Great Lakes, it didn't seem like he had gone at all. He called them whenever he could, and talking to him helped the family feel like he had never left. It was Rosemarie he missed, especially since he had no way of contacting her, other than his letters. He tried to call her uncle's apartment, but Nicky was seldom home, or when he was, Patrick wasn't able to get to a phone. The weeks went by slowly for Rosemarie as she waited for him to come home. She knew he would only be home for a short time, and he had to spend most of it with his family, so she decided to go over to the McCann's on the pretext of seeing Peggy. The day after he arrived home, she strolled over to the McCann's. Katie thought nothing of it, because Rosemarie hung around with Peggy so often it wasn't odd for a neighbor girl to stop by, but it was torture for both Patrick and Rosemarie to pretend they were just neighbors. Patrick had written to her about telling his family he had to leave a day earlier than he had to, so they could have the last day together if her uncle let them spend it at his apartment. In the McCann kitchen they sat across from each other, occasionally looking at each other in such a way that Peggy knew they were desperate to be together. Katie didn't seem to notice anything except her son, because she knew he would be leaving again. She couldn't take her eyes off of him. She prayed daily for Michael and Patrick; she felt so helpless when it came to protecting her sons. They weren't little boys like Brian and Kevin; she couldn't help them, all she could do was ask God to protect them and bring them home to her, safe and uninjured.

On his last morning with his family, Patrick awoke to the dreaded day he would have to say goodbye to them. He avoided looking at his mother, he felt guilty leaving a day sooner than he had to, but upper most in his mind was Rosemarie. He needed to spend time alone with her before he left. He would say his goodbyes and leave to go to her uncle's apartment where she was waiting for him. She was taking the day off from work. Nicky would be at work, so they would have the apartment to themselves. He was up early sitting at the kitchen table talking with his mother, waiting for the rest of the family to come in for breakfast. Peggy was going in a little late to work; she wanted to be present when her brother left. After cooking breakfast for her family, Katie watched with glistening eyes, as her eldest son packed his bag for the return trip to Great Lakes. It seemed like she was hardly used to Michael being gone. She cried so over Michael. He seemed like such a baby and now Patrick, her pride, her first born, the one who resembled her father, the father she loved and lost much too soon. She knew all the prayers she would offer would not change her sons going off to war. She looked at her other two boys quietly eating their oatmeal. At that moment she thanked God they were only ten and twelve years of age.

When Patrick finished packing, Katie handed him his warm pea coat. He looked handsome in his Navy uniform. The rest of the family waited in the front room to say goodbye. It was an awkward moment; no one said anything until Patrick broke the tension, hugging Kevin and then Brian by grabbing him from behind in a bear hug. Brian squirmed as he tried to free himself, but Patrick held him until the ten-year-old started crying and broke free. He would have none of that sissy stuff with his older brother. He was upset when Michael left, but Patrick was like a second father to him and now he too was leaving home. He didn't know how to handle the situation, so he reacted by hitting Patrick and trying to kick him, crying at the same time. He felt his older brothers were abandoning him. He ran out of the room and Peggy wanted to go after him, but Jim said, "Leave him be; let him handle it in his own way."

"Well my boy," Jim said, as he embraced his son, "Keep your nose clean and make us proud."

Patrick nodded and turned in Casey's direction. He could see his grandfather was visibly shaken. The second time Katie witnessed tears coming from the hardened old man and it caused her to turn away to hide her own grief, which was mounting by the minute.

"Good-bye Pops," Patrick said, grabbing Casey's

shoulders. He tried to give him a hug, but Casey stood his ground, kept his grandson at arms length and shook his hand and then patted him on the back.

"So's yer goin me boy, remember, yer a McCann, keep da stiff upper lip ther, don't take nuttin from no one, ya hear?" Casey tried to appear cool while holding back the sniffles and blowing his nose. Peggy went up to her brother and hugged him. When he picked up little Jean, Katie started to cry openly. He handed Jean to his Mother and hugged his father. Jim said, "Are you ready?"

"As ready as I'll ever be," he said, as he turned away from them and went towards the door.

Katie ran up to hug him one more time and the rest of the family called out to him to be careful and to be sure and write. They watched as he walked to the corner with his duffel bag slung over his shoulder and his bell-bottoms flapping in the cold Chicago wind. He looked back, gave them a last wave of his hand as he walked away.

When he arrived at Nicky's apartment, Rosemarie was waiting for him. She ran down the steps, meeting him on the landing and flew into his arms. Together they climbed up to the open door of the apartment. He dropped his bag on the floor and took her in his arms. They were locked in each other's arms for what seemed like forever before she broke away, took his jacket off and flung it onto a chair. She led him to the couch. They kissed and he held her in a tight embrace, then as he relaxed his arms around her, he looked at her intensely.

"How were you able to take off work?"

"I called in sick," she said. "It was almost impossible to make the call with the phone in the front hall. My grandmother has ears like a funnel; she hears everything. Her eyesight is poor, but there's nothing wrong with her ears. I swear, I think she can hear what I'm thinking."

Patrick began to laugh. "I doubt anyone can do that honey; it's just your imagination, or you feel guilty about what you're thinking about."

Rosemarie buried her face in his chest as they sat holding each other. She loved the smell of the dry cleaning fluid on his uniform. She thought about how she loved everything about Patrick, even that. "I love you Pat," she said, looking up at his face. She ran her fingers through his hair, she couldn't mess it up, there wasn't much hair with a crew cut but she yearned for the day she could run her fingers through his thick red hair, and just when she finally got the courage to do it, it was gone. He continued to kiss her and she encouraged him. They kissed with desperation knowing it was possible they might never see each other again. She threw all caution to the wind and she returned his kisses in a way that rendered him helpless in controlling the situation. He told her over and over how much he loved her. In her uncle's apartment, they made love. When it was over, he came to his senses and told her how sorry he was.

"I'm not," she said. "I love you Pat; I'm not sorry. We may never see each other again if you don't make it back home."

"If I don't make it back? Of course I'll be back. Honey, don't think that way; now I have a memory to take with me. Do you still love me?" he teased, afraid she was regretting what had just happened. He searched her face for any expression that would convey that she felt that way, but all he could see was her love for him. He was quiet for a few moments, and had a worried expression on his face.

"What if you become pregnant?"

"Don't worry," I won't, it's not going to happen because it's not that time of the month."

"You're sure?"

"Yes, I'm sure, I know all about these things."

He had to take her word for it. They spent the rest of the day together. The fact that it was their last day together made their continued lovemaking acts of desperation.

"What if you don't make it back?' She said, crying as she asked the question again. It was a question neither of them could answer. All she could think of at that moment was the

191

awful newsreels they viewed of the war when they went to the movies. He put his finger to her lips, "Shush, honey, I hope you don't regret anything." He was starting to feel guilty. He felt responsible for what had happened, but Rosemarie didn't care. She loved him, there was a war on, and things were different now and she was afraid she might never see him again. They had to leave the apartment before her uncle came home. He would not have approved of them spending time alone on Patrick's last day. He knew the risks; and even though they spent time there before, he'd know this was different with Patrick leaving. They knew he wouldn't trust them under such circumstances. They never bothered to ask his permission this time because they knew he would have said no. It never occurred to him to ask her to return the apartment key. On the streetcar ride to the el station, where Patrick would take the train back to Great Lakes, they sat together having eyes only for each other. They never noticed the passengers arriving and departing at each stop staring at the sailor and the girl with smiles on their faces. At the station, which was a couple of blocks from where they lived, they said their last goodbye. Rosemarie walked home alone, crying, trying to wipe her tears before they froze on her cheeks.

It was many weeks before anyone received a letter from Michael. Eventually, a letter came from him just days after Patrick wrote. Brian brought it in from the mailbox.

"Mom!" he screamed, "I think it's a letter from Mike." Katie rushed to meet Brian before he could bring it to her. Her hands trembled as she looked at the return address. It said, Pvt. Michael R. McCann 61st Platoon, Camp Elliot, San Diego, California. She opened it and stared at the date on the envelope, February 20th, he wrote it weeks after he arrived, just like Michael she thought.

She read....

Dear Mom,

We arrived in San Diego the 11th of January and boy what a place! Big O Bay, I have never seen so many camps in all my life. I am stationed at the 2nd camp, about 14 miles from the first one. We'll stay here about 4 weeks and then go on to the Rifle Range. I don't mind it too much as I'm getting 3 good meals a day and all my clothes so that's not bad. Up here in this camp, we live 3 men in a tent and we have a stove heater for the night because it gets pretty chilly out here at night. We have a full uniform and do I look good in it! You should see the haircuts; you would laugh your head off, but its growing back pretty good now. We have our own Rifles to practice with and they sure are good ones too. We have to clean them up once a day and shine them up in our spare time. We have a few classes and we also go to church on Sundays. I know you want to hear that. Can't think of anything more to say but I will write more next time. Give my best to Dad, Pops, and the kids. Did Pat leave yet? Have you heard anything about Joey Nuzzo?

Well I'll say good night for now.

Love, Your son Michael.

Katie finally sat down on the nearest chair, stared at the letter in her hands and cried a little, but they were tears of happiness. She looked up at Brian, who was the only one home from school due to a cold, and the only thing she could think of to say was, "Michael said he goes to church at the camp."

 C彡C彡C彡

In the month of March, Nora was nervous every time the mailman came. The family had not heard from Joey since his first letter in late January. He left in December after Pearl Harbor and it was over two and a half months since he left home. When Rosemarie mentioned that Katie McCann received a letter from both her boys, Nora worried. She watched her mother go through the mail this cold March morning and still no letter from Joey.

"Don't worry Ma," she consoled her mother, you know, maybe Joey's training is different. He's in the Army Air Corps and that might take special training which is different from the Navy or the Marines." She knew she was just saying that to calm her down. Rosemarie wondered why Joey hadn't written again.

When the door bell rang, Nora couldn't imagine who it could be as Benny was at work and Sammy never rang the bell when he returned from playing next door with Bobby Woods. Rosemarie ran down to the outside hall to see who it could be when she was surprised to see the mailman.

"Sorry, I missed this," he said as he handed her a letter. She took it, thanked him and ran up the stairs yelling, "Ma, it's a letter from Joey!" Nora took the letter and sat at the kitchen table with Rosemarie and Maria sitting close by. Her hand shook as she tried to tear the letter open. Rosemarie grabbed it from her and pulled the letter out and handed it to her mother. The address on the envelope said, Army Air Corps, St. Petersburg, Florida. It was dated February 15th 1942.

Dear Ma and Rosie,

I want you to know I'm doing ok down here. It's warm for being winter. They have us in a resort hotel being used as a temporary barrack. I've been in training and I'm disappointed that I washed out of pilot's training because I don't have perfect vision in my left eye. Something like stigmatism, nothing serious, I don't need perfect vision to make navigator so that's what they put me in. I hope I'll be assigned to a B-17 when our training is over. We run every day and got to keep our bunks tightly made. Our uniforms look nice and I met a lot of guys here from all over the country---

As Nora was reading, Rosemarie laughed, hearing Joey had to make his own bed. "That's a first for him," she said, knowing how messy her brother was and how he expected her to pick up after him. She enjoyed hearing that her brother was made to do something he never had to do at home. Nora continued reading---

Don't worry about me Ma, everything is fine with me. I'll be home on leave soon, not much more to write about for now. Say hello to Granny and Sammy. Don't let anyone in the garage Rosie; I don't want anyone disturbing the Ford. Write me about any news in the neighborhood. Take care of yourself Ma.

Love Joey

Nora handed the letter to Rosemarie who read it again to herself. Nora smiled as she got up to start lunch. Maria asked Rosemarie to read the letter to her again and as she did, Nora realized he never mentioned Benny. It bothered her that he never mentioned his father. What if Benny wanted to read the letter? She thought. He would see that Joey never mentioned him at all. It would hurt him and he would get angry. Nora didn't know what she should do. Maria now knew about the letter and she would mention it to him, so she had to tell him about it. Maybe he wouldn't ask to see it she thought. When he came home, Nora casually mentioned that Joey wrote and said hello to everyone and that he was doing okay. She told him where he was stationed and how he made navigator and hoped he wouldn't ask for the letter. He didn't, and she was relieved.

When the phone rang around eight one evening, Rosemarie hurried to answer it. It was Nicky; a letter had come from Patrick.

"I'll come by with it tomorrow after work," he said. Rosemarie took the phone into the hall near the door as far as the cord would stretch.

"When you come Uncle Nicky, don't leave right away, stay awhile. You know how my father gets when you rush out."

"What difference does it make; he gets that way when I come and when I leave. If I stay too long it's worse. He has more time to think up stuff. I don't want to hear how his son is

195

gone and I'm still here. Don't worry Rosie, meet me at the bottom of the stairs so I can slip you the letter before I come up," he said.

After she read Patrick's letter, she realized she wouldn't be able to keep the letter or give the opened letter back to Nicky, not after Patrick mentioned making love to her. She sat on her bed with the door closed and thought of Peggy, but the risk of Katie coming across the letter left her with only one option, Lorraine Peterson. When her uncle was about to leave, she whispered to him that she would keep the letter.

Later that evening she strolled over to the Petersons. Mrs. Peterson was happy to see her; she called to Lorraine. Lorraine came to the top of the stairs and called down for Rosemarie to come up. After the two girls were seated on Lorraine's bed, Rosemarie took out the letter from Patrick and showed it to her.

"Would you keep this for me? I can't have it at my house; I'm afraid my mother or grandmother would find it."

"You haven't told them about Pat yet? I don't blame you, I can't tell my parents anything about Michael either. My father won't even give Michael a chance, just because he's Catholic and Irish. One day I'll tell you a secret."

Rosemarie smiled. In Lorraine, she found a friend and confidant. Lorraine was like an older sister and she felt she could trust her. She left the Peterson's feeling secure in the knowledge she could always confide in her.

CHAPTER 25

One afternoon in late May, Nora was surprised when she heard the door open in the hall.

Sammy was in school and she was home alone except for Maria who was napping. When she turned to see who had come in, she screamed. It was Joey standing there in the uniform of the Army Air corps. He looked so handsome was shocked to see him in it. She screamed and ran to him crying as they both embraced. She stepped back to take another look at him and hugged him again. He took off his cap, flung it on the dining room table and with his arm around her they walked into the kitchen as she cried tears of happiness.

"I'm home on leave Ma, I have a five-day pass before I have to report back for my orders on where I will be sent next."

"Only five days? Your father will be so happy to see you and Rosie and Sammy, too. Boy, will they be surprised when they come home!"

Maria was standing in the doorway; Nora's scream had awakened her. Joey turned to his grandmother and put his arms around her. Maria just cried, but they were tears of happiness.

Later that evening, the whole family sat around the kitchen table taking in every word Joey had to say. Benny was unusually quiet. He embraced Joey when he came home but said very little.

"It looks like I'll be assigned to a B-17." Joey said. "We don't know when they will send us out. I'm finished with my twenty weeks of training." Benny looked at Joey intensely.

"Do you know where they're sending you, East or West?"

"I don't know," he said, keeping the fact that he heard his unit might be going to England to train. He heard talk of flying along the coast of France where many of the German submarines were.

The British had been doing night raids with the B-17 and the B-24 Liberator and taking heavy losses. He thought his unit might be sent over in October for flying training runs, but he wasn't sure. Benny knew he wanted to be a pilot badly, but washed out during training. He thought he would be safer as a navigator, not knowing the navigators sat beneath the pilot in the worst position, in the nose of the aircraft.

"So navigator, they do a good job, huh?" Benny asked.

"Yea Pa, without us guys, the pilots would get lost."

Nora listened intensely, not understanding much of what Joey talked about and left the table to open the hall door; she knew either Rose or Nicky had arrived. She called them earlier to let them know Joey was home. It was Rose. She rushed into the kitchen as Joey was getting out of his chair to greet her, almost knocking him over as she threw herself at him and hugged her nephew.

When she finally backed away far enough to see him in uniform, she excitedly cried, "Oh, how handsome he looks, look, look, how handsome!"

Benny rolled his eyes and laughed. "What do you think we've been doing? Looking at how he looks in his uniform! Now you look!" He laughed again. He thought Rose overdid it, made a big thing out of everything.

When Nicky arrived, Benny left the table after acknowledging him and retreated to his chair in the front room. The kitchen had become too crowded.

"Hey!" Nicky greeted Joey with a bear hug and ran his hand over the short haircut. Joey's thick wavy black hair was gone.

"Boy, they scalped you!" You ain't gonna get the girls with a head like this!" he said, laughing.

"My uniform will make up for it, especially my cap. The girls around the base, they love when we wear our Air Corps cap with the wings in front, they really love that Uncle Nicky." He went to pick up the cap from the dining room table where he had placed it upon his arrival and handed it to Nicky.

"I was awarded my navigators silver wings and commissioned a 2nd lieutenant."

Nicky just stared at the cap he held in his hands. "Wow!" was all he could say. He was proud of his nephew.

"Uncle Nicky, I'll be sent on to unit training when I report back and then hopefully to the flying fortress."

"The flying fortress?" Nicky didn't know much about planes, but he had begun to read about them after Pearl Harbor was hit.

"Yea, that's what we call the B-17; they say it's a better plane than the B-24."

"Well, keep your head down and take care of yourself." Nicky handed the cap back to Joey and they returned to the kitchen where Rosemarie, helping her mother in the kitchen, turned away from the sink to face Joey.

"Joey, where do you sit in the plane, in the tail?" she asked.

"No, the navigator sits below the pilots, way up front, but we also have guns. When I report back I'll be going to flexible gunnery school for a six-week course to learn how to use those guns. My navigation school lasted twenty weeks. With all the rest of that training yet, I don't think I'll be sent out for a while."

Benny was taking in all the conversation coming from the kitchen. He took a deep breath and smiled. In spite of all his misgivings, he was proud of his son.

Later that evening Joey presented Francie Kruger with an engagement ring. He took her in his arms and kissed her.

"I can't take you over to my family yet, but I wanted you to know that while I'm gone, you're my girl. My family has had a rough time with me leaving and springing this on them at this time would be too much, you understand Francie?" She nodded yes. He looked down to see tears forming in her eyes. "My sister plans on bringing you around as a friend of hers, you know, so they can get to know you first. Later, she'll tell them about us."

She walked him to the door when it was time for him to leave.

"Be sure to write often, I'll need letters from home to help me get through all this," he said.

"I'll write you every day Joey." She put her arms around his neck and they kissed goodbye.

CHAPTER 26

Spring of 1942 had come in like a lion, but by the month of May, when Joey came home, it was pleasant, warmer than April had been. Nora's sister, Rose, spent more time with the family, especially on Sundays when the bakery was closed. Joey had always helped whenever Rose needed an extra hand and now Rosemarie took his place. They ignored Benny's grunts and groans when Rose came over. He was alone with just the women and he grew more suspicious as time went on. He was sure that they were plotting against him in some way and he missed Joey more than he expected.

Rose was a heavy woman, but with the war on she seemed to add more pounds as the days passed, worrying and praying for her nephew Joey. She spent more time in church, lighting candles and making Novenas, not only on Joey's behalf but also for all the children of her neighbors, and the customers that kept her in business. She was a deeply religious woman, and unlike Nora and Maria, she never missed Mass on Sunday. Since Joey left home, Nora attended more often leaving Sammy with Maria. Occasionally, Rose would come on Sunday morning and together the two sisters would walk the two blocks to Our Lady of Sorrows Church on Jackson Boulevard. It gave them time together, to talk without Maria interfering.

Benny found Rose bossy and opinionated. He didn't trust the effect she had on Nora. Maria didn't help the situation when she joined her son with comments behind Rose's back.

"She puta idea ina her head," she told him. "Onea day she makea trouble for you."

Rose would tell Nora to stand up for herself. She would both console her younger sister and chide her for being too easy, too willing to be a doormat to Benny and his mother. It was the first Sunday in June and Rose had no reason to believe this Sunday would be any different.

Nora looked forward to Rose's visit again. She would come in the afternoon, with her usual bag of cakes, and pies. She would include fresh-baked bread, which angered Maria. Maria baked bread for the family and felt put out, like her bread wasn't good enough, but Rose didn't care what Maria thought. She was happy to see Rosemarie and Sammy whom she doted on.

Lately, Rosemarie spent many Sunday afternoons at the neighbors, the Petersons and the McCann's and occasionally she would drop in next door to talk with Twyla Woods, or go downstairs to chat with Mrs. Katz and fill her in on the neighborhood news about all the boys in service. Mrs. Katz's son David was in his thirties, with two teenage children. He was a reporter for the Chicago Daily News. He informed his mother he could be sent over as a war correspondent in spite of his age. If the war lasted long enough, older married men would go. Mrs. Katz spent more time with the Nuzzo family since the war broke out. After Pearl Harbor happened, Davie stopped to see his mother more often... He brought his children and it pleased her. She lost no time rushing upstairs to share her happiness with Nora.

After church Rose sat drinking the coffee Nora poured for her, and they talked about Joey. When it was close to suppertime, Rose helped Nora prepare the food, which left Maria spending the time in the front room with Benny. A knock on the kitchen door was heard, and Nora opened it to the Landlady.

"Come in Sylvia, have a cup of coffee with us. Have you had supper yet?"

She pulled up a chair for her. Rose smiled at her and filled Sylvia's cup.

"Nein," Mrs. Katz answered.

"Have you heard anything more about where your brother is?" Rose asked.

Mrs. Katz started to cry. "No, I don't know. I don't vant to know. I hear so much bad tings. I tink my brother is gone. Oy vay iz meer." She cried, which Nora recognized as o, woe is me. Nora was getting to understand more Yiddish as her relationship with the landlady had become much closer through the years.

"Stay and eat with us," Nora said, as she gave Mrs. Katz a gentle hug.

Sammy came into the kitchen, he had been playing outdoors and his cheeks were flushed. When he saw his Aunt Rose he ran into her arms. As big as he had become, he still managed to sit on her lap and she enjoyed every minute of it, planting kisses on both his red cheeks. Most boys his age would have none of that, but ten-year-old Sammy loved it.

"Look at these fat little cheeks, like apples," she said, as she kissed first one cheek and then the other. Mrs. Katz forgot her sadness and smiled until Benny entered and stood in the doorway watching the display before him. His presence changed the mood in the room. Sammy looked up at his father and upon seeing the frown on his face, slid off Rose's lap.

Benny looked at the clock on the wall, it was close to suppertime and seeing Nora busy starting the meal, he went back to the front room. Rose got up to help and whispered to both Nora and Mrs. Katz that Benny always made her feel like it was a gloomy day.

"His moods could put out the sun," she whispered. "He's all hot air and you shouldn't take him so seriously."

Nora turned and gave an exasperated look to her sister. "Try living with him for one week," she said.

Later, Rosemarie returned home, just in time for supper. She was happy to see her aunt and Mrs. Katz sitting at the table. She would find it easy to ignore her father when others were present, instead of just her mother and grandmother. He would save his interrogation of where she had been for when it was just his family, so she was grateful whenever company appeared for supper. It was the only time she came in direct contact with him. Their relationship had deteriorated since Joey left. Her brother wasn't around to support her, so she avoided her father as often as possible. Maria sat next to Benny at the table, ate a few bites of food and then excused herself. "I gotta the stomach, shesa no good," she complained, and went to her room. Rose gave a quiet giggle knowing it was probably because she helped cook the food. She passed a second helping of potatoes to Sammy, looking at Benny, expecting him to say something, but he remained quiet. He ate in silence, not speaking at all. Everyone ate in silence. When he went back to his chair in the front room and turned the radio on, the women began to speak.

"Have you heard from Joey lately," Rose asked, directing her question to Nora.

"Yes, she has," Rosemarie said. "Remember, he washed out of pilot's training because of his eyes, but they made him navigator." Rose looked puzzled.

"You know! The guys who map out where they are and where they are going on a flight," Rosemarie informed her. "He might be training with the 97th Bombardment Group flying in a B- 17." Rose listened with interest to anything about her eldest nephew; she was proud of everything he did.

"I haven't heard from him since he left after his leave," she said, "but I know he must be busy. I'm glad he writes to his mother."

"You know Joey, Aunt Rose," Rosemarie laughed. "He doesn't write too often to anyone except Ma, and he always starts his letters with Dear Ma, Rosie and family so I guess he means everybody."

Rose turned to Sammy who was still eating and quietly taking in the grown-ups conversation. "I hear they're going to make a Victory Garden in the empty lot this summer, have you heard about that?" Sammy looked up from his food and began to speak excitedly with a mouth full of food. Nora stopped him. "Swallow, swallow first," she said. After he did as he was told, he couldn't hold in his excitement.

"Auntie, they gonna take our playground away, we can't play marbles there no more."

Rosemarie gave her brother a hug and turned to her aunt.

"Is that what you heard Aunt Rose?"

"Yes, it will be at the corner of Congress Street and Sacramento Ave."

Nora looked sad and shook her head, "All the kids play in that empty lot. It has hills from the dirt the kids shoveled into piles and all those weeds they pretend is a jungle. They used to play marbles and ride their scooters over the hilly ground, but now I think they use it for a battlefield when they play army."

Rosemarie laughed, "Just think, it will help the war effort to have a Victory Garden, planting food, watching it grow, but I don't think it will happen soon, maybe next year." She looked at Sammy, "Don't worry," she said, "I'm sure it will remain a place to play for the rest of the year."

Mrs. Katz, who had not said a word, and was just content to be there, sharing a meal with the family instead of being alone, spoke up, "A Groysn Dank," she said and then followed up with "Tank you," in English as she often did. "It vas goot you ask me to supper." She turned to Sammy, "In the yard you play too. It's goot that they take avay that empty lot. My Davie, he play ther and get hurt many time ven he vas a boy." She stood up and said goodbye, thanked them again and went back downstairs to her flat.

Maria returned to the kitchen thinking Rose had left when she heard the door close. "Do you want me to warm up your plate Ma?" Nora asked. Maria shrugged and sat at the table, which Nora took to mean yes. Rose, standing behind Maria, rolled her eyes at Nora. "I think I better go home, I have things to do to get ready for Monday morning at the bakery," she said. She retrieved her coat from the hall tree and left with a wave goodbye to everyone in the kitchen. She purposely avoided Benny who was sitting in his chair with his eyes closed, as usual. The radio had been turned off. He wanted to hear their voices from the kitchen, but it had suddenly become quiet when Maria entered the room. With Rose gone, he turned the radio back on. The commentator mentioned that the battles in the Pacific raged fiercely. Benny hunched over bringing his ears as close to the radio as he could. He lived for any news on the radio or in the newspapers about the war. Most of the news was of a general nature as places of battle and casualties were kept a secret while each battle was going on. It was only after the Japs were defeated in any one place that the public found out about it. Casualties or victories were usually reported well after the fact.

It was news of the U.S. troops in Europe that interested Benny the most, even though he thought Joey was still in the states. He hardly left his chair in the evenings. He was afraid he would miss something.

When Rosemarie went over to visit the McCanns, the same scene would greet her there. She enjoyed going over to spend time with Peggy, but it was the entire family she liked being with. It made her feel close to Patrick, as though he were still there. When she was at home, she spent more time in her room or playing the Victrola, putting on all the records of songs she loved, --*There Are Such Things*, and *Stardust*, by Frank Sinatra. She started to play more Sinatra records. His songs were more of Romance and longing than Bing Crosbys. Frank's songs fit her mood. Every time she heard --*You Made Me Love You*, or *I'll Be Seeing You*-- she became melancholy for Patrick.

Nora attended Mass most Sundays and once in a while Maria managed to walk the two blocks with her. With Patrick and Joey gone, Rosemarie went to Mass less often if she could find an excuse not to go. She hated when it was communion time. Sitting at Mass one Sunday she didn't go up for communion. She couldn't bring herself to receive it after what she and Patrick had done. She found it difficult to attend Mass. If she couldn't find a way out, she would have to go and witness Maria sitting back with her knobby fingers going from one Rosary bead to another, eyes closed with her lips moving in silent prayer. Rosemarie would glance at Nora staring straight ahead as though she understood every word of Latin the priest spoke. Sammy would be wedged between his mother and grandmother finding it difficult to sit still. He would squirm and fuss. Imprisoned between them, he had little choice but to endure the hour long Mass. For Rosemarie, the Mass went by quickly as she paid little attention to the service and daydreamed the whole hour away thinking of Patrick and remembering her favorite songs. When Nora would motion for her to go up to receive communion, she pretended not to notice. That was the one thing she couldn't bring herself to do. Later, her excuse to her mother was, "I forgot I ate a piece of toast this morning," or "I had a doughnut after midnight." After a while Nora quit asking why.

Maria's health began to fail as far as her walking any distance, so she attended church less often and Nora noticed that when it came time for Maria to work in her garden behind the garage, she seemed too tired to dig with the shovel. Nora had to help her.

The 2nd of June, Nicky came to visit on Sunday. Benny had gone out for a paper and had not returned yet and Nora, Maria and Sammy were in church. Rosemarie didn't feel well and was still in bed when she heard the doorbell ring. Slipping into her bathrobe she happily let her uncle in. She greeted him with a smile and said, "Uncle Nicky, I'm the only one home. Pa went out for the Sunday paper and he usually stops to talk with anyone Italian who happens to be in Peppy's on Sunday morning."

"So, it's just you and me, huh kid?" Nicky handed her the latest two letters from Patrick. She hurried to open them and then put them in her bathrobe pocket. She would read them later in the bathroom where she could lock the door.

"You look pale,' he said. "Are you getting enough sleep or are you staying up late and worrying about Joey and Pat?"

"No, I think I'm coming down with a cold. Uncle Nicky, why can't you and Pa get along with each other? I know it's not just your fault, it's mostly him, but why does he seem so mad at you all the time?"

"If I tell you, you promise me never to let them know I told you?" He asked. She touched his arm, "Tell me what Uncle Nicky?"

"Your parents were about to get married and I was only eight years old when your grandpa Frank died. Well, he wasn't your real grandpa. He wasn't your father's father. Grandma was married twice. Her first husband died when your father was six years old."

She looked surprised, "What do you mean? Grandpa Frank was your father wasn't he?"

"Yes, but I was born after grandma married Frank. Your real grandfather's name was Joe. He was the older brother of my father. You're my father's great niece."

A look of confusion crossed her face, "I don't understand," she said.

"Rosie," he said, reaching across the table to put his hand on hers. "My father and your real grandfather were brothers. My father was your great uncle. Your father was jealous of the relationship between grandma and my father because he remembered how it was between his father and grandma. She didn't want to marry Joe; he was at least twelve years older than her. When she met my father she really loved him, he was her age, and when I was around eight years old, she told me the story of how they met. She told me that after she got off the ferry from Ellis Island to New York, my father was waiting at the pier. She said her heart skipped a beat when she first laid eyes on him. She mentioned how tall he was compared to his brother and much better looking too. Unfortunately, your father over-heard the conversation and he was hurt."

"Why did she marry my real grandfather if she didn't love him?" Rosemarie said, with sadness in her voice.

"Because she had to, it was the custom in the old Country. The parents picked who you could marry."

Rosemarie shook her head sadly. "That's terrible! But didn't they pick your father also?"

"Yes, but grandma got lucky, it was love at first sight

when she met my father. I don't think your father ever forgave her for loving my father more and he took it out on me."

"Uncle Nicky, I can't believe people would marry someone they didn't love."

She looked sad as she sat quietly sharing a cup of coffee with her uncle. She thought of how much she loved Patrick and now she understood why her father wanted to choose the boy she dated.

"He will never tell me who I can marry," she said, "Never!"

Nicky wanted to leave before the women and Sammy came back from church, but he knew he had to visit his mother. When the women returned Maria was happy to see him, and he had to stay longer than he had wanted, but he stayed for his mother and hoped Benny wouldn't come in before he left.

"You staya to eat, eh?" Marie pleaded, as she forced him to sit down. He knew he had to stay; he wouldn't hurt his mother's feelings again. He had done just that many times when there was words of anger between him and Benny.

Nora looked at the clock, it was noon and Rosemarie was still in her bathrobe. Nora believed she wasn't feeling well, and wasn't as angry with her as she had been earlier when they left for church. She didn't believe her then, thinking she lied to get out of attending the service. "Why don't you get dressed before your father gets home? She said. "You know how he hates when you walk around like that. We don't need him finding fault with another thing in this house."

Nicky laughed, "What difference does it make Nora? It won't be Rosie this time; it'll be me, just because I'm here."

Rosemarie went to get dressed and Nicky sat thinking about how it was now impossible to leave. He felt guilty about not coming over to see Maria as often as he should, but since Joey left, Benny was always in a terrible mood. Joey, the family's peacemaker was gone and it was impossible for Nicky to escape Benny's wrath. For the sake of his mother, he would have to be in the same house with his brother once more. He would remain at the kitchen table and not move to greet Benny when he came, just wait for him to enter the room. He would remain quiet, and not provoke any conversation that could lead to an argument. He sat there feeling trapped. *It's just one more Sunday, like all the rest,* he told himself; *I'll live through it, for Ma's sake.*

When Benny arrived home, he avoided Nicky by staying in the front room. He found an excuse to eat his meal alone in the dining room so he could hear the radio from the front room. Not much was said until Nicky was ready to leave. He had to pass through the room Benny was in to get to the hall door. He thought he better say goodbye to him. He called to him as he was leaving.

"I'm going!"

Benny looked up from his place at the dining room table and angrily said to Nicky,

"How come every time you come in the door, Rosie spends time in the bathroom?"

"What! Are you going to make something out of that too?" Nicky couldn't believe what he had just heard. "So! She goes to the bathroom, so what! Because, she's gotta go!" They stared at each other until Nicky shook his head in disgust and slammed the door behind him as he left.

CHAPTER 27

The last days of June had arrived and Rosemarie began to worry. She hadn't felt herself the past few months. She thought it was the flu coming on and when the nausea seemed to leave, she thought she was over it. She had gained some weight and Nora was worried about her.

"Go see the doctor!" she said, but when she told her Mother she was feeling better, Nora didn't mention it again. Sitting on the edge of her bed one morning, she wondered and worried about the fact that she had missed her period for a couple of months, or was it three or four months? She couldn't remember when she last had it. "I can't be!" she told herself and she pushed the thought out of her head. She told herself it was the war, her nerves, the worries about her brother and Patrick. *No wonder I missed,* she thought. She remembered a school friend who missed her period when her mother died. She said it was due to stress. Didn't her 12th grade Physical Education teacher tell the girls what stress could do to hormones in the body? That's what it was, she thought, and put the whole thing out of her mind. The little movements she felt, she attributed to an upset stomach.

Rosemarie lived only for Patrick's letters. Whenever Nicky came over, he would usually have more than one letter for her. They weren't coming as often and when they did it would be two or three at a time, written weeks before or even a month before. All the postmarks were California, but she knew he was on the ship The USS Enterprise. He manned the small guns on the ship; it was all he could tell them. On the news, the McCann family heard of a great battle going on, the report called it the Battle of Midway; it had been taking place that month of June. They wondered if Patrick had fought in that sea battle. Rosemarie was spending more time at the McCann's on the pretext of just seeing Peggy, but she loved being with the entire family. She could share in the letters Patrick wrote to his family as well. On one of the visits, when both girls were in Peggy's room and Peggy was sitting on the floor reading aloud Patrick's latest letter, Rosemarie got up from sitting on the edge of Peggy's bed.

Peggy looked up at her and said, "Rosemarie, you've put on a lot of weight, is that why you're always wearing your brother's shirts lately?" Rosemarie sat back down and started to cry. Peggy knelt before her, "What's wrong? You can tell me." but before she could say anything, Peggy asked, "Are you pregnant?"

"I don't know," was all Rosemarie could say between sobs.

Peggy pulled her up to a standing position and pulled up the large shirt she was wearing.

"Oh My God! Rosemarie, you're pregnant! How far along are you?"

"I can't be, I can't be," she sobbed. She knew she had to be. She had been in denial for the last few months, but deep down she knew, she always knew, but the thought was so horrifying to her to be in her family in that condition? It would break her mother's heart, her grandmother would spit on the ground she walked on, and worse, she thought, her father would kill her. She looked pleadingly at Peggy.

"I don't know what to do."

Peggy leaned over to make sure her bedroom door was locked, and both girls sat down on the bed. Peggy consoled a very distraught Rosemarie.

"Don't worry," she said, "no one must know in my family or yours. How far along are you?" She looked at her swollen stomach. "How have you hidden this from your mother? And grandmother? You both sleep in the same room; you're already showing!"

"I've been wearing large sweaters and my brother's shirts and it's been easy, but now I'm showing more. I think I'm almost five months. In another month I won't be able to hide it. I've been lucky so far that it's only been the past month that I look pregnant. I don't know what to do."

Peggy held Rosemarie close and said, "I promise, I won't tell a soul, I can't, it's my brother's and my mother can't know, it would kill her. I'll think of something, but you have to tell someone in your family. You have to tell someone who can help you, maybe a cousin, or some other relative that could take you in. Someone who lives far away from your family and the neighborhood."

"There is only my uncle, but he would... he would," she started to cry again. "It happened in his apartment when he wasn't home. He trusted us. My Aunt Rose? I couldn't tell her, she would tell my Mother, first thing. Oh Peggy, I want to disappear, I want to die. How can I face my uncle with this?"

"Don't think anymore today. Go home and make plans if you can, it's either your uncle or you'll have to go to the convent and talk to one of the nuns. There's a place they send unmarried girls who get pregnant where they can live until their babies are born, but they might expect you to give it up for adoption. Because you're eighteen, maybe they don't have to let your parents know where you are. That's your second option."

Rosemarie stood up, wiped the tears from her eyes, buttoned up her shirt, and gave Sally a hug. "I would never give my baby up for adoption; it's your brother's child too. We love each other, and we'll get married when he comes home, but I know I have to leave home before they know." Peggy unlocked the door and peeked out to check on where her mother was, in the kitchen as usual, so she quickly let Rosemarie out the front door, fearful Katie would see Rosemarie had been crying or worse ask questions about her weight gain. Katie might surely recognize the signs having had six children of her own. Peggy watched Rosemarie cross the street, trying to walk tall, hiding the bulge under her brother's shirt. As she watched her, she knew she wouldn't be able to hide it much longer. She thought of Patrick, so far away, and not knowing he was going to be a father, of what her Mother would do if she knew, or what Rosemarie's family would do. She would be the baby's aunt, she smiled at the thought and she knew she would have to support the girl her brother loved. They had been friends since they were children. She had to help her, whatever the outcome.

The next day, Rosemarie went to work at Woolworth's as usual; her dream of quitting her job and applying at Sears and Roebuck or one of the defense plants that were now hiring women as riveters on airplane parts, was now out of the question. She wasn't sure how much longer she could go into work. She knew she lasted as long as she did because the women employees were required to wear long smocks that were quite loose. She worried that someone would notice when she had to remove the garment and hang it up in the storeroom. She was able to slip her coat on quickly for the last couple of months but since the month of June the days were getting warmer. She knew she couldn't hide her condition under a coat much longer. She could hardly keep her mind on her work; she also knew she had to see a doctor soon.

Later that week, Peggy sat with her in the doctor's office. They rode the Harrison Street streetcar to Chicago's Cook County Hospital. The Doctor's office was in the hospital; the County hospital served the community's poor and lower middle classes. It was many blocks east of their neighborhood, but they worried about running into someone they knew. Rosemarie was nervous and frightened. She was relieved that Peggy agreed to accompany her for her first visit. She knew all along she was expecting a child and she felt stupid to have waited months to see a doctor. *What was I thinking?* She thought. She felt humiliated answering all Peggy's questions, as they rode to the hospital.

"Didn't your mother ever tell you anything about how you can get pregnant or how to prevent it?" Peggy asked.

"No, my Ma never talks about such things. I was only eight when Sammy was born. She never mentioned it to me until the midwife came, just before he was born." She told me I was going to have a baby brother or sister but not where he was going to come from."

Peggy looked surprised, "You never noticed your Ma's stomach got big?"

"No, she always wore a big apron."

Rosemarie was embarrassed, Peggy only a month older than her knew so much more about life.

"I never thought I could get pregnant; we only did it that one day and I thought it was at the safe time of the month. A girl at school told me there was a safe time."

"There isn't any safe time, and my Mother's proof of that. Look at us six kids, I'm sure after Kevin my parents were happy with four. I heard my mother complain after Jean was born, that Pat, a pair of twins, and Kevin was enough. I heard her say that to her brother, my Uncle John, he's a priest. She was angry when she said it."

"But I thought your parents had more children because they're such good Catholics."

"No, they had six children because they believed what the church told them, that there is a safe time. My Mother found out there isn't any safe time that works for every woman unless you use protection, but that's considered a sin by the church. I'm not ever having six children when I marry and I don't believe half of what the Church tells us. Besides what do the priests know about real life? They're not married."

Rosemarie nodded in agreement, "You sound like my father," she said. "He believes God gave us a brain to think for ourselves."

"That's the one thing I believe your father's right about."

Rosemarie was deep in thought when she heard the nurse at the desk call...Mrs. Clark! Peggy leaned over to her, "That's you," she reminded her. "Remember, that's the name we picked."

Rosemarie took a deep breath, stood up and walked towards the nurse's desk. "You can go in now, the nurse said, pointing to a door behind her. As Rosemarie went to the door, her legs felt like jelly. Her heart was pounding and fearfully she entered the room. Doctor Phillips was sitting behind a desk. He motioned for her to sit in the chair facing him. He stared at her for a moment. *Another one*, he thought, and he could see she was nervous. When he smiled it put her at ease.

"You are Mrs. Rose Clark?" he asked. She nodded yes.

"Don't be afraid," he said, still smiling. "So your husband's name is…He waited for her answer.

"Patrick," she answered before she had time to think of a name; Patrick just slipped out. "Patrick Clark," she added, her voice, barely audible.

"You needn't be afraid," he said."I'm here to help you. Where is your husband?"

"He's in the Navy, overseas." She answered with her head down. She found it difficult to look up at him. She felt her face flush. She wasn't good at lying. He looked at the sheet of paper he held in his hand. It was the form she filled out when she first arrived. He looked up at her again and then his eyes went to her left hand.

"You're not married, are you?"

"No," she whispered, feeling ashamed, she covered her left hand with her right hand. *Why didn't I think to wear a ring*, she thought.

"I'm not here to judge you," the doctor said. "You're eighteen; you have a right to privacy. I'm only here to help you. You're not the first unmarried mother I have been taking care of; in fact you're the seventh since the war started." He stood up and handed her a white hospital gown and pointed her to the exam room. She went in and closed the door. She was cold and shivering. The room was warm, but fear made her break out in a cold sweat. She undressed and put on the gown, sat on the exam table and waited. The few minutes she waited seemed like an hour. She felt a lump form in her throat and soon tears would follow. She didn't want the doctor to think she was a big baby. When he entered, a nurse was with him. She motioned for her to lie down on the exam table. After the exam, which left Rosemarie very embarrassed, he informed her she was about five months along in the pregnancy. "Come and see me again in six weeks, everything seems to be ok" he said. "Your baby is due around the middle of November."

After they left her alone to get dressed, she felt relieved it was over. She would be a mother soon; she had mixed feelings of joy and fear, shame and embarrassment. All she could think about was she was having Patrick's child, a part of him that she would always have if he didn't make it back. She hated thinking that way, but the thought that he might not come back was always in the back of her mind. When she passed the doctor, sitting at his desk, he smiled at her again, which made her feel like he had not passed judgment on her. He had a kind face which relieved some of her fears. "Make another appointment in six weeks with the nurse at the front desk," he reminded her.

She said "Thank you," as she left. At the desk, the nurse said, "That will be five dollars for the visit." That was almost a quarter of her weekly pay. On the way home, she said to Peggy, "I thought County was a charity hospital."

"It's for everyone and also for people who don't have a job. You made the mistake of writing on the form that you worked," Peggy said, "You should have marked no to that question."

Rosemarie never thought of lying on the hospital form, but after all, she was carrying the biggest lie of all, and she had to keep it from her parents. With all her father's faults, she knew lying wasn't one of them. He prided himself on being an honest man, which Rosemarie knew he was. Sometimes so honest it hurt people's feelings. Her uncle was always in the crosshairs of her father's strict principles and total honesty.

On the ride home, the girls rode a few miles in silence, then, Peggy took her hand and said, "Four months along? You won't be able to hide it much longer. Rosemarie, you've got to tell someone."

"I know, I know," she said, as she bit her bottom lip. Her

eyes were beginning to well up in tears. "I can't, I can't," she cried. "You don't know my father. He has this look he gives that kills me even when I haven't done anything wrong. When he looks at me lately I feel so... I don't know what I feel, like I've done something bad and he guesses."

"That's your imagination playing tricks on you because you know what's happened. No one else knows, but you sleep in the same room with your grandmother; it's only a matter of time before she notices your condition, tell them soon or leave before they find out."

"My father is so foreign. Honor and family and all that, it's so important to him. It's what he lives for."

"Then you better leave," Peggy said, looking at her with a sad expression.

"Where can I go except to my uncle, and what if he throws me out?"

"I can't believe he would do that. Your uncle is much too kind of a person."

"But he has had to deal with my father for as long as I can remember, and my father acts like he hates his own brother. My uncle would be afraid to take me in."

Peggy put her arm around her, "Just think about it, and if he won't help you I might be able to find someone who will. My friend Lucy has a married sister whose husband is away at war and she might take you in as a babysitter for a while. She just started working at a Defense plant."

Rosemarie started to cry. "Don't cry, it will work out somehow, you'll see," Peggy said, trying to console her.

CHAPTER 28

It had been several weeks since Rosemarie's visit to the doctor and still she was unable to make a decision about what she was going to do. A heat wave hit Chicago the past week and she was still wearing her brother's shirts, except she had to buy larger size skirts to fit her waistline. One of her co-workers at Woolworths asked her if she was pregnant and she lied and said no. The girl looked at her and gave her a look that told her she didn't believe her. Later, she noticed the girl whispering to several others, and she was sure it was about her. She knew she could not go back to work. The next morning she awakened early before her grandmother and waited until her father left for work. With one bathroom in the flat, she had to pace her time. She put on her long bathrobe and waited until her mother left the bathroom, and then she locked herself in to get dressed, but she wasn't going to work and thought of what to do next. Afraid her co-workers all knew and she was going to get fired, she decided to call in sick, knowing that in a couple of days she would quit her job. She dressed and entered the brightly lit kitchen. It was a cloudy day and about to rain. Nora had turned the large ceiling light on which lit up the kitchen brighter than when the sun was out.

"Good morning Ma," she said, as she quickly slid into a chair. Her stomach under her brother's long shirt was partially hidden beneath the tabletop. Nora turned from the stove, fried eggs simmering in the pan she held. She carried it over to the table and slid the eggs on Rosemarie's plate. Nora was looking at her with a funny expression.

"What Ma?" she asked, hoping her flushed face wouldn't betray her. She blushed so easily.

"What's this? Wearing your brother's shirt again?" Nora said, "You never stay in one place. What do you do in your room all the time, and the bathroom every night? You're avoiding us all the time."

Maria entered the kitchen. "Leavea her alona," she scolded Nora. "She no hava to tella you when she usea the batharoom!"

"It's the busiest room in the house, always someone in there, mostly her," Nora said, annoyingly.

She turned her back to them, and started cooking Sammy's eggs. He was standing behind her patiently waiting for his breakfast. She turned with the fork in her hand almost poking him in the face.

Looking at Rosemarie, she shook the fork and said, "Your father thinks something is going on with you. You never talk no more? Always with the long face!" After serving Sammy his eggs, she sat down next to Rosemarie and poured herself a cup of coffee. Patting her daughter on the shoulder, she said, "You always pick at your food, what's wrong? You don't feel good this morning?"

Sammy blurted out with a mouthful of egg, "She's fat!"

Maria looked at Rosemarie with sympathy and turned to Nora, "She no feela good, you upseta her stomach. She goa to work with the upsetta stomach."

Nora got up and returned to the stove and with her back to Maria, said, "So, she goes to work with an upset stomach! My stomach is upset every night listening to your son. What's wrong with Rosie? What's wrong with Rosie? He asks over and over, like a broken record. Are you going to tell us what's wrong?" She directed her question to Rosemarie.

Rosemarie glared back at her, "Nothing's wrong," and then she started to rise up from her chair but didn't push the chair back far enough. Her stomach brushed the edge of the table, and the shirt she was wearing became unbuttoned just as Nora turned to say something else to her. Her mouth flew open and her hand went to her mouth to stifle the scream that came through her fingers. What she observed was a very pregnant daughter standing before her. Maria looked horrified, not realizing what Nora was screaming about until she watched her pull the shirt off of a very frightened Rosemarie.

"What have you done?" Nora screamed, "My God! What

have you done?"

Maria looked at her granddaughter and her eyes took in her extended stomach as Nora held on to her so she wouldn't try to get away.

"Oh! Oh! Madonna mia!" Maria cried. The two women were in shock.

Nora screamed hysterically, "Who's the father?" but Rosemarie wouldn't answer. Nora looked at Maria, "She won't tell us," she cried. She let go of her daughter, and collapsed into a chair. Both women were crying hysterically as Rosemarie fled the room.

Mrs. Katz heard all the shouting in the flat above her and lost no time in climbing the stairs to see what was wrong. Maria let her in the back door. She entered the kitchen to see both Nora and Sammy crying. Nora had her head down on the table and Sammy was upset because his mother was crying.

"Vot is wrong?" she asked, looking at Maria for the answer.

Maria hunched her shoulders and put her hands on each side of her face, shaking her head from side to side. Mrs. Katz went over to Nora, and putting her arms around her, she whispered in her ear, "Vot is wrong darlink?"

Nora raised her head up and still sobbing she said, "Oh my God! You don't want to know."

"Tell me," Mrs. Katz pleaded.

"It's Rosie," Nora said, "I can't talk about it right now, maybe later."

She put her head down into her arms on the table and continued to cry along with Maria.

"That's ok, I go now," Mrs. Katz said."When you need me you call, I come."

Maria ushered her out the door. Turning to Nora she said, "Sure, you tella you business to everybody? We no tella Benny tonight, we wait." She sat down across from Nora and started to pray.

Annoyed, Nora left the table and dragged Sammy toward

the hall door. "Go next door and play with Bobby until I call for you," she said, as she pushed the boy out the door and closed it.

He was still crying and she felt bad about it, but she didn't want him there when she confronted Rosemarie again. Sammy started down the steps and then went back up and put his ear to the closed door. He was confused. He wiped his wet tears with the back of his hand and tried to listen to what it was all about.

Nora rushed to Rosemarie's room and banged on the locked door. "Rosie! Open this door!" she yelled, banging with her fist as hard as she could. Her shock and horror now changed to anger. The door opened to a destroyed Rosemarie, her face was very flushed and she was shaking uncontrollably. "You're having a baby!" Nora yelled, "You're having a baby? How could you do this to us? You're not married! Oh my God Rosie, you're father can't know, we can't tell him."

Maria entered the room; she put her arms around her granddaughter to comfort her. "We no tell Papa," she whispered to Rosemarie and turning to Nora she asked, "She goa somea place tonight huh?"

Nora tried to calm down and think of a plan. "Aunt Rose is coming for supper tonight, I'll talk to her about you spending a few days with her until I figure out what to do, and please control yourself in front of your father at supper. If you stay in your room again he might get fed up and come in here to get you. It would be better if you came to the table to eat with us." Turning to Maria, she warned, "Ma, we can't let Benny know yet, not while Rosie is still here. Promise me Ma, that you won't say a word. God only knows what he will do when he finds out and I don't want her here when he does."

Maria, still hugging Rosemarie, nodded in agreement. She knew her son better than anyone in the family, and she witnessed how angry and cruel he could be to his brother, how ridged his beliefs were and being a woman, she witnessed firsthand how some of the men from the old country regarded women. Men were the head of the family and they had the last word. Her second husband, Frank, wasn't too much different, but he was an improvement over Joe, so she found his control more bearable because he was kind, and she loved him. Whatever she thought and tolerated about Benny and Nora's relationship, she felt different when it came to her granddaughter. Maria shook her head in disbelief and with her face half buried into the bottom of her apron she cried, "Oh Madonna Mia!" over and over.

"Please Ma, enough!" Nora said, as she turned to Rosemarie and yelled, "What have you done? Who is going to take the hell that will come when your father finds out? Me! As well as you, but I'll get blamed the most."

Nora's shouting was unlike the mother Rosemarie knew and it caused her to crumble down on the floor hugging the edge of the bed, pulling the bed covers half off the bed. Nora's voice became softer as she tried to console her very devastated daughter.

"Tell me who the boy is that did this to you," she asked as if Rosemarie had no part in the dilemma. All Rosemarie could do was shake her head no. Nora pulled her up and made her lie down on the bed. "Try to get some rest and stop crying; we have to appear normal when your father comes home," she said as she looked at the time on the clock. The hours flew by and now it was afternoon. She had to call Sammy home and give the boy lunch if the neighbor, Twyla, hadn't already done so, but as she entered the hall she heard a noise. She went to the door and opened it to a very distraught Sammy, sitting on the top landing, crying.

"What are you doing here?" she yelled. "I told you to go next door! Get up from there!" She pulled the boy to his feet. "Stop your crying!" she scolded, as she took out her hankie and roughly wiped it over his face. How much of the confrontation with Rosemarie had the boy heard, she wondered. Bringing Sammy into the hall she said, "Go wash your face." She went to lean on the dining room table; nothing was going to calm her down. She stood with both hands clutching the edge of the table. She knew what she would have to endure when Benny found out. She tried to think of a way of keeping it from him. *Maybe I can send Rosie to stay with my sister Rose*, she had all these thoughts as she gripped the table and cried uncontrollably. She would tell Benny that Rose needed help at the bakery because one of her employees quit. When Rosemarie didn't come home, she would make up some other excuse. She would talk to Maria about it later to make sure she went along with it. She would have to confide in her sister, and she dreaded when that moment came. She knew how religious Rose was and she hoped she would accept the situation without judgment.

"What have I done to deserve this?" she cried, her hands still gripping the table edge, her head bent down. When Sammy came into the room she straightened up to get control of herself. She made up her mind that Benny could not know, he would blame her, he would say, 'You didn't watch her!' He would punish her too. In some way she would be the fault of it all. She finally got control of herself and called Rose. She held the phone close to her mouth and tried to talk in a regular voice. "Can you come over early?" she asked, but Rose could only promise to come early if she had someone to lock up for her. Still crying, she went into the kitchen to start the evening meal. Where did the time go, she thought. It was close to 4:00 p.m. and Benny would be home at 6:00. She went back to Rosemarie's room and found Maria sitting on Rosemarie's bed stroking her granddaughter's arm. She could see the girl was exhausted, and with Maria's sympathy and attempts to comfort her, she had fallen asleep. Nora motioned for Maria to come out of the room.

"Ma, remember, we don't say anything. I have a plan that maybe we don't have to tell Benny right away, we can wait." She searched Maria's expression to make sure she understood.

"You noa worry, I no say noting," Maria assured her.

The two women started the evening meal and Maria said, "You sister, shea comea tonight?" She knew the answer, but

224

she asked anyway. She knew Rose always brought bread, so she didn't bake in the morning. She made a big thing out of how she couldn't bake her own bread, how the bakery bread was dry and it would stick to her false teeth, but Nora would just let her talk, she had heard it so many times before.

Nora was in the pantry gathering a few pots for the evening meal. She had to keep wiping her nose and drying her eyes. She couldn't stop crying and using the damp hankie she now held permanently in her hand. She knew she had to compose herself before Benny arrived home. She hoped she could keep herself together until Rosemarie went home with her sister, but hearing Maria shout, "Benny's home!" crushed the plans she hoped for. He was home early, and she didn't have time to compose herself, and Rose hadn't arrived yet. She stood inside the pantry, pot in hand and very nervous, she started to shake. She dried her tears once more, took a deep breath, and went into the kitchen. Benny was in the front hall removing his shoes when he noticed Maria's face looked odd.

"What's wrong?" he asked, "Somebody died?" but Maria didn't answer. When he entered the kitchen, he could tell something was very wrong. Nora's face betrayed the very feelings she tried so desperately to hide.

"What's happened?" he shouted, in his usual loud voice. Sammy came up behind him, fearful of what his father would do. He started to cry and Benny turned to him. "What's wrong? The kids picking on you again?" He took in the grave expressions on Nora and Maria's face. "It can't be that bad," he said, as he cupped Sammy's chin in his hand and looked the boy's face over. "Where did they hit you? I don't see anything." Turning to the two women he started to laugh, "You're both acting crazy, he's not hurt, not a mark on him. Let him grow up. You treat him like a baby." With his back to Sammy, he continued to laugh and shake his head as he started towards the table, about to sit down and rest his feet. He thought, silly women, upset over nothing, the boy has to grow up and defend himself, when Sammy said…

"Rosie's having a baby."

Benny turned to Sammy, "WHAT! What did you say?"

Startled by the expression on his father's face, Sammy ran from the room. Benny's face expressed rage. He walked up to Nora, grabbing her arm to get her full attention, and yelled as loud as he could into her face. "Tell me what I just heard was a mistake!" All Nora could do was cry. "Where is she?" he shouted, and then like a wild man he ran towards Rosemarie's room. Maria quickly followed behind him, trying to pull him back but he shook her off and entered the room yelling, "Get out of that bed!" Rosemarie got up, shaking and crying. He said nothing for a few moments. His silence was more menacing than his shouting as he stared at her, taking in her condition; it became very obvious, when out of fear, she jumped up quickly. He grabbed her by the shoulders, his face a few inches from hers and screamed so loud it caused her to respond with her eyes closed and tightening her facial muscles as she tried to turn her face away from him. She felt like she was about to faint. As all the shouting was going on, Sammy opened the door to his Aunt Rose, shopping bag in hand, full of desserts and bread from the bakery. She entered the dining room and saw Maria and Nora at Rosemarie's bedroom door. She heard Benny's shouting. She placed the bag on the dining room table and rushed to see what was happening as she kept asking, "What's going on? What's wrong?"

Benny kept shouting in Rosemarie's face. "It's true, isn't it? Tell me, who's the bastard? How could you do this to me?" Still holding her by the shoulders, he continued to yell, "I never thought this would happen to me!" She tried to get free of him and her fear turned to anger as she found the courage to yell back, "It didn't happen to you! It happened to me!" With that remark, he struck her on the face with his open hand and she fell to the floor. Maria rushed in and pushing him aside bent down to console her granddaughter. Nora grabbed at his sleeve trying to pull him out of the room. Sammy was crying. Rose was yelling, "Tell me what's happened!" Rosemarie was holding her hand over the side of her face where he had hit her, now crying harder than she had before. Maria was hugging her where she lay on the floor, curled up in a fetal position.

Benny walked into the front room; he looked like a beaten man. He sat in his chair and cried into his hands, then as quickly as he sat down, he stood back up and tried to enter the room again as Rose and Nora were now trying to help Maria pick Rosemarie up off the floor as Rose looked in horror at her very pregnant niece. Maria rushed to the door to block Benny from entering. He gripped the doorframe trying to push his way in as he kept shouting "Who's the father? Who's the father? Who's the bastard?" but Maria stood in front of the open door. Her 4 foot 11 inch height might as well have been a steel door. She pushed at him with all her strength, like a bear protecting her cub. He could have pushed his own mother aside easily, but that was one taboo he would not cross. That was akin to murder in his eyes. Pushing down the one who gave him life was a greater sin than a daughter who would bring shame into his home. He backed away, went and sat down and cried into his hands again.

Maria motioned to Nora and Rose to leave Rosemarie to her.

The two were about to leave the room when Benny appeared at the doorway again crying and shouting, "Who's the father?"

Maria bent over to Rosemarie and whispered, "Maybe you shoulda tell him."

Rosemarie said, "I don't know if I can."

All Rose heard was, -- I don't know-- which caused her to run screaming into the dining room shouting over and over, "Oh my God! Oh my God!" Nora rushed after her. Maria went to the door where Benny was still yelling and she slammed it shut.

Nora sat down at the table next to Rose; she put her head down into her arms on the table and cried. They were helpless to do anything at that moment, and then Rose took out her

Rosary beads and started to pray. "Oh my God!" She repeated, " Maybe it's a miracle."

"What are you saying?" Nora asked, "It's no miracle, it's a disgrace."

Rose kept repeating, "It's a miracle."

Nora looked at her like she was crazy, "How can you say such a thing?" She scolded.

But Rose insisted; it might be a miracle. She patted Nora's hand and said, "It happened once before, wasn't Jesus born without a father?" Nora looked at her like she had lost her mind, she believed in miracles but not the one Rose thought just happened in her home.

Rose continued to pray as Nora cried until they heard Benny get up from his chair and enter the dining room. They watched him slowly drag himself into the front hall. They watched helplessly as he pounded his fists against his temples, then moaning loudly he pounded the wall with both fists and alternately with his forehead. It was the sight of a man in total agony. The sounds that escaped from his mouth were no longer that of a man but of a trapped animal. They watched as he took his hat off the hall tree, only to throw it on the floor; then he went into the kitchen. They sat motionless, straining to hear what he was going to do. Both women stayed at the dining room table, sitting rigidly in silence as they heard the pantry door open and loudly slam shut. They heard the gallon of wine placed roughly on the tabletop. They looked at each other; there would be no supper tonight.

Nora got up to go to Sammy who had fled to his room. She went to console the boy. He wouldn't understand what had happened, and she worried about how it would affect him. She could hear her husband, wailing about the shame and the dishonor brought to his family. She knew he would drink until he passed out. She heard her mother-in-law's voice praying and talking in Italian to no one in particular. She often talked to herself when she was upset. She could hear her sister's rosary beads as Rose moved them in her fingers and prayed out loud.

It pained her to hear Benny ranting incoherently in the kitchen. She would get Sammy ready for bed and bring him something to eat as soon as she felt she could bring herself to enter the kitchen. She knew she had to wait until her husband went to bed or passed out. She would talk to her sister about Rosie living with her; she knew it would be impossible for both Benny and their daughter to be in the same house. It would be like living in hell.

Rose was crying as she prayed her rosary; then she reached into the bag and tore off the end of the loaf of bread and absentmindedly began to eat it. She took a deep breath, sighing between bites. At that moment, she couldn't think much beyond the bread she was chewing and the words in Hail Mary.

Benny sat at the kitchen table; his mind was racing with scattered thoughts. They seemed to bump into each other. He was unable to make sense of his own thinking. He reached for the wine and poured another glass. He had to shut out the thoughts he had. He had to stop it, to deaden the rage he felt. He drank another glass of wine and then another. He kept filling the glass until the drink seemed to slow the battle that was going on in his mind. He wanted to slip into oblivion, to numb the pain. He was frightened of the desperate thoughts he had of putting an end to the anguish. He could have killed the bastard who was responsible if he knew who he was, and not care what happened to him. The wine eliminated such thoughts.

With sadness, Nora watched helplessly from the kitchen doorway as he slumped at the table, his head hitting the tabletop. The last drink brought the peace he so badly needed as he dropped the empty glass to the floor, scattering bits of glass all over the linoleum. She left him there, hopefully for the night.

She went back to Rose and asked if Rosemarie could go home with her. Rose looked up at her, "Are you crazy?" she said. "I run a business. I can't have her there in her condition and not married. My customers would all talk and quit coming!" Her statement made no sense to Nora. First Rose thought her niece was the Immaculate Conception, and now she was a disgrace? Nora thought she could count on her sister but she knew Rose was from the old school. Whatever Rose believed, saving face was most important.

"You might as well go home, before Benny wakes up," Nora said. She was upset and disappointed in her sister. After Rose left, she was left with the horrible feeling of being alone with the tragedy.

Later that night Nora shared Sammy's bed. She was afraid to go to her own in case Benny woke up. She lay on top of the covers next to her sleeping son. Sleep would not come and she didn't bother to undress; she was waiting for something else to happen. What? She didn't know. She told herself it could be anything like Benny waking in the middle of the night in an even worse mood and attacking Rosemarie again. She lay awake, vigilant, hearing every sound in the house. She heard Sammy's even breathing and Benny's loud snoring from the kitchen. She thought about who the father of her first grandchild could be. She only knew of one boy her daughter had gone out with and that was Vinnie Russo. Each time she saw him in her mind's eye he didn't fit the image of one who could be responsible for her daughter's condition nor one her daughter would ever be involved with. She lived to see her only daughter walk down the isle of the church, on her father's arm, dressed in a white wedding gown, and now she knew that would never happen. She was sad about that and finally cried herself to sleep.

Rosemarie was awake most of the night thinking of what she should do. She knew she had to leave before daybreak. She turned to look at the clock on the nightstand between her bed and her grandmother's. It was 3:00 a.m. Maria slept soundly, snoring and muffling the sound of any noise Rosemarie might make to get dresser drawers open or open the squeaky closet door as she tried to take a few articles of clothing off the rod.

Soon the sun would come up and she had to leave while it was still dark before the neighbors were up. She knew Mr. Peterson was up very early for his work at the newspaper company, and she didn't want to run into him as she was leaving.

She rose from bed quickly, packed a small bag of her clothing, grabbed her spring coat, carried her shoes in her hand and quickly tiptoed through the dining room. She could see the form of her father through the kitchen doorway as she went towards the hall. He was seated with his head on the table. She was afraid any noise she might make would awaken him. When she opened the hall door, its hinges squeaked and she froze for a moment holding her breath. Her heart was beating fast as she peeked back at his form, more apparent now in the early dawn hour. He hadn't moved. She was afraid to open the door any wider and squeezed through, leaving it partly open, afraid of making more noise trying to close it. She went down the stairs as fast as she could and put her shoes on only when she reached the downstairs hall. The streetlights were still on and there was a full moon, but soon the sun would give birth to a new day. She hurried past the few houses between hers and the corner, glancing up once at the McCann's place, thinking of how she could get word to Peggy on where she would be. There was only one place she could go, to her Uncle Nicky. She would endure his anger when he found out about her condition because she had no one else to turn to.

She was happy to be riding the streetcar at that hour. She was alone except for the conductor and one lone man who appeared tipsy. She was thankful no one from her neighborhood was in the car. She had the key to her uncle's apartment and quietly let herself in. She took her shoes off, dropped her bag on the floor and collapsed onto his couch without removing her coat and fell asleep. Nicky's alarm clock went off at 7:00 a.m. and awakened her, but she lay there waiting for him to discover her. It didn't take long after he dressed, and she followed the sounds of his movements from the bedroom to the bathroom off the kitchen. She waited tense and frightened, knowing he had to pass through the room she was in to leave for work.

"What are you doing here?" he asked, surprised to see her at that hour. She rose from the couch and her coat opened revealing her condition. He stared at her in disbelief. "You're not pregnant?" he yelled loudly. "I don't believe it! How could you do this? You can't stay here; your father would kill me."

"I can't go anywhere else; I have nowhere to go." She started to cry. "Please Uncle Nicky, help me."

She was his only niece and he looked at her with sadness. "Do they know?" he asked, knowing what the answer would be or she wouldn't have come to him. "It's Patrick isn't it? I trusted him. I trusted both of you! How could you do this to me? I should have never let you come here with him. I don't know what I was thinking. When did this happen?"

She couldn't answer; big heaving sounds came from her as she was in total anguish knowing she disappointed the one who always came to her defense. All she could do was cry, "I'm sorry Uncle Nicky; I'm so sorry."

"You can't stay here Rosie; I'll call Lillian, and she'll put you up until I figure something out."

He put his arm around her, trying to console her. He went to the phone and called Lillian; she was only one of several women he dated. The only girl he ever brought over to Benny's and Benny called her a Polack and a painted puttana. It was the last time Nicky took any girl to his brother's home. If ever he needed Lillian Kosinski, it was at that moment. Rosemarie sat back on the couch and dried her tears. She heard her uncle talking to Lillian. He explained that he had a problem and asked if she could help because his niece needed a place to stay for a few nights. He proceeded to explain how he would bring Rosemarie over after work that evening. He closed the call with "Thanks Babe, I owe you one." He returned to Rosemarie, knelt down in front of where she was sitting and said, "You can stay until I come home from work and then I'll take you over to Lillian, she didn't ask any questions, just said, 'Of course I'll take her.' I won't have to explain anything after she gets a look at you."

Rosemarie smiled at him, "I don't know how to thank you Uncle Nicky." He looked at her and with a half laugh, said, "Make sure your father never finds out you came here." Staring at her condition, he asked, "When can we expect this disgrace?" then realizing he called his future great niece or nephew a disgrace, he apologized. "I'm sorry Rosie, I'm not thinking straight right now." He appeared so sad when he looked at her that she felt ashamed for disappointing him and putting him in such a position.

As he turned to leave he said, "Get some rest and don't answer the telephone if it rings." Rosemarie grabbed his sleeve and hugged him, thanking him again.

"How many years have you dated Lillian, Uncle Nicky, ten years?" she asked. "You should marry her. You're lucky to have her as a girlfriend."

He looked at her and laughed, "Me? Get married? You're kidding; she's not the only girl I go out with."

Rosemarie gave him a teasing look, "How come it was her you called, huh, not one of your other girlfriends?"

Nicky waved to her as he left the room. "I'm going to be late for work; I gotta go." He opened the door and turned to her once more, "Remember, don't answer the phone." As he went down the two flights of stairs to the street below, he wondered why it was Lillian he called first.

CRITICAL

When Nora went to awaken Rosemarie in the morning Benny had left for work early, which surprised her. Maria was getting dressed. "Where's Rosie?" she asked. Maria looked surprised, "She no ina the house? I wakea early, five o'clocka and she no here." Maybe shea goa to work."

"Not this early Ma, she's not in the house?" Nora noticed a piece of paper on the nightstand, she picked it up, Rosemarie

233

had written, -- Don't worry about me Ma, I'm staying with a friend. I can't tell you who it is. Just don't worry about me. -- Rosie

Nora felt both sad and relieved, her daughter wouldn't have to face Benny again, but she knew he would ask her where their daughter had gone. She was glad she didn't know. To avoid his questions, she would keep her distance from him as much as possible by keeping herself busy with Sammy and helping Maria in the garden. She was still upset and found herself shaky with the fear of facing Benny when he returned from work. She didn't know how he managed to get up for work after the terrible night they all endured. She had to turn her thoughts to other things or she wouldn't be able to function. The vegetables needed tending and Maria needed her help, and she herself needed something to think about besides her daughter. She enjoyed working in her own garden. She felt she needed to confide in someone about her daughter and she knew Mrs. Katz was the only person she could trust at the moment, regardless of what Maria thought. She even talked Mrs. Katz into turning over a patch of ground and growing some seedlings of cabbage and carrots. Mrs. Katz wasn't much of a gardener, so Nora would find herself working her area of the garden as well. About half of the women on the block worked in their backyard gardens, and they enjoyed visiting with each other superficially. Most of them only knew each other from working in gardens they planted since the war started. If it weren't for the war, some of them wouldn't have met at all. They exchanged information over back yard fences about the war and the sons that were fighting far from home. It gave Nora comfort to know she was not alone with her worries about her son.

CHAPTER 29

Benny was unable to concentrate on anything since Rosemarie left home; anger consumed him daily and it made life difficult for his family. Nora dreaded his return from work each day. He would continue to badger her to tell him where their daughter had gone. She called everyone she knew including her brother-in-law Nicky, and no one knew where Rosemarie was. He believed she knew and wouldn't tell him. He wasn't able to keep his mind on work. The straw boss over all the men he worked with noticed he wasn't working as hard as he usually did. He would find him leaning on a shovel in a trance thinking about something. He asked Benny if anything was wrong, but all Benny could do was snap out of it and start digging again. His hands were lifting the heavy clay but his mind was elsewhere. He told himself it had to be the Russo boy. His daughter was out with him once, to her prom, but that was long ago, and he knew his son took them and brought them back home. They must have met later in secret he thought. In his mind he made plans; he was going to confront the Russos, maybe she went to them he thought, but quickly realized if she did, Mr. Russo would have called him. He was sure the Russos knew nothing about their son and soon he would make sure they knew.

Maria's health began to decline since Rosemarie left home. She would become confused and forgetful at times. She wasn't as patient with Sammy, and became cross with him over little things. Nora tried to understand what was happening with her mother-in-law. It upset her because she couldn't talk to Benny about anything, not even about his mother. She counted on the landlady more often to help her with Sammy, and as she would vent all her worries and anger, Mrs. Katz would sympathize with her. When she wanted to run an errand to her sister's bakery or the grocery store she wouldn't leave Sammy alone with Maria, so Mrs. Katz was there for whenever she was needed.

It was the month of August and the men working on the Victory Garden were almost finished. Sammy, and the McCann boy Brian, along with several other children had gathered to watch with sadness as their improvised playground was destroyed. The bumpy lot where many an army battle took place was covered with soil to even the ground. Their make-believe mounds of dirt where they played King of the Hill was now flat and the tall weeds where they played Jungle and hid from each other was gone. All the children could do was stand silently by and watch their make-believe world disappear and for a garden, they were told.

"Hey mister!" Brian McCann shouted as one workman proceeded to dump another pile of soil into one of the many holes the boys used as fox holes when they played Army.

"Whatcha gonna make here?"

"A garden," the man answered.

"What kind of garden?" Brian asked.

"A Victory Garden," the man replied.

"What's a Victory garden mister?"

The man smiled at the half dozen faces where hundreds of questions were forming behind the creases in their foreheads.

"Don't you kids know what a victory garden is?"

Brian shook his head, no. Sammy stood quietly taking in what the man was telling them.

"It grows things," the man said laughing, and then he said teasingly, "I'm going to put up a tall flag pole and a bunch of little flags will sprout up from the ground."

"Nah," Brian said, he knew better."You're gonna grow vegetables."

"In a plain garden you plant vegetables. This is a special garden, you'll see, the little flags will grow." The man enjoyed teasing the boys. "You boys come down every day and watch them grow."

He laughed and all the kids laughed with him except Sammy. This was serious stuff he thought, not like his grandmother's garden. He couldn't wait to run home and tell her they were going to grow little flags at the corner lot. When he ran home to tell her about the little flags, she became cross with him.

"Whata you talk? Little flags? No flags growa there. I planta the tomatoes, thatsa whata grow."

When the lot was finished, it was close to the middle of August and Nora thought it was too late to plant at the Victory Garden, but a few of the older women on the block mapped out their little plot and so did Maria. Every day since school was out for the summer, progress had been made. The lot was flattened, and the workmen were finished putting up the tall flag pole rising above a cement post that held all the names of the neighborhood boys serving their country. The names faced the street side and could be seen by all who walked or drove by. Michael Robert McCann's name was at the top with Joseph Francis Nuzzo's below, followed by Patrick Thomas McCann and over a dozen other boys in the neighborhood, thirteen in all, from four blocks of their street alone. The names were placed in the order of when they enlisted or were drafted.

Sammy would stand and watch for the little flags, but the McCann boys would run their fingers over Michael and Patrick's name encased in a glass cabinet mounted on the post. All the children could be found watching the precinct captain for their area, Mr. Martin, raise the flag each morning and lower it each night, and every day Sammy watched the neat rows of vegetables sprouting up out of the ground, hoping that in between them would be the little flags the man had promised.

Maria worked a little patch close to the sidewalk. Sammy stood next to his little red wagon that held the cans of water Maria needed.

"Do you see the flags yet Granny?" he asked.

"I tell you onea hundred times thesa no flags" she scolded.

"But the man said --"

"I no care whata the mana he say." She handed him the

sprinkling can, "Go filla her upa some more."

He took the empty can and noticed the two cans in the wagon were empty. "Granny, I go get more water," he informed her. He placed the sprinkling can in the wagon and with disappointment etched on his face, he began to feel stupid believing little flags would grow. He felt his face flush, the same way it did at school when he didn't know the answers to the questions his teacher would ask him. As he pulled his red radio flyer wagon behind him, he started to cry. He cried more often lately. Ever since Joey went away to war and Rosemarie left home, he was confused and felt abandoned. Nora thought he was regressing and lost all the ground he had accomplished the past year, even with the help he received from Lorraine Peterson's tutoring. He missed Joey most of all. His Uncle Nicky's visits were less often and when he did come to visit, Sammy was usually in school. When Joey was home, he made him feel different about himself; Sammy had more confidence. His father always shoved him away. He was too busy with his ear to the radio every night, or he had his face behind a newspaper. Sammy missed his siblings.

He wiped his cheek with the back of his hand where it had become wet with tears, tears that flowed freely as he pulled his wagon home. He knew he wasn't good at understanding some things, but he had feelings. Except for his mother, only his brother and sister seemed to understand, and now they were gone. He carried the sprinkling can to fill with water from the hose in the backyard and then filled each bucket with the sprinkling can. It never occurred to him to fill each bucket from the hose. After he filled the last can, he sat on the porch step and rested, and then his eyes took in the pile of newspapers stacked under the porch. He was saving the papers for the war drive. He always searched the back alley for discarded papers. He would bring them to school after Labor Day. The pile of newspapers had grown into a high stack collected over summer vacation. He wanted the gold star the teacher promised to the child who brought in the most paper.

Early that summer, Benny yelled at him to get rid of the papers. 'If there's a fire, the whole place could go up with all that paper under there!' he yelled. All Sammy could think of was the more paper that he brought in at one time might earn him the gold star. He sat thinking about the compliment his teacher, Miss Rocky, gave him for bringing in the most scrap paper on the last day of school before summer vacation. She pasted a gold star on his spelling paper, even though most of the words were misspelled. He got up and took the cans out of the wagon and began to stack the papers in it. He was thinking about the gold star. He forgot all about Maria waiting at the garden. Thinking of how happy his teacher would be with his war effort brought a smile to his face and the next thing he knew, Maria was standing above him, with an angry face. She pushed his stack of papers out of the wagon and yelled at him.

"Whata you do here? I calla you, you no hear?" She gave him a slap to the back of the head, which shocked him; she had never hit him before, for any reason. He looked at his neatly stacked papers scattered on the ground and he began to cry. She was angry with him, "I waita and I waita and you no come?" She put the filled cans back in the wagon and handed him the handle and ordered him to pull it back to the Victory Garden. He followed her, crying all the way. Some of the neighbors were on their porches watching and now his humiliation was complete. He thought the Victory Garden was just another thing for him to get into trouble over. One of the neighbors, watching the boy and his grandmother walk down the sidewalk, was Katie McCann. She noticed the grandmother appeared angry and the boy was crying as he followed behind her. Later that night she mentioned it to Peggy. Peggy had returned from work and found her mother at the window watching the goings on at the Nuzzo home.

"What are you looking at Mom?" Peggy asked as she entered the room.

"Oh I'm feeling so sorry for that family, all they are left with is that poor child," she said, turning to look at Peggy who had come over to the window. She shook her head sadly, pointing to Sammy who was now sitting on his front porch steps alone, looking so forlorn. She said, "Look at that poor kid, I'm sure he misses his brother and sister. I never expected that girl to leave home. Can you believe she would do such a thing? They were so strict with her, too strict; they wouldn't let her go anywhere. I heard she might have gotten in the family way and they sent her away."

Peggy pretended to look surprised. "Mom, where did you hear that?"

"Everyone in the neighborhood is talking about it; some girl Rosemarie worked with said she was expecting when she quit her job at Woolworths. Katie shook her head sadly.

"It's gossip Mom; I wouldn't believe everything you hear."

"Just the same, it has to be true; why would a girl like that disappear?" Katie asked. "What boy would be crazy enough to get a girl like that pregnant and from that family? That uncle of hers might hire someone to kill him."

"Oh Mom, he's not like that, you don't know him; why do you say such things?"

"I only mention it because Mrs. Peterson told me that's what her husband thinks. "That poor family," she said as she shook her head sadly and went into the kitchen. Peggy stood alone watching as Mrs. Katz came out to the porch and took Sammy by the hand and led him into the house. Peggy knew where Rosemarie was. Lillian called her one evening shortly after Rosemarie left home. Rosemarie couldn't make the call herself; Mrs. McCann might recognize her voice and so after Lillian asked for Peggy, she handed the phone to her. Katie just thought it was one of the many friends her daughter had.

In the middle of September, Rosemarie was two months away from giving birth, and Peggy spent as much time going over to Lillian's as she could. Rosemarie asked her to retrieve the letters Lorraine Peterson had kept for her and in the process Lorraine had confessed to Peggy that she had married Michael

Donovan. Peggy felt safe in telling her about Rosemarie, assured that Lorraine would never say anything to anyone. After all, she had a secret of her own.

CHAPTER 30

Lillian brought a letter into the kitchen. It was from Patrick, she handed it to Rosemarie.

"I guess he got the change of address," she said, as she took the letter. She couldn't open it fast enough. She sat at the kitchen table and read...

Dear Rosemarie,

It seemed like I would never hear from home again but all the mail came today. I guess it was held up somewhere and it came all at one time, seven letters, three are from you. Things have been pretty rough out here. I got myself---and the next words were blacked out---I hope you're doing ok. I was surprised that you want my letter's to go to your uncle's girl friends address, why? Won't he take your letters anymore? I hope you're doing ok and miss me because I miss you something awful. I think of you all the time when things are quiet above deck, which isn't too often. I know all this will be over one day and I can't wait to come back home. I miss you Rosemarie and all of my family, and Congress Street. Send me news of how everyone is on the block. Tell Peggy to write more often. I get plenty of letters from you and my Mother though. Don't worry about me, when this war is over with them Jap's we'll tell our parents about how we feel about each other. They will have to accept it. Then we'll have that wedding you want. Joey will be back and he can drive you to church in his Ford, all decked out for our wedding. It seems like it's been such a long time since I last held you. Take care of yourself. Did you get that job at Sears and Roebuck?

Until we meet again, I love you and miss you.

All my love, Pat.

She folded the letter and cried as she put it back into the envelope. She thought, If only he knew, there wasn't any job at

Sears, she no longer lived at home, and his baby would be born soon, illegitimate, in disgrace, without a father to look upon it for the first time, to hear it cry, and to comfort them both.

"What did he say?" Lillian asked.

"He loves me and wishes he were home." She dried her tears.

Lillian sat across from her and pleaded, "It's time Rosemarie, to tell him about the baby so you won't feel you're going through this alone. Maybe you can get married by proxy, you know, let someone stand in for Pat."

"That's not a marriage; I wouldn't feel married to him. I'll write to him about the baby but I worry that he might not be happy about it." She remembered how he worried about her getting pregnant when they were together that day in her uncle's apartment. She went into the bedroom to put the letter away when she paused in front of the little crib Lillian had borrowed from a friend. She smoothed her hand over the baby quilt Peggy bought for the baby and cried. She felt guilty taking Lillian's room, the only bedroom in the small apartment and Lillian had to sleep on her couch. If it weren't for Lillian and her uncle, she didn't know what would have become of her. She knew she could count on her for help, but she was her uncle's friend and she felt she was imposing on her too much. Peggy promised she would try to be with her at the hospital when the time came and so did Lillian, but all she wanted was her mother.

Rosemarie thought of how many years Lillian dated Nicky, waiting for some kind of commitment from him, but she never knew how much Lillian loved her uncle until she got to know her better. Lillian would do anything for Nicky, hoping against hope he would finally ask her to marry him. Year after year, she hung on to that hope. Rosemarie thought, when he sees what she is doing for his niece, then maybe he will realize how much she cares for him. She avoided going out of the apartment except for visits to the doctor. She hated the looks she received from the other tenants. She was a pregnant girl,

243

living with another women who lived alone. She felt guilty about what she had done. She felt guilty about everything. She mentioned how the other people in the building looked at her when she passed them in the hall.

"Oh, just ignore them," Lillian said. "They look at me the same way, and I'm not in your condition."

"Why, because my uncle comes here?"

"Don't you know? It's not just that, it's because I'm a women in my thirties who lives alone. You know what they think of a women who lives alone that isn't old or a widow?"

Rosemarie nodded yes, "They think you're a tramp," she said.

"That's right; you're not supposed to move out of your family's home until you're properly married. It doesn't matter what age you are. I never had a real home; my mother died when I was seven. I went to live with my grandmother; she died when I was twenty-two. I met your uncle where we both worked, and he helped me find this apartment. He was very kind to me. I think he felt sorry for me. When my grandmother died he helped me with her funeral; we were just friends back then. I was totally alone and if it wasn't for his help I don't know what I would have done. My father was never in my life. He abandoned us when I was small. I know what it's like to feel alone and in need of support."

Rosemarie put her arms around her and hugged her tight; she was getting to know the women her father called a puttana. She knew she wasn't at all like the kind of person her father thought she was. If only he knew what a kind person she is and how she loved Nicky, she thought. Her uncle didn't realize what he had in a girl like Lillian. Rosemarie was determined to make sure he knew.

Peggy arrived after work one evening. She was surprised to see that Rosemarie had started a nice supper. "This is a treat," she said as she hung her purse over the back of a chair.

Rosemarie gave her a hug and said, "Lill will be home soon and I asked my uncle to come over also. We need to talk about how to let my mother know. I really want her with me when the time comes."

Peggy gave her a hug and touched her stomach, which was quite large. "Does it kick much? Did you write and tell Pat he's going to be a father?"

"Yes, I did, but I haven't heard from him yet. I hope he isn't upset about it."

CRUCRUCRU

On the day Patrick received the letter, he slowly sank down on the deck to his knees as his eyes took in the words …you're going to be a father and I hope you're not upset about it… He stared at the words and couldn't believe it at first and then remembered it had to be true, after all he was just as responsible, and he felt helpless to do anything to help her. He was frightened for her, but happy to know she was staying with Lillian, and then he thought of his mother. He would write Rosemarie, and tell her he was happy about the baby even if he didn't feel happy at the moment. Being so far from home, he felt responsible and helpless in the situation.

When Rosemarie finally heard from him, she was relieved that he was happy about the baby, but worried about what would happen if his Mother ever found out.

When she informed Peggy, she smiled, "So he's worried, I knew he would be. He wrote me too and I called the baby a he when I wrote to him. I told him not to worry."

"How do you know it's a he" Rosemarie asked, "It could be a girl you know."

Peggy laughed, "I don't know, just guessing. I think Pat would like a boy." She looked seriously at Rosemarie,

"I'm glad you told him before the baby's born, give him something to really want to live for and to be careful on ship. The name of his ship has been safe so far, the Jap's haven't been able to sink her or we would have heard. He wrote to tell me to please make sure my mother doesn't get word of it. He feels responsible and wants to tell her himself when he's able to return home."

Rosemarie reached over to Peggy and held her hand, "I was afraid he would worry about us."

She looked at Peggy with a concerned expression, "What are the neighbors saying, what about your mother, does she ever say anything about me, the fact that I left home?"

"She thinks you're expecting and your family sent you away. She keeps asking if it's true. I tell her it's a rumor, but I don't think she believes me. If it wasn't for that darn girl you worked with at Woolworths; she spread the gossip and somehow Mr. Peterson heard it from someone and told his wife."

"Oh no! And she was the one who told your mother, right?"

"Yes, but I try to tell her it's not true, and Lorraine tells her mother the same thing. I hope you don't mind Rosemarie, I told Lorraine all about it, not where you're staying but about the baby."

"You didn't! Why?"

"I went to get your letters and she asked about you over and over, and when she told me that she and Michael Donovan are secretly married, I trusted her. I'm glad I did. Can you imagine when her mother told her about it, she would have been shocked and agreed with her, but for now she is covering for you, telling her it's only a rumor, after all, she has a secret of her own."

Rosemarie smiled, barely a smile, her lower jaw trembled slightly,

"Look what I've done, I ruined everything, you're the only relative looking forward to the birth. My uncle is upset over it, even though he acts like he has accepted it; I know it still bothers him. Our parents are about to be grandparents and they should be happy, but instead mine are horrified and yours don't even know about it."

"Why do you keep saying you ruined everything? My

brother had something to do with the situation. It takes two, you know."

"No, I don't feel that way," she said.

"Why? Do you think you forced Pat?"

"No, it's just the way I was raised. The girls always wear the skirts, my father would say."

"What's that supposed to mean?" Peggy laughed.

"I don't know; all I ever heard was the girls wear the skirts."

"Yes and the boys wear the pants," Peggy replied.

"I never heard my father say that."

"I guess he wouldn't. My mother always thought Italians would never blame their sons if they got a girl in trouble. It would always be the girl's fault. Isn't that true?"

Rosemarie thought about that. She thought about how much freedom they allowed Joey.

"I think your mother's right," she said.

CHAPTER 31

The third week of September was over and Sunday marked the first day of the fourth week. Benny got up early to get the Sunday papers. He was gone before Nora was up to make the coffee. Sammy was still sleeping, and she let him sleep. After she set the coffee pot on the gas burner, she went to check on Maria. The old woman was in bed, awake, staring up at the ceiling.

"You want to sleep more Mama, I put the coffee on, take your time getting up." Nora said.

Maria just nodded and continued to lie with her eyes wide open. Maria didn't talk as much as she used to, and she spent more time lying down. Nora was worried about her but didn't mention it to Benny. If she tried to engage him in conversation, he would ultimately turn the conversation to Rosemarie, and it would end with him shouting in anger because Nora would walk away from him. She ceased talking to him about anything. The stress she felt would have broken her had she not been able to confide in Mrs. Katz. She told the landlady everything. She held nothing back and the advice, care and concern Mrs. Katz had shown her was her salvation. She had no one else to turn to. Her sister Rose was a disappointment. She was judgmental and unable to sympathize with what she was going through. She never had children, she didn't understand and was unable to support her in the way she needed; that is what Mrs. Katz explained to Nora when she complained about her sister. It made Nora less angry with Rose.

Benny came home with the newspaper, poured himself a cup of coffee and brought it into the front room and turned on the radio to catch any morning news about the war. Maria came out of the bedroom and went straight to the kitchen. She avoided her son as much as possible. His anger upset her. Both women were sitting at the kitchen table drinking coffee, waiting for Sammy to wake up before Nora would start breakfast. The past month she had not gone to Mass on Sunday morning. It was an ordeal to get Sammy ready and to have him sit there for a full hour. She didn't want to leave him home with Benny and Maria, so she used Mrs. Katz to care for him for what she thought were more important errands. Missing Mass was the least of her worries, she thought.

Benny came into the kitchen, went over to the stove and both women remained silent thinking he was getting himself another cup of coffee but he turned, put his empty cup on the table and announced it was the day he was going to confront the Russos about their son.

Maria shook her head no. "You makea a fool of you self," she scolded.

Nora remained silent. Anything she could say would only make things worse. She felt that knot in her stomach. It came more often lately. She knew Vinnie Russo was not responsible. All one had to do was look at him and know he wasn't capable of such a thing. She didn't think he ever went near a girl until he was forced to take Rosemarie to her prom. She sat quietly drinking her coffee until they heard the door slam shut. She looked at the clock, it was only 10:00 a.m. "Where is he going so early?" she asked, looking to Maria for an answer.

"He go to the Russos, no?" Maria said, hunching her shoulders.

"But Ma, they could be in church this early."

"He know they goa to eight o clocka mass."

Nora put her face in her hands and leaning on her elbows, she shook her head from side to side. She would never be able to face the Russo family again.

CRBOCRBOCRBO

Angie Russo heard the doorbell ring and went to answer it. She was surprised to see Benny at her door, so early on a Sunday morning.

249

"Come in, come in!" she repeated several times, before he stepped inside. She turned to call her husband, "Salvatore! Mr. Nuzzo is here."

Mr. Russo came over to Benny who was standing in the front hall and reached to shake his hand. Benny gave it reluctantly.

"Come, sit down," he pointed to a chair in the room off the hall but Benny remained standing near the door, looking nervous.

"I came to talk to you about your son."

"My son?" Mr. Russo looked puzzled. "About what?"

Benny looked down at the floor and hesitated for a moment.

"My daughter is in the family way and your son is the only boy she ever went out with."

Mr. Russo stood shaking his head, no. "You're wrong! not Vinny," he said. "It can't be!"

Angie screamed, "You're crazy! My son would not do such a thing."

Mr. Russo took Benny by the arm and tried to reason with him, "My son took your daughter to her school dance, but that was a long time ago."

Mrs. Russo yelled louder, "How dare you accuse my son!" Vinnie heard all the commotion and came into the hall. "What's happened?" he asked, unaware it was about him.

His mother went to him and held onto his arm, "He's accusing you of getting Rosemarie pregnant," she said, as her voice rose in anger. Vinnie looked down at the floor; it appeared like he was about to collapse. He put his hands on the sides of his face, then covered his eyes, tried to say something but stuttered badly. He started to sweat, and took out his handkerchief to wipe his face. His face turned red, and he was shaking. He was being accused of something that he knew wasn't his fault.

His father pointed to him and then turned to Benny, "Look at my son! Does he look like he would do such a thing? He took her to the prom, but that was a long time ago."

Benny stared at Vinnie; he had to admit to himself, he didn't look like the sort of guy who would take advantage of a young girl.

"It's not me!" Vinnie managed to say in a quivering voice. "I never went out with her; I never took her to her prom. I went with Joey to a restaurant. We just dropped her off."

Benny looked confused, "What do you mean; you dropped her off, where?"

Vinnie paused, he didn't want to tell on Patrick, but he felt he didn't have a choice; he was being accused of something he didn't do.

"We dropped her off at school; it was Patrick McCann who took her to her prom, not me."

He stared down at the floor; he felt terrible because he promised her brother he would never tell, but here he was breaking that promise. He wished Joey were home taking some of the blame, instead he had to face the lie alone.

Benny stood speechless; he felt foolish standing there, staring at a young man who was overweight, a bit immature, and a son who stood next to his mother trembling like a big baby. Just looking at the boy, he realized he couldn't be the culprit he envisioned. *How could I have been so blind, so stupid to believe it could have been him*, he thought. He had made the biggest fool of himself and saving face with the Russos would now be impossible. He would never be able to face them again. He apologized and backed out the door, turned and went down the porch steps as quickly as he could before any of them could say anything more. His walk back home was the walk of the damned. He walked quickly with his head down. He thought about all the neighbors, how long it would take for the news to travel about his daughter. He made things worse, now the whole neighborhood would know. He felt terrible; what if it wasn't the McCann boy? The father is a policeman and the family could sue for something like their reputation being ruined or lies about their family, and now everyone would know his family business. He wouldn't be able to walk the street in broad daylight. Maybe the father would arrest him for slander; he thought of all that, as he was becoming paranoid. He was his own worst enemy.

He looked over at the McCann house as he approached his front porch. He would not confront that family. What if he was wrong again, he thought. His daughter had left home; maybe people were talking, but without her walking around they couldn't know for sure, now they would all know. Angie Russo was the neighborhood gossip. *Why did I go over there?* He asked himself as he walked up the stairs with a heavy heart, full of regret.

Nora was waiting anxiously for his return. When he entered the hall, she wanted to ask him what happened but the look on his face told her to remain silent. He said nothing and quietly removed his coat and sat in his chair. He didn't turn the radio on, just sat with his eyes closed. The tension in the house was unbearable for Nora. She remained in the kitchen with Sammy who was eating a late breakfast. Maria had gone to lie down in her room. After Sammy finished, she took him with her down to the landlady's.

Mrs. Katz was happy to see them. She took cookies out for the boy, poured Nora coffee and asked, "Now, vot did he do?"

"He went over to the Russo's to blame their son for Rosie's condition, but he came back all quiet and I was afraid to ask anything."

"Vot he has is chutzpah," Mrs. Katz said.

Nora nodded in agreement, "What happened over there, I don't want to know," she said. Mrs. Katz nodded in agreement and changed the subject,

"My son Davie, he vants to go over to Europe as the news man. He vrites for the paper and now they vant to send him vit the Army. Vit two big kids he has, he vonts to go? Such a mentsh, my son. He start to tell the kids about their Jewish blood. I ask you? Vot for? Too late he does it."

Nora smiled, "It's never too late in times like these. Who

knows how long this war will last."

Mrs. Katz shook her head up and down in agreement.

"Mine son, Now! he vants to be Jewish. He hears all the news about Hitler and vot he is doing vit the Jews, chasing them out of Germany, now he vants to go over there. I'm afraid he vill soon go."

Nora thanked her for the coffee and Mrs. Katz handed Sammy a few more cookies before they went back upstairs.

It was time to start supper, and Nora looked into the front room to see what Benny was doing. He was sleeping in his chair with the radio on and Maria had just come out of the bedroom. She seemed a little disorientated and not too steady on her feet.

"Are you alright Ma?" Nora asked.

Maria nodded yes. "I gonna sita here," she said, as she slid into a chair at the table.

She didn't look too well and Nora was concerned. Nora went into the front room with Sammy; it was time for the Henry Aldridge radio program that he loved every Sunday evening. Benny was asleep in his chair. It was getting late and she hadn't started supper yet, so she hurried to put on the program and return to the kitchen to prepare the meal. Since Joey and Rosemarie left, and Maria wasn't feeling like she cared to eat, the family was having Sunday supper later. Benny seldom came to the table to eat with them; he usually preferred to take his gallon of wine and his plate into the dining room with the excuse of wanting to hear the news on the console radio in the front room. He never had much to say anymore, and Nora felt like her family was falling apart. Every night brought a death-like atmosphere to the home when he was there. He made grunting noises to whatever questions Maria might ask until she stopped asking him anything. Nora kept her distance from him, but Maria had less patience with his inability to be civil to them.

Sammy had the radio turned up. It woke Benny up. He got out of his chair with great effort and went into the kitchen to turn on the small radio on the shelf above the sink to hear the evening news, but the small radio had too much static so he returned to the console. The sounds from the radio in the kitchen interfered, so he asked Nora to turn it off, and without a word to Sammy changed the program to the news.

"No!" Sammy cried. Benny ignored his plea.

Nora walked in and looked at him with disgust. "Why did you shut it off? You could turn it down; he's listening to his favorite program." She bent down to Sammy, who was crying, to comfort him and she turned his program back on, lowering the sound. "Sit closer," she said, as she patted him on the head. When she returned to the kitchen Benny followed and picked up the gallon of wine from the pantry floor. Maria put her face into her hands and lines around Nora's mouth began to appear as they both feared him drinking before they had started supper. Nora knew it would be one of those nights she dreaded. After she put the pot of soup on, she handed him the latest letter from Joey, it had come the day before. He took it, looked at it and handed it back to her.

"Why are you handing me this? You know I can't read his writing. You have to read it," he said angrily.

She unfolded the pages. "Don't read it now," he said.
"I wanna hear the news." He brushed her hand away and knocked the letter out of her hand. She picked it up and gave him a look that showed how hurt she was, but he never noticed. He never looked at her; he avoided looking at any of them. He sat drinking his wine and giving his attention to the news on the kitchen radio. He was seated at the kitchen table and made no move to go to the dining room, so when the soup was ready and the bread was sliced, Maria filled two bowls and took them into the dining room for her and Sammy. They kept the boy away from him to avoid him finding fault with how he sat at the table or drank his milk. Lately, the boy couldn't do anything right. Maria wanted to spare another night of her grandson crying at the table. The stress of it all was taking its toll on her. She alternated between feeling sorry for the boy

and attacking him herself. Benny ate alone as Nora joined them in the dining room. He hardly noticed or cared that they seldom sat at the same table with him. Lately, much of their communication was nonverbal. Both women were afraid of saying anything that might antagonize him further. When Nora finished half of what was in her bowl, she busied herself with cleaning up. Lately, she never felt like eating as much as she normally would. Her stomach was often upset. She passed him in the kitchen as she went to the sink. She could see that he was getting drunk. He seemed to get that way on less wine. She knew it was going to be another one of those long nights where he would rant and cry and talk to himself. Maria would go to her room and close the door, and Nora would have to take Sammy and find refuge downstairs with Mrs. Katz.

Nora stood at the sink with her back to him. As she washed the pot and bowls she could view him in the mirror above the sink. He sat hunched, his head almost in his bowl of soup which he hardly touched. His face had haggard lines, deep lines that formed down the sides of his face. His lips moved like he was speaking but not a sound emanated from them. He was speaking silent words, words of anguish only he could hear. He banged his fist hard on the tabletop, downed another jelly glass of wine and banged the table again. Nora refused to watch anymore of his antics and left him alone. She went to the front room where Sammy had returned to his spot on the carpet in front of the radio. Another one of his favorite programs was about to begin. Maria had gone to her room leaving her bowl and spoon on the table. Nora left them there; she wasn't about to go back to the kitchen just yet.

She sat in her chair with Sammy at her feet and watched him smiling as the sounds of the Abbott and Costello program started, when she noticed Maria come out of her room and pick up her bowl from the dining room table to carry it into the kitchen. She was worried about another argument that might provoke her husband, but it was his Mama, and it had been quite a while since Maria had scolded him about anything.

255

Maria stared at him with a look of sternness in her features; she was disgusted with his behavior.

"You gonna sita there all night?" she scolded.

"Go, go on," he yelled, waving his hand for her to leave the room, to leave him alone. "Leave me in peace!" he shouted.

"Peace? You wanta peace Benny?" she shouted back, anger rising in her voice. "Peace you getta ina the grave, not ina life. Ina life there isa no peace." She paused to watch him, and then she bent down close to his ear, "Like a goat, you pusha Rosie away," she said.

"What are you talking about?" he shouted back at her as he poured another glass of wine.

"You know what I talk," she said. She was standing holding on to the back of the chair to steady her hands as they began to shake. She started shaking lately for no reason. Nora noticed and planned to call the doctor to visit her. The shouting brought Nora back to the kitchen. She took Maria and led her back to her room. "You better lie down Ma, it's not good for you to upset yourself. Tomorrow, I'll call Doctor Scola to come and see you. I don't like how your hands have been shaking lately."

Just as they reached the bedroom door, Benny appeared behind them, and now Nora noticed how very drunk he was. He wasn't steady on his feet. Ever since he had gone to visit the Russos that morning, he looked miserable. He was drinking more lately. He started to yell at Maria.

"You know who's to blame? Your baby, that's who. He never shows his face around here no more since she left. He knows where she is. Ask your baby, ask Nicky!"

Nora helped Maria to her bed and turned to Benny who stood leaning in the doorway, a full glass of wine in his right hand. "Nicky doesn't know where Rosie is," she said.

"He knows, he knows, that's why he never comes around here anymore. Do you think I'm stupid?"

"He comes to see us when you're not home, why should he come and have to listen to you," she answered back. She surprised herself, raising her voice to him. It wasn't like her, but her visits to Mrs. Katz helped her to assert herself more.

She remembered her landlady's words, 'Vats he going to do? hit you? You call the police, or verse, you call me. I tell him I kick him out of mine house. That's vot I will vel tell him.'

"He knows, he knows," Benny shouted. "I know what's going on. Do you hear me! You think I don't know what's going on? He's afraid to show his face around here!"

Maria yelled back,"Stopa, you yella so loud, the dead, they hear you."

He went back into the kitchen to fill his glass with more wine. He carried the full glass into the front room. Nora was seated back in her chair near Sammy; his attention was still on the radio program. Benny stood weaving back and forth in the middle of the room. He directed his attention towards them. He stared at the boy, and Nora watched his expression change. His brow line came down, almost touching his eyelids, his mouth turned into an ugly twisted grimace. Nora could plainly see he was in a fighting mood. She pretended to be listening to the radio but was watching him out of the corner of her eye as he walked over to where Sammy lay on the carpet, facing the radio with his chin resting on his hands; he was oblivious to his father standing above him. He was engrossed in Abbott and Costello and laughing.

"What's he gonna do? Huh?" Benny asked.

Nora ignored him.

"What's he gonna do?" He asked again, a little louder. "He can't add two and two; you women baby him. He'll never be a man." His voice was loud as he cried a drunken cry. "Who wished this on me? What do I have left? For all my sacrifices, what do I have to show for it all?"

Nora remained silent; she twisted the handkerchief in her hand over and over until it resembled a piece of rope.

"I work and work and for what?" He cried, "I dig ditches to put roads in for the government to take away my son! I work

for a daughter who brings me disgrace! I work to feed him!"
He points to Sammy with the hand that held the glass of wine,
spilling some of the wine onto the boy's head, causing him to
look up at his father. "I work to feed him!" he shouts. "He was
to be my walking cane in my old age, to take care of me! How
can he grow up to take care of me? He'll never be able to take
care of himself! I've been cursed!"

Sammy crouched down, looking up fearfully at his father.
Nora rose from her chair and tried to take Benny's arm to steer
him away from their son. He jerked away from her grip and
stumbled to the window. He paced back and forth ranting
incoherently. Looking out the window, he now had a clear
view of the McCann's house and that deflected his tirade away
from his son. His voice was so loud that Maria appeared at the
bedroom door, shook her head sadly and went back in and
closed the door behind her with a loud bang.

"Over there!" he shouted, pointing his finger and pulling
on the curtains. "That's where it happened; she was always
over there! She was never in this house where she belonged."
He turned to Nora, "It's your fault! You didn't watch her!"
Pointing to Sammy, who had run to his mother and was hiding
behind her, he said, "You spend all your time watching him!"
Turning back towards the window, he cried, "What kind of
house do they run over there? A policeman's son, who
disgraced my daughter? I obey the law for a policeman's son to
disgrace my daughter? He's busy arresting innocent people on
the streets when he should have had his eyes open in his own
house."

A look of horror came over Nora's face. He was accusing
wildly, first the Russos and now the McCanns. "If you go over
there, you're going to make a fool of yourself," she said.

"I'm already a fool for not watching the comings and
goings in my own house. I'm the laughing fool of the
neighborhood. They all know, and they're all laughing. I can
hear them laughing."

"Nobody's laughing, it's all in your head Benny", she said.

"It's the wine that's laughing in your head." She started to back away from him as he stood by the window looking out between the curtains and continued to rant.

Downstairs, Mrs. Katz could hear all the shouting upstairs. She knew it would only be a matter of time before she would hear Nora and Sammy's footsteps on the stairs. She went into her pantry to retrieve the cookie jar.

CHAPTER 32

The Western Union boy rode his bike down Congress Street. It was a windy day. Clouds had formed all morning shutting out the sun. It looked like rain was in the making. Katie McCann raised her window shades higher to let the late morning light in. Grace Peterson came out to pick up the morning newspaper. A strong Chicago wind was blowing, the kind of autumn breeze that was still warm enough to allow the neighbors to open their windows one more time and air out their homes before the winter chill set in. The second week of October 1942, brought changeable weather. One day there were touches of the departing summer and the next day the approaching specks of winter. This day, a quiet Monday, men had left for work, children had gone to school and women were in the factories doing their part for the war effort or home tending to household chores. Windows were open a few inches here and there as the bottom of curtains fluttered from the breeze.

Katie was the first to notice the messenger boy lean his bike against the porch stairs at Mrs. Katz's and go to the door and ring the bell. She watched him enter, closing the door behind him. It was Mrs. Katz who heard the piercing scream coming from upstairs. She lost little time in rushing up the stairs. The Western Union boy was standing just inside the hall door. Nora had sunk to the floor, a telegram crumbled in her hand. After that first scream, her mouth was screaming without sound. Maria was trying to rush to her from the bedroom just as Mrs. Katz reached her. The messenger boy kept saying he was sorry, but no one heard him. He slowly backed away and went back down the stairs. He never got used to delivering bad news. He thought they didn't pay him enough to go through it over and over again. He thought he should have left before the lady opened the telegram, but sometimes he stayed. If it had been his mother alone with such news, he would want someone with her.

Grace Peterson had the newspaper under her arm when she spotted the mailman coming down the walk. She was waiting for him when she heard the scream from the open window of the Nuzzo's flat. She watched the messenger boy peddle away on his bike. She went down to the sidewalk. Katie was looking out her closed window. She wasn't able to hear anything but when she saw Grace walk to the curb, looking up at the Nuzzo's open window, she went out to Grace.

"Oh my God!" Grace said, "I heard a scream, I hope it isn't about their son."

Katie said, "Maybe we should go over there. I think the women are alone."

Grace agreed. The two women crossed the street. "Maybe he's wounded." Katie said aloud, hoping for any declaration other than -- Killed in Action.

Twyla was coming out of her front door as Grace and Katie crossed the street.

"Did you see the Western Union boy who just left?" Katie asked Twyla. Twyla nodded yes.

"If it's Joey, it will all be too much for this family," she said.

The three women climbed the stairs to the Nuzzo's flat. The door was open, so they walked in. Twyla rushed to Nora who was sitting on the floor in Mrs. Katz's arms. Maria was lying on the couch crying out words in Italian. Mrs. Katz motioned for the other women to go to Maria. Grace went to Maria; she could see the old woman was in a bad way.

"Mrs. Nuzzo I'll get you a glass of water," she said, as she gave her one of the pillows from the couch and placed it under her head. She went into the kitchen and helped herself to glasses from the pantry.

Twyla helped Mrs. Katz pick up Nora and sit her in a chair near the fireplace. Then she went over to the window and closed it the six inches it had been opened. The two Nuzzo women were shivering badly. Katie went over to the fireplace and checked to see if she could turn the gas fireplace on. Mrs. Katz, still hugging Nora, said, "The old burner, she doesn't vork anymore."

"Can we get some blankets for them?" Katie asked. Mrs. Katz motioned towards Maria's room. As Katie went to take blankets off of the beds, Grace came in with two glasses of water for the women. Twyla pulled in two chairs from the dining room. Nora was slumped in Benny's soft chair, crying into her hands. Mrs. Katz and the neighbors felt helpless in the presence of her pain. The crumbled telegram was still on the floor where Nora had dropped it. Twyla picked it up and her eye went to- Killed in the service of his Country, - It was all she needed to see. She placed it on the dining room table and motioned to the others with her lips but no sound that Joey was gone.

"We have to get news to someone in the family," Twyla said.

Mrs. Katz left Nora's side to retrieve the little book Nora kept on the shelf in the telephone table. She scanned the pages and came upon the number of Rose Scali. She dialed the operator and gave the number of the bakery.

Rose wiped her hands on her apron and picked up the receiver. "Hello!" she said. Mrs. Katz handed the phone to Twyla.

"Are you Rose, Nora's sister?"

"Yes, Yes," she recognized Twyla's southern accent."What's wrong? Is it my sister?"

"No, it's about your nephew. They received a telegram and your sister and her mother-in-law are in a bad way." Rose didn't wait for any more information, "I'll leave right away," she said.

Twyla went back to the front room. "Her sister Rose will be here as soon as she can," she informed them. Nora was drinking some water, her hand shaking, she handed the glass back to Grace. "Thank you, thank you," she said.

"Can we get you anything else?" Katie said.

Nora shook her head no and thanked them again. "Will you stay until my sister gets here?" she said, and asked them to look for her brother-in-law's work number. "We never call Benny at work, he's never in the same place and there's different numbers for the work trailers," she informed them. She tried to compose herself as she looked over at Maria.

Maria lay with her eyes closed. "I have to call the doctor again," Nora said. "She hasn't been well lately."

Nora was still crying softly as she spoke. "Nicky will have to break this to my husband," she said, and then she started to cry even more; she couldn't stop.

Katie said, "I'm so sorry Mrs. Nuzzo, we all are." The other women nodded in agreement.

"Her sister, soon she vel be here, if she caught the streetcar right avay. On Paulina, near Marshfield Avenue the shop is," Mrs. Katz said.

Grace went to the window, looking towards the corner, she kept checking until she saw Rose turn the corner and hurry down the walk.

"Your sister is coming Mrs. Nuzzo. I think we can go now," she said as she looked at Katie. "Is it alright Mrs. Nuzzo?"

"Yes, yes, thank you, thank you," Nora answered.

The women reached the porch just when Rose was about to climb the stairs.

"It's my nephew, isn't it?" Rose asked, even though she knew the answer. Her lower lip trembled. Grace and Katie nodded yes, words were too painful to express. Rose said, "Oh no!" as she raced up the porch steps. Crossing the street, nether of the women spoke. All Katie could do was think about her two sons with apprehension. Grace thought of how lucky she was not to have had a son to worry about.

Upstairs in the Nuzzo's flat, there was much to do. Rose was good in a crisis, any crises that didn't include something that would shame or disgrace one. She embraced Nora and even Maria, she cried with both of them and then she made a call to Delta Star, the plant where Nicky worked. She made coffee, she called the doctor for Maria, and she went into the kitchen to prepare something, anything, to eat. Even if no one would eat, food was the answer to any crises for Rose. Twyla left with the promise to keep Sammy at her place when he came home from school with Bobby. She would watch for them, she would feed Sammy his supper and keep him with her until they called for him. Sylvia Katz stayed to help Rose. They would all wait until Nicky arrived. The flag with the blue star in the window would soon turn to gold.

The doctor had come to treat Maria and just after he left, Nicky arrived. He parked his '39 Ford coupe at the curb and ran up the stairs two at a time. When Nora saw him she broke down again. All Nicky could do after he read the telegram was hold Nora and cry with her. When he arrived, Sylvia thought it was time for her to go back downstairs. She didn't want to be there when Benny came home.

"Where's Ma?" Nicky asked. Nora pointed to the bedroom. He entered Maria's room and bent down next to her. "How are you Ma?" he asked, knowing she was in a bad way. She opened her eyes and when she saw it was him, she cried in Italian, over and over, "Madonna mia! Madonna mia! Guiseppe morta!"

He kissed her and looked at her with sadness; he worried about what this would do to her. He knew she wasn't well. The doctor had visited her a couple of times the past month. Mrs. Katz told him they tried to keep Maria from knowing, but she knew what a telegram looked like even though she couldn't read English. With Nora going to pieces in front of her, she didn't need to know what was written on it, she knew something terrible happened to her grandson.

Nicky tried to talk to her, to comfort her, but she was beyond being consoled. He was mourning the death of his beloved nephew along with them. When he came out of Maria's room, he went to Nora.

"We have to let Benny know; I'll drive downtown to look

264

for him. Do you know what worksite he's at?"

Nora handed him the little book of phone numbers, it had a couple of numbers Benny gave her only to be used in case of an emergency. Nicky finally reached the correct number for Benny. He told the foreman on the jobsite that there was a death in the family and not to say anything to Benny that he was coming to take him home. When he pulled up in front of the construction trailer, the foreman sent for Benny. Nicky watched with apprehension as a very tired-looking Benny walked up to him and he dreaded telling him. Benny thought something had happened to Maria.

"It's Ma, isn't it?" Benny asked. He could see how distraught Nicky appeared. Nicky didn't answer, but led Benny to the car; it was after they were in the car that Nicky turned to his brother and had difficulty speaking.

"It's not Ma," he said in a shaky voice as he labored to get the words out. "A telegram came. Joey was killed somewhere overseas." *My God! I thought he was still in the states,* Nicky thought. He stared straight ahead as he drove, afraid to look at Benny after he said the terrible words, but not a sound came from Benny. When he turned to look at him, he could see he was in shock. "Ben, did you hear what I just said," he asked. The wail that came from Benny was almost a whisper. He had a vacant stare on his face. On the ride home, Benny never uttered a word.

When they returned home, Benny walked in asking for the telegram, like he wouldn't believe it until he read it for himself. Rose handed it to him. He stood just inside the dining room and held the piece of paper in his hand. Nora had come to his side and he could see her face, how badly she was crying and still he held the telegram tightly in his fist, crumbling it more than it had been, still not reading it. It was as if it was all a lie if he didn't see the words for himself, like it never happened. Nora had never seen him like this, head down, eyes closed, not moving, not uttering a sound, just clutching the piece of paper that would change his whole world once he read it. But for those few moments as he stood there, he could stop time, regardless of what Nicky said, or how Nora looked, or why Rose was there looking at him with a kindness she never displayed for him before. In his mind all that didn't matter as long as he kept the terrible words hidden in his fist, a fist that squeezed the paper into a wrinkled ball. Nicky grabbed the ball of paper out of his hand and began to smooth it out. He handed it to Benny, but he wouldn't take it, his hands hung by his side, his eyes remained closed, his face down so low his chin touched his chest, so Nicky began to read…

"We regret to inform you that 2nd Lieutenant Joseph Francis Nuzzo was killed in the service of his Country on October 6th, 1942." Benny grabbed the telegram from Nicky before he could read another word and went into his room, closing the door behind him. Nora went to rush after him, but Nicky stopped her. "Leave him alone Nora, he wants to be alone." They stood together in the dining room, not sure of what to do.

"Joey was trained in a B-17," Nicky said. "They're supposed to be safer planes, not like the B-24's; those are called flying coffins, they have a bad casualty record. I just read about that in the papers."

He wasn't sure of what he should say, and he was sorry he mentioned it to them when they heard a piercing low moan coming from Benny's room, the sound of a man in total agony. Nicky asked Rose to check on Maria and then took Nora aside. When Rose was out of the room, he put his arm around her and led her to a chair in the kitchen.

"Nora, I'm going to have to tell Rosie."

Nora looked surprised, "You know where she is?"

"Yes, she came to me and I had to help her, but you can't ever tell Benny, promise me Nora."

She shook her head yes as she continued to cry, wiping her eyes with a very damp hanky. "Don't worry," she assured him, "I will never tell him anything."

"She's staying with Lillian, a friend of mine. You

remember Lillian?" Nora nodded yes. "I'm going over there now. I won't tell her anything until Lillian's home from work Nora, because Rosie's only 4 weeks away from having the baby, and I have to tell her in person, do you understand Nora? She needs you; you will have to find a way to see her." Nora nodded yes. The tears running down her cheeks were now bittersweet. She had lost her son, but she found her daughter.

 come come come

Nicky waited until they were finished with the supper Rosemarie prepared. She didn't think anything of her uncle's visit. He often came to Lillian's for supper. When they were settled in the front room with Rosemarie sitting on the couch, he went to sit next to her. He looked at Lillian across the room. He wished he had a chance to tell her first, but there wasn't time to be alone with her when he arrived. He took Rosemarie's hand and she looked surprised.

"Rosie! I have some bad news, now please try to remain calm; you know if you don't hold yourself together, it won't be good for the baby."

"It's Granny isn't it?"

"No, it's not Grandma, it's Joey."

"Oh my God! He's wounded?" She tightened her grip on his hand as he held her now tightly in his arms. He could feel her heart racing.

Nicky cleared his throat, as it started to swell, "No, Rosie, he was killed. I think his plane went down; the telegram came today."

She stared wide-eyed and then slumped into his arms. He yelled for Lillian to get some water. She sat for a moment across from them not sure if what she heard is what he really said. She ran into the kitchen and came back with a wet cloth and applied it to Rosemarie's face. She had fainted and the cold water on her face revived her. She sobbed into Nicky's chest as Lillian held her hand and stroked her arm. She tried to hold back her own tears but seeing Rosemarie going through such agony, caused her to break down. All three of them hugged each other and cried. There wasn't anything else they could do. Nicky thought it was the cruelest thing he ever had to do; to him it was worse than telling Benny, mostly because of how close Rosemarie and Joey had become, and because of what his brother put his niece through, he didn't have much sympathy for him. When he thought she was going to be all right, and Lillian could handle the situation, he said to Lillian,

"I have to return to my brother's place, I'm worried about my mother."

"I understand Uncle Nicky," Rosemarie said, "I'm worried about Granny too." She was still sobbing. "Will you go over and tell Francie, she has to know." She thought of Joey's girl even in her sorrow.

"Don't worry, I will," he said. He dreaded having to tell Francie. "I'll be at my brother's if you need me Lill, just call me over there."

When he arrived at Benny's, Nora came to the door, she whispered to him, "Benny's in a bad way, please don't say anything to him. I can't talk to him, he's so angry, and he shouts at us, and he's drinking again, and accusing everyone of everything. He blames Roosevelt for Joey. He blames you for Rosie. I don't know if you should be here now."

"It's Ma I'm worried about, not him Nora, so don't worry, I can handle him."

Nicky walked past her going toward Maria's room and when Benny saw him, he lost no time following after him. Before Nicky could reach the door to Maria's room, Benny stopped him. He grabbed his arm forcing Nicky to turn and face him. Nicky pulled away from him.

"What the hell is wrong with you?" he said, he could see he had been drinking more than usual. Benny's anger erupted.

"I lost my son! I lost my son, he was MY son, he wasn't your son, what do you know about losing a son?"

Nicky couldn't believe what he was saying. "Are you

crazy!" he shouted back, "You don't think I cared about Joey, I loved him too, he wasn't my son, but he was my nephew. You're not the only one suffering here, what about your wife and Ma? Your son, your son, he was Nora's son too!"

Benny yelled back, "That's what happens when a son serves his Country. What do you serve? They didn't send you away to die, and for nothing, he died for nothing, he just got there, was he even fighting yet?" He was crying and Nicky could see he was very drunk. He tried to put his arm around him to calm him down and get him to sit in his chair, but Benny would have none of his sympathy. He angrily pushed him away, "Save your sympathy for the puttana you made out of your niece," he said.

"What are you saying?" Nicky shouted, not surprised at Benny's accusation.

"You know what I'm saying, you know," he repeated. "You can stand there and lie to me? You don't know what I'm talking about? I'm talking about Rosie! You know where she is!" he yelled.

Nicky tried to answer, but he cut him off and continued the confrontation. His anger flowing out freely now, directed at his brother. "All the time, you coming here, encouraging her to go out with boys when I say no! Sneaking around here giving her lessons on how to disobey her father. You! Who have amounted to nothing, even the army don't want you!"

"Wait a minute!" Nicky shouted back. "It's not my fault, I'm not classified yet. I'm almost forty-years-old. When they need me I'll go. I'd go in a minute, don't make me out a coward, and Rosie? She's nineteen; she has a mind of her own. She's not a piece of furniture you place in the corner of the room, and stays there to suit you!"

They were both shouting at each other; their dislike of each other took precedence over their mother lying in the next room hearing their angry voices. Any concern they had for her was lost in their confrontation as Nora stood nearby pleading for them to stop. Nicky turned away from Benny and finally walked into his mother's room and shut the door.

Nora went to Sammy's room. In his room she could be alone. The boy was spending more time next door or downstairs with the landlady. She sat on his bed, the bed he shared with Joey and cried until she was exhausted. She felt very weak as she lay down on her side and sobbed until she couldn't cry any more. She looked around the room, the room her two sons shared. She could still smell the after-shave Joey used; it seemed to hang in the air of his room. She felt closer to him in that room, as if he were still there. She wished her sister Rose was with her, but Rose was not one she could confide her troubles to. She was bossy and opinionated. Finally, she dried her tears and thought about her husband; he was getting worse, and she thought of what the loss of their son would do to him, and he was drinking more lately.

She started to feel anger; she knew he could never keep her from seeing their daughter. The anger fueled the courage to do what she had to do in spite of Benny. She wouldn't cater to him like she had in the past. She remembered Mrs. Katz words, 'So vat can he do?' She felt a giant weight lift off her shoulders. She lay there making plans to see Rosemarie. It was a comfort to think of only that now. She stood up to comb her hair. It was past Sammy's bedtime. She would go next door to get him. It would fall to her to tell the boy about his brother.

CHAPTER 33

It was after midnight when Nicky's phone rang; he was sitting in the kitchen, having a beer. He hadn't slept much since the day he received the news of Joey, and he was still upset with his brother. He walked over to the phone, expecting it to be Nora, but it was Lillian.

"Nicky, you've got to come," she said. "I think Rosemarie's in labor."

"Already? I thought she had another month. I'll leave right now."

As he reached for his car keys, he thought about the baby coming too early. He worried about that when he had to tell her about Joey. He was glad he hadn't gone to bed. On the drive over to Lillian's, he thought about how he was going to notify Nora. He couldn't call her at that hour, not with Benny there. He would have to wait until Benny left for work in the morning.

☙☙☙☙☙☙

Nicky and Lillian helped her walk into the lobby of the hospital. The pains were coming closer together and more intense. They walked her over to a chair and sat her down.

"I'll go up to the desk; I'll tell them whatever you want me to tell them," he reassured her. "What should I tell them?"

"Please Uncle Nicky, give them the name Rose Clark."

He gave her a quizzical look. "You should give your right name."

"I will after the baby comes," she said. "When they ask me for the baby's name, I'll give the right name. I was too embarrassed to give it when I first came here."

He went up to the registration desk. He wasn't sure what they would ask him. The nurse looked up at him.

"Can I help you?" she asked. He pointed to Rosemarie

271

sitting across the room slightly bent over in pain.

"It's my niece, Rose Clark; I think she's ready to have her baby."

"Is her husband here?" she looked past Nicky over to the two women across the room. "Oh I guess he's in the service. Most of the women come in here alone or with one family member," she said it as an afterthought as she shuffled papers to find the folder with the name Rose Clark.

Looking up at him, she asked, "Is her mother here? So many women come in here with their mothers. It's a sad time to be having a baby for these young women, especially with their men away at war." She handed him a form for Rosemarie to fill out; it had a line for the mother's name and father's name. He walked back to Rosemarie.

"Rosie, you might as well fill out the correct names."

On the line for Mother she wrote in parentheses, Rose Clark and then Rosemarie Nuzzo. For the father's name she wrote Patrick Thomas McCann. A nurse came with a wheelchair and helped her into it. Nick and Lillian followed them to the elevator. At the elevator door the nurse informed them that only the husband or mother was allowed in the upstairs waiting room. They would have to wait there and the nurse at the desk would notify them after the baby came.

The last thing Nicky said to her before the elevator doors closed was, "We'll be waiting Rosie."

"It could take hours, maybe even into all day tomorrow," the nurse said. "Maybe you should go home. Call the hospital and they will let you know how she's doing."

Nicky looked at Lillian, "What do you want to do? I can call work and take the day off. You might as well stay home too, whatever you decide," he said.

Lillian took his arm, "I'm staying home Nicky, I've been with Rosemarie all these months and I don't mind waiting." Nicky smiled and put his arm around her as they walked towards the entrance. "Thanks Lill," he said, we'll wait together."

The nurse helped Rosemarie into bed. The room was full of women. The room was large; the nurse called it the labor ward. Rosemarie looked around at all the beds filled with women in labor. In the bed next to her was a slightly older woman. When Rosemarie cried out in pain, the woman asked if she could help. "I'm Mary McLoughlin," she said. "Is this your first baby?"

"Yes," Rosemarie answered. Her face showed the increased pain she was beginning to experience.

"I thought so, you look rather young. This will be my fifth; I hope it's a boy, for my husband you know, he tells me he is tired of being surrounded by women. We have four girls, the oldest is twelve, and I think she'll make a good babysitter."

Rosemarie smiled and nodded. She didn't feel like talking. She was in too much pain. The women rattled on…

"Is your husband in the father's room, or is he away at war?"

"He's in the Navy," she barely finished the last word; the pains were coming closer together.

When she cried out "Ma!" The woman got up and went over to her and took her hand. "What do you hope for, a girl or boy?"

"I don't know, I never thought much about it, only that it's born healthy."

"We all wish for a healthy baby don't we?" the women said. She held Rosemarie's hand. "Now, when you feel the next pain coming don't tighten up, try to relax and the pain won't feel as bad. Lord knows, I've been through this many times, I should know." She laughed as she said it.

Rosemarie nodded, yes. She was trying to do as the kind woman said, but all she could think of was Sammy and the fears she had for her baby. Deep down she worried. She didn't understand Sammy's problem, but she knew what some of the neighbors thought about his condition. "Please God," she prayed silently, "Please don't let it be like Sammy." It was her greatest fear.

"It will be healthy, won't it," she asked the nurse. "Why wouldn't it be?" the nurse said, reassuring her. But she remembered hearing her mother and Mrs. Katz talking about Sammy and how Sammy was the way he was because he didn't get enough air, something like that. She was young then and never asked her mother to explain it to her. She was afraid to know the details. Now lying in pain, it was all she could think of. She remembered when she was around twelve and Sammy was four, they realized he was different, much slower than her or Joey at that age. He wasn't talking well, and he walked much later than most children his age. She remembered her grandmother blaming it on a curse, a punishment for her father, because of her father's treatment of his brother, and the way her two sons never got along. Her mother said she didn't believe in such things, and that Maria was from the old country where uneducated people made up stuff when they didn't understand. Her other grandmother, Anna Scali was a young women when she came to America. Nora was a generation removed from all the superstition Maria believed in. Anna died when Nora was a young girl. Rosemarie wished she could have known her. In between pains she was thinking of all that, trying to keep her mind off of the pain and frightened of not having a healthy baby.

She was happy that Mary, the kind lady, was there for her. The room was full of young women, but Mary seemed to be older than most of them and a great comfort to her. She wanted her mother, but if she couldn't have Nora, Mary was there to comfort her.

In the delivery room, she was afraid. She was given something to make her sleepy. After awhile, she started to drift into being half asleep. She could hear the doctor and nurses around her talking, but they sounded like they were far away. She thought she was in a dream. She thought she saw her grandmother float by her, shaking her finger at her. Was she trying to tell her she was going to be punished for what she had done? She didn't believe in such stuff. She wasn't sure how long she was dreaming. She heard a voice call, Mrs. McCann! Mrs. McCann! That's funny, she thought, Mrs. McCann lives across the street, why are they calling her? She thought she was back home on Congress Street, and that is why she heard someone call Mrs. McCann. She felt like she was drifting or floating somewhere. The voices became louder. "Mrs. McCann! Mrs. McCann!" Now she heard it much clearer, it sounded like the voice was in her ear. She opened her eyes and realized she wasn't dreaming. The young nurse with the nice smile that encouraged her in the delivery room called her Mrs. McCann, how strange, she thought. Her mind was still foggy. She was trying to wake up.

"Your baby's here," the nurse said.

Rosemarie was tired; she was trying to wake up completely. *Did I imagine I heard her say my baby's here*, she thought. The next time she heard her, she was fully awake.

"Your baby's here, it's a boy."

"I have a boy?"

"I'm sure you want to see him, but he is rather small, he was a little premature."

"Is he ok? I mean, is he healthy?"

"Of course he is, didn't you hear him cry? He has a great set of lungs."

"No," she said, but she was happy it was a boy. She was sure Patrick wasn't angry with her for getting pregnant after he received her letter, but she knew he worried about her. When he finds out he has a son, she thought, she was sure he would be happy about the baby. She was relieved it was over.

"Can I see him?" she asked, as she watched the nurse move about the room getting her ready to bring her back to another room. "When can I see him?" Rosemarie wondered if anything was wrong.

"He is just too small, and we had to bring him to the nursery and put him in an incubator. It's just a precaution; he will be fine," the nurse informed her, but Rosemarie didn't believe her and started to cry. The kind nurse came over to her,

"Honey, you can see him as soon as we get you settled in your room and you're able to get into a wheelchair; then we'll take you to the nursery." As another nurse was getting her ready to be wheeled from the delivery room, she asked again, "Is my baby alright; is he healthy? When can I hold him?"

"Oh honey, he's too small to hold. He has to stay in the incubator until he gains weight. He was less than five pounds," the nurse said, as she pushed Rosemarie to her room.

When Nicky and Lillian called the hospital around 8:00 a.m., they were told the baby had not come yet. They sat around the apartment until 10:00 and then Nicky said, "I'm not waiting; I'm going to call again." He picked up the phone and dialed the operator. After the call went through, he said, "Hello, I'm calling about my niece, Rosemarie Nuzzo, has her baby come yet?" The smile on his face told Lillian that the baby was born. He said thank you and placed the receiver back on the phone and hugged her. "I have a great nephew," he said. "He was just born at 9:33 a.m. Lill, I'm going over to see Nora. No use waiting, I'm not going to call first. Sammy's in school and I can take her the hospital. They said visiting hours are from 2:00 to 4:00 this afternoon." Lill nodded yes, handed him his coat and hat. He hugged her and thanked her for all she had done. "I'll call you later," he promised.

She walked him out to the porch below.

"I'll be home all day, no use going to work when I called in sick; call and let me know how Rosemarie and the baby are doing."

"I'll come over after I take Nora back home after visiting hours are over."

He turned back to her and went up to the stair she was standing on and kissed her. She watched him go to his car. She thought of how many times in the past he had said that, and he didn't show up or was later than he said he would be. Something in the way he kissed her told her he would be back.

Nora wasn't surprised to see Nicky at her door this particular day; she knew how worried he was about his mother.

She was a little surprised that he wasn't at work. She would have expected him after work but figured he didn't want to run into Benny again.

"Come in Nicky," she said. She was happy to see him; she dreaded being alone all day with her grief. He could see she had been crying again, maybe all night, she looked terrible. He knew Maria wouldn't be much comfort to her, not in the condition she was in. He looked for Maria.

"Is Ma still in bed?" he asked. Nora nodded yes. He followed her into the kitchen.

"I have the coffee on, would you like a cup?" she tried to smile, but she looked so sad.

He thought of how happy the news he was about to give her should make her, but wasn't sure of how she would feel about the baby being born out of wedlock.

"Nora I have some good news."

"You're going to marry that girlfriend?"

He laughed, "No, no, nothing like that. Rosie had the baby this morning at 9:33 a.m.; it's a boy."

Nora started to cry; all she could say was "Oh, thank you, Jesus. Is Rosie and the baby ok?"

"They're fine; he came almost a month early, but the nurse told me it all went well. We took her to the hospital at 1:00 a.m. and she said the baby weighed less than five pounds. He came too early, and they have him in an incubator."

Her tears were a mixture of sadness and joy. He felt sorry for her. She had always been kind to him; she never judged him, and he loved her for that. He sat drinking the coffee she offered him, and thinking, if he could ever do anything to make her life easier, he knew he would do just that.

"I'll go in to see Ma now," he said, "get ready to go to the hospital around 1:30, visiting hours are from two to four. I'll drive you there."

She rose up from the table, dabbed at her eyes, and said, "I need to call Twyla to take Sammy after school; he gets home a few minutes after 3 and I'll let Mrs. Katz know so she can come up and check on Ma, but I have to be sure we get home before Benny, you know, sometimes he comes home early."

Nicky went over to her and put his arm around her, "Don't worry about him. So what if he comes home early, you have to stand up for yourself Nora. He'll change when he sees you're not afraid of him. You have to assert yourself more. Ma isn't able to stand up to him and put him in his place anymore, so you have to do it."

She shook her head no, looked at him and said, "I don't know if I can, I want to, but, I don't know."

"What's he gonna do? Hit you?"

"No."

"Then what are you afraid of?"

"He gets so mad and he drinks more."

"So he gets mad. Let him get mad. If he yells and starts to drink, stay away from him. You have to get the upper hand here; after all, Rosie is your daughter. You should feel free to see her."

CЗ∞CЗ∞CЗ∞

Rosemarie was engrossed in what a stocky woman in the next bed was telling her, of her ordeal giving birth to a nine pound baby the day before. She didn't see Nora enter the room until Nora reached for her. "Mommy!" she cried, she hadn't called her that since she was a child. Mother and daughter hugged and cried together.

"I have a little boy, Ma."

Nora kissed her face over and over, "I know, I know," she said.

"You're not mad at me?" Rosemarie looked up at her sobbing, "I'm sorry Ma; I'm so ashamed."

Nora hugged her again, "Let's not talk about that, just think of the baby and that he's healthy."

Rosemarie was afraid to mention Joey. Nora didn't mention anything about the telegram. They both avoided it and tried to talk about the baby.

Nora sat in a chair next to the bed holding her daughter's hand.

"Rosie, are you going to tell me who the baby's father is?"

"Yes Ma, I'll tell you what I named the baby. His name is Joseph Patrick McCann."

Nora fell to her knees as she reached for Rosemarie again, hugging and crying as she thanked her for naming her grandson after her beloved first born.

"Oh, Joey, Joey," she cried, "We lost Joey, we lost him Rosie."

Both of them hugged and cried. The nurse ran over to ask what was wrong. The women in the next bed who knew about Rosemarie's brother said, "She just told her mother she named her baby after her brother; he was killed in the war." The nurse looked on feeling helpless in the face of such a display of both tragedy and joy.

"Excuse me," the nurse said, as she approached them. "Would you like to go to the nursery now, to see your baby again?" Rosemarie nodded yes, and with the nurse and Nora's help, Rosemarie got into the wheel chair. When they reached the nursery window and looked at all the little cribs lined up, to Rosemarie every infant looked the same, but Nora spotted a round little head in an incubator off to the side. It looked familiar; the same shape her children's heads were when they were born, round and well-shaped. "Is that him?" Nora asked.

"Yes," the nurse said. "I'll go in and roll him closer to the window."

When the little incubator was wheeled over, Rosemarie could see how he looked just like Patrick. His features were a tiny version of his father. His hair was only light fuzz. He was just lying there, moving around and not crying as some of the other babies were.

"Oh Ma! Look how cute he is!" Rosemarie said. Nora began to cry, "He's so tiny," was all she could say as her eyes went to the tag on the crib with the name McCann.

"Rosie, why didn't you tell me that you and the McCann boy were seeing each other?"

"I couldn't tell you Ma, I was afraid you would tell Pa."

Nora thought about that, she had to agree, she herself might have told him once, but now she knew she would never tell her husband anything, ever. She stared at her grandson; a smile came over her face as she said, "Rosie, I think I see a little red in his hair."

Rosemarie looked closer through the glass. The light from the room did make the little peach fuzz on his head, as the nurse called it, look like it had some red in it. When they went back to the ward, it was time for Nora to leave.

"It's too bad your uncle can't come up to see him but I know only husbands or mothers are allowed," Nora said sadly.

"Uncle Nicky can see him as soon as they allow the baby to go home." Rosemarie assured her.

Nora looked at her, "Where will you go? Back to that girls place?"

"Where else can I go Ma? Lillian is kind enough to share her apartment with me, but please make sure you never say a word to anyone about the baby, what he looks like or about Patrick and me. His mother can't know, not until Patrick comes home and tells her."

"Does his sister know? I know you and Peggy have been close." Rosemarie nodded yes.

"I feel sorry for Mrs. McCann not knowing and under the circumstances, not being able to enjoy the fact that she has a grandson," Nora said. "Did Patrick know you were expecting?"

"Of course, Ma. He said he was happy about it, but he worried about me. He understood why I left home, and he wrote that he was more worried about his mother finding out before he could tell her himself, so Peggy said she would make sure she wouldn't find out about it. Mrs. McCann's very religious and I don't think she would find the baby a joy, knowing we're not married, but Patrick and me, we love each other, and we'll get married as soon as he comes home."

Nora smiled a strained smile, *As soon as he comes home?* She thought about what happened to her own son and she wasn't sure of anything. All she could think of was the situation her daughter and grandson were in.

"Are they going to put Patrick's name on the birth certificate," she asked.

"Of course Ma, where it has father's name, it will be Patrick's."

Nora thought of the word illegitimate, afraid it might be on it as well, but said nothing to Rosemarie. She was unaware the word was outlawed years before.

When Nora got up to leave, she bent over to kiss her daughter goodbye. Rosemarie held on to her hand for a moment and said, "Ma, tell Uncle Nicky to notify Peggy. He might forget. He'll ask Lillian to call over to the McCann's and ask for her. Peggy needs to know, she has been real good at supporting me and she came to see me often."

"I'll tell him," Nora said, giving her daughter one last hug. Rosemarie watched her walk across the large room to the door until she was gone.

When Peggy received the call that evening, she couldn't talk, her mother was standing nearby. She nodded yes and after a few minutes she thanked the caller and hung up the phone. Katie, standing close to her asked, "Who was that?"

"Oh, no one important, a girl from work."

Katie looked at her suspiciously… She rushed to pick up the receiver and then she says nothing? She thought about that for a moment and shook her head as she went about cleaning the kitchen. What had she been doing before the phone rang? She was worried about everything lately. She worried about her two boys; she didn't sleep well ever since the Nuzzo's received the news of Joey. It could have been one of her sons. She stared at Peggy who came into the kitchen to get a coke out of the fridge. Peggy's face looked flushed. She wondered what the call was really about. She started hearing rumors about Rosemarie from some neighbors who lived at the other end of the block. Something about Rosemarie not attending her prom with Vinnie at all, something about her going out with another boy. She had a lot of suspicions going through her head. Peggy was acting strange lately or so she thought. After what happened to the Nuzzo girl, she was worried about her own daughter. Would Peggy get into trouble? With the war on, she thought anything was possible. *I will have to keep a keener eye on her and her whereabouts,* she thought. After all, she reasoned, Peggy was given a lot more freedom than Rosemarie and yet, look what happened to her in spite of her parent's vigilance. *I need to pray more,* she thought.

Peggy showed up at Lillian's a few days later. She went straight over after work, knowing Lillian usually arrived home around the same time. Peggy got there first and sat on the top step of the inside stairs. She pulled her coat tighter around her as the winter wind sent chills through her. A few minutes later Nicky's car pulled up with Lillian. They weren't surprised to see her waiting there. Peggy congratulated Nicky on being a great uncle.

"How about you?" he said, "You're an aunt now."

Peggy smiled, "How are Rosemarie and the baby doing? I sure wish we could see them."

"Rosie should be home in seven days but not the baby. He only weighed four and a half pounds; she named him Joseph Patrick and put McCann as his last name. She's going to write and let him know the baby was born," Lillian said.

"She named the baby Joseph? I'm glad, losing her brother has to be the worst kind of sadness. Pat needs to know. It'll give him something to fight for. My mother is another story, another hurdle. We can't let her know anything until Pat comes home to tell her, and God only knows when that will be." Peggy said sadly.

The hospital released Rosemarie after seven days. When Nicky prepared to drive her back to pick up the baby a few weeks later, he called Nora to meet them back at the apartment. Rosemarie had just settled Joey in his crib when the doorbell rang. She scurried as quickly as she could to greet her mother at the door. Nicky was behind her as she let her mother in. Nora hugged her and without taking her hat or coat off asked, "Where is he?" Rosemarie led her to the bedroom where the baby lay awake, opening and closing his eyes. Nora leaned over to look at him and when he opened his eyes, she excitedly proclaimed, "It looks like he has large dark brown eyes like Joey, but they could change."

"I know Ma," was Rosemarie's reply."His features are exactly like Patrick's, and I think his hair is going to be reddish, don't you think so?"

Nora bent down to get a closer look, "Can I pick him up?" she asked, as she proceeded to lift him out of the crib. She carried him over to the window where she could inspect the light fuzz that covered his head. "Oh! Look, look, it's red," she said. Nicky walked over to have a look. "Wow! He's going to be a carrot top," he said. "Don't bring him too close to your neighborhood as he grows; it wouldn't take much for someone who saw him to figure out who his father is." As soon as he said it he knew he had hurt Rosemarie's feelings.

"Uncle Nicky, I'm not that dumb," she said, "and don't call him a carrot top."

Nora looked on with a sad expression. All she could think of was this beautiful baby who should bring two families such happiness, but instead would be an object of scorn. She said a silent prayer for his father to return home safely, to marry her daughter and claim his son. Filled with mixed emotions, she shed a few tears as she carried her grandson over to the couch and still wearing her coat and hat, she cradled her first grandchild in her arms.

CHAPTER 34
1943

When Rosemarie returned home from the hospital, she quickly mailed a letter to Patrick, but it had been over a month since she received any letters from him. It was now January of 1943. She knew it took time for letters to go through during the past summer. His ship was in the battle of Midway. It wasn't until the USS Enterprise was going through repairs at Noumea, New Caledonia in November of 1942 that mail would have been dropped off from his ship. It went through repairs after sustaining damage in the Battle of Santa Cruz, and had to be repaired to be able to take part in the Naval Battle of Guadalcanal in the second week of November 1942. She wasn't aware of any of that or where Patrick was and worried constantly. It was now January and her little son was almost three months old. The few letters she received from Patrick gave no indication he received her letter about the baby's birth.

Nora visited them as often as she could, which wasn't as often as she would have liked. Rosemarie took a job at a defense plant after her son was six weeks old. She worked the late night shift, and Lillian took care of the baby when she was at work. She had to find work to help pay her own expenses and didn't expect her uncle to subsidize her financially any longer. Nora would arrive whenever she could get Mrs. Katz to sit with Maria, who couldn't be left alone. She didn't want to ask any more than one or two mornings a week, even though Sylvia was willing to help. Her visits made it possible for Rosemarie to get a few extra hours of sleep, but not as much as she needed to be able to work at night. The baby being so young and sleeping most of the morning made it possible, but she knew when her grandson was older he would sleep less, so she worried about her daughter getting enough rest. She also worried about her mother-in-law. Maria was frail and not the same mother-in-law she had been in the past. She seemed kinder to Nora, more thoughtful and willing to please. She appeared happy to know she had a great-grandson in spite of the circumstances of his birth. Nora felt bad that Maria had not been able to see him. She was afraid to take a chance having Rosemarie bring the baby anywhere near her home, and Maria wasn't able to travel away from home. She worried that the neighbors might see them or worse, Benny might come home unexpectedly. She worried about everything.

CR&OCR&OCR&O

When Patrick sat behind one of the guns he manned aboard the ship, Rosemarie was never far from his thoughts. The last battle took on a few casualties. The sailors who handled the guns hadn't a spare minute to think of anything except trying to bring down the Jap zeros. Earlier the ship sustained some damage and it had returned to an Island for repairs, but on this day they were back in the battle. It would be some time before they would see land again. When they were in port, they picked up many weeks of mail, and by the time the sailors in the mailroom were able to sort it, the men were back behind the guns, or flagging the Hellcat pilots to begin their sorties off the ship's deck and once again engage in battle. So far, Patrick had been lucky. When the mail came, it was during a lull in the fighting. It had been two months since he had received any news from home. Uppermost in his mind was Rosemarie and the baby. He thought the baby was due sometime in November, and it was now near the end of January. He received a stack of mail and knew he might not have time to go through it all, so he only opened letters from Rosemarie. After opening the letter with the news of the baby's birth, he stood up and shouted to all his buddies nearby, "I have a son! I have a son!" as he waved the letter over his head. The men cheered and congratulated him, no one cared if he was married or not; they had more important issues to think about. He sat back down and read the letter again, his hands shaking as he held the pages.

October 26th, 1942
Dear Patrick,
We have a son, he was born on October 18th at 9:33 in the morning, he came almost a month early and weighed only four pounds, three ounces but he lost a few ounces, which they tell me is normal. He is still in the hospital and will be released when his weight reaches five pounds. He's healthy and doing fine. I don't know if Peggy wrote you, but the baby was born after my parents received news that we lost Joey. I guess the news caused me to go into early labor. I don't know how to feel about it all. I know it's silly but I can't help thinking maybe I'm being punished for something and yet I know that's crazy to think that way. I hope you don't mind, I named him Joseph Patrick. I will always miss my brother and I know you will too. Uncle Nicky finally told my mother where I was and she came up to the hospital. Together we went to see the baby in the nursery, but they had to place him in an incubator, just to be safe, he's perfectly healthy. He looks just like you Pat; we can see a little red in his hair. I can't wait for you to see him. I'm home now and as soon as the baby comes home, I'll take pictures to send you.
I miss you. I can't wait until you're safely back home, and please be careful.
I love you, Rosemarie

He held the pages of the letter tightly in his hands and pressed them to his chest as tears fell. He felt anxious, guilty, excited and sad all at the same time. He felt bad about Joey. He knew nothing would be the same without him. He was glad the baby was named Joseph, mostly because he knew it was a comfort to Rosemarie. When he shouted he had a son, he felt a little embarrassed because he wasn't married until Jack his close friend yelled, "Hey guys! We have to keep Pat alive, and make an honest man of him, so he can go home and marry the girl." They all cheered and laughed and patted him on the back. He didn't have time to read another letter. All he cared about was that he had a son. That was good enough. Suddenly, he had to turn his attention to the gun he manned, Zeros were approaching.

CRBOCRBOCRBO

Back home in the states, goods were rationed. Nora kept count of how many coupons she had left in the little coupon books, which were part of every shopping day. She was short of sugar coupons often, especially with Mrs. Katz borrowing sugar she seldom returned. Nora couldn't bring herself to ask her to return any of it because she knew what a huge sweet tooth she had and also because she was so helpful with Maria and Sammy. She sat at the kitchen table counting her coupons. She knew Sammy was hard on shoes and when he wore out a pair she tried to make do by putting cardboard inside when the weather was warm, but it was early March and winter still hung on. With light snow on the ground from the last snowfall a week earlier, she would have to get him a new pair of shoes. She had to go to Benny for everything unless it involved food. She could buy whatever she needed from the little grocery store in the neighborhood. The owner, Mr. Farnelli, would mark down everything she bought and he knew Benny was good for it, usually coming down the next day to pay the bill in full. Nora felt the humiliation of never having any amount of change in her purse, and although the family was never deprived of food, Benny was stingy with everything else and kept a tight hold on the purse strings. She had to beg for anything extra. She dreaded approaching her husband about the shoes; he would yell that the boy was reckless, pointing out how he didn't have the sense to stay out of mud or water puddles. She remembered how Joey at the same age was hard on his shoes, but if she mentioned it to Benny he would only deny it. Lately, she dare not mention Joey's name at all. If it wasn't for her daughter and her sister Rose, she would be alone with her grief over Joey. She felt nervous, often, as she tried to balance Maria's needs with her desire to spend more time with her daughter and grandson and she would have to be watching every move Sammy made. When he left his sled on the walk at the bottom of the back porch stairs the past winter, Benny went into a rage. If his marbles or jumping jacks were left on the front room floor, it was another reason for Benny to get angry, yell, drink, or take out all his frustrations on the poor boy. The stress Nora felt was taking its toll on her in the form of not being able to eat. As a result she lost weight. Benny didn't seem to notice. He never noticed the boy either, just everything he did wrong, which was often.

She dreaded facing another summer with Sammy home from school. She would have less time to visit Rosemarie. Sammy didn't know the baby was born and Benny never asked. She didn't dare tell the boy anything; he would forget and say something to his father. When she mentioned her daughter and grandson, it was only when she was in the company of Mrs. Katz or Twyla. She knew they would never tell anyone. If it weren't for them, she would have gone mad. Her sister Rose cut her off when she mentioned the baby had been born.

"After she's married, you can tell me about it," she had said, and then changed the subject. Rose was uncomfortable with the whole situation and Nora respected her feelings. Lately she spent her time doing the household chores without her favorite radio programs. She never turned the radio on during the day. She ceased listening to her favorites like Stella Dallas or Molly Goldberg and some of the melancholy music on the stations made her feel very sad. Benny used to have the radio on loud to hear the war news, but since they lost Joey he wasn't interested in the war. He just sat in his chair and slept or pretended to sleep. It was all becoming unbearable. She found herself thinking only of her daughter, and in spite of what she had done, she knew she could never give up her daughter.

She found everything changing since the war, and she was changing too. She no longer brought her husband his coffee; she thought he was perfectly able to get out of his chair and pour it himself since he hardly spoke to them. Maria would occasionally come into the kitchen and pour his coffee and call him to come to the table; but mother and son had fewer words to say to each other. Except for Nicky's visits whenever he knew Benny worked on Saturday, it became a sad and silent household.

CHAPTER 35

Spring of 1943 had come and gone with many outbursts from Benny over real and imagined slights he thought he perceived on the job or from his family. He was a spiritually broken man who withdrew into himself. At work he did what he was told and nothing more.

Summer kept Nora on her toes, watching every move Sammy made to avoid his having any involvement with Benny. She looked forward to the day he returned to school because she could visit her daughter and the baby in the mornings. All summer, she had to pick a Sunday when Mrs. Katz would take the boy for a few hours so she could take the streetcar over to see Rosemarie, usually during the time she was to be at Sunday Mass. On Saturdays, she asked Sylvia if she would work at the Victory Garden. Maria was unable to walk down to the Garden. The women kept busy weeding and after talking with her neighbor Angie Russo, who never mentioned Benny's visit, she felt better. Angie liked Nora and felt sorry for her, but even though she loved to gossip, she never mentioned Benny's visit or that Vinnie had blamed the McCann boy, and she ordered her son to never mention it was Patrick to anyone.

Going to one dance with Rosemarie didn't prove he was the boy, she reasoned. Benny had forbidden Nora to ever mention their daughter. He told her his daughter was dead to him, and he didn't have a daughter. When summer was over and the month of October had arrived, Rosemarie informed her that Joey would be a year old on the 18th and she was planning his first birthday at Lillian's with Nicky and Peggy.

"Ma, you've got to come. It's his first birthday," she said.

"If your father works that Saturday I'll come, but if he doesn't, what excuse could I give for leaving the house on Saturday," Nora said, "We don't talk, but if I go somewhere he wants to know where I'm going."

"Ma, that's because you never went anywhere, only to the

grocery store or to Aunt Rose's. You let him get away with all the control he has and now when you want to go somewhere you have to tell him or ask permission like a child." Rosemarie appeared upset. "You deserve to feel free to come and go as you please without answering to him for everything you do."

Nora thought of what both her daughter and brother-in-law had been telling her, that she had to stand up for herself.

Joey's birthday would be celebrated on Saturday. Nora wouldn't know if Benny would be home because he wouldn't know until the Friday before. When he returned home on Friday, she asked him if he was working on Saturday, when he said no, she was disappointed. When Saturday came, she got up the courage to speak to him.

"I need to help my sister this morning," she said. "Sammy will be playing with Bobby next door. Twyla will keep him until I get back," she was informing him, as he ate his breakfast.

"What if Ma needs something?" he said.

"You're here, aren't you? She can still help herself in the kitchen."

She went to put her hat on, pinning it to her hair, making sure it would stay in place to survive the strong gusts of wind coming off of Lake Michigan. With early arrival of winter nipping at October's heels, she dreaded the cold months. Benny would be home more often and she wouldn't feel free to leave on Saturdays. She would run out of excuses. She talked it over with Rose; she counted on her to keep her secret when she was visiting Rosemarie. If Benny called the bakery, which he was known to do on occasion, Rose would tell him Nora was busy helping with a customer. She was happy to have that support from her sister. Whenever Nora tried to defy Benny, Rose was delighted and encouraged her.

On the streetcar ride towards Ashland Avenue, she could see all the blue stars hanging in the apartment windows above store fronts. She noticed a couple had turned to gold since her last trip to Rosemarie's. She remembered how she couldn't bring herself to replace her blue star after Joey died. After all, she thought, he died so soon after leaving the states. To keep the blue star made her feel he was still alive until her sister came with the new flag and replaced it for her. Rose said he died for his country and deserved a gold star. She cried all over again every time she had to raise the window shade. There it was, a constant reminder of her son's death. Until the flag was replaced she could pretend that maybe he was still alive somewhere and they had made a mistake. Maybe it was some other young man, some other mother's son, but eventually she had to accept the truth and the gold star helped her face what she was unable to do for at least several weeks after she received the telegram. *Oh, I hate this war,* she thought, *I pray and pray for it to end, when will it ever end?* Now her worry was for her grandson's father. She prayed for Patrick every day. When the conductor called out, Ashland Avenue! she was deep in thought and missed her stop. She emerged from the car at the next stop and hurried along the walk, her coat and dress blowing in the brisk wind. Clouds were forming overhead and she looked up and hoped it wouldn't rain on little Joey's first birthday. She called him Little Joey but Rosemarie had admonished her. It was cute at first, but she could still hear her daughter's words, 'Ma, stop calling the baby little Joey, it will stick. He won't want to be called little Joey when he's older.' Remembering her daughter's words brought a smile to her face; she was so happy he was named after her son, but like a dark cloud, sadness was never far from her feelings. The baby wasn't a blessed baby from a marriage. The baby was a year old now and still not baptized. Her daughter couldn't bring herself to go and ask the priest because she had heard that their parish priest, Father O'Malley, refused to christen a child born out of wedlock. Rosemarie told her he would be baptized as soon as Patrick returned and they were married.

When she reached the apartment building, she could see her daughter standing in the window holding the baby and waiting for her. Once inside, she lost little time taking Joey out of her daughter's arms; she smothered him with kisses and then noticed Lillian, Nicky and Peggy in the room.

"Oh my goodness!" she said, "I missed my stop and I'm out of breath, I walked as fast as I could to get here." She said hello and then looking at the clock she realized she had to make the most of every minute she had. Nicky kissed her on the check and Lillian offered to take her coat but she hung on to Joey.

Pointing to Lillian she said, "Look, what a nice girl you have," she directed her statement to Nicky. All Nora could see was goodness in everyone, unlike Benny who couldn't see much good in anything. "Your brother is a bitter man," she said to Nicky, "He's to be pitied. Look what he's missing."

CHAPTER 36
1944

It was the month of March. Joey was 16 months old and walking all over the apartment; he was an active baby and kept Rosemarie and Lillian busy. On a few weekends when Lillian and Nicky took Rosemarie out to a movie or shopping, Peggy would babysit for them. Lately, Nicky was spending more of his time with Lillian. The other women he dated seemed to have fallen out of his life to Rosemarie's delight. Rosemarie stayed close to the neighborhood around Lillian's apartment. Afraid of running into anyone from her neighborhood, she would usually shop on the east side of Ashland Avenue. She would have used a bakery nearby, but the past year the shop had closed. Her aunt's bakery wasn't far, but she didn't dare take Joey with her, knowing how Rose felt about what she had done.

She would take the chance and go to the bakery four blocks east of her family's neighborhood. She knew the old couple that owned it would be there alone. They wouldn't remember her. They had a son, who ran the business for them before the war, but he was drafted and his wife worked in a defense plant. The parents were back behind the counter. She would get there right after it opened for the day and hope to avoid anyone she might know.

"Can I help you," the old women asked, looking at Joey who squirmed in his mother's arms. The weather was still cold and Rosemarie had the boy bundled in his snowsuit and woolen stocking cap. Joey tried to get out of her arms; he twisted his cap and she had to adjust it to cover his ears.

"Two loaves of bread," she said.

"That's a cute little boy you have there," the old woman said.

"Thank you," was all Rosemarie said. She looked at the clock and soon other customers would be entering the shop.

She was nervous and wanted to be out of there as soon as possible, but the old women took her time behind the counter. She heard the bell on the door ring as a customer entered the shop. The old women looked past Rosemarie.

"Good morning, Mrs. McCann!"

Rosemarie froze. She turned her face away as Katie came up to the display case. The old woman put the wrapped bread on the counter. "That will be twelve cents," she said. Rosemarie tried to get her purse open to count the change. Standing a few feet away was Katie, busy looking into the display of cakes until Joey who had tried to wiggle out of his mother's arms began to scream. Rosemarie dropped the change on the floor and she had to put him down to retrieve it, while trying to keep her back to Katie. Joey's crying drew attention to the child. Katie looked at the boy and smiled just as he stopped crying, and then turned her attention back to the bakery goods but something bothered her and she turned back to look at him again. Something about him looked familiar. Where had she seen him before? She took a few steps around to look at the mother.

"Rosemarie! Rosemarie Nuzzo, is that you?" she asked, surprised to see her. Rosemarie stood up shaking badly. She couldn't speak. Of all the people she might have run into, Patrick's mother was the last person she wanted to see.

All she had to do, she thought, is smile, say hello, put the money on the counter, grab her baby and her purchase, and leave, but Joey had other ideas. He had toddled away from her and in the process pulled the knit cap off of his head. The child's flaming red hair stuck out like a beacon of light in the dark. Katie stared in disbelief, her mouth open. There was no mistaking where she had seen that face before. The hair, the features, Katie was mouthing silent questions as she looked back at Rosemarie. She saw the horror in the girls face and thought, *"Why is she shaking and so nervous? Why does she look so afraid? How could her illegitimate child be the very imagine of my eldest son when he was a baby?"* All the questions racing through her mind and none of them were able to reach her mouth, and before they could, Rosemarie had picked up Joey and dashed out of the store, leaving her purchase behind.

The old woman hadn't moved, she stared at the two loaves of bread she so carefully wrapped, still sitting on the counter.

"What's wrong with that girl?" she asked. Katie didn't answer. She was still looking at the door where Rosemarie had fled. When the woman behind the counter looked at Katie, her face was pale, as though all the color had drained out of it. She tried to compose herself to answer.

"I don't know," was all she could offer. She stayed long enough to buy a quick dessert for supper and left. The four-block streetcar ride could have been two miles as far as she was concerned; her mind was racing with questions *"How could Rosemarie's baby look so much like one of my own?"* A terrible fear crept into her thoughts, but how could it be, she had never seen them together, Patrick never mentioned her, whose baby could it be? There were other boys in the neighborhood with red hair, wasn't there? Maybe the father wasn't from their neighborhood, maybe he came from north of Van Buren Street where all the Irish lived. The baby looked Irish didn't he? But why would the girl run out of the store like that? Of course, she knew why, she was embarrassed; everyone knew she had a child out of wedlock. The whole neighborhood knew. By the time she arrived home, she had sufficiently convinced herself of how silly it was to think that it could be her son, when all babies look alike, especially babies with red hair.

She thought about the incident for the rest of the month, afraid to mention it to anyone. She wanted the memory of that little boy to go away. She thought back to all the rumors that circulated through the neighborhood about the Nuzzo girl. Thanks to Angie Russo, everyone knew that Rosemarie never went to her prom with Vinnie but some other boy. Everyone was wondering who the boy could be. Angie made sure she never told on Patrick, just said she didn't know who the boy was. Katie remembered the Greek women who lived on the next block, whispering to someone in Farnelli's store about the Nuzzo girl once being seen walking with a red-headed boy near Douglas Park. But she never thought anything of it. She knew of the Kelly family in her parish, they had several red-headed sons around Rosemarie's age, so she thought it might be one of them. She never had any reason to think otherwise. She tried to push any thought of the boy resembling her children out of her mind, but from time to time she would think about it and it left her feeling anxious. As the months went by she busied herself with other things to think about. Grace Peterson called and invited her for coffee one morning and she went, hoping she would hear more neighborhood gossip, maybe something to resolve her doubts about her own fears. After the two women sat at the table and Grace poured the coffee, she started to cry.

"What's wrong?" Katie asked.

"Such terrible times we are living in," she said. "Look what happened to Joey across the street. I worry every day."

"But Grace, you don't have to worry about sons like I do," Katie said.

"Oh, but I do, I do, you have no idea what I worry about. I have to tell you, but you can't tell anyone. My daughter informed me that she is married, but Ralph doesn't know. We are afraid to tell him."

Katie looked surprised, "When did she get married?"

"They were married just before he left for the Army, so you see I do have a boy to worry about."

"Who did she marry?"

"A boy she had been dating for a year. You know how Ralph is, he doesn't like most people," Grace said, afraid to say her husband didn't like the Irish.

Katie looked at her sadly, "You can say it, and he doesn't like the Irish. I've known that ever since I heard him complain about my boys, but he doesn't like the Nuzzo's or Mrs. Katz, or the Woods family either, he calls the Woods family

Hillbillies. You can't hurt my feelings telling me that."

Grace felt relieved to have Katie so understanding about Ralph. "Lorraine married Michael Donovan," she said.

"You mean the one whose father is an alderman?"

"That's who she married, and she's afraid to tell her father."

"Well, at least they're not shanty," Katie said, "They have money." Changing the subject Katie asked, "Have you heard any more rumors about who the father of Rosemarie's baby could be?"

"No, I haven't, but some people think it's one of the boys that hang out on Van Buren Street. Someone thought they had seen her walking with a boy near Douglas Park, and thought he might be one of the Kelly boys."

Katie breathed a sigh of relief that what she heard in Farnelli's store was confirmed. There were redheads in the Kelly family and one was about nineteen.

She remembered them from church on Sundays. After the visit to Grace, she felt so much better. She thought about how she and Grace Peterson became much closer since the war. She thought about most of the neighbors, they all seemed friendlier; they would stop to chat whenever she ran into them on the street. She seldom saw Nora outdoors unless she was walking to catch the streetcar on Harrison Street. She often thought of her and felt sorry for her, but couldn't bring herself to go over to talk to her when she did see her. She would wave and Nora would wave back, but she wouldn't know what to talk to her about. She couldn't ask her about her son, he was dead, and she couldn't ask about Rosemarie after knowing the situation.

She hurried into her home, closing the door behind her as a gust of wind went in with her. It was getting warmer outdoors and she was looking forward to summer. She dreaded when December and Christmas would come. It wouldn't be the same without Michael and Patrick at home. It would be the third Christmas without her complete family all together. She wouldn't think about that; it would make her sad. She promised herself she would concentrate on her other children; they deserved the best holiday she could give them, in spite of the war.

She looked at the clock in the front room as she went into the kitchen. Soon her family would be home and she needed to start supper.

Peggy was the first to arrive home. She peeked into the kitchen.

"I smell corned beef and cabbage; that's Pop's favorite," she said, as she came behind her mother at the stove. Katie seemed to be in a good mood. "I had a nice visit with Mrs. Peterson," she said. "She told me something that no one knows and you can't tell anyone if I tell you."

"Mom, I know what you're going to say, Lorraine and Michael Donovan are married, right?"

"How did you know?" she looked surprised that Peggy would know that bit of information.

"Lorraine tells me everything, Mom; girls talk, you know that."

"Since you tell each other secrets, have any of your friends ever mentioned where Rosemarie disappeared to?" Peggy looked surprised, "Why do you want to know," she asked.

"I just wondered. You're not going to believe who I once ran into at the bakery in March."

"Last March?" Peggy asked, "How come you're mentioning it now? So, who did you run into?"

"Rosemarie, and she had her little boy with her."

Peggy's face became flushed and she suddenly appeared nervous, "She did? What did she say?"

"Nothing, she ran out of the store… why are you looking like that?"

"Looking like what?" Peggy turned away from her on the pretense of going for something in the fridge.

"Do you know who the child's father is? He has red hair. Peggy! You know something, don't you?" Peggy looked frightened. "I don't know Mom, really, I don't."

"If you know it's one of them Kelly boys, don't worry I won't say anything. Grace thinks it's one of them."

Peggy took a deep breath, relieved her mother was on the wrong track about Rosemarie. "I don't know, but it could be one of them," she said.

Something in Peggy's demeanor left Katie with an unsettled feeling. She watched her daughter leave the room and thought, something's not right with her.

Later that evening, she wanted to mention her fears to Jim but thought better of it. She was afraid if she did, he would think her foolish. She tried to think of how many times her son went over to the Nuzzos, but it was for Joey, she reasoned. She wondered why Joey seldom came to her home, but then realized it was Joey who had the Ford the boys loved to ride around in. She couldn't get the face of that little boy out of her mind. She would pay close attention to the features of the Kelly boys when she attended church on Sunday. Then her thoughts shifted to the fact that another Kelly brother was in the service. It could be him, she thought. She hardly kept her mind on preparing the evening meal until her two younger boys noisily entered the house. She was grateful for the intrusion.

Sitting across from Peggy during supper, she tried to engage in small talk, but her mind would wander. She hardly heard the banter between Jim and his father or anything her other children were saying. She noticed Peggy was extra quiet, but then she never talked much since her older brothers were gone, she reasoned, but every time she looked at Peggy she felt unsettled. *I've been so occupied with worry for the boys,* she thought. She told herself that she was just imagining her daughter appeared to be avoiding her, ever since she first mentioned running into Rosemarie. After arriving home, Peggy stayed in her room instead of helping in the kitchen, and she didn't talk about what went on at work as she often did.

CHAPTER 37

On June 6th, 1944, the invasion of Normandy commenced, and it was all over the news after it happened. Eisenhower planned a surprise attack on the Germans, and everyone was hopeful it would bring the war to an end in Europe. Fighting on two fronts was a terrible burden for the Country and for the familys who had husbands and sons who were doing the fighting.

December came, and still the war raged on, and soon it would be Christmas. Nora looked out at the window. She noticed the Christmas decorations Ralph Peterson had strung around his window and the large wreath on his front door. He was always the first to decorate for the holidays. Benny had mentioned how crazy it was for an atheist to decorate for Christmas, but Nora knew Grace and her daughter both attended church, and that Ralph catered to them. He saved his war on religion for the neighbors. She understood Ralph was a man of contradictions. It seemed to her that her husband never understood anyone and she was unable to reason with him about anything. She tried to get up the courage to mention that Rosemarie had the baby, and before she could tell him he cut her off sharply and said he didn't want to know anything, and forbid her to ever mention their daughter again. Somehow she mustered up the courage to yell back at him, "You can't ignore them, they're not dead!" He yelled back, "There are things worse than death, and disgrace is one of them!" She knew he was beyond ever convincing otherwise. It would be a sad Christmas. All she could do was pray that Patrick would make it back to marry her daughter. Her heart wasn't into putting up a Christmas tree, but she had to do it for Sammy. She wasn't looking forward to Christmas, and foremost in her mind was going to confession to receive communion for Christmas. She had missed mass too many times. She was afraid to confess to the priest that she hadn't attended Mass at all the past year. She worried about his reaction when she told him about all the lies she was telling Benny when he thought she was working in her sister's shop. She worried about everything, especially about her grandson never having a baptism. God forbid anything should happen to Joey, the fact his little soul would be stuck in a very dreary gray place called limbo, forever, is what bothered her most.

When she arrived at the church, the lines to the confessional of the old priest, Father O'Hara, who was partially deaf, was very long. The line for the young priest Father O'Malley was short. She surveyed the situation, and then went to the long line hoping more people would take up the slack in Father O'Malley's line. She ran out of luck when the last person came out of Father O'Malley's confessional and he looked over at the long line across from him. He walked over to the line she was in, and to her dismay told the woman in front of her that she and everyone behind her were to go over to his side. She hated going to him and now she was stuck. As she waited in line, she watched children younger than Sammy take their turn, and wondered what they needed to confess.

When it was her turn, she knelt down and found herself confessing about the lies to her husband, about this and that, trying to avoid any mention of how many Sundays she missed Mass until the last minute. When she got up the courage to mention her grandson, born out of wedlock, she asked if he could be baptized and before she could explain that the parents planned on marrying as soon as the war was over, Father O'Malley stopped her explanation and said rather coldly, "The baby's parents aren't married? He was conceived in sin. I cannot condone that by performing a baptism at this time."

"But Father, the boy is away at war," she cried, "What if he doesn't come back." Her throat swelled with emotion as she took out her handkerchief and dabbed at the tears forming in her eyes.

"Well, they should have thought of that," Father O'Malley said. "Say ten Hail Mary's and ten Our Father's," and then he slid the little door between them shut with a bang. It left Nora feeling worse than if she had not gone to confess her sins at all. When she arrived home, she stood in the outer hall and leaned against the door and cried. She screamed for Sammy to come down and shovel the porch stairs and walk. The snow was getting deeper and it was the one chore she asked him to do when she left for church. Mrs. Katz heard her outburst and opened her door to a very distraught Nora. She was astonished to see Nora display such anger.

"Get your coat and galoshes on and get down here right away!" she ordered Sammy. When she turned and saw Mrs. Katz standing behind her, a look of surprise etched on her face, she lost all composure completely; her face was a crimson color first from the cold, and now from the anger. The landlady had never seen her like this. She was crying and leaning against the door as if her legs had lost their strength. Mrs. Katz held her up, trying to comfort her.

"Vot is wrong?" she asked, but all Nora could do was cry. She led her into her flat. She walked her into her kitchen and sat her in a chair. She helped her get her coat and scarf off.

"Oh, Sylvia I tracked all the snow in, look at your floor," Nora said.

"Don't vorry, it's only vauter," Mrs. Katz assured her. "It's Rosie, is it? Something vrong vit her? Vit the baby maybe?"

"No, no, they're ok. It's everything," Nora said, wiping her eyes as she tried to explain the emotional pain she was feeling.

"Sylvia, the priest won't baptize the baby."

"Vie?" Mrs. Katz asked. She didn't understand Christian decorum.

"Because the parents are not married, and according to the church, they committed a sin."

Mrs. Katz shook her head in disbelief, "The baby? A sin he committed? A baby has no sin."

"I wish I could believe that," Nora said sadly, "In my heart

I believe it, in my head I have trouble. I don't know what to believe anymore."

Mrs. Katz showed her concern and sympathy, in hopes of eliminating Nora's pain. It was all she could do; having lost faith in mankind, even in God himself since fearing the Nazis killed her brother and his family. It had been years since she heard from him. After four years she lost all hope because if he were alive, she reasoned, she would have heard from him. She was sure they were all dead.

When Nora calmed down enough to go back upstairs, she noticed Sammy had gone outdoors to shovel the porch stairs without putting his galoshes over his shoes. Almost thirteen years old and he always forgot something. She found herself having to repeat her orders over and over until he could remember to do as he was told. She was grateful that Benny was home so she could slip over to the church for confession. She was finding it more and more difficult to leave and go anywhere lately with Maria's health declining rapidly from week to week. The old woman spent more time lying down as each day passed. All Nora and Benny could do was check on her often. The last time the doctor had come, he informed them that there wasn't any more he could do because she had little mini- strokes, and eventually it would lead to a major one and just to watch her and keep her comfortable. Maria could still speak, but with slurred speech it was hard to understand her. Nora had begged Rosemarie to come and see her grandmother before it was too late, but she wouldn't bring the baby in broad daylight to Congress Street, especially after having run into Mrs. McCann that one day in the bakery. Finally one day, she left Joey with a girl she became friends with in the apartment building and took the morning to visit Maria. She found her so different from the grandmother she remembered. Old and frail, the old women looked up at her as she tried to smile a crooked smile. She closed her eyes, and then opened them again as if to make sure it was really her Rosie, her beloved granddaughter.

"I'm sorry, Granny," was all Rosemarie could say sitting

on the edge of the bed, and holding her hand. She took out a picture of Joey and showed it to her. Maria lifted her head up and looked at the picture, and with a crooked smile crossing her face, she tried to say, "Bella, Bella." Rosemarie wished she could have spent more time with her but she had to leave after a couple hours. She was happy to have seen her grandmother, and that Maria was able to see what her great-grandson looked like.

CHAPTER 38
1945

The month of January brought in the new year of 1945. Sammy Nuzzo turned thirteen and the war was still raging on. It had been a full three years since the boys in the McCann family left home. The people in the nation wondered when the war would be over. The weather was bitter cold and Nora rose early one morning and sent Sammy off to school. When she went in to check on Maria, she found her unresponsive so she quickly called the doctor. When the doctor arrived, he checked on Maria as Nora stood in the doorway. It was after 9:00 in the morning. The doctor turned to Nora and shook his head to signify there wasn't much hope.

"She had another stroke during the night and she is in a coma," he said. "It's best if we call an ambulance and have her taken to the hospital. She could go anytime now and you don't want it to happen in front of your boy." He understood about Sammy and thought it best to shield the boy from her dying and witnessing the removal of his grandmother from the house.

Nora began to cry, dabbing her eyes she said, "If you think it's the best thing to do doctor, I'll call my husband." She went to the phone and then realized Benny wasn't easy to get hold of; she never knew what jobsite he was sent to. She called her brother-in-law instead. When Nicky came to the phone, she hesitated, to get control of her emotions, and then told him about his mother.

"Call the ambulance Nora and I'll meet it at the hospital" he said. "I'll leave right now. I'll try to reach Benny."

Nora and Mrs. Katz watched sadly as the medical attendants removed Maria carefully down the flight of stairs on a stretcher. When the ambulance left she went downstairs with Mrs. Katz. She didn't want to remain in her flat at that moment, she knew the landlady would give her emotional support, support she badly needed.

"I don't want to be alone right now," Nora said, as they entered Mrs. Katz's flat.

"Maybe I should have gone to the hospital, but what could I do, Nicky will be there with Benny."

Later that morning, after Benny had returned home, changed his clothes and left for the hospital, Nora could only sit and wait. When Sammy returned from school, she was waiting for him in the downstairs hall. She wanted to give him the news of why his grandmother wasn't there, before he ran up the stairs with his usual routine of running into Maria's room to say, "Hi Granny." She told him to call as soon as he had any news, but he didn't call until well past midnight.

"Ma's gone," was all he could say with a choked up voice. "She passed away at 2:15 a.m. She went peacefully. I'm leaving the hospital now to make the funeral arrangements with my brother." She heard the phone click without a goodbye. Benny never said goodbye when he hung up the phone. She would have to call Rosemarie. She dialed the number, not realizing the time; it was 3:00 am. She forgot Rosemarie might be asleep after arriving home from her late night shift. When she heard her daughter's voice, she began to cry.

"Rosie, it's Grandma. She had a stroke during the night," she managed to say.

"She had a stroke? She's going to be ok isn't she Ma?"

"No, she died about an hour ago."

Now she could clearly hear her mother crying. "Oh Mama, I can't believe it, not Granny." It never occurred to her that one day her grandmother would not be with them, even though she had seen the condition of her grandmother a few months before.

"I'll come home Ma," she assured her.

"No, no you can't!" Nora's voice changed; fear replacing the sorrow she heard in her mother's voice. "You can't come home and you can't come to the funeral either."

"What do you mean; I can't come home or go to the funeral? He can't keep me from seeing Granny."

"Please, please Rosie," her mother pleaded; "if you come I can't promise what will happen. I'm sorry, I'm sorry, he won't let you in if you come."

"You have nothing to worry about Ma, don't cry, please don't cry." Then she said goodbye to Nora.

Maria was buried on a cold January day. It seemed to be the only day Benny and Nicky were civil to each other, but it wouldn't last. Nora was upset over the way Benny treated Sammy; he tried to force the boy to go up and kiss his grandmother in her coffin. Sammy became hysterical, crying and hanging onto his aunt. She was grateful that Nicky and Rose intervened. Rose took the boy out of the room. With Maria gone, she worried that her brother-in-law would have less reason to visit them. She was grateful to Nicky for arranging the after-hours visit so her daughter could see her grandmother, to say goodbye. The funeral director understood and was accommodating.

CHAPTER 39

Spring came early to Chicago in April of 1945. The cottonwood trees that lined the parkway on both sides of Congress Street were already shedding their caterpillar seeds, and they began to fall to the ground. Katie McCann came into her kitchen and removed the March page off of the calendar to welcome the first day of April. It had been a year since she ran into Rosemarie with her little son. A whole year of occasionally wondering who the child's father could be. It filled her thoughts. She wrote faithfully to her two sons. She hadn't heard from either of them in over a month but expected to get some letters soon. Patrick was usually good at writing to her and Peggy, even a couple of letters to his grandfather. He would address it to Pops McCann, and the old man would get excited and wait until his grandson Kevin, who at the age of fifteen was a tall teenager, would read it to him.

On April 12th, the newspapers and the radio informed the country of President Roosevelt's death at Warm Springs, Georgia. The nation was in mourning, except for Casey, who never forgave him for helping the British. When the announcement came that Vice President Truman would be sworn in, Casey commented about how worried he was, because he didn't trust him either. Katie dismissed his comments; she had more important issues to worry about.

She wondered why Michael would ask about the Nuzzo family in his letters after hearing about Joey, but Patrick never mentioned the Nuzzos. Maybe he didn't know Joey died. She was sure she or Peggy wrote to him about it. What bothered her was precisely that he never mentioned them. She went about her chores around the house, but her thoughts were never far from the little red- headed baby who took her breath away. She had convinced herself it was just the color of his hair that conjured up such suspicions. She could not face such a calamity, nor believe what she found unbelievable. To do so would destroy all she believed in, all she lived for. The devastation of all her dreams would surely kill her. Maybe Michael, he was just like Pops, but not Patrick she reasoned, he was the good son, the most pious of all her children. She thought of all that as she prepared supper. Soon everyone would be home. She looked forward to her family coming home because she was finding it harder to be alone with her thoughts. It was only when she was alone that the image of Rosemarie's little boy haunted her. She was afraid to tell Peggy of her fears, afraid that her daughter might tell her it was true.

She had just finished setting the table when Brian came rushing in from playing outdoors; at thirteen he spent most of his after school time playing in the street with the other boys.

His shouting, "Mom! Mom, come quick," startled Katie.

She ran to the door to meet him on the porch as he pointed towards the elevated train station a block east of them at California Ave. A lone figure was walking in the distance; Katie's heart began to race. Oh, it couldn't be, she thought. As the Marine got closer, she could make out his uniform, the bag slung over his shoulder, the walk, and then the features of his face came into view. She screamed and ran down the porch steps and a full half block to the arms of her son Michael. She was overcome with emotion, crying and hugging him. Michael hugged her and then he laughed.

"Mom, didn't you get my letter that I was coming home on an extended leave?"

Katie could only shake her head no, and cried tears of happiness. "What a surprise!" she managed to say as they walked together with Michael's arm around her.

"Oh, Michael, Michael," was all she could say as they walked quickly towards the corner. Brian ran up to Michael and wrapped his arms around his waist as Katie looked on overcome with emotion. They were in front of their home when they noticed half the houses around them had heard her scream, and the occupants came out to see what it was all about. Mrs. Katz was walking her dog Mitzi when she heard

Katie scream and stopped in front of her house to watch the happy reunion between mother and son. Grace Peterson stepped off her porch and called to her husband to come out. Ralph stood on the porch, a slight smile on his face as Grace clapped her hands and then waved to Katie. Bobby Woods and his little sister Betty were playing with Sammy Nuzzo, but they stopped their roller skating on the sidewalk to watch the scene across from them. Twyla Woods stood on her porch to witness the happy reunion. Mrs. Katz thought of calling Nora, but then thought she shouldn't. It might make her sad, knowing her Joey would never be coming home to a welcome like that. She would tell her about it later.

That evening all the McCanns were a captive audience in anticipation of Michael's war stories. They admired the medals and the three battle stars he wore on his uniform, but Michael remained quiet and pensive. They could see he didn't want to talk about anything, except to hear what they were willing to tell him about the other boys serving from their neighborhood or about his own family. Katie respected his wishes and motioned to other family members not to ask Michael any questions. "When he's ready, he'll tell us," she said.

"I have a two-week leave," was all he would say.

Katie looked at him with pride. "They won't be sending you back overseas again, will they?" she asked with apprehension.

"No Mom, I'm all finished with that. I have to report back to Camp Pendleton, and then I don't know where they will send me, somewhere stateside I think. This war can't last much longer. We've been bombing over 60 cities in Japan the past few months and they have to cave in and give up soon."

"Dem Japs is one stubborn bunch," Pops added, "Dem Marines is gonna git it to dem."

Michael laughed, "I don't know Pops, it looks like the Army Air Corps flyers will have to finish the job over Japan itself. Ever since the Doolittle raid over Tokyo, flying 16 B-25's off the USS Hornet, we have been bombing them, and they still don't give up."

"Enough," Katie said, as she and Peggy placed the supper on the table and when the entire family was seated, Katie bowed her head in a prayer of thanks as they all followed her example. *I only have Patrick to pray for now,* she thought.

C3⬛C3⬛C3⬛

That night in the Peterson kitchen, Mr. Peterson watched as his wife and daughter bowed their heads in prayer. He was used to them doing that ever since the war started. He figured it was a sign of respect for all the service men. He had no way of knowing it was especially for one soldier, one who had become a member of his own family.

That same evening, Nora went downstairs to Mrs. Katz. Sammy had run in earlier in the day to tell her of the return of Michael McCann. She waited until Sammy went to bed and Benny was home in his usual spot, his chair, sleeping or pretending to sleep. They seldom ever spoke to each other and although he wasn't drinking as much as he used to, it didn't improve his mood. In fact, it made him very quiet and crabby. Nora sensed he was depressed. Maria was gone, his brother never came over when he was home, Joey would never come home again, and Rosemarie was absent forever, as far as he was concerned. He was alone and feeling sorry for himself. Nora couldn't stand being around him for long, and she found any excuse to leave and visit Mrs. Katz or Twyla. When he wasn't working on Saturdays, she would take Sammy and visit her sister Rose. She found it possible to visit Rosemarie during the week one or two mornings with Sammy at school, and on a Sunday morning when she was supposed to be at church, she would leave her son downstairs with Mrs. Katz, or Twyla for a full couple of hours. After she put Sammy to bed, she went downstairs to visit Mrs. Katz. Always happy to visit with her, the landlady greeted her with a big smile.

"Come in, come in," Mrs. Katz said as she led Nora to the

312

kitchen. "The boy, ver is he?"

"He's in bed," Nora sighed, with an exhausted expression.

"Var voos? Too big he is," She looked at the clock, "So early?"

"It's eight, if he stays up, I have a hard time getting him up in the morning." Nora shook her head with a sad expression. "Thirteen years old and he still has to be reminded of everything, he forgets two minutes after I tell him. I don't know what will become of him. Benny ignores him and I feel so alone with the problem."

Mrs. Katz put her arm around Nora's shoulder to comfort her. "I have something to show," she said, and held up a letter to Nora. "'It's from my Davie, in Belgium he is, vit the newspaper, vit the paratroopers. The war over there, she is almost over, he vrites.

Nora smiled, "I hope he comes home soon. My Joey, they never found his body. His airplane went down near the coast of France, the whole crew they didn't find. He just got there and I think he was only on a training mission. We couldn't mourn him the right way." She started to cry. "I don't know what I would do if I didn't have you to talk to."

"Come, have the coffee, better you vel feel." Mrs. Katz poured her a cup and sat down next to her, "Someday vee vel all feel better," she said. "Here, vood you read the letter, mine eyes not so goot." She took off her thick glasses to rub her eyes. Nora took the letter and began to read…

February 25th, 1945.
France…End of Censoring
War Correspondent, PFC David Katz

Dear Mama,
Received your swell letter and valentine. I know it's been a long time since I wrote you, but sometimes we are in a spot where we can't write. We had a very busy trip coming back from Germany to France. Seen some badly damaged German

cities, Boy, I mean they were completely wrecked! Also went through the famous Siegfried line. How are my children? Do you see them much? They are old enough to visit you themselves. Does Ellen come to see you? I bet this war won't last too much longer. Take care of yourself and God willing I will be home soon.

Your son, David

"Vot is this Siegfried he vrites?" Mrs. Katz asked, but Nora wasn't sure what it was.

"Maybe it's a battle he went through," she said, "when were your grandchildren here to visit?"

"Two veeks ago they come to see their Bubbie now, ven they can. The children, teenagers they are, but they stay vit her mutter ven she vorks and me they see too."

"I better go back upstairs," Nora said. "Thanks for the coffee."

She was tired and hoped Benny had gone to bed. She quit sleeping with him, preferring to sleep in Maria's room where she would be spared his loud snoring when he did go to bed. Half the time she let him sleep in his chair, afraid if she woke him, he would start in on all his perceived slights and how life had dealt him a lousy existence. She didn't want to hear any of it, especially over and over again.

On April 28th Mussolini was captured and hung by the Italians and Benny took the news with satisfaction. At first he was angry with Roosevelt for Joey's death, now he blamed Mussolini for joining the war against America. "He got what he deserved," was all he would say. On May 2nd the news reported the fall of Berlin. By May 8th, the war with Germany was over. People rejoiced in the streets. Taverns on Van Buren Street were full of people celebrating the end of the war in Europe. Later in May, Mrs. Katz received another letter from her son and brought it upstairs for Nora to read. It was May the 20th, but the letter was dated May 9th, 1945.

Nora read it aloud.

5-9-1945
V-mail service--passed by censor--Germany
War correspondent, PFC David Katz
Dear Mama,
Received your dear letter and was glad you're feeling in good health. As you know, the war has ended in Europe. I sure waited for this day to come. I was up on the front lines taking pictures when it ended. The German people and the soldiers were all in a panic trying to get away from the Russian Army. They were more willing to surrender to American and British forces. Now that the war in Europe is over I don't know what's next for me. I sure hope I don't have to go to the South Pacific. Yesterday I had the experience of going through one of the slave labor camps here in Germany. I tell you Mama; it was one of the worst sights I've ever seen in my life. Thousands of dead people, and many more people were starved and dying, and they were mostly Jewish people, our people Mama; I wouldn't have believed it until I actually viewed it with my own eyes.

You can believe all you read about these concentration camps in the papers back home. It's true. How did the people back home take the news that the war was over? Did they celebrate? Up here it was just another day, nothing to celebrate after viewing that camp. I had to document everything in the camp.

Until I see you again, Love, your son David

Mrs. Katz started to cry, wiping her face where tears had fallen she said, "That's ver mine poor brodder vent, maybe, in von of those camps."

Nora tried to comfort her, "Maybe they sent him somewhere else, maybe he's still alive," she said, but deep down she was only trying to comfort her. She knew from the news and the newsreels, the radio and word of mouth, that Hitler had conspired to kill off all the Jews and now the discovery of the camps proved all the rumors where true.

CHAPTER 40

On May 25th, a late Friday afternoon, Katie McCann was going about her daily chores.

She received a letter from Patrick and even though it was weeks late, dated May 2nd, she was happy to hear from him, and that he was okay. She was in a good mood, knowing Michael was in the states and the war in Europe was over. She looked at the time; it was close to getting supper started, and soon her boys would be bounding in from school, happy it would soon be summer vacation. Kevin was in the tenth grade and Brian was in the eighth. Her father-in-law had not been feeling well, and was sitting on the back porch feeding the early robins that flocked into the yard to peck at the seed he threw from the porch. Usually he would be with his old friends at O'Conner's Bar, but not this day.

Katie had just finished setting the table when her boys came in, throwing their books on the hall table. Two hours after the boys had gone outdoors, the doorbell rang. When she entered the front hall, she could view from the curtain-covered glass on the door, the form of a man wearing what looked like a policemen's hat. When she opened the door her knees went weak. It was the Western Union boy, the same boy she remembered, who visited the Nuzzo's home. She tried to call out to someone, her boys, Pops, but no sound came out of her mouth as the boy handed her the telegram. She could barely sign the receipt he handed her, and with shaking hands she ran into the kitchen, sat in a chair and held the message in her hands, in her lap, unopened. She smelled the stew boiling over and stood up to attend to it with legs that didn't feel like her own. She turned the gas jets off under the pot, turned and slowly sank back into the chair. She held the unopened telegram in her hands. She sat as if paralyzed, not daring to move. She could not bring herself to open it. All she could say was "Oh God! Oh God!" She was in shock. She watched the clock, it was almost 5:00 as the big hand moved; each second seemed like an eternity. The sound of the screen door's squeaking hinges as Pops opened it to enter the kitchen took her out of her trance. It was then that she started to shake. She stared at him with eyes wide open, still clutching the uncertainty of her world in her hands. Casey stared at her. Her face appeared as white as chalk.

"What's wrong wit ya girl?" he asked, but she couldn't answer. Her lower lip trembled. He sat across from her and when she brought up both hands still clutching the telegram and laid them on the table, he reached across and patted her hand with his, gently keeping his hand over hers. "Open it," he said, but she was unable to do so.

"I can't," was all she could say. Just then, Jim and her boys came in from the opened front door. The scene that greeted Jim at the kitchen table looked odd, his father and his wife sitting there together, and Pops was holding her hand? He knew instantly something was very wrong.

"What happened?" he asked, as he came behind Katie and looking at their hands he spotted the paper clutched in her right hand. He took the telegram from her and seeing the War Department stamped on it, he opened it quickly. He read it silently to himself first as Katie held her breath and Pops didn't move. Time stood still, until Jim said, "Oh my God! Katie girl, he's alive, our Pat's alive. He's been wounded; he's in a hospital in Hawaii. It's okay Katie; don't you know what that means? He's out of the fighting."

She began to cry, Pops let go of her hand and put his handkerchief up to his nose and took a deep breath. Jim handed the telegram to Katie, and she was shaking as she reached for it.

"We don't know how badly he is wounded," she cried, as she read it.

"He's alive, that's all that matters right now," Jim said, "We can deal with it later."

When Peggy came home she found them still sitting there

together, no one said anything but she spotted the telegram in her mother's hand and reached for it. Her eyes found the line— "We regret to inform you that your son, CPO Patrick Thomas McCann was wounded in action on May 11th, 1945 and is now residing in the Naval hospital at Pearl Harbor, Hawaii. It was signed by the Navy Department.

"Wounded, wounded it said," Katie kept repeating, as she looked up at Peggy.

"Yes Mom, it said wounded, it doesn't say killed."

"Oh My God!" Katie cried, "What if it's bad?"

"We just have to wait until we hear more," Jim said, patting her arm. "If it were real bad, they would have mentioned it, don't you think?" he tried to reassure her.

"It could be just a minor wound Mom, but they still have to notify you," Peggy said, hoping to comfort her mother. She was still holding the telegram and in the excitement she said, "I have to go over to Rosemarie and let her know," and then she realized what she had said but it was too late, Katie stood up and grabbed the telegram out of her hand.

"What do you mean you have to go tell Rosemarie? What for? What has she to do with this?"

Peggy was nervous, she didn't want them to find out this way, not at a time like this but she had slipped up and now she had to explain herself.

"Mom, Dad… Pat and Rosemarie, they have been a couple ever since they were teenagers, and they were afraid to tell anyone because of you Mom, and her parents. They thought you would never accept the relationship." Peggy stopped explaining and held her breath. Katie looked shocked, turned to Jim and cried, "It can't be true!" but then she remembered the little red-headed boy, and she started to lose her balance as Jim caught her and sat her down. She laid her head on the table and cried, great racking sobs. Peggy and Jim tried to comfort her by putting their arms around her, but she pushed them away. Looking up at Peggy, she asked with anger in her voice, "Is Rosemarie's baby Patrick's?"

"Yes Mom," was all Peggy could say.

Jim remained silent, taking it all in, and he looked as confused as Casey who hadn't said a word.

Peggy waited until her mother tried with much difficulty to compose herself, and then she told them the entire story, about how Patrick and Rosemarie loved each other, and if they had been allowed to date in the proper way, maybe none of it would have happened. How Mr. Nuzzo disowned her, but Mrs. Nuzzo knew all about it just before the baby was born, and supported her daughter.

"Mom, he looks just like Pat," Peggy said, as Katie cried uncontrollably. Casey stared at her, she looked so vulnerable, not at all like the daughter-in-law who never had a kind word for him, and he was savoring the moment. When Katie seemed so docile, so kind, even towards the likes of him, and allowed him to hold her hand, he felt privileged to share such a moment with her. He felt worthy; for the first time, his presence counted for something in his son's home. Katie dried her tears; she was exhausted from crying and turned to Peggy.

"Has her mother seen the boy?"

"Of course Mom, she was with her at the hospital after he was born."

"What did she name him?" Katie asked.

Peggy put her arms around her mother, "His name is Joseph Patrick." She said.

"Oh, she named him after her brother, that's nice."

"We have a grandson, that's all that matters," Jim said. Turning to Pops, he said, "You're a great grandpa, Pops." The old man smiled.

Peggy could see her mother was slowly and painfully trying to accept the situation.

"They plan on getting married as soon as Pat is back home," she said.

Part of Katie clung to the illusion that her God, the one she talked to all her life in the form of daily prayer would not repay her loyalty by allowing such a disgrace to befall her family.

She felt her control of her world slipping away. If God couldn't control wars, she reasoned, she couldn't hold him responsible for her son's indiscretion.

Peggy took out the picture of Joey she kept in her wallet. He was wearing a sailor suit in one of the little dime store photos. She handed it to her mother. Katie stared at it and a slight smile crossed her mouth; she held it up for Jim and her father-in-law to see.

After a minute of silence, while the men stared at the little boy in the sailor suit, she said, "You can't see it in the picture but he has red hair just like Pat."

Peggy took the telegram and prepared to go to Rosemarie when Katie lifted her head up from the table where she had started sobbing again and said, "Is it alright if I go with you?"

"Are you sure you want to go, NOW? You're so upset. I don't know how Rosemarie will take the news and I think she might feel uncomfortable with you there at this time. Let me prepare her, I'll tell her that you know about it first."

Jim agreed with his daughter and said, "We'll invite her here with the boy, give her a chance to receive the news about Pat first." Katie nodded, still wiping her face of tears that continued to fall. When she looked up, the frightened faces of her boys, standing at the doorway with their little sister Jean caused her to stand up and compose herself.

CROCROCRO

When Peggy arrived at Lillian's, Lillian had just returned from work and greeted Peggy in the downstairs hall. "Before we go in I have to tell you that my brother was wounded. I want you to know before I tell Rosemarie."

Lillian's hand covered her mouth; she shook her head no and said, "Oh God! I hope he's going to be ok." Together they entered the apartment as Rosemarie walked toward them with Joey in her arms. They sat her down and told her, but before she could cry or say anything, Peggy assured her it couldn't be a bad wound or they would have been told. "The most important thing to think about is he will be sent home," she said. She handed her the telegram and Rosemarie took it with trembling hands and read it. Putting it to her chest and with her eyes closed she took a deep breath and let the tears fall. All she could think about was her son's father was coming home. She would take him in any condition because she loved him.

CHAPTER 41

The first week of June, Grace Peterson answered a call from Michael's mother. Mrs. Donovan called to tell Lorraine about Michael. It was the 2nd time Grace had spoken to the woman. The first time, Grace called Mrs. Donovan to let her know that Lorraine told her about the marriage, and she was ok with it, but her husband hadn't been told. Together the two women talked for over an hour, getting to know each other. Grace knew all Michael's letters to her daughter went to the Donovan's home because they were addressed to Lorraine Donovan and they couldn't take the chance that Ralph would see them. She thought the call was about the letters, but Michael's mother tearfully confided to her that their son was listed as missing, somewhere in Belgium.

"It can't be!" Grace said, "That war is over, when did you get the news?"

"This morning," was all the woman could say before she broke down. "Will you break it to your daughter and when she's up to it, tell her to come over."

"I'll come with her, is it ok if I come with her?" Grace asked.

"Of course, I wish we had met under better circumstances," Mrs. Donovan said.

Grace worried about how to break it to her daughter. She was shaken up and sat down to compose herself. Getting such news right after hearing about her neighbor Katie's eldest son getting wounded was too much to take in. She put her head into her hands and cried.

When Ralph returned home from work, Lorraine had been home a good hour and became hysterical after getting the news about Michael. Grace tried to be as gentle as she could, explaining that missing did not mean he was dead but her daughter fell apart and ran up the stairs to her room. She was still crying when her father entered the front hall. The first thing he noticed was his wife's eyes; they were very red.

"What's wrong?" he asked. "Something happened?"

Grace was standing at the bottom of the stairs and they could both hear their daughter crying.

"Is something wrong with her?" Ralph asked.

"Yes Ralph, quite a lot is wrong," Grace started to cry, and as he started for the stairs she stopped him.

"Before you go up to her, you better hear me out," she said, "Her heart is breaking; she loved that boy, Michael Donovan. She loved him, and it didn't matter if you didn't like him, she loved him, and they were married, but she couldn't tell you, and now he is listed as missing in action from the war, and don't you dare say anything to her. She's hurting enough without your misguided judgments being thrown at her. Until you accept the situation, don't go near my daughter," she screamed, as she turned and ran up the stairs to Lorraine before Ralph, who stood there alone in the hall and in shock, could respond. His very gentle wife had torn into him like he had never seen her do before. It left him speechless. He sat on the bottom step, put his head down into his hands and listened to the sounds of anguish coming from the two people he loved the most. All his defenses came down around him as he felt their pain.

Later that night, he sat alone at the kitchen table; he was left to his own devices when it came to supper. There wasn't any. His wife and daughter had left for the Donovan's and he was left to ponder his place in their lives. He loved his daughter more than life itself and after many hours of sitting alone with his thoughts, thoughts about the war, the pain his neighbors had to endure, all the neighborhood children the war had taken, the very children he complained about through the years were getting wounded, or giving their lives for the cause of their Country, his Country. The very neighbors he never liked were sacrificing their sons for his freedom, and his right to express himself. By the time his wife and daughter had returned home, he was a changed man.

One could not say the same about Benny Nuzzo. The war had changed him, but not in the way his neighbor Ralph Peterson had accepted the changes the war had brought. Benny was a broken man. Nothing mattered to him. The war had taken the only one he lived for, his son Joey. He felt Joey died for nothing because he died so early in the war. He turned inward, full of bitterness. He wished to be alone with his thoughts and seldom spoke to Nora, and as far as Nora was concerned, he acted like Sammy was her son, not his. Sammy was thirteen years old but still acted like an eight-year-old. He was a loving child, but only Nora and her sister Rose were around to show him their love. Nora felt his every joy and also his pain and frustrations of trying to cope. At times she didn't know where his feelings left off and hers began. They were merged together, mother and son, her only son. She unselfishly gave herself to his needs and absorbed his constant struggle. Since Maria was not there to share the burden, she assumed it all. Benny retreated into a world of his own where there wasn't room for her or their imperfect boy. He didn't acknowledge them at all, even when sitting only a few feet from them at the supper table.

CRROCRROCRRO

Katie McCann waited a week after she was told about Patrick's baby before she gathered up the courage to pay a visit to Nora. She went to Nora after she witnessed Benny leaving for work one morning. It was an awkward moment for both women, but they weathered it well. The two women talked about their new grandson and they apologized to each other for their children's lack of judgment. Knowing the baby wasn't baptized, Katie's concern was for his soul.

"I went to Father O'Malley," Nora said, "He refused to do anything because they aren't married,"

"I'll take care of that!" Katie said, sounding like she would take charge of the matter, "Lord knows I've done a lot for that church."

The following Saturday found Katie very upset as she walked home from a meeting with the priest. By the time she arrived home she was in a fighting mood. Unfortunately, her father-in-law was at home, sitting at the table, enjoying his cup of tea. Except for little Jean playing on the kitchen floor with her dolls, the house was quiet. Peggy had gone over to her friend Lucy, and the boys were out on the street with their friends, leaving their sister in the care of her grandfather.

Katie entered the kitchen and told Jean to go and play in her room. When the child had left, she turned on Casey.

"Old man! A fine example you set in this house. You! With your wild stories of your days working at the railroad and me trying to raise morally good sons with manners. Michael and Patrick were always getting into fights in the neighborhood, and now Brian and Kevin following, using the language you bring home from O'Connor's. You made such an impression on their young lives, even the bars of lifebuoy soap I stuck in their mouths when they were using your gutter words didn't stop them, but Patrick was different, he never seemed influenced by what you said, he was a gentle boy, like my brother John."

She was crying and stopped to wipe her nose with a hankie. "Now, he has done worse than using your street talk and fighting ways! It's all your fault!"

He felt like a prisoner sitting there, taking the blame, unable to get away. She would only follow him to his room and he would still hear her outside his door, so he chose to just stay and take it. He told himself he might as well sit there and wait until she finished.

"It's all your fault!" she continued, "Pat's baby can't be baptized because they aren't married."

"How is it me fault?" he said, sorry he asked, the moment the words left his mouth.

"He followed your example, didn't he? Jim was conceived out of wedlock wasn't he?"

"But how'd he know dat?"

Katie had no reply, she gave him a look he knew well, and to his surprise, she left the room. He lost no time in grabbing his hat and taking a deep breath, he left the house as quickly as his old legs could take him. He would grab a bite to eat at O'Connor's, and stay out of her way the rest of the day.

On Sunday morning Katie would miss Mass and join Nora for the trip to visit Rosemarie and Joey. Peggy told Rosemarie her parents took the news about the baby well, and that her mother would pay a visit to Nora. She told her that Katie was anxious to see Joey. The two women met at the streetcar stop on Harrison Street and rode together. On the ride, Katie talked about her confrontation with Father O'Malley; she was disappointed in the priest and very angry. Nora tried to calm her down.

"If only the old priest would talk with us," Nora said. "I've accepted that Joey will have his baptism when the kids are married. What can we do? Nothing."

"Oh yes, we can," Katie said, "I remember one Catholic rule; in an emergency anyone can perform a baptism with water if someone had an accident and might die. Well Joey was an accident through no fault of his own and I'll take him to church with me one afternoon, to another parish, and sprinkle some holy water on his forehead and say the words; then he'll be covered until his parents are married." Nora looked at her with a frown but said nothing. What does it matter, she thought. She was beginning to believe like Mrs. Katz, that Joey was innocent.

Both women continued to talk about their grandson, agreeing that he was a beautiful child.

Katie greeted Rosemarie with a smile, to Rosemarie's relief. She embraced her, and then Nora who had picked up Joey handed him to Katie. Katie started to cry as she held the boy. "He looks just like Pat," she said and then added, "But he has large brown eyes, like your brother, he's beautiful." Rosemarie smiled, "Guess what? I got this letter from Pat, he'll be shipped to Great Lakes Naval hospital in Chicago." She handed the letter to Katie.

Katie read it." "He doesn't say what his wound is, do you know?

"I don't, but it can't be too bad, he sounds so happy in the letter. He mentioned only that his ship was hit. Only seven casualties he said."

Rosemarie was happy that Katie chose to pay her first visit to see Joey with Nora. It made it less awkward for all of them.

In July, Patrick was at the naval hospital at Great Lakes. The call came to Rosemarie early on Sunday morning the first of July.

She picked up the phone, "Hello!"

"Hi baby."

"Who is this?" she asked. The voice sounded husky.

"Don't you recognize me?"

Suddenly, she realized it was Patrick. "Oh Pat, Pat," she started to cry.

"Hey, I didn't come all the way home to hear you cry," after a pause, he said, "I love you Rosemarie"

"I love you too, where are you?"

"At Great Lakes Naval Hospital. We got in last night. It was too late to call. Our plane landed at Douglas Airport and we had to be driven up here to the hospital."

"Can I come to see you?" she asked. She wiped her tears with the back of her hand, stranded by the phone without a hanky.

"This afternoon between 1:00 and 3:00, those are the visiting hours.

"I will die until then,"

"No you won't."

When Nora received the call from Katie that Patrick was home, she was calling for Rosemarie because she would never call her mother on a Sunday, her father might answer the phone. Nora was so happy; she rushed downstairs to share the news with Mrs. Katz "I have good news," she said excitedly as she entered the door to the landlady's front hall. "Sylvia, Patrick is home at Great Lakes!" Then noticing the sad expression on Mrs. Katz face, she asked, "What's wrong?"

"Oy Vay! A deaf man should be so lucky, the tings I hear on the vadio these days."

Nora pulled out a picture of little Joey. "Look at Rosie's baby; he'll be three in October."

Mrs. Katz took the picture in her hands and smiled. "Vat did Benny say?"

"Benny doesn't want to know anything; I can't mention Rosie in front of him. He's so bitter."

Mrs. Katz shrugged her shoulders and shook her head back and forth, "Vot can vee do, we accept or we sit Shiva. Your Benny sits Shiva. A terrible ting, this vour. It kills, it brings new life, the whole vorlds meshuge."

At supper that evening, Benny was quiet as usual until half way through the meal, and then he said, "I'm thinking we should move."

Nora frighteningly asked, "Why? Where?"

"Back to the old neighborhood," he said, determination in his voice.

"The old neighborhood, Why?"

"You have to ask why? I'm disgraced here. Everyone knows our business."

"But we've been here over fourteen years, Benny, this is our home. I don't know anyone in the old neighborhood, everyone has moved," she said pleadingly. "It's mostly immigrants and old people who live there now."

"What's wrong with that?" he said angrily.

"Nothing Benny, but I like it here where the people are not all greenhorns."

"Greenhorns? That's a laugh; greenhorns were good enough for you when you met me. Did you forget that I wasn't born here? I will always be a greenhorn."

She tried to explain, "I didn't mean it that way, I meant to say, I'm used to living here and I'm forgetting the language.

Since your mother died, I seldom hear the language anymore?"

He stared at her, "I was more comfortable there," he said.

She knew that wasn't the real reason. It was the McCann's he wanted to avoid. He insisted it was the McCann boy who was involved with his daughter, but he was afraid to confront them on the possibility he might be wrong again.

"Well, my kind of people live on this street," she said, "Remember, I was born in this Country!" "How can I forget," he answered, "You throw it up to me, every chance you get. Maybe, away from these people you admire so much, you'd show more respect for me, like you used to."

She decided not to answer him. It was useless to continue the conversation, but she was upset at the thought of going back to where little old ladies dressed in black and sat on their front porches with nothing better to do than gossip. Her every move would be talked about. Maybe it was the wine talking again, she thought, as she watched him put the half empty gallon away when he left the table. Soon after, he went to his chair and the newspaper. She called Sammy from the room and together they went to sit on the back porch swing. She put her arm around the boy and pushed them back and forth. The cherry tree in the backyard was full of cherries. Sammy got off of the swing and looked over the banister.

"Mama, look at all the cherries," he said.

She got up, walked over to him and put her arm around him. "You know Sammy, that tree was planted by Granny and Mrs. Katz in the spring, after you were born." She looked at his smiling face. His cheeks were puffy and red. He had put on more weight again, since turning thirteen in January. He had grown taller too, as tall as she was. He was so sweet, she thought, and she knew he would always need her.

"Are we moving Mama?"

"Goodness, no!" she said, "We can't move, that tree was planted for you, it's grown just like you have," she put her arms around him. She looked at him and thought, would he ever marry or have children? She worried about his future, but as long as she could view the tree producing an abundance of cherries every season, well, she knew then she could never leave his tree. It would be like leaving part of her son behind.

CHAPTER 42

Patrick lay in the hospital bed, the back of his head cradled in the palm of his hands. All around him were service men with mending wounds. A young sailor named Ensign Taylor lay with his head covered in bandages; only his nose and mouth were visible. Periodically, nurses appeared to put a straw in his mouth so he could take water, medication and food. He screamed one night and awakened Patrick, and that is when Patrick learned the sailor was blind due to an explosion aboard his ship. The scream came as he awakened from a dream. In the dream, the wounded man could see. Upon awakening, he remembered it was only a dream. He would never have his sight again. Patrick tried to lean over to comfort him. It was then he realized his missing left leg wasn't the worst thing that could have happened to him. He said a prayer of thanks that his eyes were unmarred, and he would soon see his child for the first time. For that privilege, he could accept the missing leg. That afternoon, he waited in anticipation for visiting hours. His parents, with Peggy and Rosemarie were to visit him for the first time. When he called them, they asked about his wound but he told them not to worry about it. He couldn't tell them over the telephone, preferring to wait until they would see him in person and know that he was going to be okay, in spite of his loss.

Jim and Katie entered the room shortly after 1:00 p.m. He watched his mother rush across the room, past beds filled with the wounded. He greeted her with a wide smile as she threw her arms around him.

"Hi Mom!" he said. She kissed him and then looked down at his covers where his legs were. The flatness of the sheet where his left leg should have been startled her. She began to cry.

"Mom, Mom, look! It's not that bad." He tried to reassure her that he would be all right.

331

Jim came up and gave him a hug. "You will do fine son," You're home, you're safe, that's all we care about."

"He'll never be able to return to the Fire Department again will he?" Katie asked, wiping the tears that ran down her cheeks.

"Mom, I think there was a bill passed by the government last year, allowing servicemen to attend college on some kind of G. I. Bill. I'm going to look into it," Patrick said. "Don't worry about me, I'll be fine. As soon as I'm ready, I go to rehab to be fitted with a leg. I have my knee, see," he bent his knee, which accentuated his loss and Katie cried again. "That's the important thing Mom." Jim smiled, "Katie" he said, "Just think, our Pat will be the first in the family to go to college, if that bill was passed." He turned to Patrick, "So you're doing okay? That's my boy."

Patrick felt awkward because they hadn't mentioned his son when they first arrived. Rosemarie told him the family knew about the boy. Before he could mention it first, Katie said, "Your little boy looks just like you. Rosemarie and your sister are downstairs waiting to come up to see you." When his parents left, Patrick watched the doorway, and as soon as he spotted Rosemarie he called to them. The girls rushed in and Rosemarie bent down to embrace him. Her eyes filled with tears when he explained the loss of his left leg. She looked down and cried openly, but then quickly composed herself; all she cared about at that moment was that he was home. Peggy hugged him and said, "If I know you Pat, you aren't going to let anything stop you from doing whatever you want to do."

Rosemarie pulled out the latest picture of Joey and handed it to him. "Can you believe he will be three in October?"

"Is he talking much? At almost three I guess he is," Patrick said.

"Is he talking?" Rosemarie laughed, "We can't shut him up and he looks at your picture and says Daddy. He used to say Dada but that was when he was younger."

"I sure wish I could have heard that, I've missed most of

his first three years," Patrick said sadly.

"Maybe we can find a way to bring him here, you know, downstairs in the waiting room when they'll let us wheel you down. Whenever you're ready," Peggy said.

The time went by too quickly and they hated to leave, but visiting hours were almost over. "I'll try to come as often as I can," Rosemarie promised. Peggy kissed him and walked over to a sailor a few beds away from Patrick's. The wounded man was eyeing Peggy ever since she came into the room. Peggy thought he was flirting with her so she engaged the sailor in conversation, giving Rosemarie and her brother a few minutes without her. They wouldn't be alone, not with a room full of wounded sailors. Peggy and the sailor exchanged names and she couldn't help noticing how handsome he was. She asked him about his wound and was happy to hear he was going to be okay. He was a Navy medic wounded by gunfire trying to rescue another man.

It was the third week of July when Patrick finally met his son. Peggy and Rosemarie waited in the waiting room and when the elevator doors opened and Patrick's parents wheeled him toward them, Rosemarie ran to him, embraced him, and then Peggy placed Joey in his lap. All Patrick could do was try to hold back the tears he felt were about to emerge, and all he could say was, "The poor kid, he really does have my hair!"

Joey's little face wrinkled up and large tears fell; he didn't know this stranger, so he tried to pull away from Patrick. He was confused by all the grownups around this strange man in the wheelchair. Patrick held him closer and then Joey let out a wail and reached his little hands up for someone to rescue him. Patrick kissed him before Rosemarie picked him up to stop his crying.

"Mom, would you call Father O'Malley and arrange a time for us to get married." Patrick said, smiling. "They said I could leave for a couple of days before I go to rehabilitation as long as I can use the crutches. Rosemarie needs to take a blood test; I've already had mine. Do it as soon as possible."

ᏮᏇᎷᏇᏇᎷᏇ

The wedding was set for Saturday, August 4th. Nora was afraid to mention it to Benny but thought he might feel different when he was told his daughter was getting married.

She was up early on Saturday and he noticed she was dressed in her best dress and wondered where she might be going.

"Why are you all dressed up?" he asked.

She looked at him, took a deep breath and tried to remain calm.

"Benny, our daughter and Patrick are getting married this afternoon. Father O'Malley is going to marry them. I think we should both be there."

"Are you crazy?" he said loudly, "How can you show your face there? So! It was him all along, I was right. He took advantage of her and she was stupid. He caused the damage and I don't wanna see either of them."

"What damage Benny?" she said, as she raised her voice in anger.

"What good is going, when the cart came before the horse?"

"I don't know what you're talking about," she shouted. "Rosie is our only daughter, not a horse and I'm going." She called Sammy to get ready, "Sammy has a right to see his sister again and his little nephew for the first time." She thought he looked flushed when she said nephew; he hadn't known the baby was a boy. He would never let her tell him anything about Rosemarie whenever she tried to mention her.

"I heard he has one leg. How's he going to support her with one leg?" he said angrily.

"What a terrible thing to say," she started to cry. "I don't care what you think, I'm going, if you don't like it, too bad!" She couldn't believe she spoke to him in that way, she felt emboldened for the first time.

After Sammy was dressed in his Sunday best, they walked

out the door without another word to him. He couldn't believe she would defy him, so he walked over to the open window hoping to get the last word in, but she went downstairs to Mrs. Katz. They would wait there until it was time to leave for church.

Rosemarie wore a light blue suit and matching hat in church. Patrick was in his Navy Blues. He walked with crutches; his left pants leg was pinned up. All the McCanns were there except Michael. Peggy invited Steve Pavlik, the wounded sailor she met at the naval hospital. They had been seeing each other since he was released from the hospital. She introduced him to everyone, and then Father O'Malley told everyone to be seated. The service was a short one and Nicky and Peggy were witnesses. After the service, Lillian showed everyone her engagement ring. Nicky had finally made a commitment to her. It made everyone happy. After the ceremony, Peggy and Nicky stood at the baptismal font with little Joseph Patrick McCann, as he was christened. After the service, they all went to Nicky's apartment; Nicky and Nora would cater a little wedding party with cake and ice cream. It should have been Benny's responsibility. The McCanns offered to have it at their home, but Nora thought it would be too awkward for all of them to be there with Benny brooding across the street, alone in his misery.

"I knew he would never show up for this," Nicky said.

"I don't care anymore, I'm fed up to here with him," she raised her hand up to her eyebrows. "Let him feel sorry for himself," Nora said.

Nicky laughed and gave her a hug. He was pleased to see the change in her.

Two days after the wedding, Mrs. Katz called for Nora. She sounded excited.

"What is it Sylvia?" Nora shouted, from the top of the stairway landing.

"Put the vadio on!" she yelled back," Soon the vour vill be over!"

Nora ran back into her flat and turned the radio on. Benny was sitting in his chair, reading the paper. "I don't wanna hear that now," he said.

She ignored him, and turned it on, "Something has happened, Sylvia just yelled to turn the radio on."

The broadcaster was excitedly announcing that the atomic bomb was dropped on Hiroshima Japan at 8:15 a.m. Japan time. It was August 6th. Nora and Benny moved their heads closer to the radio to catch every word. They heard the plane that carried the bomb was named The Enola Gay.

"I think the Japs will give up now, don't you think, Benny?" Nora said, hoping to get a response from him.

"What do I care, the end of the war won't bring Joey back," he said, with anger in his voice.

Nora stood up and looked at him for a moment. She knew she couldn't have a decent conversation with him about anything. She shook her head in disgust and left the room. She checked to see where Sammy was and then remembered he had gone next door to be with Bobby Woods. She decided to go downstairs and join Sylvia; they would hear the war news together and she needed to talk to someone. She felt so angry with Benny most of the time. Lately it was almost impossible living with him, and being alone in the house with him with no one else to defuse the tension was becoming unbearable. If Sammy were different, she might not feel so alone, but he was what he was, and she accepted him as he was. She needed the support that only Mrs. Katz could give. Once in a while Twyla would sympathize with her, but it was mostly Mrs. Katz, she was older, like an older sister, the kind of sister she wished Rose could be.

Sitting in Mrs. Katz's front room near the radio, the two women listened to the entire broadcast on the bombing. When the report was over, Mrs. Katz turned the radio off and the women went into the kitchen to have coffee and talk.

"That big bomb, such a ting, all the innocent children, vot did they do? Var is no goot for nobody." Mrs. Katz said, shaking her head from side to side. "No goot," she repeated.

Nora brought up Benny and how she was finding it impossible to live with him.

"He will never forgive Rosie," she said, "and it's tearing us apart."

Looking sad, Mrs. Katz said, "You know Nora, my Sol, so bitter he vas when Davie married Ellen, she vasn't a Jew. He wanted to sit Shiva, but Davie vas our only child and I beg him to accept. For mine sake he try like he did, but I know in here" ---She pounded her fist over her heart---"He never did. I have all the insides taken out after vee had Davie so vee couldn't have more children. I vouldn't sit shiva for mine only child. Sol thought Davie have no respect for the ancestors for vat he did. I tell you, I felt the same vay. The vay Benny feels, I tink I know. The vorld is changing, better maybe that things get all mixed up. I tink maybe mine brutter, he be alive, if he vas all mixed up. Den vat can they do? Hate the part that vas only Jewish maybe? If he vas a little this or dat, den vat part vould they hate, huh? The leg, the arm? Vere vould they find the part they vould hate? How much of him vould they hate?" She looked sad as she said it.

Nora never thought of it that way, but it made sense to her. Sylvia poured herself another cup of coffee and spooned a heaping spoonful of sugar out of the sugar bowl, she held it up close to Nora, "Look, you see vat this is," she dumped it into the coffee. "The sugar, she is still in der but now you von't see it, it's all mixed up." Nora smiled. Mrs. Katz took a deep breath and sighed, "You know, dis vour is a terrible ting but something goot maybe come from it."

Nora took a swallow from her cup of coffee and sighed. For her, the only good that came out of the war was her little grandson.

CHAPTER 43

On Friday August 10th Benny arrived at the worksite feeling a bit under the weather. All the men were excitedly talking about the second bomb dropped on Nagasaki, Japan the day before and how the war would be ending soon, but he wasn't in a talking mood about anything. Mr. Marini was the foreman Benny hardly tolerated most of the time, and this particular morning he felt angry and out of sorts. It wouldn't take much for him to blow up at the man. He never did like him, and he knew this was the day he was ready to snap. He kept to himself most of the morning, and then after lunch, went off to the side, pulling on the long rubber boots over his work shoes. It had rained the night before and the ground was very wet. The deep trench he would have to climb down into had several inches of water at the bottom.

For several weeks the men dug the trench and shored up the sides with planks. Soon, plumbers would go down and lay the sewer pipes. It was the construction crew, usually referred to as the ditch diggers, who went down and set the pump, to drain the water out and check the temporary plank walls. Mr. Marini called out two of his men, of which Benny was one, to do the job. A narrow wooden ladder was eased down the side of the deep trench. Benny was the first to descend down to the bottom, as fellow worker, Frank Piermani, followed. Benny waded along the long water-filled ditch, checking the plank sides as Frank stayed at the bottom of the ladder waiting for the pump to be lowered down to him. There was a slight bend in the dirt wall where Benny was inspecting, about twenty- feet from Frank. The walls of dirt appeared wet and a bulge pushed the planked wall forward. Benny pushed on the wood to check its strength, when without much pressure from his hand, it gave way, and before he could react, the heavy soil came down around him. Up, down, left, right, it was all the same now. The earth was closing in on him, blocking out all view of the sky above. The shouting voices seemed to get further and further in the distance until all he heard was silence. He couldn't move and he struggled to breath. The heavy gray soil felt soft and cool. He thought, this is what death must feel like, like soft wet flannel. He welcomed it, embraced it, as he automatically tried to take a deep breath but it wasn't there to take, and he didn't care.

The call to the Nuzzo home came at a quarter after three in the afternoon. Nora answered, expecting it to be her sister or Rosemarie. At the wedding, Rosemarie said she wouldn't be afraid to call the house now that she was married.

"Hello!" Nora answered cheerfully, expecting it to be a women's voice. The rough voice on the other end startled her.

"Mrs. Nuzzo," the voice said

"Yes," she answered.

"I'm Mr. Marini, Mrs. Nuzzo, there's been an accident. Your husband has been taken to County hospital."

Nora didn't reply. She had a hard time taking in what the man said. She told herself it couldn't be. Finally, she repeated his words. "My husband had an accident?"

"Yes, yes, there was a cave-in at the worksite. The ground gave way, too much rain."

"No, no," was all she could say. He could hear her muffled cry.

"He was taken to Cook County Hospital, I'm sure he's going to be ok Mrs. Nuzzo." He tried to assure her, although he wasn't sure himself.

"Thank you," was all she could reply. She hung up the phone, and with her hands shaking she dialed for the operator. She gave the number of Nicky's work place. It rang four times, "Delta Star," a voice answered.

"I'm calling for Nick Nuzzo," she said, "It's an emergency." She heard the voice yell above the noise of the punch press machines, "Hey Nick, for you. It sounds important!"

Nicky shut off his machine and walked to the phone. He

picked up the receiver.

"Yeah, who is this?"

Nora broke down crying when she heard his voice. "Nicky, it's Benny, he's in the hospital, there's been an accident at work. The man just called, I don't know how bad it is. He was taken to County Hospital."

"I'll leave right now; I'll go straight to the hospital. Meet me there," he told her. He could hear her sobbing into the phone. "Nora, it might not be as bad as you think. Stay calm and take the streetcar and I'll meet you there." He knew she was closer to the hospital, but he would drive and get there first.

"Ok, I'm leaving right now."

She hung up the phone, removed her apron and looked at the clock. Having just returned from school, Sammy was on the back porch with Bobby. She wasn't sure how long she would be at the hospital. "Sammy! Go downstairs to Mrs. Katz," she ordered. She sent Bobby home, and followed Sammy downstairs to inform Sylvia of the bad news. She knew she could depend on her to bring Sammy upstairs and put him to bed if she hadn't returned in time.

She went back upstairs to get her purse and left as quickly as she could, never bothering to check her hair as she usually did whenever she left home. Her heart was beating fast as she half ran to the streetcar stop. Looking down the track, she watched for an approaching car. There never seemed to be one when it was needed. As she waited, she thought she should have called someone else in the family, Rose, Rosemarie? And then thought what would she tell them when she didn't know anything about his condition herself.

On the ride to the hospital she sat close to the exit, ready to jump off as soon as the streetcar stopped in front of the hospital. She thought of how she had been so disgusted with her husband's behavior and thought, *Oh God! I wished him away when I couldn't stand his anger. I wanted to be free of his anger, and now look what my wishing did.* She felt guilty. She was sure in some unexplained way, she was the cause of his accident. His attention to anything, his caring about anyone had disappeared since they lost Joey, and Rosemarie left home. *I should have been more understanding,* she thought, as she cried softly into her hanky; grateful for the near empty car she rode in, she didn't try to hold the back the tears. She couldn't think straight. Logic wasn't part of her thinking when the unexpected occurred. She always tied it to something that was thought about, or wished for. She never would have believed her husband would have an accident after all the years of telling her he worked in safety. For her, this sort of tragedy was unexpected.

She would laugh at Maria who believed in the evil eye when something bad happened, and would only agree with her to placate her. Her children didn't believe in such things, and would hold her up to ridicule when she agreed with their grandmother, but this day, she couldn't shake the feeling that somehow she was responsible. When she arrived at the hospital, Nicky was waiting for her in the lobby. He didn't want her to see Benny before he had a chance to prepare her for what he found when he walked into the hospital room.

"Benny's in a deep sleep," he gently told her. "The doctor said they expect him to wake up soon. They sedated him heavily because of the severe pain he was experiencing when they brought him in. Don't worry, he'll come out of it, you know how stubborn he is."

"But what if he dies?" she asked, with a worried expression.

"What! Benny die? Benny won't die. People like him live on, they cause people like you and me to die," he laughed, hoping she would take it as a joke.

She could only see it as resentment toward his older brother. She didn't blame him. Benny had never been kind to Nicky, even when he was just a boy and she first met the family, she could see how Benny treated him. Back then she felt sorry for the boy; she observed the animosity, the jealousy, and she had a hard time understanding the Nuzzo family's strained relationship. She could only judge them by her relationship to her own children. She had loved her children equally. If it appeared she catered more to Sammy, it was because of the boy's condition. Joey and Rosie were never jealous of Sammy, she was sure of that.

She held on to Nicky's arm as they walked into Benny's room. The nurse met them at his bedside.

"Are you Mrs. Nuzzo?" she asked. Nora nodded yes.

"He is heavily sedated, but doing as well as can be expected, in spite of his injuries," the nurse said.

The scene that greeted Nora filled her with apprehension. She walked over to the side of his bed. He was under an oxygen tent to help him breathe. She called his name but there wasn't any response. Nicky stood at the foot of the bed. The doctor came in to check his vital signs and introduced himself. He motioned them into the hall. Nicky followed him, but Nora remained at his bedside; she hadn't noticed the doctor wave them out.

"I'm his brother," Nicky informed him, "Doctor, what is his condition?"

"He has several broken ribs, that alone is painful but it's the right leg we are concerned about. It's his femur bone, it was crushed, and it might not heal as we hope it will. Only time will tell. All his injurys are on the right side of his body. That's the side that took the weight of the heavy planks and soil that caved in on him. Also, his breathing has to improve. He was unconscious when they pulled him out. His airways were obstructed for a short time, and he has a collapsed right lung. He's lucky to be alive."

Nicky thanked the doctor and returned to the room where Nora was still trying to talk to her husband.

"He can't hear you," Nicky said, "He's going to be ok, don't worry. His right leg is broken and his ribs on the right side too." He wasn't going to explain all the details to her just yet. He knew how worried she would get. No use telling her things she couldn't understand and telling her what the doctor feared would only upset her more than she needed to be.

For the next couple of days, Benny lay sleeping. Nora was able to see him every day by leaving Sammy with Mrs. Katz or Twyla. On the fourth day, she found him awake. She looked down at him with sympathy.

"How are you feeling?" she asked.

He moaned and hunched his shoulder, looked at her and then closed his eyes. He didn't talk, just lay there and she didn't know what else to say to him.

A week later, she looked at the time on the clock. It was early afternoon. She had gone to the hospital every afternoon since he was brought in. She felt uncomfortable leaving Sammy with the neighbors every afternoon. She felt she was imposing on Mrs. Katz too much, but Rose's bakery was too far out of the way to bring him there, and she didn't want to burden her daughter by bringing him there, afraid the boy might tell Benny where he had been. She wouldn't go this afternoon, but wait for her brother-in-law to come over after work, she would feed him supper and together they would return to the hospital for the evening visiting hours. The McCanns offered to take Sammy one evening and also Grace Peterson, but she declined sending him over to Grace. She wasn't sure how Ralph would be with the boy. It was mostly Mrs. Katz who took Sammy, every time she was needed.

When Nora and Nicky entered the hospital room a week after his accident, they found him without the oxygen tent and Nora was relieved. She leaned over him and asked how he was feeling. He had a very raspy voice but managed to speak in a whisper. He said some words she couldn't understand. She bent her head closer to him

"What? Benny what did you say?"

Nicky asked him to repeat what he was trying to tell them.

"I hid the money," he said.

"You hid what?" Nicky asked, not sure he heard right.

"I hid money in the basement; Nora will need money for

food."

"Where? Where did you hide money? Where in the basement," Nora asked, looking surprised.

They both looked at him with frowns on their faces; they couldn't believe what they were hearing.

"I don't remember where," he said, "I put it there a long time ago for safekeeping.

"He's still living in the depression," Nora said, "He doesn't trust banks."

Nicky laughed at such a ridiculous reason to hide money in a basement.

CHAPTER 44

After Nicky and Nora returned home, they went into the basement. They searched for the money knocking over a coal shovel in the process, and the clanging noise brought Mrs. Katz and Sammy to the top of the basement stairs. Nora wanted to find it and go back upstairs without Mrs. Katz knowing about the money, so they entered the basement from the outside entrance, under the back porch.

"Vats going on down dere?" Mrs. Katz called from the top of the stairs. Soon both she and Sammy were in the basement.

"Benny told us he hid money down here", Nora said. "We have to find it."

"Vat Money? Money he hid! Meshugener!" Mrs. Katz yelled.

"What did she say?" Nicky asked, as he slid his hands behind pipes.

"She's calling Benny crazy and I thinks she's right," Nora said.

Before long, Mrs. Katz joined in on the search with Sammy following. They looked under everything, an old workbench full of spider webs that hadn't been used since Mr. Katz died. The pipes in the basement were damp and the damp basement smelled musty of mold, and coal dust was everywhere.

"I can't believe he would hide money down here!" Nicky said, laughing.

Nora was as surprised at her brother-in-law. "I can't believe he let us know where he hid it," she said.

"I think he told us because he thinks he's in worse shape than he is. If I know my brother, he thinks he's dying.

"You know your brother, always crape hanging and feeling sorry for himself," Nora said.

Nicky tried to get behind water pipes, running his hands behind everything but all he came out with was spider webs and coal dust. The light from the few light bulbs left the area dimly lit, casting shadows everywhere.

"Maybe he removed it and forgot, you know he was still groggy from all the medicine they gave him when he told us," Nicky said.

He spotted an old wine barrel in the corner; the smell of stale wine still permeated the air around it.

"What's this?" he asked.

"That's mine Sol's vine barrel, in prohibition he make the vine, for the Passover." Mrs. Katz explained.

The part of the basement they were in was at the back corner, away from the coal furnace. The air near the old barrel and a rusted wine press had a hint of fermented grapes and mold.

"I could get drunk just breathing the air in this corner," Nicky said, shaking his head in wonderment that after so many years the smell hung on.

The four of them tore the basement apart looking for the money. Sammy asked, "What are we looking for, Uncle Nicky?"

Nicky laughed, "For a treasure."

As Sammy joined in the search, even the coal bin wasn't overlooked. He became filthy with coal dust. They were about to give up when Nicky noticed a large drainpipe coming from the bathrooms upstairs. He reached his hand around the pipe, running his hand up and down between the wall and the large pipe. Toward the top, his hand hit wet paper stuck to the wall behind the pipe. There was barely enough room between the pipe and the wall for his hand. He pulled the object loose. His hand brought out a thick damp dirty envelope. He shouted, "I think I found it, I found it!" as they all ran to see what he had found. The wet envelope fell away from a wad of bills. They stared, wide- eyed, in total silence. Sammy's face was black, and his eyes stuck out like two white spots, which caused them all to laugh.

"Look at this!" Nicky said, "I can't believe it. Didn't he

ever hear of a bank?"

"Let's go upstairs," Nora said, leading the way. The four of them hurried up the stairs to Nora's kitchen. They rushed to sit at the table and watch Nicky count the money. They were covered with coal dust.

He started to count the damp bills and when he got up to two thousand, he stopped. "I don't believe this!" he said, holding the few bills not counted, for the others to see. Nora looked angry. She turned to Mrs. Katz, "And to think I was sitting up late at night crocheting and knitting until I was cross-eyed trying to make a little hush-hush money selling doilies, money Benny wouldn't know about. Damn him!" Mrs. Katz put her arm around her to comfort her. Nicky continued to count five-hundred dollars more. He spread them out on the table to dry.

"These had to be in the basement for years," he said.

"That cheap son-of-a!" Nora said, and then realizing what she was about to say, she covered her mouth with her hand as quickly as the first words were out. She couldn't believe she almost said them and in the presence of Sammy, but the boy's attention was on all the money that covered the table. Nicky started to laugh, soon they were all laughing. Something snapped in Nora. She grabbed a fist full of bills and held them up.

"This should have been for the new washing machine he said we couldn't afford." She grabbed another handful of bills, "And this should have been for Ma's train ticket to New Jersey to see her brother, a trip she wanted to make for years but he always said he couldn't afford it. He's a miser!" she cried.

"Boy, oh boy! The chickens have come home to roost Nora, you got to take the upper hand like I been telling you. He ain't gonna be in no condition to give orders to anyone," Nicky said.

She nodded in agreement, she felt strange, like the feelings she had when she ignored him and left for the wedding. She felt stronger.

"Don't mention we found the money," she said to Nicky, and then looking at Sammy, she worried he might say something. "Sammy, remember, if you want that new bike you always wanted, forget we found this money."

"Where did the money come from, Mama?" he asked.

"Oy Vay," Mrs. Katz said. She put her arm around the boy. She understood Nora's worry, "You see Sammy, mine Sol, in the basement before he die, he hide the money."

Later that evening, with Sammy in bed, Nora and Nicky talked about Benny and hoped he wouldn't remember telling them about the money. "He was half asleep, he's not going to remember," Nicky assured her.

With Benny away from home, and money in her possession, she felt a freedom she hadn't felt since she was a young girl helping her family in the bakery. Some of the neighbors heard about the accident and stopped by to ask how her husband was doing, and to offer any help she might need. Katie was a frequent visitor, she now thought of Nora as family. Twyla was a big help with Sammy whenever she was asked to relieve Mrs. Katz from having the boy every afternoon. Benny was slow to heal and the leg seemed to give him the most trouble. Grace Peterson stopped by one morning to ask about Benny. Since Joey died, Nora had gotten to know her better and found her to be a sweet woman, although more reserved than her other neighbors. They sat together in the kitchen, and Grace talked about her son-in-law.

"Did you know Lorraine's husband was found? He was in a German prisoner of war camp. Michael is back home now."

"How is Ralph handling it?" Nora asked.

"He has accepted Michael. The kids are living with Michael's parents temporarily, they have more room, and Lorraine is more comfortable there. I can't blame her, the way Ralph was."

"At least your husband has accepted. My Benny, he will never accept, never forgive Rosie for leaving home. You know the situation, and they are married now but still he won't forgive her. He's too set in his ways, too stubborn," Nora said sadly. "Rosie won't go to the hospital, but she calls me every day to ask about him."

"Everyone has their breaking point Nora. With Ralph, it was seeing the pain our daughter was in when Michael was listed as missing, and the fear he might lose her. This war has brought so many changes to everyone."

Nora nodded in agreement, but thought the change it brought her husband wasn't for the better.

CRITICAL CRITICAL

Benny had been in the hospital two weeks. He was improving greatly, but being able to walk was questionable. They waited, holding their breath, hoping he wouldn't mention the money. He didn't. He was wide awake, alert, and feeling better. The doctor mentioned he might be released soon. Nora was at his bedside.

"Do you know when you'll be coming home?" she asked.

He shook his head, no. He wasn't talking much. He seemed subdued, quiet, not like the belligerent Benny they were used to. They didn't know what to make of it. Nora thought he felt embarrassed because the brother he treated so badly was there for him in spite of the strain in their relationship. Nicky, his lifelong nemesis, thought his silence was just plain stubbornness.

When a priest entered the room and introduced himself as Father David, he explained he was the pastor that visited all Catholic patients in the hospital, and he checked on Benny every day but always found him asleep. This was his first visit where Benny was doing well and wide awake. The priest smiled at him.

"Would you like to receive communion in the morning Mr. Nuzzo?"

"How much is it?" Benny asked.

Nicky started laughing, but Nora was embarrassed. The

349

priest had no way of knowing the patient never went to Mass.

"It's free," The priest said, "Unless they charge you for it when you get up there," he pointed his finger in the air.

CHAPTER 45

It was the last week of August 1945, and everyone knew the war had come to an end. All the Japanese had to do was sign the final unconditional surrender. It was to take place on September 2nd. Benny was to be released from the hospital and Nicky was bringing him home. Nora and Sammy sat on the front porch like two people waiting for a storm to arrive. They were nervous about having him home again and not sure of what to expect. Mrs. Katz and Twyla waited with them. Nora told them how his leg was slowly healing and he couldn't walk without the aid of crutches, which he was unable to use; he said it hurt his arms. He would be confined to a wheelchair. It was Sunday, the 26th of August, and Nora spent the last couple of days preparing for his return.

When Nicky's car pulled up to the house, she could see Benny sitting in the passenger seat. She thought he looked depressed. Twyla went to get her husband to help carry him up the stairs. Nicky then returned to his car for the wheelchair. When he had settled Benny in his blue chair, he asked him if he wanted to sit by the window in the wheelchair.

"Ok," he said, "The wheelchair." Those were the only words he spoke since he arrived home. Nora stood watching him get settled by the window where he could look out on the street below and watch the neighborhood children playing. There wasn't anything else he was able to do besides read the paper or listen to the radio. She raised the window shade to let the sun in and the flag with Joey's gold star hung there, in his face, like a matador's cape in front of a bull. She held her breath, not sure of what he would say, but he said nothing. *I should have removed it before he came home*, she thought. He had to sit by the window, with the reminder that he lost his son, inches from his face. Nora walked away and went into the kitchen. There was nothing more to do. Nicky joined her.

"He hasn't mentioned the money," he whispered to her. "I

don't think he remembers telling us. It must have been years since he hid it there. The envelope was ready to fall apart and the money would have dropped to the floor."

"I put it in the bank with my name on the account too," she said, looking worried. "What if he should ask about it?" *I'll cross that bridge when I have to*, she thought.

"I'm afraid he planned to use the money to move us back to the old neighborhood," she said.

Nicky walked to the doorway to view Benny at the window, hunched over in his chair. Turning back to Nora, he said, "The only plan he's going to make is how he's going to get to the bathroom after I leave."

"Oh, I never thought of that," Nora said.

"Don't worry; I'll stay until we put him to bed."

During supper, he sat quietly, never speaking, he felt humiliated to have had to rely on his brother. Earlier when Nora was preparing supper he heard them talking in the kitchen but couldn't make out what it was about. They were talking about Sammy and the celebration that was to take place at the Victory Garden the following Sunday, September 2nd, the very day Japan was signing the surrender. He could see the change in his wife and he felt threatened. After supper he tried to wheel his chair back into the front room again, but he had to use his arms and he was still in pain. He wasn't able to do it. The kitchen doorway was narrow and Nicky had to help him through it. He could see that Nora wouldn't be able to handle him alone.

"Nora, I think I should stay for a few days. I'll go home and get some clothes and be back tonight. I'll sleep in Ma's room; at least for this week, you need the help."

"Thanks Nicky," she said, as she gave him a hug, relieved she wouldn't be alone with Benny. Maybe by the time the week is over, he could manage by himself, she told herself.

Later that night after Nicky returned, and they had gotten Benny to bed, they sat with Sammy and talked about the planned Labor Day weekend, and the end of the war celebration to take place at the Victory Garden.

"So, you're going to get a reward, huh Sammy," Nicky said.

"Yeah, Uncle Nicky, I gotta wear my uniform, all the Boy Scouts have one too. Mama got me the new uniform, ya wanna see it?" He ran into his room and retrieved the crisp new uniform hanging on a hanger. He looked so proud as he showed it to his uncle.

After Sammy went to bed, Nora and Nicky talked late into the night.

"Remember Nora, you hold all the cards now, get the upper hand and don't let him boss you around. Who's he got? Tell me, who's he got? Only us. He's in no position to order you around or make plans for anybody." She agreed with him, and they spoke of the coming celebration.

"They're going to honor all the boys whose names are on the flag pole monument, and also the Boy Scouts for all they had done for the war drive," she said. "The eighth grade band from the John Ericsson Grade School will play. Everyone from our neighborhood will be there. Mr. Brown the Boy Scout leader, and our neighborhood precinct captain, Mr. Martin, and the air raid warden, Mr. Rizzo, also old Father O'Hara, from Our Lady of Sorrows Church. Pastor Ed from the Messiah Baptist church will be there. The children from the grade school choir will sing. The music teacher, Miss Van, will lead them. Nicky, our Sammy is getting a reward for collecting the most scrap for the war drive."

"Well, I'm not going to miss that!" he said. I'll bring Lillian too."

"What should I tell Benny?"

"What do you mean, what should you tell him, tell him his son is getting an award and he's gotta be there."

"He'll never go; his excuse will be the wheelchair."

"Don't worry Nora, then don't say anything and let me handle him."

On Saturday, Benny was in a foul mood. He sat all

morning where Nicky had placed him, in the wheelchair. He pretended to sleep, keeping his eyes closed. Nicky had taken Sammy with him to run errands, and Nora found herself alone with her husband and his unpredictable moods. When the doorbell rang, she was happy to see Grace Peterson at her door, but surprised to see Ralph standing behind her.

"We came to see how Benny is doing," Grace said.

"Come in, come in," Nora said smiling. They followed her into the front room.

"Benny! Mr. and Mrs. Peterson are here."

The Petersons coming to his home surprised him; he was unaware that Grace had visited Nora since he was in the hospital. He managed a weak hello, and then pointing to a chair across from his, he motioned Ralph to sit. The two women went into the kitchen leaving the men alone. Ralph looked concerned.

"How are you doing Mr. Nuzzo?"

"I'm doing."

Ralph sat forward in his chair, "When we heard about the accident we couldn't believe it. We were hoping you would be ok."

Benny looked at Ralph, and arching his eyebrows he said, "I don't know what happened. The last thing I remember is a man yelling, next thing I know I'm waking up in the hospital. My leg's in a cast and my chest hurt real bad."

Ralph nodded, "It's is a shame that it had to happen."

There was a pause in the conversation, neither man could come up with something more to say. Finally Benny looked out the window and said, "Your grass looks good. You put a lot of work in it, huh?"

Ralph accepted the compliment with a smile. "Yes, I guess I do. You know, my father built my house and several others on the street."

Benny looked surprised, "Your family, they been here a long time then?"

"Yes, I think so, the homes were built in the 1880s and

1890s. When this neighborhood was new, it was beautiful. Of course it's still a nice neighborhood, just older, a lot has changed but some change is good don't you think?"

Benny was silent for a moment, and then shaking his head, he said, "It all depends, if it's good change or bad change." He was wondering to himself about the change in Mr. Peterson. He didn't seem like the hostile opinionated neighbor he remembered not too long ago.

So many changes, Benny couldn't keep up with them. What confused him most was the change in Nora.

Sitting at the kitchen table over cups of coffee, and Nora's homemade pound cake, the women couldn't believe their so very different men were having a conversation that was meaningful.

"Ralph seems so friendly lately," Nora said. "He never fails to say hello or wave to me when I'm outdoors. He never used to do that."

Grace smiled and adjusted her glasses, put her hand on Nora's and said, "It's the war, it was a bad time for everyone, but for Ralph, it scared the living daylights out of him. He was always so fussy about everything, he would complain, complain, and during one of our blackouts one night when the planes flew over, when we were sitting on our porch," -- She kept her voice low and looked towards the men in the front room—"after years of hearing him complain, about the McCann boys, Mrs. Katz's dog, the weeds, everything, and then some young people went by in their car and threw some trash on the street, a paper bag or something, and did he get in a bad mood. Look up there Ralph!" I said; pointing to the sky, "You call this neighborhood trash? If that plane were a Jap plane dropping bombs instead of our planes dropping slips of paper, then you'd see real trash. He shut up after that. I knew he was like a yappy dog, all bark and no bite. He has feelings Nora, Joey's death affected him, and when Patrick was wounded, I could see the sadness in his expression when I told him."

"Men are never happy, no matter how we try to please," Nora said.

"You know what my mother used to say about men?" Grace laughed, "She would say that men are like kings. They have to feel like they are the rulers of their kingdom. A king is never wrong; he thinks he makes all the right decisions. Then my mother would laugh, because quietly in the back room of the castle the queen is really controlling what is going on. The only thing the queen can't control is what's outside the castle. He makes all the decisions for his subjects and they have to go along with it, that's why the king can start wars. Underneath men are really scared little boys," then Grace laughed a hearty laugh. "Like Henry the eighth, he knew it was really the queens who ran the show; that's why he tried to get rid of them."

Nora didn't know who Henry the eighth was; but she laughed along with Grace. They could see their men in the other room looking their way, wondering why they were laughing. Benny wondered if it was about him.

"What else can men do, work and complain, that's all," Grace said.

"They can't cook a good pot of spaghetti; they can't carry children, they can't cry, and get their feelings out," Nora said. She almost felt sorry for them as she said it.

After the neighbors left, Nora tried to engage Benny in conversation, but he wasn't responding. "Can I get you anything?" she asked. He nodded no. She left him alone where Nicky had placed him, by the window, and went about her household chores, hoping her brother-in-law and Sammy would be home soon. She worried about how Benny would react when he realized the whole neighborhood would be at the Victory Garden. They wouldn't tell him, just wheel him down.

CHAPTER 46

Sunday, September 2nd the morning of the Victory Garden celebration had arrived. Benny had been home a week, and was able to manage the apartment with the wheelchair. Nora would get him through a doorway once he wheeled himself from room to room. She was pleased that he was getting better and able to do more for himself. The two of them were alone; Nicky had taken Sammy with him to pick up Lillian. He stayed most of the week with Nora, and she was grateful for his help. Benny knew nothing about the celebration that was to take place that afternoon. The fact that Sammy never mentioned what he was very excited about to Benny surprised Nora. Sammy was getting older, and he remembered her cautioning him not to say anything to his father. She kept telling herself that maybe her son would catch up one day. She needed to think that, even knowing that the scouts in his troop were all eight to ten years old. At thirteen, Sammy stood a head above most of them and he was still in 4th grade. With more help, Nora hoped she could look forward to his graduating one day.

She was nervous and worried, afraid Benny would fail to attend what would mean so much to their son. It would be the boy's greatest day. Nicky wasn't going to tell him until the last minute, so he would have a harder time refusing to go. Her sister Rose planned to attend. She knew it wasn't going to be easy, getting Benny to face some of the neighbors. They wouldn't tell him all the facts about the celebration, just that it was for Sammy's Boy Scout troop. She passed through the living room to adjust a doily on the back of the couch, when Benny wheeled his chair around to face her. "What did you do with the money?" he asked in a loud voice, it startled her. She felt a rush of heat rise to her face.

"What do you mean, what did I do with the money? You said it was for food; we had to live while you were gone.

357

Sammy needed a new Boy Scout uniform; he outgrew the used one I managed to pay for with my knitting money, no thanks to you. You watched him leave this house wearing a uniform too small; you didn't care how he looked. Did you ever look at our son? I don't think so!" She was on a roll and couldn't stop herself. "All you could think of was yourself, saving face, saving face, your damn face, that's all I ever heard that was important to you!" she raised her voice in anger, in a way he had never witnessed before.

"That money was also for a rainy day!" he yelled.

She had an expression on her face he had never seen before. "A Rainy Day? A Rainy day? Benny, living with you the past four years, it rained every day!" She turned and left the room.

She didn't speak to him the rest of the morning. She made his lunch and placed it on the dining room table where he could wheel himself over to it. She stayed in the kitchen planning the supper she would make when they returned from the celebration. It would take place at 2:00 p.m. Benny wouldn't dare refuse to leave the house, not in front of both Rose and Nicky, she reasoned.

At 1:00 p.m Nicky returned with Lillian and Sammy. Benny heard laughter as Nora met them at the door. He turned his wheelchair around expecting to see Nicky and Sammy, but when Lillian came in he was surprised.

"You remember Lillian, don't you?" Nicky said as he took her hand and brought her over to Benny. He stared at her. It had been years since she was brought over to his home. He called her a Pollack, and one of Nicky's puttanas back then. Now he thought she looked old.

Nicky could see the disapproval in his brother's eyes, as Benny just nodded at her.

"We're engaged," Nicky said, as he took Lillian's hand and held it out so Benny could see the ring.

"So, how many years you two been dating?" Benny said, with a disgusted look on his face.

"Does it matter?" Nicky replied, irritated by his brother's tone of voice, "We plan on getting married, I thought you might like hearing that!"

"How are you feeling Mr. Nuzzo? I'm so sorry to hear about your accident," Lillian said.

He managed to answer, "I'm doing." That was more than Nicky could ask for. At least he didn't ignore her completely like he had done in the past.

In the kitchen Sammy asked loudly, "Is Papa coming to the Victory Garden?" Nora put her finger to her lips, "Be quiet," she said, "He doesn't know about it yet, but he's going."

"What if he don't go Mama?"

"Oh don't worry, he's going, even if he don't like it, he's going. Uncle Nicky will make sure of that!"

When Nora heard her sister Rose's voice as she entered the hall, she went to greet her. They went into the dining room. Rose was congratulating Sammy on what was to take place at the Victory Garden, and Nicky introduced Lillian to Rose. Benny shouted, "What's going on?" He wondered why they were all there.

Nicky went to Benny, and the rest of them followed Nora to the kitchen.

"Benny, Sammy is being rewarded as a Boy Scout today at the Victory Garden and you have to be there with us," he announced, in a firm voice.

"I'm not going; I can't go in this chair. Who's going to be there anyway?"

"Only the Boy Scouts," Nicky assured him.

"All the neighbors? If everyone is going to be there, I'm not going!"

Nicky could see he was nervous; he didn't want to run into the McCanns.

"The McCann boy isn't in the Boy Scouts anymore," Nicky assured him.

"I can't go."

"Oh yes you can!"

Nora heard their loud voices and came into the room. "He isn't going is he?" she asked, she sounded upset.

"Don't worry, he's going if I have to drag him all the way down," Nicky informed her. He called to Sammy, "Sammy go get Mr. Woods, it's time to leave."

Benny was angry, he thought, *all these people in my home, my brother telling me what to do and now he calls for the neighbor next door?* He gripped the arms of the wheelchair so tight, the veins in his hands protruded. He felt he was losing control of his life. *I'm a prisoner in this damn chair,* he thought. Lately, all he had control of was his thoughts.

When Mr. Woods and Twyla came into the flat, Benny felt as though he couldn't breathe. Nicky pulled Sammy in front of him, "Look at him, Look at your son!" he shouted. Sammy stood wearing the crisp new scout uniform. Benny barely looked up at him. Nicky motioned to Mr. Woods, and the two of them wheeled Benny to the top of the landing. They decided it was easier to leave him in the wheelchair and go down the steps one at a time, Nicky pulling him down each step slowly in front of the chair, while Mr. Woods held on to the back of the chair. When they reached the sidewalk, Nicky looked around and was relieved that none of neighbors had left for the Garden yet. It was early, and he planned on getting Benny there before he realized it wasn't just for Sammy and the Boy Scouts.

He parked Benny on the parkway between the sidewalk and the street, facing him towards the flag pole with the engraved servicemen's names. On the other side of the walk were bleacher benches someone had set up where the boys would sit. A few people who lived close to the corner brought out kitchen chairs to sit on. Nicky and Lillian stood behind the wheelchair, blocking Benny's view of the street behind him. Nora, Rose and Sammy were to follow with Mrs. Katz and the Woods family a few minutes later. Benny looked around, and he could see more people arriving, more than he expected.

360

Every time he tried to turn his head and look down towards his home, Nick and Lillian blocked his view. A few more people arrived and took up spots around Benny's chair, along with Nora, Rose, Mrs. Katz, and the Woods family. Others sat on the grass and waved to him or came over to ask how he was doing. He was feeling uncomfortable, and he started to sweat. The hot sun was shining down on his bald head. He took out his handkerchief and wiped his face and the top of his head.

When Mr. Russo came up to him and asked how he was doing, he was nervous and could barely answer, he hadn't spoken to the Russos since he went over to their home and made a fool of himself. This was the last place he wanted to be and wished he were home.

"Hello Ben, we heard about your accident, I hope you're doing ok," Mr. Russo said.

Benny shrugged his shoulders and said, "I'm Ok," with his head down. Mr. Russo could tell he didn't want to talk so he said a few more words of pleasantries and left. Benny looked around and could see it was becoming very crowded. Mr. Martin, the precinct captain of their street was there, along with the two clergymen from both the Catholic and Baptist churches. They were the nearest churches in the neighborhood. When Mr. Brown, the Scout leader came up to Benny, and held out his hand, Benny shook it reluctantly.

"You must be proud of your boy," Mr. Brown said. Benny nodded and smiled sheepishly, and watched as the Scout leader gathered all the boys together, all ten of them, and had them sitting on the bleachers. Benny looked at the other boys with Sammy, all younger and a head shorter than his son. Their uniforms were neatly pressed. Sammy's new uniform had become wrinkled, and damp from perspiration somewhere between the house and where he now sat.

Benny felt uncomfortable and all he could think about was how messy his boy looked, all rumpled, with damp curls of hair stuck to his forehead. The other boys looked neat compared to Sammy. He thought about how the boy ate too

361

much, and how heavy he was. As he looked at him sitting there, he thought of how the boy embarrassed him. He thought it was all Maria and Nora's fault. They always overfed him as if food were the answer to all the boy's problems, as if food could make him into the boy he should have been, smart like his brother Joey. He was thinking all that, and didn't notice the crowd behind him becoming larger.

Nora and Rose stood next to Nicky, along with Mrs. Katz and the Woods family. They watched the school band forming off to the side of Benny. He turned to his left, and he could see the street was packed with people. He realized it was more than just the neighbors from his block, but also the surrounding area, people he didn't know from both the Irish and Italian neighborhoods. He recognized Mr. Stine from the 12th Street area whom he got to know riding the streetcar to work every day. Mr. Stine owned a store in the neighborhood, and took the same streetcar as Benny. What is he doing here? He doesn't live on this street, he thought. He sat wondering what this was really about. He now knew it was for more than just a few Boy Scouts. He tried to turn and look behind him; he feared the McCanns were attending, and they were the last people he wanted to be in close proximity to. Old Father O'Hara led the crowd in a short prayer, and Mrs. Katz elbowed Nora to look over at Mr. Peterson across from them, he was actually bowing his head. "I don't think he's praying," Nora said, "he's looking down; that's all it is." She waved to Grace. Lorraine was holding hands with her young husband as they stood with her parents.

Mr. Martin led the crowd in the pledge of allegiance. Benny couldn't stand so he sat with his hand over his heart. The crowd cheered after the band played the *National Anthem* and *God Bless America*, and when they finished, Mr. Martin gave a speech about the end of the war which was taking place with the signing of the unconditional surrender on the Battleship Missouri that very day. The crowd cheered again. The band played *Anchors Away*. Pastor Ed James from the

Messiah Baptist Church read off all the names of the boys listed on the flagpole monument. Ten names, representing all the branches of service, two were Robert and Russell James, the pastor's sons. Two had gold stars at the end of their names: Joseph Francis Nuzzo and Thomas Daniel O'Reilly. Old Father O'Hara from Our Lady of Sorrows Church, which was the main Catholic Church in the neighborhood but was at the beginning of the Irish area, said, "I bless this memorial we have here today, to honor the boys who served so valiantly in the service of their country, and to the two Gold Star mothers, Mrs. O'Reilly and Mrs. Nuzzo who made the ultimate sacrifice to keep our country free." He yelled out the words because he was hard of hearing. The old priest appeared visibly shaken.

Nora and Mrs. O'Reilly were called up to the monument. They were presented with a certificate, and corsages of white mums were attached to their dresses. Nora wiped the tears that fell on her cheeks. Benny sat stiff and still in his chair with his head down. He wanted out of there badly, so he turned to look up at Nicky behind him.

"I don't feel good, take me home," he said, but Nicky ignored him and held on to the chair, afraid he might try to wheel himself back. He sat feeling angry and frustrated, trying to see where the McCanns were, if they were there. He was afraid of facing them, he would lose all face, all his dignity, because the shame would show on his face. He was sure of it. He had so many feelings welling up inside of him.

Nora returned to be with the others around Benny when she felt a hand touch her shoulder, she turned, and there was Rosemarie. She gave her daughter a hug. Patrick walked up to her and she hugged him. He had his new leg on but still needed the aid of a cane. He was wearing his white Navy uniform. Nora hugged Katie who was holding Joey. Nora could feel herself shaking inside, afraid of what Benny might say when he saw them. Her sister Rose came up to them and met little Joey and Patrick for the first time. It pleased Nora because she knew Rose could only accept them if they were married. Rose could not bring herself to attend the wedding, and it hurt Nora, but once it had taken place she knew Rose would feel differently. Rosemarie introduced them to Francie who came to honor Joey. Peggy was introducing her sailor boyfriend Steve to everyone. The crowd was noisy; the band played one patriotic song after another. Benny couldn't see behind him or make out any distinguishable voices. He was unaware of all the McCanns, and his daughter behind him.

"Who's here?" Benny asked nervously, he feared facing the McCanns most of all. Nicky leaned down next to him. "Everyone's here to honor the servicemen, to honor the Boy Scouts, to celebrate the end of the war!" He said loudly into Benny's ear, "It's not about you, no one's looking at you! Is it hurting you to be here?"

Benny sat quietly, feeling trapped and humiliated. He sat with his chin on his chest, barely looking around anymore. Waiting for the moment Nicky would wheel him away. He felt anger and shame but proud that Joey was honored in some way. He was thinking of Joey as he tried to keep his emotions in check. He could feel a lump in his throat begin to form; it stayed there, pride refusing to let it dissipate into the tears that would dissolve it. He wouldn't look for Nora for fear of losing his composure, so he sat with his chin on his chest, with his eyes closed, and fingers intertwined tightly in his lap.

After Pastor James of the Messiah Baptist church led the crowd in prayer, Mr. Brown told all his scouts to stand. "I'm going to present the medals the boys have earned," he announced loudly. He introduced the scouts, and gave each boy his medal. Behind Benny, neighbors were admiring the little red-headed toddler who went from Katie's arms to Nora's. Everyone, knowing the parents were safely married, made the embarrassment of the child born out of wedlock more acceptable, and enabled them to admire the child in front of the young parents. Benny stared straight ahead, oblivious to all that was going on behind him. Seeing his boy standing there looking so proud caused the lump in his throat to swell. He coughed, tried to clear it, to dislodge it, but it stayed there, as stubborn as he was.

Mr. Brown told every boy except Sammy to sit. Sammy stood straight and tall, his arms straight by his side waiting in anticipation for the extra reward he knew would be coming. Benny looked at his face; it had an expression of pure joy and innocence. There he stood, his only remaining son, looking so happy and pleased with himself. Benny always thought of him as a lost cause, but Mr. Brown was praising him.

"I want to introduce you to Sammy Nuzzo," he told the crowd. "This boy deserves special recognition for what he has contributed to the war effort. Sammy did so much to win this terrible war, which took his brother. He worked very hard every day after school, and all the past summers collecting paper, metal and tinfoil for the war drive. While other children played, Sammy could be seen pulling his radio flyer full of scrap down the street and alleys of the neighborhood to help Uncle Sam. He never tired of pulling that wagon." Looking at Sammy, he said, "Children sometimes laughed at you, huh Sammy, while they played marbles or stick ball in the street, you answered your country's call."... Benny could feel the blood rush to his face as Mr. Brown continued ... "When Sammy heard, Your Country needs you, he took it personal and for that we are here today to also honor and award Sammy Nuzzo with a fifty dollar war bond contributed by the shops in the neighborhood."

Benny felt ashamed, he thought of all the times he could have helped the boy and didn't. *Maybe I was responsible for the way the boy is. I never did anything to encourage him,* he thought.

He felt guilty over the way he treated the boy, dismissing him when he needed his father the most. He knew he had problems. *What did I do to help him?* He asked himself.

He was having all these feelings of regret. The lump in his throat grew larger; he found it harder to swallow. So many emotions left him frightened and emotionally vulnerable.

After Sammy was handed the war bond, the crowd cheered and Nicky noticed one of the boys cheering off to the side had been one of Sammy's tormentors. Benny was afraid of losing his composure. When he asked himself, 'What he could have done for the boy,' he knew the answer. He was feeling ashamed, but at the same time, he felt pride in his son for the first time. Mr. Brown had final words before closing the Boy Scout ceremony, and then the band played *God Bless America*, as Sammy came up to show Nicky his war bond. He was standing in front of the wheelchair holding it up for his uncle to see it when Benny painfully tried to stand on the good leg, holding on to the arm of the chair with one hand, he pulled Sammy to him with the other, and hugged the boy. He choked back the lump, trying to hold back the tears he felt might come, but he didn't dare allow it, not in front of all the people, he had his pride; he held on, the lump stayed. Sammy looked surprised that his father was hugging him, but no more surprised than his uncle. Nicky looked at Lillian and smiled. For once my brother showed some emotion for the boy, he thought. Sammy was hugging him back, and then Benny said, "I have to sit, my leg," he said it in a whisper, he could barely talk. He tried swallowing again with difficulty. Sammy's face just beamed. His cheeks were red, and the damp curls still stuck to his forehead. He appeared so happy.

Benny felt bad that he was ever ashamed of the boy. He could barely hold on, and he knew if he didn't go home soon he would make a fool of himself. Nora came up to give Sammy a hug as well as his Aunt Rose. His uncle gave him a slap on the back, and congratulated him; he left the hugs to the women, he treated him like one of the guys. Sammy liked that. Nora cried at Benny's feeble attempt at affection, and was pleased that he acknowledged the boy with the difficulty he had standing. Sammy showed his father the bond and said, "Look Papa, now I can get a new bike." Benny smiled, he couldn't talk, and his throat felt like it was closing up on him. Nora watched his sad expression change to a strained smile and she knew it wasn't easy for him. The crowd began moving away from them as the band continued to play another song, the *Halls of Montezuma.*

"Let's go," he said to Nicky; he couldn't take much more emotion. Nicky started to turn his wheelchair when Rosemarie appeared. "Hello Pa," she said. Benny looked up. Here was the daughter who had shamed him, whom he had disowned; he hadn't laid eyes on her in over three years. He looked away from her. He was afraid of this, his heart beat faster, and he wouldn't speak. He didn't want to acknowledge her; he was angry and hurt at what she had done. *How could they trap me this way*, he thought. "I'm sorry about your accident Pa," he heard her say, still he would not look at her, even though a part of him wanted to see her. He was trying to hang on to protect the lump in his throat from escaping, and making an even bigger fool of himself. Rosemarie ignored his silence.

"There's someone here to meet you," she said, and before he could think or feel anything more, Jim McCann came up with the little redheaded boy, and sat him in Benny's lap.

"This is your grandson Joey," Rosemarie said. Joey looked up at him with large dark brown eyes, and Benny appeared to be in shock. He couldn't breathe; he thought he would pass out. His heart felt like it was about to beat out of his chest. The name Joey echoed in his head, Joey, Joey, Joey, is all he heard. Those eyes looking up at him, they belonged to his Joey, but the hair was wrong, his Joey's eyes on this redheaded little boy? The lump in his throat became so large it was about to cut off his breathing. Little Joey stared up at this strange old baldheaded man, and watched as huge tears began to roll down his cheeks. The lump had dissolved like a burst dam, as he wrapped both arms tightly around the toddler. He cried now with total abandon as he hugged his first grandson, his son's namesake. He stood the boy up and buried his face in the boy's chest as he held him close. At first he felt the embarrassment of crying in front of the crowd that was forming around him, because he was a man, worse, a grandfather crying. He hugged

Joey until Joey started to cry, then he held him a little away, so he could look at him again.

Rosemarie put her hand on her father's shoulder but he kept looking at the boy, and with one arm holding onto Joey, and his eyes never leaving the boy's face, he reached his free hand over and patted her hand. She knew then she was forgiven. What a spectacle he made of himself, this old man in the wheelchair crying like a baby for everyone to see, but he didn't care anymore. He wasn't aware of the crowd of people around him, staring. When Patrick approached him and held out his hand, he took it, and shook it without reservation. Holding onto his squirming grandson, he looked up at Jim McCann standing next to him, and asked with a voice full of emotion, half laughing, half crying, "What kind of grandson is this with my Joey's eyes on an Irish face?"

Jim McCann said, "The best kind Mr. Nuzzo, an American grandson."

The crowd began to dissipate, walking past the old man in the wheelchair who was holding the child, and some wondered why he was crying, wondered what it was all about. The school band played the *National Anthem* for the last time. Mr. Martin gave the flag one final salute.